A Cape May Kind of Love

KIMBERLY BRIGHTON

This book is dedicated to the readers who
provided such positive feedback on my debut
novel, *The Way to Cape May*, you inspired me
to keep going with *A Cape May Kind of Love*.
I'm truly humbled by all your kind words.
You gave me encouragement, joy, and hope,
and told me you couldn't wait for the second
book in the series to see what happens
to these characters.

In honor of you, here it is!

May

Marley

AFTER AN EXHAUSTING DAY AT HER LAW FIRM INTERN-ship, Marley Maguire looked forward to an evening indulging in her favorite guilty pleasure. She changed into her comfy clothes when she got home—leggings and an oversized Eagles' sweatshirt—and settled into her plush couch, waiting for her best friend to join her. The best friend who, as destiny would have it, was now her boyfriend.

Sam sauntered across the room, wearing a sultry smile, and did a little salsa shuffle before handing her a Dock Street beer. He plunked himself down on the couch and slung his arm across Marley's shoulder, clinking his frosty bottle against hers.

"Cheers to a new season," he said. "Bring on *The Bachelorette*."

Watching reality TV dating shows was their mutual obsession, something they'd started back when they were "just friends." It provided a perfect escape from the harsh rigors of law school and an excuse to get to know each other better. They dissected the stars' love lives, sharing their own thoughts about dating and relationships, unaware they were planting seeds from which their feelings for one another would begin to grow.

"I'm hoping for juicy drama this season," Marley said with a lascivious grin.

"That's you, *National Enquirer*. Bring on the tears and sob stories." He smiled, then added, "Theirs. Not ours."

"No drama here," she said, sipping her beer as she rested her head on his shoulder.

The show began as the host promised this season would be "the most dramatic ever, in the entire *Bachelorette* history," as he did every premiere.

Sam hopped up from the couch. "Forgot the grub. Keep it running."

As he salsaed his way to the kitchen, Marley's eyes were drawn to his hips, swaying in sync with his broad shoulders and tight glutes. His perfect physique and sexy dance moves were just two of the many reasons she'd fallen hard for Sam. Boy was hot with a capital *H*.

Onscreen, a limo pulled up to the house, signaling the arrival of contestants. Man after gorgeous man stepped from the vehicle. The camera trained on expensive shoes before panning up to reveal designer suits, buff bodies, gleaming smiles, and perfect hairstyles. Each man more stunning than the last.

None more stunning than her real-life bachelor, still in the kitchen rifling through a potato chip bag and singing a Taylor Swift song in pitch-perfect falsetto.

When the final contestant's foot emerged onto the gravel path, Marley gasped.

No freaking way. She'd know those shiny red Nikes with orange laces anywhere, even on the screen of her television, where it made no sense for them to be—outside an L.A. mansion, attached to a hopeful bachelor. The camera swept higher, revealing the next dead giveaway as to the final bachelor's identity: his cringe-worthy outfit. Tan khakis and a blue blazer were a stark contrast to the other men's stylish garb. No slim-fitting designer suit for this man. He owned one— that wasn't the issue—but he claimed the suit pants made a tent in his crotch when he sat down, raising eyebrows and suspicions and (in some cases) false hope. He insisted on pairing the jacket with better-fitting khakis instead. If "paired" was the right word.

The sound of his voice eradicated any lingering doubt. The last time she'd heard it was the night they broke up.

Sam returned with a bag of chips and flopped down next to her. "What's wrong?"

Marley pointed at the TV, mouth gaping.

Sam did a double-take, spewing beer all over her brand-new Ikea coffee table. "Is that—"

"Ergh," Marley gurgled in disbelief.

"No. Fucking. Way!" Sam exclaimed.

"Hello, Brie," the man on the screen cooed as he kissed the cheek of the flaxen-haired, sequin-clad bachelorette. "It's a pleasure to meet you. I'm Richard Alabaster Smith the Third. But you can call me—"

"Rick!" Sam yelled, laughing as he wiped beer from his chin. "On the fucking *Bachelorette*? Are you serious right now?"

Yes, it seemed—as serious as reality TV could be.

Richard Alabaster Smith—aka Rick, aka Marley's farm-bred, socially awkward ex-boyfriend—was on the fucking *Bachelorette*.

Rick. The guy who became tongue-tied around anyone outside his immediate social circle. The guy who hid behind wire-rimmed glasses, avoiding human interaction at all costs. Yeah, that guy. Somehow, he'd managed to put together an audition tape and beat out thousands of handsome, muscle-bound, Instagram-worthy hunks to be selected as a contestant on the wildly popular dating show. This had to be a joke.

"Good God," Marley whispered.

Sam punched the air. "I'm so *here* for this!" He gave a hearty laugh and spun toward her. "Marley! Rick's on *The Bachelorette*!"

"No shit, Sherlock. I see that."

"Those damn sneaks of his." Sam shook his head, his expression a combination of admiration and astonishment as if Rick had just ripped one on national TV. "You go, dawg."

Marley had to be hallucinating. This couldn't be real. Rick was the last person to put himself out there.

Onscreen, Brie tipped her head and smiled. "Hello, Rick. The pleasure's all mine."

Rick pulled a sock from his pocket. "I'm here to *sock* it to you," he said, straight-faced, as the lovely bachelorette doubled over in a fake laugh.

"That was *darn* good," Brie quipped.

Sam laughed out loud. Marley groaned. There was no way Brie the Bachelorette was keeping Rick the Corny Jokester past the first episode.

"What a dork," Marley muttered.

"Oh, Mar," Sam said, aqua eyes wide with revelation, "I heard chicks dig dorks now. It's a whole new thing."

"Thanks, *Glamour* magazine. I'm pretty sure dorks have always been in."

"Am I a dork?" Sam asked eagerly.

Marley chuckled. Sam was anything but a dork, although the fact he'd asked the question brought him closer. "The dorkiest."

"Good."

The premiere progressed as Brie met with each of the men. Marley's shock soon turned to dread when it was Rick's turn to chat with her in the garden.

"Have you had many girlfriends?" Brie asked.

"Just one," Rick said, giving her a shy half-smile. "And she broke my heart. Shattered, more like it."

"Oh, please," Marley whimpered. "Please don't go there."

Her heart pounded. As his only girlfriend, she was terrified he'd tell their story and tarnish her name in the process, but Rick flipped the script and asked Brie about her past. She, too, had suffered a broken heart—*de rigueur* for the formulaic show. Marley's relief was only temporary as Brie excused herself and picked up a rose.

"Oh God," Marley mumbled, hoping he wasn't the intended recipient of the first impression rose, which would mean he'd be kept on the show for another week. "This can't be happening."

"Oh, it's happening, Mar!" Sam exclaimed as he stood up and did the floss dance. "Go Riiick! Go Riiick!"

Marley, dumbfounded, watched as her current boyfriend cheered on her ex. "Do you really want Rick on our show?"

"Of course!"

"I thought you hated him?"

"Only because he was dating you." Sam plopped down on the couch and clasped her knee. "Now that I've got you, Marley McMarley, I want the dude to find love."

Marley raised an eyebrow.

"Look at him!" Sam said, pleading his case. "Poor guy's not gonna find it otherwise."

Sure enough, Brie handed Rick the rose. "You made the best first impression. You're genuine, exactly what I'm looking for."

The only thing Marley was looking for just then was a barf bag. Better yet, the remote. She grabbed it but Sam yanked it away.

"Oh no. We're doing this."

Marley slunk back on the couch and covered her face with a throw pillow. She cringed, remembering the dramatic ending of their otherwise drama-free relationship and how she'd broken his heart. Brie was spot-on, sensing his genuine nature upon meeting him. Still, if someone had offered her a bet, Marley would have wagered all ten of her toes (with a couple fingers thrown in) that there was no chance Rick would end up on a world-televised dating show.

She likely would have stayed with him forever if her feelings for Sam hadn't toppled the dam she'd so carefully built against them. Despite valiant efforts, she was incapable of denying the crush that had slowly burned for six years. After all, the heart wants what it wants. And what her heart wanted—had always wanted—was Sam.

Who could blame her? Her best friend since their freshman year of college, Sam was the most fascinating person she knew. He had a great propensity for goofiness and an uncanny ability to make her laugh, even in the direst of situations.

Sweet yet strong, with an amazing legal brain and sexy AF, he consumed every one of her senses. He was beautiful, with tousled, sun-kissed hair and eyes the color of the Caribbean Sea. His deep voice and hearty laughter were music. Her skin tingled every time he touched her. His kisses tasted like honey, and he smelled like a sunny day at the beach. She'd never loved anyone like she loved Sam.

Looking at him now, slunk back on the couch in his faded Sea Isle t-shirt and sweatpants, her heart fluttered. She took in his perfect profile, the long sweep of his lashes, the way he bit his lower lip whenever he was sleepy, aroused, or deep in thought. He rubbed her back with one hand as he held the neck of his beer between two fingers with the other and took a sip like a badass. No matter what he did, what he wore, what he said, he just oozed sexiness, and Marley was grateful she no longer had to hide her feelings for him.

"I know what you're doing, Mar," he said, not taking his eyes off the TV as it went to commercial.

"Oh yeah?" She curled her legs under her and teased her fingers through his hair. "What am I doing?"

"Undressing me with your eyes. I feel like a cheap piece of meat, Perdue."

"Busted."

Sam set his beer down, hit pause, and pushed her into the plush cushions, emitting a lustful growl as he grasped her bottom and slid his knee between her thighs.

"Please don't ever stop looking at me like that," he whispered as his lips brushed hers. He kissed her lightly, grazing his teeth against her lower lip, playfully biting it, releasing a soft whimper as his teasing tongue probed deeper. She rolled them over, straddling him, her auburn waves falling around his face as she took her turn teasing his sensuous lips.

This was exactly what she left Rick for. The wild, untamed, full-throttled passion she felt for this man who gazed up at her, helpless against her intentions.

He slid his hands inside the back of her leggings, his warm fingers clasping her cheeks. She slowly, seductively, undulated against his rigid hardness, straining to be released. His head thrust back into the cushions, and he gazed at her with sheer rapture.

"God, Marley," he moaned, "look what you do to me."

Marley pulled the waistband of his sweatpants down, her fingers frantic to find her prize. Sam let out a low grunt as she clasped his throbbing member, fondling it before he flipped her on her back. He ran his fingers, light as a feather, down her navel and slid them into her leggings, past her soaked panties, until he found her sweet spot, satiny with anticipation.

"I'm about to rock your world," he whispered, his fingers swirling their magic.

"Oh, God." Marley's back arched, not able to take any more.

They tore at each other's clothing and gave in to raw desire; the air between them practically combusted. Working each other to a frenzy, their passion erupted as they came together. As always.

"World...rocked..." Marley panted afterward, fully sated.

It had been a year, almost to the day, since Sam had confessed his love for Marley—when they scrambled out of the friend zone and dove into the relationship they'd been denying themselves for years. It felt as if they'd made love a million times since then, yet each time was better than the one before, each encounter thrusting her further into an other-worldly dimension. Just what a simmering, sizzling, slow burn will do to friends destined to be more.

"God, I love you," he said as he fell against her, spent, chest heaving.

Her head spun, and dopamine coursed through every inch of her being, rendering her powerless against movement.

His raspy voice asked the question she pondered every time. "How does this keep getting better?"

"I don't know," she said, looking up at him. "It just does."

He clasped her hand, squeezing hard as he gazed at her. "You are the love of my life," he said. "Can I please marry the hell outta you now?"

She kissed the tip of his nose. "You know my answer. Not until we pass the bar."

They'd only just graduated from law school, and the monumental bar exam loomed a month ahead. She didn't want to make any major life changes until she found out she'd passed. One step at a time: she had to meet her primary goal before planning any future ones.

"What if you meet someone else before then?" he whined.

She gave him a wry grin. "I guess that's a chance you gotta take."

"Alright." He sighed. "Just be warned. If you ditch me, mine will be the next shattered heart stepping out of a limo on *The Bachelorette*. Only with better footwear."

She swatted him with a couch cushion, and he laughed. He might have been joking but they both knew the truth. Marley and Sam were in it for the long haul. Nothing would ever come between them.

Charlotte

CHARLOTTE DRYSDALE WANTED TO BE ANYWHERE BUT here.

Here, at La Belle Salon, when she should be at work instead.

She wasn't sure if it was the nauseating smell of chemicals smacking her in the face as she opened the door, or the sound of new-age music that suggested she was on another planet. Maybe it was the sight of People Who Salon sipping champagne on a Thursday afternoon (yes, the afternoon!). Whatever it was, Charlotte instantly regretted the preposterous decision to have her hair professionally styled.

Not that it was her decision. In truth, Charlotte had never stepped foot in a salon before. Her grandmother had cut her shoulder-length mousy brown hair into the same bob, free of charge, her whole life. After Grams passed, Charlotte had taken over the job herself.

Instead, this particular foray into vanity was the result of a gift certificate presented to Charlotte last Christmas by her boss, Tom Jervis, and his wife, Tiffany. Warning it would expire at the end of the month, Tiffany had instructed Charlotte's assistant, Jasper, to make the appointment for her.

If Charlotte was anything, she was frugal, not inclined to waste a gift certificate. With her annual performance happening tomorrow, it was prudent to have her hair trimmed professionally—to appear more like a potential law firm partner and less like a person who cut her own hair with a pair of kitchen shears. Not that looks had any bearing on one's leadership qualities, but Charlotte, who'd spent a lifetime being judged for her looks (or lack thereof), knew the rest of the world disagreed.

"You'll love it there," Jasper promised as he wrote the details of her appointment on the back of a business card.

Standing here now, peering through the half-open door, she wished she'd refused. It looked expensive. Indulgent. Peoply. She was hating every second of this experience and hadn't even stepped inside.

"Come in, *mon cherie*." The receptionist waved to her.

His slaughtered French was not lost on Charlotte. Not that she'd ever been to France before. She hated planes—they were nothing more than flying petri dishes—but she'd studied the language so long, she spoke it like a native.

"Here, let me get that for you."

A man who looked like he should be in a movie came up behind her and held the door open. Charlotte gestured for him to go first, hoping to observe the customary exchange between salon receptionist and patron since she wasn't certain how to behave in this scenario.

"Sam Adams," he said as he approached the desk. "I have a one-thirty with Yvonne."

Three women scurried to greet him—one offered him a champagne glass, one batted her eyelashes, and the other twirled her hair. As they ushered him to the back, giggling over something he said, Charlotte wondered if a bevy of beefy men would assist her. The humorous thought almost caused her mouth to slide into a smile. Almost.

She stepped toward the receptionist. "Charlotte Drysdale. I have a one-thirty with..." She reached into her purse and pulled out the card. "Suzette."

A diminutive woman with spikey hair led her to a station. Before Charlotte sat, she retrieved a Wet One from her purse and wiped down the chair, pausing to let it dry. She shuddered to think of the germs lurking there. The hairdresser smirked, but Charlotte ignored her. A practiced germaphobe, she was accustomed to odd looks from people. She slid into the chair, grasping her purse in her lap, careful not to touch the arms.

"I can put that over here for you if you want," Suzette offered, indicating the vanity in front of them.

"No." Make that *hell no*. The place could be crawling with purse snatchers.

The stylist asked what "they" were doing today.

"A trim."

"Do you want to stay with the same style, or can we do some bangs? Layers, a little color, maybe?"

"No."

She raised her eyebrows. "Can I get you a drink? Champagne, perhaps?"

"Absolutely not. I have to work."

The woman cloaked her with a smock and began snipping away. Charlotte had planned to read but decided she should keep a watchful eye on Spikey Suzette in case she tried something sneaky. Without her face in a book, Charlotte was forced to watch the strange, unfamiliar world around her. Women soaked their feet in water as other women squatted before them, massaging their legs. A drag queen swept a teen girl's hair into an updo, dramatically reacting to a "promposal," whatever that was. A man, or so it appeared by the shoes extending beyond a screen, yelped as if he were being tortured. Charlotte shot a fearful glance at Suzette.

"Eyebrow waxing," she explained in a low voice, smiling at Charlotte in the mirror. "Men are such babies sometimes."

Charlotte likened the man's reactions to some of the meltdowns she witnessed in her law firm—grown-ass men carrying on like petulant toddlers when things didn't go their way.

One chair over, another stylist worked on movie-star man. He had crystal blue eyes and a friendly smile. Charlotte was drawn to their conversation as the stylist snipped at his wavy blonde hair, asking questions. The man talked about "going down the shore" last weekend with his girlfriend. Charlotte's eyes lingered on his face, familiar for some reason. Maybe because he resembled a very young Robert Redford in *The Way We Were*, one of her favorite old movies from her grandmother's VHS collection.

"Hey," the man said, smiling as he caught Charlotte's lingering gaze in the mirror. Embarrassed he'd caught her staring, she quickly looked away.

"Wait," he said, squinting. "I know you from somewhere. My name's Sam. Have we met before?"

"I don't think so," she answered. She'd remember meeting someone like him.

"I'm going to turn your chair now, Charlotte," Suzette warned.

"Charlotte!" Sam said, snapping his fingers. "Now I remember. My dad's firm—you used to intern there. Adams and Bennett."

Of course. Sam was the son of Phillip Adams, partner of the firm where she'd interned in law school. He was the college kid being groomed for lawyer-hood who'd sometimes shadow his dad. She'd liked working for them. The partners were decent and treated her with respect.

"Sam. I remember. Are you a lawyer yet?"

"Just graduated law school," Sam said. "Next stop: the almighty bar. We'll see where I end up. My money's on Applebee's."

"The bar exam isn't so bad," Charlotte said. She should know—she'd aced it. "I'm sure you'll do fine."

"I hope so. That means a lot coming from you. I recall you were totally instrumental in the Dixon-Blanchett merger. What are you up to now?"

Charlotte told Sam about her firm, Jervis Mahoney. Sam said he knew it well; the founding partner, Tom Jervis, was a close friend of his dad's. That made sense—both men were smart, kind, and level-headed, unlike many lawyers she knew, who had egos the size of small planets.

"Has Tom held his annual beach retreat yet?" Sam asked.

"End of June," Charlotte said, swallowing the rising lump in her throat. She'd rather drink battery acid than attend a work retreat with her asinine co-workers. Having endured several such trips to hell, it would promise to be a horrific few days. While she loved Tom Jervis, she couldn't stand the rest. Charlotte wished there was a way of getting out of it. There wasn't. To get her mind off it, she inquired if Sam planned to join his dad's firm.

"Nah, but don't tell my dad." Sam smiled. "I'm going into criminal law. I've been interning for Howe and Clemson, working with the Innocence Project. Hoping to make it a permanent gig."

Charlotte knew of the firm and the project. Sam could keep that area of law. Too messy. Inundated with rule-breaking people. Charlotte loved rules and detested that people broke them. Business law was easy, clear-cut. Devoid of emotion, at least for her.

When Sam was finished, he stood and offered her a handshake. She gave him a little wave instead.

"Okay, then. Nice seeing you, Charlotte."

After she finished, Charlotte handed Suzette three dollars, which the hairdresser accepted with a smirk before the receptionist tried to rob her of eighty dollars.

"For a trim?" Charlotte demanded.

"Your gift card's worth a hundred. You can use the balance on your next visit. I can set that up now."

"Absolutely not," Charlotte retorted. Not if she'd have to pay the difference on that exorbitant price.

On her way out, she caught the eye of an older woman in the waiting area who reminded Charlotte of her late grandmother. She handed her the gift certificate. While she wasn't known for her generosity, Charlotte Drysdale wasn't known for the whimsy of impractical spending, either. She wouldn't be returning to a beauty salon again if she had anything to do with it.

Back in her office, Charlotte dug into the pile of work on her desk. She was guilt-ridden over taking time for folly, despite Tom Jervis's insistence that staff take their lunch hours. Not Charlotte. It was her first time. It would be her last.

A few minutes later, the intercom on her desk phone crackled to life.

"Hey, Ms. Charlotte," Jasper's voice came over the line. "Rhys has summoned you to his office. Something about your review."

Charlotte expelled a disgusted sigh. "Right now?"

"Don't shoot me. I'm just the messenger."

What could that nimrod want? Rhys and his sidekick Declan were fellow associates; peers, if one could say that with a straight face, considering they were at least a hundred points below her on the IQ scale. They were the top alpha dogs, connected to the old boys' network of partner-track associates by a still-intact umbilical cord, and the most insufferable assholes she'd ever met. She considered ignoring Rhys's summons, as he'd have nothing to do with her review, but worried Tom Jervis would get wind of her refusal. She had to play their game if she didn't want them badmouthing her to the powers-that-be.

Charlotte entered Rhys's office to find him and Declan lounging back in their chairs, legs parted and outstretched like the typical entitled men they were.

"Come in," Rhys said, salivating like a rabid dog. "Have a seat."

Except there were no open seats.

Declan pointed to his lap. "You can sit here."

"Perfect," Charlotte said, giving him a terse smile. "Where shall I put my sexual harassment claim?"

"Whooaaaa!" both men said in unison, laughing.

"Give it up, girl," Rhys said, offering a high-five. "Good comeback."

There was no way she was reciprocating the gesture, not with the fifteen hundred micro-organisms dwelling upon each centimeter of a human hand. Not that he was human.

She crossed her arms. "What do you want?"

"We just had our performance reviews and wondered how yours went," Declan said.

"None of your business."

"It is our business. We're all gunning for partnership, and we need to know if you've put us all to shame. Again."

"Not gracing that with a response."

"Of course she did," Declan said. "She even got a new haircut for the occasion."

"I wish you'd told us, Charlotte. We woulda gotten our hair cut too."

"Was it for your review or for Tom Jervis?" Rhys asked, and the two cackled.

"You're disgusting," she said. "And you're wasting my time."

She wasn't about to stand here all day chattering with these imbeciles. She turned on her heels. Well, they weren't so much heels as they were flats—her practical, comfortable office shoes.

"They're promoting two new partners," Rhys called out as she stormed away. "May the best associates win."

Figures the firm handled their reviews first. Nothing new. Charlotte was always chosen last for everything. That would all change when she made partner. They'd better watch out.

Bella

BELLA BAXTER SPUN IN FRONT OF HER BEDROOM MIRROR, passing time while she waited. And waited. Her date should've been here fifteen minutes ago, and her stomach was beginning to knot. Maybe the rumors were true.

She pushed the thought from her mind and regarded her reflection. She almost didn't recognize herself in this dress, the way it clung to her in all the right places, making her look more like a woman than a ten-year-old boy (for once). Tiny opaque sequins twinkled on ivory silk, creating the illusion of elegance. Her strawberry-blonde hair was swept into a sophisticated updo, and her makeup—compliments an Instagram tutorial—made her blue eyes pop. Her date was going to fall over when he saw her. If he ever showed up.

Robbie Gentry wasn't the average prom date. He was the lifeguard at their pool, a star swimmer, the hot junior she'd been crushing on for two years, one month, and six days. Not that she was counting.

Facts: boy put the "rizz" in charisma.

She couldn't believe it when he'd asked her to the junior prom, and neither could anyone else. Bella ignored the rumors swirling through the halls of Belvedere High—that Robbie was intending on asking her friend, Sophie, until one of the senior football players beat him to it. Bella trusted Robbie wouldn't ask her if he wasn't truly interested.

She was thankful (shocked, more like it) when her mom agreed to the extravagant dress purchase. Their shopping trip had actually been fun—rare for a fifteen-year-old with wisdom beyond her years and a mom who lived to suck the fun out of everything. The day had started out with her mom admitting to knowing nothing about fashion (really? no!).

"I don't even know where to get a prom gown these days," her mom had said.

"Oh, Lisa," Bella had teased. "There's so much I need to teach you. For starters, it's a dress, not a gown. I'm not getting married."

Although she loved calling her mom by her first name, Bella instantly regretted her snark. She was hoping for a splurge in the dress department and didn't need Lisa to issue her typical "I'll turn this car right around" threat.

"Just kidding. I was thinking maybe Fantastique."

Fantastique was the Main Line boutique shop where the richies shopped for prom. Bella had held her breath, expecting her mom to object. Their dresses ranged in cost from a couple hundred dollars to a semester at Penn. But this was where having a fashion-challenged mother could finally pay off. Lisa wouldn't know Fantastique from Walmart until it bit her in the wallet. Assuming the suburban force majeure known as "Facebook Moms" hadn't spilled the tea, Lisa wouldn't see the prices until they were deep in the clutches of a pushy salesperson. By then, they'd be safe. Her mom was cheap, but not cheap enough to publicly out herself as a Karen, demanding to know how the fashion industry justified charging hundreds of dollars for a flimsy piece of fabric.

When Bella had finally found the Perfect Dress, she'd anticipated motherly objections over its cleavage-revealing neckline (which would've been great, had she any to reveal). But all Lisa did was:

A. Point out she had nothing to reveal;
B. Insist on shoring that right up with a safety pin anyway; as she
C. Pinched the fabric together to demonstrate.

In the end, even an overly protective relic like Lisa understood the importance of choosing the Perfect Dress for such an event, even though the last time she'd been to one, they still called it "*the* prom." (Wasn't it funny, though, when Lisa couldn't find the thing of safety pins? Bella took the fifth on that one.)

"Bella!" her mom called from downstairs now, jolting her back to the present. "He's fifteen minutes late. Are you sure you gave him the right address?"

"No, Mom. I thought it would be hilarious if I gave him the wrong address to see if he could figure it out."

Of course, she'd given him the right address. Just to be sure, Bella scrolled through her texts, relieved to find she had.

Her phone dinged with an incoming text from her friend Zachary.

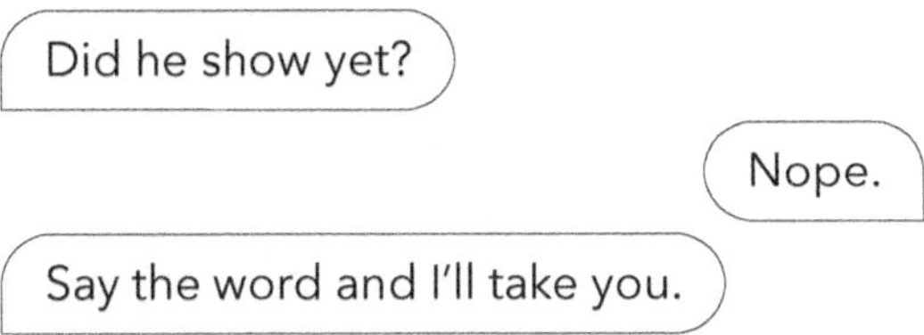

Bella smiled at the sweet gesture, but Zachary attended the Catholic school in town, and prom was limited to Belvedere students. Plus, he was like a brother to her, while Robbie was a demigod. She'd wait until the end of time for him to show before calling in platonic backup.

When the doorbell finally rang, Lisa announced he was here (thanks, Captain Obvious). Bella had practiced for weeks how she'd glide down the steps and steal Robbie Gentry's heart right from his swim-shaven chest. She began her descent as practiced, except there was one thing she hadn't counted on—Eli, her stupid dweeb of a little brother, had left a man behind. In this case, a Lego man. Her spiked heel impaled the plastic policeman right in the Kevlar vest, causing her to topple sideways. She grabbed the railing and did a half spin down the remainder of the steps, landing with a thud at the feet of Robbie Gentry, who responded with a hearty guffaw.

Today's tally—Bella: 0, Lego Land: 1.

"I told you those were too high," Lisa screeched. "You girls with these ridiculous shoes."

"Thanks, Mom, always helpful," Bella muttered as she scrambled to her feet while everyone stood there watching—except for Eli, who came and offered her a hand.

Lisa turned to interrogate Robbie as if he was one of her wards. She was a probation officer, accustomed to grilling people on the details of their lives, hoping to find inconsistencies. She launched into a full-blown investigation of Robbie's life to the point he looked ready to invoke his right to an attorney.

Dude, welcome to my life.

When Lisa ran out of questions, she whipped out her circa 1890 phone and snapped pictures until she'd captured them from every conceivable angle.

"We're good," Bella said when she'd had enough.

She'd waited too long for this night. There was nothing she wanted more than to start it with Robbie Gentry in the Perfect Dress.

Except for some cleavage to go with it.

Aside from one fast dance together, Bella hadn't seen Robbie since they arrived at prom. He'd spent most of the time with his friends by the refreshments while Bella hung with her theater friends.

"Go to him!" her friend Hanna urged. "I mean, he *is* your date."

"I dunno," Bella said, chewing her lip.

Should she? Shouldn't she? There was a definite pecking order to high school. Did she, a freshman, have any right to march up to a group of juniors? What would she even say? *Hey guys, can I see your drivers' licenses? Since I won't be seeing one 'til I'm twenty?* (For reals, her mom had once threatened that.)

Hanna was right, though. She was his date—that should account for something. Tired of feeling like a dateless doofus, she turned to make her way over to Robbie just in time to see Sophie approaching the guys.

"Oh no," Hanna said. "She's making her move."

They watched as Sophie rubbed Robbie's arm.

"Look at her. She's practically hanging all over him," Hanna announced.

"She wouldn't do anything with him," Bella said to assure Hanna but also herself. "She knows he's my date."

Hanna gave her a look.

"What?" Bella asked. "Sophie's my friend."

"Maybe, but not a good one. I heard her in the bathroom telling someone she wished she'd come with Robbie."

Bella felt gut-punched. She trusted Sophie. She'd never told anyone about her crush on Robbie until Sophie had demanded to know who Bella liked. She denied liking anyone, but Sophie was relentless. Bella shared her secret, begging her friend not to tell anyone. A week later, a girl in gym said she'd heard Bella liked Robbie. Bella confronted Sophie, demanding to know if she'd told anyone her secret.

"Oh, relax, Bella. My God," Sophie said, waving her off. "Every girl in this school likes Robbie Gentry. Get over yourself."

Cruel, but that's who Sophie was. An alpha female, the kind of person who'd talk crap on anyone, even those she called friends.

"Girl, I wouldn't trust either one of them. Sophie or Robbie," Hanna said.

Bella wasn't sure what to do. She didn't want prom to be ruined any more than it was. Doing nothing would make her look spineless in front of her friends, while going over to him might make her look desperate. Spineless or desperate?

Bella was about to make her choice when someone slammed into her from the side. A wave of blue juice splashed from the guy's cup and down the front of her beautiful ivory dress. The guy apologized profusely while her friends ran for napkins. Bella stood in utter shock, torn between a tirade and a torrent of tears.

A chaperone took her arm and hustled her to the bathroom. "We'll get this cleaned up, honey. Don't you worry."

Bella was beyond worry. As the older sister of a klutzy kid who, ironically, was addicted to this very same juice, she knew it wouldn't come out. Despite valiant efforts not to cry, Bella's resistance crumbled as the chaperone's kindness brought on her waterworks. Not just over the dress but the whole night.

To add insult to juice stain, they encountered Sophie in the hallway on the way to the restroom.

"Geez, Bella! What on earth did you do?" she asked, snark cloaked in giggles.

Bella was too choked up to answer.

The chaperone tried to work out the stain, which had taken the form of a whale. A big-ass blue whale. But it was futile. Bella sobbed until she got ahold of herself. It was bad enough Bella the Beluga Whale had to face Robbie the Hot Lifeguard in a soggy, stained dress. She didn't have to make it worse by blubbering. There was still time to turn this night around.

On her way back to the gym, she saw two figures making out in the darkened hallway. With no alternative route, Bella forged on (*awkward!*), head down, hand shielding her face to give the groping couple privacy. She'd just passed them when she heard someone say her name. It was Sophie.

"Hey, Bella," Robbie said as he detached from Bella's so-called friend, his shirt untucked and rumpled, looking guilty as hell. "Sorry, we were just—"

"How's your dress?" Sophie snickered.

Bella turned away to escape her mounting humiliation.

"Hey," Robbie said. "I'm sorry, Bells. I kinda have a thing for Soph. I hope we can still be friends."

Bella nodded, blinking back tears as she tried to save face.

"I'm good," Bella said. "I have enough real friends. But if I'm ever in need of another asshole, I'll be sure to look you up."

"Aww, Bella," Sophie sighed, giving her a pout. "We didn't mean for this to happen."

She sounded sincere, but Bella knew better.

"I'm sure you didn't, Soph," she said. "Good luck with that STD."

As Bella took off down the hall, she heard Robbie ask, "STD?"

Marley

MARLEY OVERHEARD A GROUP OF HER CO-WORKERS talking in the breakroom the day after *The Bachelorette* premiere.

"Adorable," one said.

"So unlike other contestants," said another.

"His awkward shyness is kinda hot."

It didn't take Marley long to realize they were talking about Rick. She tried not to throw up in her mouth.

"Marley, you're a *Bachelorette* fan. Did you see it last night? We're talking about Rick, the IT guy. Super cute, down to earth. I think he'll go far."

Fortunately, no one had picked up on the fact that Rick, the IT guy, was her former boyfriend. She'd worked with some of these women back when they were dating, but Rick's visits to Philly were few and far between in the last year of their relationship.

"Wait, wasn't your ex named Rick?" Sarah, one of the administrative assistants, asked. "And wasn't he—"

Marley was out the door so fast she left a veritable cartoon swoosh.

An hour later, Sarah slunk into the chair next to Marley's desk.

"Here's something funny," Sarah said as she scrolled through her phone. "Remember our office holiday party the first year you interned here?"

"Yeah," Marley muttered, only half listening as she continued working on her brief.

"I photographed the event for the firm's social media pages. Look what I found."

Sarah held up her phone to reveal a picture of Marley holding a glass of champagne. Next to her, Rick.

Marley looked up in defeat. Sarah hitched an eyebrow over a knowing stare.

"The look on your face in the kitchen when I mentioned your ex got me thinking," Sarah said. "Hmm, Marley dated a shy, awkward IT guy named Rick. I put two and two together."

She shrugged off Sarah's inquisitive look, hoping to downplay the whole thing.

"*Mar-leeeey!*" Sarah cooed. "Your ex-boyfriend's on *The Bachelorette*! And he got the first impression rose! Any regrets?"

"Absolutely not," Marley said. "I ditched him for Sam, for good reason."

"What reason?"

Marley cocked her head. "Have you met Sam?"

"Oh yeah," Sarah said, chuckling. "Can't blame you there. Total hottie."

Marley ignored Sarah's comment. It wasn't the first time she'd been caught in his fangirl wake. Hell, she'd served as his wingwoman for years.

"Please keep this to yourself. I'm hoping for an offer from the firm, and I need all the respect I can garner. The fact that my ex is a dating show contestant doesn't say a lot for my judgment and decision-making skills."

"Gotcha."

"So we can dispense with further discussion of Rick?" Marley asked.

Sarah gave a wry smile as she turned to leave. "Rick, who?"

Marley hoped she could trust Sarah. Not that she'd have to worry about it much longer. Brie the Bachelorette would certainly send Rick packing next week.

After a long day at the office, Marley headed to her yoga class, ready to namaste her way into the evening. The room was abuzz when she entered, more crowded than usual. Great.

She was hoping for a zen experience, vastly more achievable with fewer attendees. As she lay down her mat, she overheard two women talking.

"He's so different. My money's on him to win."

Marley ignored them. They could've been talking about anything.

"There's something dreamy about him," the other woman said. "Shame on his ex, breaking his heart like that."

Marley picked up her mat and searched for the class attendee least likely to watch *The Bachelorette*. She found an older woman at the end of a row.

"Hello, sweetie," the woman greeted her. "I'm Peg."

Marley introduced herself and focused on stretching, hoping to relay she wasn't interested in small talk.

"Look at you, pretty little thing," Peg said. "I love your curls. Anyone ever say you resemble Emma Stone?"

Marley chuckled. "A couple times."

"Those big green eyes and such a cute little figure. I bet you have all the fellas chasing you."

"Thank you," Marley said, blushing, "but there's only one guy in my life."

"What a shame. Let me know if it doesn't work out. My grandson would adore you."

Marley smiled politely, not wanting to encourage the woman.

"His name is Richard. He's an IT whiz," Peg continued as she lowered her head for a hamstring stretch.

Marely was relieved Peg couldn't see the look of terror crossing her face until she remembered both Rick's grandmothers had passed. Unlikely that a dead grandmother had reincarnated into her yoga class. Or so she hoped.

Sam was already at her place and making dinner when Marley got home. After a quick shower, she blasted their favorite playlist. Sam twirled her around the kitchen, stealing kisses as they danced. He lifted her onto the island, running his hands up her thighs, his lips landing softly on hers until their tongues took over the dance. Marley wove her fingers through his hair as he moaned.

"Dinner's gonna have to wait," Sam muttered, his voice husky with desire as he spoke between kisses, "because I can't."

He grabbed her hips and yanked her closer. She clenched her thighs around him, and he descended upon her with another kiss, this one more intense, leaning her back on the counter.

Her phone buzzed on the island next to them. "Kate's FaceTiming me," she said.

Sam moaned. "Tell her she's gotta wait. I'm not done with you yet."

Marley hopped down from the island. Pouting, Sam went to stir something on the stove.

"Hey, girl!" Kate cried out.

The two women had met a year ago during wedding festivities for Kate's sister, Delaney, with whom Marley and Sam worked. They'd become close after the two couples co-planned a bon voyage party for Delaney and Dalton's move to London. They'd often spend weekends together—in DC at Kate and her boyfriend Ryan's condo or in Philly when it was Marley and Sam's turn to host.

"You're so tan! How was your trip to Cabo?" Marley asked.

"Spectacular," Kate crooned.

"Lemme see this tan," Sam said as he grabbed Marley's waist from behind and rested his chin on her shoulder.

"Hi, Sammy," Kate said, blowing him a kiss.

"I think my Jersey tan trumps your Cabo any day. Just sayin'."

"I challenge you to a tan-off the next time we come north," Kate suggested.

"Will that be soon?" Sam asked.

"We'll be up for July Fourth weekend," Kate said as Ryan appeared in the background and waved. "We'll be coming in on Thursday night if you guys want to meet for dinner in Philly."

"It's a plan," Sam said.

"Great, because we have something to share."

Ryan wrapped his arms around Kate and kissed her as she raised her left hand to the screen. A diamond sparkled from her ring finger.

"Oh my God!" Marley screamed.

Sam laughed heartily. "No way! Congratulations!"

"He totally surprised me," Kate said. "You guys are next!"

Sam kissed Marley's cheek. "Not until the bar exam, she tells me."

"You're such a Delaney," Kate teased. "Always putting career first."

Marley laughed. "I worked hard to get through law school, but I'm not quite over the finish line. Thanks for the compliment, though—Delaney's an excellent attorney."

"Well, she's overseas now, and you're my friend. I'm gonna need your help planning this wedding, so pass that bar already!"

"You don't have to worry about Marley," Sam said. "She graduated top of our class. It's me you should worry about."

"We'll keep our fingers crossed for you both, but I don't think you'll need it."

"Sam, you up for some golf that Friday?" Ryan asked, swinging an imaginary club in the background.

"I'm in."

Kate suggested a girls' night sleepover on Thursday after dinner.

"That would be fun!" Marley squealed. "I haven't had a sleepover for a long time."

"I don't count?" Sam joked.

"Not 'til you let me paint your toenails and gossip about boys," Marley said.

"Like we don't already do that every night." Sam rolled his eyes in fake exasperation.

After they ended the call, Marley asked Sam if he'd be okay sleeping at his place to give them some girl time. Marley still lived in her law school apartment, and Sam lived with roommates from college, but he spent most of his nights at her condo.

"The question is whether you're gonna be okay without me here to undress with your eyes."

"I'll try to survive," Marley said.

"Don't survive too well. I'll be back." He grasped her waist, pulling her closer. "I think we were in the middle of something."

He hoisted Marley onto the kitchen island again and kissed down her neck. "When are you going to ask me to move in?" he asked as he tucked a curl behind her ear.

It was a conversation they'd tentatively broached since they'd started dating. She enjoyed having her own space and wasn't quite ready to cohabitate, especially since her conservative Catholic family didn't approve of it prior to engagement. Not that it was their decision. She just didn't want to deal with family drama or the mess of moving until after the grueling bar exam.

"Someday. Soon."

"Promise?"

"Promise. Nothing's stopping us after this exam."

Charlotte

CHARLOTTE DRYSDALE WANTED TO BE ANYWHERE BUT here.

Here, on the Broad Street Line, as it clacked its way toward her home in North Philadelphia. A perfectly horrific ending to a perfectly horrific day.

It was ten p.m. when she'd finally finished her work. As she was about to leave, an email came through from Tom Jervis, postponing her performance review originally scheduled for the following day. Charlotte was furious. She'd spent hours preparing. Annual performance review was a much-anticipated event in her life. In fact, it was her only anticipated event.

As an associate attorney in her law firm, Charlotte worked a minimum of eighty hours a week, including most weekends, to rise through the ranks and be noticed. She strove for perfection in all she did—details crisply ironed, deadlines met early. She wouldn't dream of leaving until all her work was completed each day. Performance review was when it paid off, when she felt most proud, as the partners routinely extolled her stellar performance. For six years now, Charlotte had achieved the highest accolades, not to mention a handsome salary raise. She didn't do it for the money. She did it to achieve her ultimate goal: to become partner and reign supreme over her co-workers. Her snotty, mean-spirited, condescending co-workers.

After completing her work, she called for the firm's car service to take her home but learned a tractor-trailer had overturned on 95, and the driver was stuck in traffic. The dispatcher informed Charlotte her only hope was to take the train or they could call her an Uber. Hell no. She didn't trust Uber unless she could see the driver's record. She'd asked once, the first and only time she'd tried the ridesharing service. The driver refused and told her to get out of the car. Ubers, like planes, were petri dishes on wheels, filled with myriad passenger microbes. If the germs didn't kill her, the driver likely would. No thanks.

So here she was, instead, on the filthy Broad Street (clackety-clacking) Line like some sort of commoner. Late on a Thursday night of all times, when the drunks and degenerates were out. Still, SEPTA offered a lesser likelihood of certain demise than a rideshare. At least there'd be witnesses.

She hugged her purse tightly to her chest, strap around her neck, as she eyed the guy across from her, mumbling about eagles. Charlotte wasn't sure what type of eagles were the bane of his existence: the actual birds themselves, or the high-ranking Boy Scouts. Whichever it was, he was pretty angry. Then it dawned on Charlotte—he was spewing about Philadelphia's football team.

She couldn't care less about football or any sport for that matter. Her firm owned a stadium box, and she often heard the men-babies weeping over their games on Monday mornings. Crying, over grown men chasing balls. Yet these were the people she was competing with for a coveted partner position.

The doors of the train car slid open, and a man with a guitar entered. He began serenading the women—except Charlotte. No matter. Lacking both outward beauty and a personality to excuse it, Charlotte spent her life being overlooked, passed by, ignored. She was fine with that, in most cases, except when it came to making partner. People respected law firm partners. As a partner, her salary would more than double. Along with the handsome savings she'd accumulated over the years, she could move from the duplex she'd inherited from her grandmother and into a mansion on the Main Line. Charlotte even had her future home selected. She just needed the current owner to move out.

"Hey, pretty lady." The guitar man approached. "What's your name?"

"I have no cash," Charlotte said tersely as she waved him away.

"No worries, I Have No Cash," he said, smiling. He began singing to her a song Charlotte recognized from the movie *Pretty Woman*. In fact, it was that exact song.

"Please stop," she whispered, humiliated. She wasn't accustomed to this kind of attention. She didn't want the man thinking she believed the words he sang to her. With thick glasses and plain looks, Charlotte knew she wasn't pretty. Never would be, no matter how many fancy salons she patronized.

The teens sitting across from her began tittering. Laughing at her—at the lyrics being sung to her.

"Pretty woman," one of them said, a sarcastic edge to their voice. "I wasn't even sure that was a woman."

His comment was met with raucous laughter. Charlotte looked away, trying to pretend she hadn't heard him. A tear slid down her cheek. She tried to wipe it away so they wouldn't see they'd gotten to her. She wasn't sure where the tear came from. She never cried. Most days, Charlotte didn't even feel.

"Don't listen to them," the singer whispered, holding out a bandana to wipe her tears.

"I'm good," she said, waving the man away again. She had no idea where that bandana had been.

The man shrugged. The train lurched and chugged to a stop. The teens got off, and the singing man moved on to a new car. Charlotte was left alone with the reality of her life.

She didn't belong here. Here, on this train. In a salon. At work, among a group of competitive men.

In fact, Charlotte just didn't belong. Anywhere.

A neon flash lit the night sky as she disembarked from the train. An ominous rumble of thunder followed, signaling an incoming storm. Charlotte quickened her pace for the three-block walk to her house. The last thing she needed was to be struck dead by lightning.

She was so focused on making it to the safety of her porch, she didn't see the thing until it was too late. A soft squish under her foot, followed by a high-pitched yowl, alerted her to the fact she'd stepped on some sort of animal. She leaped back in horror to find the mangy-looking thing glaring up at her. She assumed it was a cat from the way it hissed and swiped at her leg, but its fur was so matted and patched it was hard to tell.

"Get out of here," Charlotte said, keeping her distance. God only knew what kind of bugs, worms, or skin diseases it had. "Scram."

Instead of scramming, the cat gave one last hiss, staring up at her as if daring her to come closer. "Leave me alone, disgusting creature."

The cat's glare suggested it takes one to know one.

A gust of wind kicked up as fat drops began to fall from the sky. Charlotte scurried up her porch steps and turned to see the cat still watching her.

"Don't think for a second you're coming in."

She hoped the wind would swoosh the thing away. Not that she wished it harm—she just didn't want it near her house. Slamming the door behind her, she caught a glimpse of herself in the foyer mirror. The wind had whipped her hair into a mess, making her, too, look like a feral creature.

Pretty woman, indeed.

Bella

SOPHIE SENT BELLA A TEXT ON MONDAY MORNING.

> Sorry about prom. I'll make it up to you. My house after school?

Bella wasn't sure why she was being summoned to Sophie's house but was hopeful a more heartfelt apology would be forthcoming. Or maybe Sophie would disclose she and Robbie weren't going to be an item after all. Not that Bella wanted Robbie back, but she couldn't deny a bit of sweet revenge if something pulled them apart. She wasn't sure what hurt more—her crush blowing her off, or her good friend stealing her man. Both equally shitty. They almost deserved each other.

But all hope for a breakup proclamation was soon dashed as Sophie proceeded to talk nonstop about Robbie. Bella felt the knife twisting in her back with every step she took on their way to Sophie's parent's mansion on the outskirts of town. She wanted to turn back, feign illness, get struck by a passing car—anything to keep from hearing about their budding relationship—but knew better than to steal the spotlight from Sophie.

Especially once they arrived and Sophie began pulling brand-new clothing from her massive walk-in closet, handing it to Bella.

"I'm upgrading my wardrobe and purging last year's fashions. I figured you'd like them. Most of them should fit, although some will be too small."

Bella scrunched her face. "Why do you think I'd want your hand-me-downs?"

Sophie sighed, giving Bella a look of contrived patience. "Isabella. No offense, but your drip is so last year. I've barely worn most of these; they're like new. Why wouldn't you want them?" Then added, "If you're embarrassed, don't be. I won't tell anyone."

Truth was, Sophie was right about her wardrobe. When Bella had hit eighth grade and developed the fashion requirements of a teen socialite (according to Lisa), she'd been told she'd have to earn her own money if she wanted to spend a fortune on clothing. She signed up for every babysitting gig she could find, from watching her twin cousins and neighborhood kids to offering her services to vacationing families in summer. It taught her a valuable lesson—making bank felt good. The more she made, the less she wanted to hand it off to greedy clothing designers. Instead, she'd set her sights on saving for a new iPhone after her parents shot down her request for an upgrade, hoping cheaper fast fashion finds would suffice. According to Sophie, however, her drip had dropped.

She accepted the proffered clothing, trying not to act too excited when Sophie handed her a Hollister shirt Bella had eyed for months before deciding she couldn't afford it, price tag still affixed.

If Sophie expected her generosity would make up for the Robbie thing, she was right. If this was her way of making amends, Bella was there for it.

June

<h1 style="text-align:center">Marley</h1>

Marley headed to the library to meet sam for their Wednesday night study session, a tradition that began in college. They were in the final stretch, one month before they sat for the exam. It would be another two months until they'd learn their fate, and Marley's dream of becoming a lawyer would finally be realized.

She couldn't wait to see Sam, who'd been on loan to his dad's firm to assist with case prep that day. Work was boring without him.

A block from campus, she ran into her friend Gwen, a fellow attorney who worked in the district attorney's office. When Gwen asked how she was, Marley told her she was spending all her free time studying.

"I can't even think about it without crying," Marley reported.

"It's not so bad, and that's coming from someone who took it twice."

Marley recalled Gwen had failed on her first attempt.

"You'll do fine—just don't stress too much," her friend offered. "I learned the hard way the more confident and calm you are, the better you'll do. Trust me."

Easier said than done. Marley had a lot riding on this exam. Not just a job but a sense of worth. Legitimacy. Having been cast as "less than" when she was a kid had made its mark on her, and she'd spent her life trying to climb out from under the shadow of others. She had to pass the bar to officially become a lawyer and prove to everyone—herself included—that she was smart. She was enough.

She'd just settled at their favorite corner desk when her

phone blared the Rocky theme, Marley's personalized ring-tone for Sam.

"Hey, sweetheart, I'm gonna skip the books tonight," he said.

"Again?" It was the third time he'd blown off studying. "Sam, aren't you worried about failing?"

"Nah," he said. "If I do, it'll just free me up to pursue my true interest."

"Which is?"

"Origami. Someone has to fold little pieces of paper, and that someone is *me*."

"You need to start taking this seriously if you want the firm to hire us."

"Relax, Mar. There's no way we're failing the bar."

Easy for him to say. Sam always had his family's firm to fall back on—they'd hire him in a heartbeat, with or without a license to practice. Hailing from a long line of attorneys, Sam had law in his blood—he could probably pass the test in his sleep. If not, his laissez-faire attitude would enable him to laugh it off as if he'd just spilled soda on himself.

Marley didn't have that luxury. She had to work hard for everything. If she failed, humiliation and depression would weigh heavily on her because it would expose something about herself she'd forever been trying to disprove—that she wasn't the capable, independent person she fronted as.

She tried to focus on her studies, but her attention was drawn to two college kids pretending to study while stealing glances at one another. It reminded Marley of when she and Sam sat in this same library under the guise of platonic friendship. Pretending to study when, in fact, they were memorizing each other's features, searching for something to talk about to prolong the night. Not that they had to search very hard. Conversation was as natural for them as breathing.

She wished she could share her hard-earned wisdom with them. Be honest about your feelings. Spare yourselves years of faking-it torture, or worse—risk losing the other to someone else, as Marley and Sam almost had. She was reminded daily how lucky she and Sam were to have aced the friends-to-lovers trope, their favorite rom-com movie theme. From the safety of the friend zone, they'd lean together, whispering about the characters, carefully trying to avoid the other's hand in the popcorn bucket. At the same time, hoping for an accidental brush.

She texted Sam.

> I'm in the presence of two best friends stealing glances at one another. Remind you of anyone?

He texted back immediately.

> Me and my own true love.

> Aww, sweet. You're mine, too.

> I meant cheesesteaks. Wait, did you think…oh. #awkward

> You're a jerk.

> A jerk suffering serious withdrawal. When you coming home?

> By home, do you mean mine or yours?

> Ours.

> K. In that case, not until I pass the bar.

Back in her condo, Marley was greeted by the smell of pizza. She hoisted herself onto a stool as Sam uncapped two beers.

"I need an M-n-S night," he said, dimming the recessed lights over the kitchen island. Marley, knowing what he meant, put on their soft jazz playlist. They climbed onto the island and sat cross-legged, facing each other, pizza between them. It was what they did when they had something important to discuss.

"What's on your mind?" Marley asked as she lifted the lid and smiled.

A message, written on the pizza in parmesan cheese, spelled out *My True Love*. Pizza parm messages were one of Sam's love languages, each one different than the last.

"He's still at it," Sam said, frowning as he took a swig of beer.

Marley knew he was talking about his dad, who'd been trying to get Sam to join his firm for years. Sam had zero interest in practicing business law, his dad's area of specialty. Like Marley, criminal law was his passion.

"When is he going to accept that we're going to work for Howe once we pass the bar?" Marley asked. Irish superstition taking over, she added, "If we pass."

"We'll pass," Sam's Anglo-Saxon bravado predicted. "Your guess is as good as mine."

Despite suffering pre-exam nerves, Marley felt confident about a job offer from their firm. She felt it in her bones. Hopefully it was imminent, so she could have one less thing to be nervous about.

Charlotte

PERFORMANCE REVIEW TIME. CHARLOTTE'S NOTES WERE pristine, files organized. She'd even created a spreadsheet highlighting her successes. Armed and ready to go, she made her way to Tom Jervis's office where he and another partner waited.

"Charlotte! My favorite associate," Tom exclaimed, holding out a chair for her.

She wouldn't let his hearty greeting go to her head. He said the same thing to everyone.

"I've prepared some files," Charlotte said, lowering herself into a chair.

"I'm sure you have." He chuckled.

"What cases would you like to know about?" she asked, opening the top file.

"Charlotte, we know you're an excellent attorney," Tom began.

"Probably our best," Bill, the other partner, agreed. "As you know, we'll be promoting two associates to partnership this year."

"I'm ready. I've been working hard toward this, and I'm prepared to accept an offer."

Charlotte wasn't sure whether it was professionally appropriate to jump in with that, but appropriateness wasn't her forte. Nor was word mincing.

The partners looked at one another.

"A lot goes into being a partner, Charlotte," Tom finally said. "Beyond the cases and the workload, which you've certainly mastered."

"But there's also the social part of it," Bill said. "And that's where we're uncertain..."

Charlotte blinked, trying to make sense of his words. What on earth did one's social skills have to do with being partner?

"Jervis Mahoney does a lot of charity work in the community, as you know," Tom said. "We host events throughout the year. As a partner, you'd be expected to co-host each one, along with other partners."

"Let's face it, Charlotte," Bill put in. "You're not exactly the most social associate we have."

Charlotte didn't know what to say. Of course, she wasn't social. When did that become a requirement of partnership?

"What do I need to do to prove myself?" Charlotte inquired.

"For starters, you could try to bond with fellow associates, especially those on partner track. You guys will lead the firm one day, and you'll need to get along. From what I hear, you aren't exactly on good terms."

"We're a team," Bill added. "We have to act like it—in the courtroom and the community."

She swallowed hard. Telling her to be social was like telling her to bungee jump off the Ben Franklin Bridge. Actually, she'd prefer that.

A recluse of sorts, Charlotte had spent a lifetime teetering on the edge of, then plunging headfirst into, social awkwardness. Raised by a single dad who worked two jobs to keep food on their table, Charlotte had had no guidance in understanding social norms of human behavior. Her father was a man of few words with little time for idle chit-chat. He was only home for thirty minutes between jobs, six nights a week. The two would eat dinner in silence, broken only by his one question: what did you learn today? Charlotte chose her words carefully, not wanting to waste his time.

In college, she learned the rest of the world didn't work that way. It seemed people who made it to the top knew how to use their words—many of them—to convince others of their importance. Similar to primates in the wild, banging on their chests in a show of strength or social status. She found it extraneous, but her performance evaluation suggested otherwise. Tom Jervis made it clear—if she wanted to succeed, she had to pretend to like people. To be like people.

"What, exactly, must I do?" Charlotte asked, wringing her hands. A consummate rule-follower, she'd do whatever they asked, no matter how wretched.

"Help each other with cases. Attend our events, go to happy hour. Schmooze a little. Follow the examples set by Rhys and Declan."

"Great team players," Bill added.

True, if what they were looking to assemble was a team of baboons.

Still, a partnership hung in the balance. Dread crept through her over the prospect of being social with the people she hated most, but she had no choice. There was only one way to achieve her goal. As mortifying as the prospect was, Charlotte was willing to do anything, even attend a happy hour. More like unhappy hour.

The mangy creature had returned. It sauntered toward Charlotte as she scurried home, trying to avoid another Philly-famous summer storm.

"Shoo!" she yelled, tossing a rock a few feet away from the cat—not wanting to hit it, just scare it away. The last thing she needed was an animal cruelty charge. She'd heard the feral cat situation had become bad in their neighborhood. She'd have to call Animal Control as soon as she was inside, but the cat beat Charlotte to the bottom porch step and sat smack dab in the middle. No matter how she tried to sidestep it, she was still within swatting range. The second to last thing she needed was cat scratch fever.

"I said, 'scram!'" Charlotte yelled louder, stamping her foot in its direction.

The cat just sat there, defying her order. Charlotte stared it straight in the eyes. It gave her a slow blink as if trying to win her over.

"Not gonna happen," she said, giving it another menacing look. "I hate cats."

The thing wasn't budging. She lunged at it, screaming. That did the trick—the cat scurried away. If only she could do that to people.

Having no time for feline folly every time she returned

home, Charlotte called Animal Control. It was after hours so she left a message to come and take the animal away.

Later, staring out her rain-streaked window at the storm-swaying trees, she wondered where stray cats and other creatures went when it rained. She felt lucky to be human and privileged enough to have shelter from nature's fury. Then again, cats weren't under the same pressure humans were to socialize in order to be accepted. Housing aside, Charlotte had to admit a bit of envy over animals' ability to behave anti-socially without being judged for it.

Bella

"COME ON, BELLA! I NEED TO PEE!" ELI YELLED AS HE banged his fists on the bathroom door.

"Calm down," Bella snarled.

She finished applying her mascara before relinquishing the bathroom, knowing felony charges would swiftly follow if her marathon makeup session caused The Precious One to wet his pants.

Eli darted past her and slammed the door as Bella left. She made her way down the hall, passing the Dallas Cowboys shrine known as Eli's bedroom. He'd just turned eight last week, and his only birthday wish was a Cowboys-themed bedroom. Despite the rest of the fam being die-hard Eagles fans, Eli had somehow missed that gene, choosing instead to march to the beat of his own blue and silver drum.

"You can do what you want in your own room," Bella had lectured from the doorway as their mom helped Eli decorate. "Just don't go wearing their merch in public, or you'll be pummeled into oblivion."

"That's enough, Bella," Lisa had said, trying to hide a smile as she turned to Eli. "No one's pummeling you."

She was impressed by her mom's defense of her traitorous offspring, given she herself hadn't missed an Eagles game in years. Bella was certain if you cut her mom open, she'd bleed green.

Then again, Eli could do no wrong in Lisa's eyes.

Bella spent the first seven years of her life in only-child bliss, sharing attention with no one. At first, she enjoyed being an older sister, but the older Eli got, the cuter he became—with big blue eyes, freckles, and hair the color of dark chocolate. He was sweet and loving, no matter how much Bella taunted him. Naturally, everyone adored him for it, which made her feel jealous and insecure. She couldn't help it—her brother was smarter, sweeter, and more loveable than she'd ever been. Ever would be.

Besides, she hadn't asked for a baby brother. She'd asked for a sister. Bringing home a boy was her parents' first mistake. Their second was trusting Bella would grow to appreciate him. She didn't believe her mom when she told her that one day she would, and they'd become friends. Oh sure, maybe when she had nothing else to live for. In Bella's current life stage, everything that mattered came from her iPhone or her friends. Nowhere else.

Eli now appeared in her bedroom.

"I hope you washed your hands," Bella warned.

"I did. Here, smell." Eli charged across the room, hands outstretched.

"Gross, get out of here!" Bella yelled as she tossed a stuffed animal to ward off the encroaching danger. There was nothing grosser on the planet than an eight-year-old boy.

Eli placed the animal back on Bella's bed. She made a mental note to have it fumigated.

"Mom said we're leaving in an hour. Will you be ready? I want to get there before the boardwalk closes."

The family was heading to their Ocean City beach house for the summer. She knew without having to ask what lurked behind Eli's Major Motivation. He was obsessed with a board-walk ride called the Viper, a gross, rickety wooden roller coaster. He'd been waiting his entire life to ride it, but was still too short last summer to meet the height requirement. As a result, he'd spent the year eating all his vegetables and stretching so he'd be tall enough to ride it this summer.

Except there was a major design flaw in his plans.

One day, Bella found Eli hanging by his hands from a bar their dad had installed at the top of his bedroom doorway.

"What are you doing, freak?" she'd asked as she skirted past his swinging legs.

"Stretching, so I can be tall enough to ride the Viper."

Bella felt a Grinch grin cross her face. She turned slowly to deliver her soul-crushing news.

"You're not going to get taller doing that, you know," she told him. "The only thing that'll do is stretch your arms so long they'll drag behind you like an ape."

Later, she found Eli hanging upside down by his knees.

"Does Mom know you're doing this?"

"She's the one who helped me up. Bella look. Guess what I am?"

Eli closed his eyes, crossed his arms on his chest, and stuck his upper teeth out in fang-like fashion. She couldn't help but chuckle. Most of the time, her little brother was an annoying twerp, but sometimes his quirky little personality made her laugh.

"Um, werewolf?" she false-guessed, deciding to play along.

"*Vym a vampire!*" Eli hissed between his menacing fangs. "*I vant to bite your neck!*"

"Oh no, let me get my cross! And garlic!" Bella teased as she dashed to her room.

"I'm just kidding," Eli called out. "I'm not really a vampire."

Bella now recalled the incident with a chuckle, sizing up her little bro, worried his goals of growing taller hadn't worked. Well, at least she'd stopped him from having ten-foot arms.

Cruising down the AC Expressway on their way to the shore, Bella could hardly contain her excitement. She loved spending the summer in Ocean City, where she got to hang out with her beloved uncle Jake, who lived down the coast in Avalon. Jake was the coolest person she knew over the age of thirty. He ran boat cruises and planned to sail solo around the world one day. Bella thought it was lit, but the women in her fam didn't get it. She often overheard her grandmother, mom, and Aunt Amy talk about Jake's inability to settle down and find a woman, as if it were a character flaw. Bella saw no reason to get married until you were closer to death, like your forties. They accused Jake of chasing a "pipedream," to which Bella said, "You go, boy." It made Jake even cooler in her eyes. She only wished she could stow away on his boat and escape life at Belvedere High for a few months.

She was also looking forward to spending time with her Ocean City friends, including Zachary, who was both a hometown and shore friend. They'd met on the beach as little kids and discovered they both lived in Doylestown. Their moms would get them together for occasional playdates when they were younger. Now attending different high schools, they mostly kept in touch through texts and social media, and occasionally in person. Summer was when they really hung out.

Zachary had been there for her the night of the Robbie Prom Debacle. She'd texted him after she ran into her date locking lips with Sophie. Zachary didn't have his license yet, so he did the next best thing—he rode his bike to her school to rescue her, like a knight on a white Huffy. She ran out like a runaway bride in her ruined dress, jumped on his handlebars, and they sped off into the night, ending up at their favorite ice cream place. They shared a goopy sundae sitting on a worn wooden picnic table. Zachary made her laugh about Robbie,

Sophie, and the Big Blue Whale Incident, deciding if they ever started a band, that's what they'd name it. By the time their spoons hit the bottom of the sundae dish, she was over it.

They finally pulled up to their house, and Eli's bid for a boardwalk jaunt was vetoed by their parents in favor of unpacking.

"Okay," Eli said, easily accepting his fate. "That's one more night to stretch."

Bella helped her parents unload the car, although her version of helping might have differed slightly from theirs. Hers consisted of taking her own luggage to her room, after which she flopped down on her bed to check her texts. She was exhausted from the long car trip and needed a break. She snapped a selfie and sent it to Zachary, announcing she'd survived two hours of hell, aka family road trip.

Her dad appeared in the doorway. "Thanks for helping, Bella," he said, sarcastic AF.

"What? I did my part."

"Your willingness to go above and beyond is remarkable. Make sure you include that in your college essays."

"I'm not going to college."

Of course, she was going to college. She only said it to jack him up. College was her ticket out of her parents' house. Her life's hall pass. Her Get Out of Jail Free card. She couldn't wait to escape the familial binds that tied her.

What was his deal, anyway? She'd unloaded her stuff. What did she look like—some sort of Sherpa? Then again...

"I'll help if I can get a new iPhone," she offered.

"No."

Oh well. Worth the try.

Eli popped out from behind his dad. "Don't worry, Bella. I helped them unload everything so you could relax."

Her dad guffawed as he turned to walk away. "Don't encourage her."

"But, Dad," Eli said. "You always say Bella works overtime to annoy us. I'm pretty annoyed right now, so she must *really* be tired!"

Marley

MARLEY WAS SUMMONED TO A MEETING ON A NEW EM-bezzlement case Friday morning. While property crimes weren't her favorite, she was grateful to be chosen for any team—a sign that an offer for permanent employment was forthcoming.

Sam was on loan to his father's firm again. She couldn't wait for him to be done with that project so they could resume their daily routine—working together by day, enjoying steamy activities by night. Their friends often asked how they successfully maintained both a professional and intimate relationship. It was easy for them. They enjoyed each other's company, and it never felt like a chore being together all day. Quite the opposite.

As she returned to her office, she sensed several pairs of watchful eyes. One co-worker passed with a smile. Three peered at her from an office. Two stood at the end of the hall, tittering. Something was up. She noticed her office door was closed. She'd left it open.

"What's going on?" Marley asked the nosy admins.

"You'll see."

She opened the door to find her office had exploded in tulips. Vases of Marley's favorite flower filled the room, looking like Holland in springtime. In the middle of it all was Sam, holding a bouquet.

"Happy anniversary, sweetheart."

Marley clasped a hand over her mouth and giggled. "I thought you were at your dad's?" She hugged him, breathing in the intoxicating scent of Sam's aftershave and fresh tulips.

"A little fib so I could spend the day sweeping you off your feet."

Someone had discreetly closed the door behind her, leaving Marley and Sam alone.

"For you." He handed her the tulips. "Your favorite."

He hadn't forgotten. Last summer, Sam had pretended to enlist her help in telling the woman of his dreams how he felt about her. Marley had assumed he was courting his ex-girlfriend, Jenna, who'd recently reemerged in his life. Marley suggested giving her tulips as they stood for new beginnings—having no idea, at the time, that Sam was actually in love with her.

"Come here," he said, pulling her in. "A year ago today, you made me the happiest man on earth by agreeing to be my girlfriend. I couldn't let it go without celebration."

Sam spun her around, leaning her against the desk. She hiked her leg around his thigh as he slid his hand under her skirt.

"I want to take you right here," Sam whispered breathlessly, forehead to forehead, as he inched his hand higher, his pants unable to hide his growing arousal. She curled her fingers over it.

"Oh, God..." he muttered, falling into her. "You gotta stop, or we're gonna have a mess on our hands."

Which, of course, was an open invitation to keep going. It was thrilling, fondling Sam like this during work hours. It wasn't the first time they'd been intimate in the office—they'd enjoyed a few R-rated moments when they worked late but never took it all the way. Now, knowing others were in the building, adrenaline dared her to give in to the passion coursing through her as Sam groaned and his eyes rolled back.

He pulled away. "Not here," he said, his voice gruff.

"Aww," Marley whined. "Why not?"

"I thought we'd covered this. I'm not a piece of meat. You can't sink your teeth into me and ravish me just anywhere."

"I can't help myself."

"Who can blame you? Besides, we have somewhere to be tonight, so try to keep it in your pants until then."

"Ooh, where are we going?"

"It's a surprise."

"Wee!" Marley gave a little clap.

"And it's starting now." He took her hand and guided her to the door.

"I have a meeting—"

"No, you don't," he said, cupping her face with one hand as he kissed her again. "I saw to it. Let's go."

"How long are we gonna be? I should let Maxine know—"

"She already knows. I'll have you back by Monday."

Marley's mouth dropped open. "It's a weekend thing?"

"Yes."

She hesitated, thinking of all she had to accomplish. She couldn't afford time off and didn't want to jeopardize her chance at being offered employment. But the way Sam was looking at her...screw the assignments. He flung the door open to applause and cheers from a handful of admins.

"Happy Anniversary!"

Marley was embarrassed by the attention Sam's grand gesture had garnered, especially when they were only celebrating a year of dating.

"Thanks for all your help, ladies," Sam said. "Now, I must whisk this beauty away for a romantic weekend."

He led her down the hall as a swooning chorus echoed behind them.

"Your chariot awaits, my lady." He gestured to a white stretch limo parked in front of their building. She wasn't sure where they were going, but a limo seemed over the top, even for Sam. Once they were tucked in the back, he tapped on the glass partition. "Hit it."

A song began playing.

> *I wished upon a star above and found a Cape May kind of love.*
>
> *Like endless waves upon the shore, we were once friends, and now we're more.*

"What song is this? I've never heard it before," Marley asked.

"I heard it the other day," Sam said. "Reminds me of us."

Marley listened to the next few lines.

> *You took my hand and then my heart, in hopes that we will never part.*
>
> *Just like the stars that shine above, it's in Cape May where we found love.*

The song seemed to tell their story.

"It's beautiful," Marley said, snuggling next to Sam.

"It makes me think of us. I'd been falling for you all those years in Philly and summers in Strathmere, but it wasn't until we were at Delaney's wedding in Cape May that I knew I'd never have another first date again."

Marley's heart skipped several beats. Not just from love but also a tinge of anxiety that something else was coming. Something she wasn't quite ready for.

A proposal.

Sam was, without a doubt, her person. She couldn't wait to spend her life with him but wanted to get her career started first. Or, at least, pass the grueling bar and get beyond her nagging imposter syndrome before planning the next phase of her personal life.

"Where are you taking me?" she asked with a nervous chuckle.

"To the scene of the crime," Sam said.

"What crime?"

"The one where you killed all chances I'd ever date someone else."

The song suggested they were heading to Cape May, but the limo pulled off the Garden State Parkway at Exit 17 and headed north into Strathmere, where they'd summered for the past few years with friends.

"Welcome to the tour of our love story," Sam said as the limo stopped at their beach entrance.

A path of tulip petals led to a blanket where flickering faux candles surrounded a basket containing wine and grapes.

Marley gasped. "For us? But how—"

"A magician never reveals his tricks," Sam said. He led her to the blanket and turned to face her. "On June sixteenth of last year, at approximately seventeen hundred hours, the suspect fled Philadelphia in hot pursuit of the only woman he'd ever loved. She'd finally, *finally*, broken free from the chains that bound her to a very kind yet insufferably boring boyfriend. The suspect found his intended target here on this beach, sucking down a bottle of wine to drown her sorrows."

Sam turned toward the dunes as if to address them.

"Ladies and gentlemen of the jury, do NOT think for one second she was crying over her broken relationship! Nay, her tears were over the prospect of losing the man of her dreams to someone else. Man of dreams being me, the suspect in question."

"Sam!" Marley giggled a warning. He was drawing the attention of other beachgoers, talking to the dunes as he was.

"Don't harsh my attorney vibe. I'm in the middle of my closing argument."

"Wouldn't dream of it, Perry Mason."

"His attended target was *hot*—those curls, those sexy eyes, looking at him like she is right now. Can you blame him? Her kisses are like nothing on this earth. I DIGRESS! She was here, ladies and gentlemen, wearing the SEXIEST bikini ever donned by WOMANKIND when he finally found the words he'd been seeking for SIX LONG YEARS!"

A woman walking by ushered her kids toward the beach path, eyeing him with caution.

"Sorry," he called out. "I'm a major dork."

"The biggest," Marley reassured her.

"Where was I?" he asked after they passed.

"You were about to open this bottle of wine." Marley pulled it from the basket, appreciative of his showmanship but ready for a drink. Hoping this wasn't leading to something more.

"IN CONCLUSION!" Sam yelled as he lifted an arm and pointed dramatically at her. "I urge you to find this woman GUILTY! GUILTY of stealing his heart!"

"Wait, I thought *you* were the suspect?"

"You catch my drift. But you did steal my heart. Actually, you ripped it from my chest and devoured it."

Marley got chills as she always did over Sam's big pronouncements of love. He was dramatic, passion-filled. Her calm, modest nature was a perfect yin to his yangity-yang-yang.

He pulled her close. "We'll get to the wine in a minute. I just want to tell you how much this damn beach means to me. Not only for all the summers we spent here in school but because it's where you told me you loved me."

They sat on the blanket and watched the sun dance on the waves, just as she had a year ago. Nursing a wounded heart, unaware love-struck Sam was racing to the shore to offer his.

Back in the limo, Sam announced they were heading to the second crime scene: the Deauville Inn.

"In case you don't recall the testimony, ladies and gentlemen—"

Oh God, we're still on this.

There was no stopping Sam's penchant for drama, so she went with it. They bellied up to the bar where he ordered two Shore Crush cocktails, her favorite drink of their beloved summer hangout, apropos of their once crush-laden friendship.

"Mere days before our suspect stole this poor man's heart, she was here, dancing with another man. And while our victim—"

"Wait. You're the victim now?" Marley teased as she sipped her drink. "I can't keep up with your ever-changing roles."

"Yes, a victim of your then-unrequited love," Sam said. "In any event, this was the place our poor victim realized he did not care one iota for the woman he once dated. We shall call her Jenna. Because, across the bar, the woman he did love was dancing with another man. And then she left without a trace."

"You really didn't care about Jenna that night?" Marley asked, caught on that fact. She had been convinced Sam was hung up on his ex and that he and Jenna were in the process of getting back together. Thus the left-without-a-trace part.

"If I had zero shits to give, it would've been too many."

"Wow. You do know how to charm a woman."

Sam broke character. "Is it working?"

"Lemme deliberate."

They finished their drinks and crunched their way across the gravel parking lot. Marley linked her arm with Sam's and gazed up at him. She was tipsy from the wine and cocktail but mostly drunk on love.

"If I forget to tell you later," she whispered, "I had an awesome time tonight.'"

"Night's just begun, my girl."

They had dinner at Carmen's, the bayside seafood restaurant in Sea Isle, where they'd had their first official date. Afterward, they stopped for a drink at the Oar House on the other side of Sea Isle's Venetian-inspired waterway before continuing down the coast to Cape May.

"Congress Hall was booked, unfortunately," Sam said as the limo pulled up before a charming bed-and-breakfast. "I figured we'd try something new."

Cape May was known for its bed-and-breakfast accommodations, perfect for a romantic getaway. But, upon checking in, they learned the only room available was in the third-floor attic. And had twin beds.

"Oh, and our air conditioning unit is on the fritz," the desk clerk said apologetically.

Sam looked crestfallen.

"It's okay," Marley said as they dragged their luggage up the narrow stairs to the top floor. "We're together, nothing else matters."

Except for space. And maybe oxygen.

As they entered the room, roughly the size of a closet, a hot blast of air smacked their faces. Marley tried to A. breathe and B. fight off the feeling of foreboding. She'd clearly been hanging around Kate too much, who strongly believed the universe doled out signs. Was this a sign? Maybe this is what they got for cutting out of work early, especially when they were both hoping for job offers.

"I'm sorry, Marley. I wanted this to be special."

Marley wiped the sweat from her forehead and, with it, the look of disappointment likely showing on her face. She took a drenched Sam in her arms and hugged him.

"It *is* special. You could've booked us into a dumpster, and I'd still be over the moon. At least here we have beds."

"Bonus: we don't need our jammies," Sam said, "since I lowkey forgot to pack them."

Marley laughed. "Who needs jammies when we have each other and an oven for a sleeping chamber?"

They pushed the beds together. Despite the heat, maybe

because of it, they made slow, sweet love. He sang as Marley drifted off to sleep in his arms.

> *A summer breeze, a salty kiss, a boardwalk stroll, hearts full of bliss*
>
> *Two souls connect and sparks ignite; a passion filled with love's delight.*

Marley woke hours later. She went to put her arm around Sam, but the bed was empty. She heard the faint trace of his voice, still singing the same tune.

> *A king-size bed, now torn apart; I rolled away to hide a fart*
>
> *And plummeted to earth below; come help me Mar, I'm on the flo'.*

Marley, half asleep, rolled over and found herself plummeting as well—into the gaping hole between the beds.

"Oof!" Sam exclaimed as she landed face-down on him. Somehow, during the night, he'd fallen between the two beds and had become lodged there.

"I knew I could make you fall for me again," Sam said.

They burst out laughing.

"Welcome to the floor, where it's cooler by a half-degree," he joked.

Pulling the comforters off both beds, they made a nest for themselves. Perhaps it *was* a sign—no matter where they went or what the universe put them through, they'd always make it work. Laughing all the way.

And there, on the hardwood floor of the antiquated bed-and-breakfast, lodged between two fugly metal beds in three-hundred-degree heat, Marley fell for Sam all over again.

Charlotte

CHARLOTTE DRYSDALE WANTED TO BE ANYWHERE BUT here.

Here, inside this fancy-schmancy restaurant called "The Clink," for her first expedition into the life of Schmoozing Socialites. Otherwise known as hell.

The large, sprawling place was filled with people shouting at one another to be heard over the din of a three-piece band, but all Charlotte could see were millions of bacterial microbes.

"*Char*-Char!" Jasper sang as she arrived at the corner of the bar where her co-workers huddled like a bunch of drunks. "Good to see you out, hon!"

"No way!" Rhys exclaimed. "What the hell, Charlotte? Some sort of nerd conference here tonight?"

Charlotte ignored him.

"What's your poison?" Jasper asked.

"I—don't know what that means."

Jasper laughed. "What would you like to drink?"

"Ginger ale. Please."

"Charlotte, is that you?" A male voice came from behind her. She turned to see her salon friend, Movie Star Sam. Beside him stood a girl with curly hair.

"Charlotte, this is Marley, my girlfriend," Sam said. "Marley, Charlotte. She interned at Dad's firm when we were in college. She's a kickass mergers attorney with Jervis."

Marley smiled and held out her hand to shake, but Charlotte just waved.

"Where do you work, Marley?" Charlotte asked.

Score one schmoozer point for me.

"I intern at Howe and Clemson with Sam, hoping for job offers after we pass the bar."

"As long as you study, you should pass."

"See?" Marley said to Sam. "I'm not the only one who finds value in studying."

Jasper announced a table had just opened up, and they were heading over. Charlotte bid Marley and Sam farewell and followed Jasper to the table. Her colleagues filled each of the seats, and Charlotte stood there awkwardly, uncertain what to do. She knew what she wanted to do—end this ridiculous charade and go home. But she had to stay and prove herself to be "social," even though she'd rather be lying across Vine Street Expressway at rush hour.

"Here's a chair," Jasper said, pulling one from another table.

Charlotte perched on the edge of her seat, clutching her purse and drink, trying to follow the conversation around her. In the sea of noise, she couldn't hear a thing.

One of the women turned to her. "Charlotte, are you excited for the retreat next week?"

Excited, yes—if you all promise to go swimming with bloodthirsty sharks. Otherwise, no.

"Yes," was all she offered.

The co-worker nodded, then turned back, rejoining the group conversation.

One hour—that's as long as Charlotte would stay. A glance at the large clock on the wall revealed only fifteen minutes had passed. She prayed for an act of God to rescue her.

While the vibrating phone in her purse wasn't exactly what she'd hoped for, it was something—a perfect excuse to get out of this social nightmare. Assuming it was a client in need of her assistance, she leaped from her seat. In her haste to pull the phone from her purse, she knocked over her glass. Ginger ale raced across the table and streamed into the laps of her unsuspecting co-workers. They scrambled to stand, grabbing their belongings before they were saturated by the carbonated rapids.

"Jesus, Charlotte," Declan exclaimed as a wet spot the size of a dinner plate spread across his crotch. "What the fuck?"

"I'm—sorry," Charlotte said, glancing fervently around the table for napkins, but others were already on it. She scurried outside to take the call before the caller hung up. Too late. It had already gone to voicemail. She dialed in to listen to the message.

"Hi, this is Animal Control returning your call regarding a feral cat. It's important not to provide food or shelter for the animal, as that will only cause the colony to grow. If you can do so safely, it's best to trap and bring it to your local office for neutering."

Right. Like she was going to capture a wild animal and take it anywhere. She listened to the rest of the message, assuring they routinely patrolled the area and would be on the lookout.

Through the large picture window, she observed her co-workers inside as they schmoozed with one another. She felt a stab of envy that the gift of gab seemed to come so naturally to others but not her. It had never mattered before, until it became a prerequisite to partnership. She debated going back inside, but there was no need. She'd made the effort, tried being social, and yet felt invisible the entire time. Except, of course, when she doused them all in soda. It wouldn't matter to anyone if she left. In fact, they'd probably prefer it. Not that they'd even notice she was gone.

There was that damn cat again. This time sitting on the porch in front of her door.

"Git!" she yelled, swinging her purse toward the beast.

It raised its paw and gave a half-hearted swat, which looked more like an ill-fated attempt at a high-five. It almost made her laugh. Charlotte thrust her neck out, giving it a look of terror, hoping to intimidate it. The cat widened its eyes in return and stared her down before giving her a staccato meow.

"Look, there's a mouse!" Charlotte exclaimed, pointing down the street. "Get it before someone else does!"

The cat continued to sit there, staring at her.

"I guess you don't speak human," she mumbled.

It meowed in return.

"You dodged a bullet," she said. "You're lucky I hate cats. Animal Control wants me to trap you and take you somewhere, but that's not happening. You're gross. Disgusting. Putrid."

As more words of disdain poured from her snarled lips, Charlotte flashed back to the day in second grade when the teacher wouldn't excuse her to use the bathroom. Unable to hold it in, urine puddled across her seat, dripping at her feet. She sat in mortified silence, terrified someone would notice; her body's only movement was the tear rolling down her cheek.

"Gross!" one of the boys yelled once he noticed. "Charlotte peed on the floor!"

The kids around her scrambled from their desks as if she was spraying them with it.

"Eww!" the girls screamed in horror.

"Disgusting!" others chimed in.

For the remainder of the year, no one would sit with her at lunch or play with her at recess. Whenever she came close to other kids, they taunted her about her accident. She never fully lived it down; her classmates referred to her as Charlotte Wetsdale well into high school.

"I'm sorry," Charlotte now whispered to the cat, recalling how ostracized she'd felt that day. Every day. No need to do that to another being—human or not.

The cat tilted its head and meowed as if it understood her words.

"I know you enjoy your freedom, so let's make a deal. You stay away from me, and I won't have someone trap you. Deal?"

She could swear the cat's meow sounded just like *Deal*.

Bella

BELLA WAS EXCITED FOR HER FIRST FULL DAY OF SUMMER vacation, until Lisa asked her to take Eli to the boardwalk. As if she had nothing better to do with her time.

"But mo-*o*-om," Bella objected, "I want to go to the beach. Can't we do it tonight?"

"I'm not crazy about the boardwalk at night. It gets pretty wild out there," declared Lisa, Prophet of Doom, Slayer of Good Times. "What do you think, John?"

"Please, Dad? Can we go tonight?" Bella pleaded, then went for the mother-of-all winning arguments: "I'll watch Eli so you guys can have a dinner date."

Bella could barely get the words out. That was how disgusted she was, envisioning her parents on a date. But she had to appeal to them in some way.

"Okay," Lisa said. "You can go to the beach today and save the boardwalk for tonight."

In a rare moment, she and Eli looked at each other and smiled.

He held out his hand for a high five. "Just you and me, Bell!"

Bella lifted her hand to reciprocate but quickly pulled it back. "Psych!"

Hours later, looking in the mirror, Bella decided her tanning strategy hadn't been her best work. Thanks to creative application of sunscreen and limited knowledge of SPF, her face was the color of a Jersey tomato. She'd opted for one application of SPF 30 despite her mother's pleas for repeated applications of SPF 50. She'd only been out for a few hours. It shouldn't have been a big deal, but now it was. Bella didn't want to admit it, but her mom might have been right about this one.

Today's tally—Lisa: 1, Bella: 0.

"Bella, can we go now?" Eli banged on the bathroom door for the fiftieth time. "I wanna get there before the line gets too long!"

"Chill out, dweeb!" she snapped, making her mascara face and wincing as she swept her lashes.

"Vi-*per*! Vi-*per*! Vi-*per*!" Eli chanted along to a corresponding *thud*. Bella ignored him and took her time applying her makeup. When she finally opened the bathroom door, she found Eli lying on his back, feet banging the wall. She stepped over him and made her way to her bedroom as Eli scrambled to his feet.

"Ready? Ready? Ready?" He bounced along the hallway behind her.

"Yes, yes, yes," Bella said. "Calm down."

She longed to dip herself into an ice bath and get some relief from this burn, if only she hadn't agreed to boardwalk babysitting tonight. Bella's parents had already left for their "romantic dinner" (barf, gag). She couldn't renege on her agreement now, and even if she could, that would only make Lisa go apeshit. Not worth it.

They headed out to the deck, where Eli withdrew a lightsaber from his holster and fought imaginary threats, nearly swiping Bella's head. She grabbed the stick and almost snapped it in half until she realized the penalty for breaking her precious brother's prized toy would be life in prison without possibility of parole until her mid-thirties. It was the first night she and Eli were let loose on the boardwalk, and she had to prove to her parents they could trust her. A small step for her parents, perhaps, but a huge leap for teen-kind. At fifteen, one simply couldn't have enough Sweet Freedom.

Eli bounded down the steps, and Bella turned to lock the door when she heard a noise. Someone was standing on the deck next door—a cute guy, from what she could tell. He waved, and Bella reciprocated before scurrying to the steps so he couldn't see she was hanging out with her dorky brother.

"Goin' to the boards?" he called out.

"Yeah," Bella answered over her shoulder like it was no big deal for her to be *goin' to the boards* alone. As if her life wasn't one big G-rated movie, and she roamed the earth without restriction on a routine basis. As if a foray into the wilds of the Ocean City Boardwalk—at night and completely devoid of parental stranglehold—was a natural occurrence. She was just glad Eli was out of his range of vision. She wouldn't want him knowing her date for the night was an untamed, saber-wielding, third grader.

"Maybe I'll see you there," he responded.

Eli's excitement was palpable as he bounced the entire ten blocks to the Viper.

"Wow." He sighed, looking up at the ride. "Tonight, I will finally soar to the highest heights of my young life! I just hope I don't throw up."

"You won't," Bella said, chuckling. She found herself almost hoping he'd make the height requirement. Almost.

They made their way to the entrance when a teenage ride operator stopped them. "Hey, champ, step over here. Let's check your height."

Eli bounded over to the height chart. The closer he got, the more apparent it was he was still too short. He looked crestfallen but stood tall, thrusting his shoulders back, trying hard to gain the additional half inch he needed. Bella marveled at the kid's optimism.

"Oh, dude, I'm sorry," the ride guy said to Eli, sounding sincere. "You're a smidge shy of the mark."

"But I spent all year stretching!" Eli said.

Bella might otherwise have laughed, but the look on Eli's face broke her heart. It was one thing for her to dash his dreams—as his older sister, it was her inalienable, firstborn right. But when others threatened to do so, Bella couldn't help but feel a surge of protection over the tiny doofus.

"Can't you let him slide?" Bella asked.

Obvs the rule was there for a reason, but Eli was so close to being tall enough. Not that she wanted to endanger her brother, although the thought of him being catapulted into the Atlantic was kinda funny. But he missed the mark by such a teensy amount, he'd probably be fine.

Ride Guy looked at her with a sad face. "I would, but I don't want him to get hurt. And that guy over there is a real stickler about height," he said, pointing to an older man in a red polo.

Squatting to Eli's eye level, he asked how old he was.

"Oh man, when I was eight, I wanted so badly to go on this ride, too," he said sincerely. "I know exactly how you feel. Trust me. You'll get there."

It was pretty decent of the kid to share his own experiences. He could've been a jerk and sent them packing.

"Sorry, buddy," Bella said, backing up Ride Guy's decision. "They have rules for a reason."

She widened her eyes at the guy to convey the need for a teachable moment. She knew analytical Eli would get it if he understood the rationale behind the height chart. Ride Guy seemed to pick up what she was putting down. He launched into an explanation of the ride's design and the physics behind keeping someone safe.

"How long are you down here for, Eli?" he asked.

"The whole summer."

Ride Guy nodded. "Tell you what. I'm gonna be here all summer too. Why don't you keep stretching and come back periodically so we can measure you. If you're still not tall enough by the end of summer, I'll let you on the ride. Let's say, Labor Day weekend. Our schedules are set for the entire summer, and I'll be working alone that Sunday night when the height sticklers won't be here."

Eli nodded enthusiastically. "Do you mean it?"

"I do, but here's the deal. You must do at least three nice things for people between now and then."

Eli bounced up and down. "I'm in!"

Ride Guy stood and faced Bella, smiling. "I know that sounds weird, but it's what my grandfather says whenever I ask for something. It really does make a difference in how you approach your goal."

Weird wasn't the word that came to Bella's mind. Just because a grandparent would say that didn't mean a Gen Z-er had to repeat it. Whatever. He had a nice smile, so she decided to cut him a break.

Eli asked Ride Guy what he needed to do to uphold his end of the bargain. He was an old soul that way—he loved school, following rules, and doing chores. The guy's plan was right up his alley. Bella, on the other hand, would've told him to beat it.

"Help someone who's older. Offer to carry their beach stuff," Ride Guy suggested.

"Like my sister? She's older," Eli asked in all seriousness.

"No, I was thinking someone slightly older, like maybe someone in their—"

"Thirties. I get it. Like my aunts and uncles."

Bella and Ride Guy chuckled, and Bella clarified he meant someone more like Grandma and Grandpa's age.

"Oh, you mean ancient. Okay. What else?"

As Ride Guy gave other examples, Bella wondered how she could benefit from this deal, maybe unload some of her chores onto the mini-man. She'd have to give this some thought.

Eli shook Ride Guy's hand, agreeing to come back and report his progress.

"Bring your sister, too," Ride Guy said to Eli as he gave Bella a smile. She felt herself blushing. He had kind brown eyes, and she liked the way he talked to Eli.

"Sure!" she said. Anything for Eli.

Wait, what? Did she really just agree to take this kid to the boardwalk multiple times throughout the summer? *Somebody slap some sense into me.*

Marley

MARLEY AND SAM'S SUPERVISOR CALLED THEM INTO A meeting Monday afternoon.

"I've got bad news," Maxine said. "The firm was hoping to hire you both after the bar, but we're downsizing. We'll only have one spot open this fall. I'm sorry."

Marley's heart sank. This was the worst possible news, other than failing the bar itself.

"That sucks," Sam said.

"I know." Maxine nodded. "You're both valued members of our team."

Marley fought back tears. It was her dream to work for this firm alongside Sam as they had for two years now.

"How will you decide which one of us you're hiring?" Sam asked, his jaw tightening.

"All things about you being equal, the only fair method is your bar exam scores."

Maxine's announcement added a whole new layer of stress. Now, it wasn't just a matter of passing the bar, but scoring higher than Sam. Her boyfriend. Her heart.

"I can't believe this," Sam muttered as they left the meeting. He side-punched the wall. "Utter bullshit."

Marley sucked on her quivering lip as tears broke free. Sam guided her into his office and shut the door. He ran his hands through his hair as he looked out the window, his back to Marley.

"It's yours," he finally said, turning back and leaning against his desk.

"But Sam—"

"No, Marley, this has been your dream firm. I'll go tell them now. I'm out of the running."

"What will you do?" she asked.

"Origami," he said, through a defeated half-smile. "Maybe I'll make a tiny law firm out of paper, and you and I can shrink ourselves down and work there together."

"Seriously."

"I'll work for my dad."

"But you don't want to!" Marley said, taking his hands. "Why are they doing this to us?"

"All's fair in love and law, Mar," he said, shrugging. "They're not doing it to us. It's just business. We can't take it personally."

"We've worked here for two years, and they practically promised us jobs after graduation."

"I'm just pissed they're trying to pit us against each other. That's why I'm out of the running. I'm not fighting against you. The job's yours—I'll tell them."

Sam kissed the top of her head and walked to the door.

"Wait," Marley called out. "What if they're just going after low-hanging fruit? Let's not make their decision for them. Let's force their hands; see what happens. The bar results aren't due until October. By then, they could change their minds. When others get wind of the downsizing, maybe they'll jump ship and both our spots will open up."

Sam returned to Marley and cupped her face, kissing her. "This is why I love you. You're brilliant."

"Your dad's firm is the ace up your sleeve. Since you have that open-ended offer as a backup, let's ride it out."

It was also Marley's ace up her own sleeve. Even if Sam scored higher, he'd just agreed to go to his dad's firm. She didn't want that for him, but drastic times and all. She was selfishly relieved he was willing to make that sacrifice. It meant the job was hers either way, a win-win. While it would be a bummer not to work together, a lot could change before then.

"I never knew you to be the gambling type," Sam said, smiling down at her.

"I'm not ready to fold just yet," she said. "Plus, knowing I have to score better than you will up my game."

Sam laughed. "Is that why you want me to stay in the running, to wipe the floor with my piss-poor bar exam scores?"

"Pretty much."

"Okay, Maguire. Game on. May the better lawyer win."

"I plan to," Marley said as she headed for the door. "Looking forward to visiting you at your dad's firm."

Sam's laughter filled the room like music as she closed the door behind her.

Bella

BELLA'S FAMILY ARRIVED AT THE DOCK FOR A MORNING of back-bay fishing with Uncle Jake and her mom's other siblings, Ryan and Amy. Everyone was in town for the long holiday weekend and Bella was excited to spend time with her aunts, uncles, and toddler cousins. They'd be joining other passengers on the boat where Jake worked, which offered fishing charters by day and sunset cruises by night.

"Ahoy, matey!" Eli called out to Uncle Jake, who was waiting on the dock.

"Ahoy, Captain!" Jake saluted Eli. "Ready for your big fishing adventure?"

"*Yessir*, I am, sir!"

"At ease, sailor," Jake said, ruffling Eli's hair.

Jake greeted everyone with hugs. When he got to Bella, they did their special handshake.

"Girl, I swear you look older every time I see you. How's college going?"

"I got a tattoo, took up smoking, and joined a sorority. How 'bout you?"

"OMG, same!" Jake said and gave her a fist bump.

"Got any coffee in this jawn?" Bella asked, ruing the decision to stay up Snapchatting with friends until three.

Jake pointed to a walk-up window on the dock. Bella scored a piping hot cup of life-affirming java just as Aunt Amy and Uncle Michael arrived with their toddler twins, Violet and Petunia, whom Bella often babysat. Uncle Ryan and his bride-to-be, Kate, arrived next. While she wasn't yet an official aunt, Bella adored Kate. She was closer to her in age than her other relatives and hadn't forgotten what it was like to be a teenage girl. She knew Bella's friends by name and always gave great advice.

"Since when do you drink coffee?" Ryan teased Bella as he hugged her. "Weren't you born, like, yesterday?"

"She was born fifteen years, two months, three weeks, and four days ago," Eli said. "I figured it out in the car yesterday."

"Then it's five days ago if you figured it out yesterday," Bella corrected him.

She delighted in proving Eli wrong the one or two times a year it occurred. She wasn't a math geek like him and didn't see the need to be. That's what phones were for.

"Nope, already calculated it. Do the math, Bella," Eli said.

Bella stuck out her foot to trip him, but he jumped over it. She knew he'd been coached by her mom "not to react" when Bella taunted him, which only made her want to do it more.

Once other passengers arrived for Jake's fishing trip, they all climbed aboard.

"Uncle Jake put me in charge of fishing gear," Eli explained to Bella as he handed her a rod. "It's my first good deed."

"That isn't a good deed," Bella said. "You're doing Uncle Jake a favor. Ride Guy meant do something you normally wouldn't do."

Eli nodded. "Got it."

Out on the bay, the wind kicked up. One of the passengers, an older man, cried out as a gust of wind deposited his hat in the water. Without hesitating, Eli dove into the water and swam toward the hat.

"Eli!" Lisa shrieked. "What are you doing? John, go get him!"

"He's fine," Eli's dad said, waving her off. "You're fine, right?"

Eli gave a thumbs up and lifted the hat from the water. Everyone cheered.

The man retrieved the hat from a wet and shivering Eli, who read the inscription aloud. "US Army Vietnam Veteran.

Wow. Thank you for your service."

"This hat reminds me every day of the friends I lost over there," the man said. "I can't thank you enough."

Eli told the man he was just doing what anyone would do.

"Now, that's a good deed!" Bella said as she wrapped a towel around him.

She was surprised and impressed by her brother's quick thinking and fearlessness. Bella wouldn't have jumped into the bay for any amount of money because #sharks and all. Okay, maybe for a million bucks. Or a new iPhone.

"I just did the right thing," Eli said. Proving, once again, her brother was a better human.

No wonder everyone liked him more.

Charlotte

CHARLOTTE DRYSDALE WANTED TO BE ANYWHERE BUT here.

Here, unintentionally sprawled on a dock as her co-workers jeered at her from the upper deck of *Sea Urchin! A Party Boat!*

Slipping and falling wasn't the impression she'd been hoping to make with the senior partners of Jervis Mahoney. She was here to prove she was a team player. A schmoozer. Worthy of partnership, not a neck brace. Tumbling off a boat had not been in the plan. But here she was.

She'd joined her boss and co-workers in Stone Harbor for the dreaded three-day retreat, much against her free will. The sunset cruise was the first of many planned activities. According to Tom Jervis, the annual retreats provided an opportunity for current and prospective partners to bond, but after years of attending them, Charlotte felt no more bonded to her co-workers than she did the stray cat that had taken up residence under her porch.

Charlotte would have preferred to spend the weekend in her office, where she wouldn't have to interact with other humans. Not that her co-workers would qualify as such. Simians, perhaps—then again, that was an insult to knuckle-dragging primates. But, if Charlotte was anything, she was precise and obedient. As much as she hated it, the retreat could be her chance to show them all just how well she fit in and what a good partner she'd make. If only she could figure out how. She suspected that wiping out on the dock wasn't the way.

"Have another one, Charlotte," Rhys called out.

"Ah, leave her alone," replied Declan. "At least she makes the rest of us look less drunk!"

Charlotte wasn't drunk. She had an absolute limit of one drink per outing, and this outing was no different. In fact, she'd only taken one sip of her piña colada when she accidentally dropped her sweater onto the dock below. She made the executive decision to retrieve it before the boat crew lifted the ramp, but the steep slope and slippery surface were too much for even her practical flats to handle. Her feet slipped, and kerplunk she went. Her drink, held high in her hand, survived the fall.

"I got you." A kind stranger helped her up with a smooth pull of his muscular arm. As he steadied her, she looked up into a pair of indigo eyes matching the polo shirt he was wearing, on which *Sea Urchin Crew* was embroidered in white thread.

"Sorry," Charlotte instinctively muttered as she stepped back from him. He had dark, wavy hair and a bright smile. She was immune to the charm of attractive men, believing good-looking guys to be cocky, shallow, and unintelligent. But this one seemed—different. His eyes were kind, the look on his face genuine.

"No worries." He handed her the sweater. "I'm Jake."

"Jake." Charlotte registered his name aloud to remember it. "Thank you. Jake."

"Nice job on the drink, but the way." He winked at her still upright piña colada.

It was one thing to fall, but Charlotte wouldn't allow herself to add insult to injury, spilling the only drink she was allotted that night, thereby having to purchase another. She was practical that way. Case in point: she lived in a major city on a fraction of her income, in a house she'd inherited. She packed her lunch every day, never went out, and didn't take vacations. After groceries and bills, the remainder of her six-figure salary was socked away for the purchase of her future Main Line home.

Jake took Charlotte's elbow as if to guide her. She instinctively yanked it away.

"I'm good," she snapped. The last thing she needed was to be molested by a boat person.

"My bad." Jake held up his hands as if Charlotte had pulled a gun on him.

She made her way back up the ramp, carefully this time, relieved her rubber-necking co-workers had shifted their focus to small-minded cocktail talk.

Charlotte sought refuge on the lower deck, wrapping her sweater around her shoulders to block the breeze as the boat pulled away from the dock. No sense in risking a summer cold. With another big project looming on the horizon, she couldn't spare a day for sickness. Which reminded her—the boat man had touched her hand. She pulled sanitizer out of her purse. She never traveled without it. Or tissues, Wet Ones, and a book. Especially a book for times like tonight when conversation would prove tedious.

She thought about the man who'd helped her. Jake. She was appreciative of his kind gesture, assisting when co-workers didn't. She should repay him, perhaps tip him after they docked. Three dollars should do it.

An announcement came over the loudspeaker, but she couldn't make out the words. A chorus of "oohs" wafted down from the deck above. Charlotte wondered if it was a *Guaranteed Dolphin Sighting!* as the cruise brochure promised. She wasn't sure how the company could command such compliance by wild mammals and whether a refund was in order if they couldn't.

She finished her drink, preparing to join co-workers and earn points. After all, that was the whole point of her being here. The drink helped soften her usual anti-social edge, almost to the point she was ready for inane chitter chatter.

"Can I get you another drink?" a familiar voice said from behind her. Jake.

Charlotte had reached her one-drink maximum. They were now on open water, and the boat had started rocking. It was too late for Dramamine as she'd already consumed alcohol and wasn't about to add a drug interaction to this already awkward night. She declined his offer but remembered she needed to thank him for his earlier good deed. She retrieved her wallet and handed him three crisp bills.

"For helping me earlier."

"Oh, ma'am, that's generous, but I couldn't," he said, a hint of humor in his voice. "Please, save it for something else."

He was right. She should save it. Charlotte tucked the bills back into her wallet.

"Besides, you already thanked me," Jake said as he pulled a chair over, spun it around and straddled it. He rested his tan arms across the backrest and nodded towards the upper deck. "You part of this group?"

"Yes."

Jake narrowed his eyes at her. "You don't seem like one of them."

"In what way?" she asked, terrified it was that obvious she didn't fit in.

"Well, you're not as—hmm, how shall I put it?"

"Imbecilic." Charlotte nodded, cutting to the chase.

"Fun...is, actually, what I was going to say."

Charlotte recoiled as if he'd slapped her. "I'm fun!"

"Yeah? Then why are you sitting down here by yourself?"

She looked away.

"Business trip, I take it?" he asked.

Charlotte realized she could practice small talk with him, since she frankly didn't care what he thought of her if she happened to say the wrong thing. Her IQ was clearly superior to his. After all, he worked on a boat.

"Yes, a work retreat. I was told I have to socialize. I guess that's not happening with me sitting down here."

Jake pushed the chair back and stood.

"Come on," he said, summoning her to follow. "Let's mingle."

Jake led her to a narrow metal stairway. Charlotte ascended to the top deck and turned to say something, but he was gone. As she made her way through the crowd, raindrops began to fall. The captain came over the loudspeaker to confirm an approaching storm and announced they'd be turning around. The crowd groaned, but he promised the bar would remain open and they could stay aboard until the scheduled end of the cruise.

Suddenly realizing she'd left her purse downstairs, Charlotte backed down the steps, holding on for dear life. She didn't need another fall tonight. When she didn't find her purse where she'd left it, full panic set in. It had to have been that deckhand.

Between her asinine co-workers and the kleptomaniac boat crew, Charlotte was done with this whole trip. In fact, she was on her way to tell the captain about her stolen purse when she heard a voice behind her.

"Hey, Charlotte, how'd it go up there?" Jake asked.

"Where's my purse?" she demanded.

"I tucked it away for safekeeping."

He retrieved her purse from a locked closet and handed it to her. She inventoried its contents.

"Don't worry, I didn't steal anything," he said, laughing as he reached in his pocket. "Except a tissue, but I'll return it."

She recoiled in horror.

"Just kidding."

Charlotte was relieved. One could never be too certain. "Thank you. I guess I owe you for that, too."

"You can repay me by telling me how it went up there. Were you the life of the party, as expected?"

As Jake wiped down the bar, he inquired about the law firm and her area of specialty. She explained she handled mergers and acquisitions, to which Jake posed a series of questions suggesting he knew something about the world of business and finance. Charlotte wondered how he would know such things. He didn't look like someone who could *spell* Wall Street, much less know what it was.

It was getting late, so she said goodbye and went upstairs, only to find the boat deck and parking lot empty. Her co-workers had left without her.

"They're gone," she said as Jake joined her. "I'm not sure how I'm getting back."

"Where are you staying?"

"My boss's house in Stone Harbor."

"No worries. I can take you. I just need to clean up first, if you don't mind."

Charlotte weighed her options. She could call Tom Jervis, but she didn't want to bother him. Jake was her only choice unless she wanted to take an Uber, which she absolutely did not. He wasn't setting off her stranger danger radar, so he was probably the safest bet. Bonus: she'd already memorized his features if she later had to do a composite sketch.

It began pouring, forcing them to return to the lower deck.

"I still have more to do, but I can take you now if you're anxious to get back to your co-workers."

"I'd rather do time in a maximum-security prison," she said.

Jake laughed out loud. "Okay, but I'm gonna put you to work."

Fair enough for a free ride home. She was grateful to have something to do other than rejoin her co-workers, especially since nobody had thought to wait for her. Not even Tom Jervis.

Jake kept the conversation going as they secured the lower deck, asking her questions about herself. He listened intently, posing thoughtful follow-up questions.

"What made you choose law?" he asked.

She paused to consider her answer. Nobody had ever asked her that before.

"I like rules," she said after giving it some thought. "The law, when followed, provides order and consistency in our world. I like that."

"If you like law and order, why didn't you become a prosecutor?" Jake asked.

"I tried." She wasn't sure she wanted to tell him the story, but frankly didn't care what he thought of her since she'd never see him again. There was something calming about him that made talking easy. Maybe because he actually listened.

She told him about her first ill-fated trial and how she threw up in the middle of testimony when the assault victim described his injuries. Tom Jervis had been in the courtroom that day and took pity on her, telling her he was impressed with her attention to detail and "regurgitation" of the facts. He gave her his card and told her if she wanted to work for a private firm to give him a call. So she did.

Charlotte asked Jake questions in return. Not that she cared about the details of his life, but she understood communication to be a two-way street. She had to pretend to care if she wanted to be a good communicator.

"Have you always wanted to work on a boat?" she asked.

Jake laughed. "No, it's just a way to make some cash before I'm off to follow my dream."

"What's your dream?" Charlotte asked, hoping she didn't sound as condescending as she felt. What dream could possibly be achieved working on a boat?

"To sail around the world."

"Why?" Charlotte felt her face scrunch with judgment.

"Freedom. My love of the open sea. Being one with nature."

"Wouldn't you rather get a real job and make good money?"

"Money isn't everything. Trust me," Jake said.

How would he know? He probably hadn't earned enough to know what kind of difference money could make. "No, but you can do a lot with it."

"What's your dream, Charlotte?" he asked.

"Make partner at my firm and buy a house on the Main Line."

"Hmm. I don't see you on the Main Line."

"Probably because you don't know what it is."

"Sure, I know what the Main Line is," he said. "I grew up on the Jersey side of the city, so I know all about the wealthy 'burbs of PA. Lots of people with preppy names live there."

He was right. Most everyone she knew who lived on the Main Line were co-workers and clients with names suggesting they should have college buildings named after them.

"Drink?" Jake asked as he went behind the bar, poured two small glasses of whiskey, and handed her one. Charlotte shoved the drink away. She'd already reached her one-drink maximum.

"Come on, relax a little," Jake said. "I don't want to drink alone."

It didn't matter to her one bit if he drank alone. A rule was a rule. But he'd been kind to her, the only person on the boat interested in talking to her. She made an exception to her rule, deciding it would be rude to refuse.

"To new friendship," Jake said as he clinked her glass with his.

She was thrown off by his comment. It had been a long time since someone wanted to befriend her. She took a sip of the pungent liquid and grimaced.

"Not a big drinker, I see."

"I don't like to lose control."

Jake laughed. "You don't say?"

Charlotte liked the twinkle in his eye. He reminded her of a young James Marsden in *The Notebook*. Another favorite movie from Gram's collection.

Jake downed his drink. Oh my. And he was her ride home?

Charlotte considered her next steps, as she never took any without thorough contemplation. The glass was small, so there wasn't much in it. She could pour it out when he wasn't looking, nurse it all night, or—

Quand à Rome...

She threw her head back and drained her glass. Her throat and eyes stung. For a second, she thought she might vomit.

"Impressive," Jake said.

Reeling from the throat scorch, Charlotte removed her glasses and wiped her burning eyes. He smiled as he poured another drink for each of them. She hoped it wasn't because he'd slipped her a molly.

"You have pretty eyes," he said.

Charlotte hugged her purse to her chest, not sure what he was up to. Was he trying to flatter her, get her drunk so he could have his way with her? Steal her money?

"They're such a unique color," he continued. "Golden, like crispy pancakes."

Charlotte laughed despite her fears. Maybe from nerves. Or

whiskey. Perhaps both. She'd received the occasional compliment on her eyes but never comparing them to breakfast food.

As Jake shared funny stories about other sunset cruises he'd run, Charlotte felt herself loosening up. She wasn't quite sure what had come over her, but she liked talking to this guy. He was giving her good schmoozing vibes. She'd definitely have to tip him after this was over. Maybe she'd offer five dollars this time.

"I made good money once," Jake said, swirling his glass, watching as the amber liquid coated the sides. "I was a New York investment banker."

"Ah." Charlotte nodded. "Thus, your knowledge of M&A."

It made sense. The average Joe Boater wouldn't know as much about finances as he did.

"Yep, I was all in," he continued. "Lavish lifestyle, wealthy friends, great apartment overlooking Central Park. But I was working so much I couldn't enjoy any of it. I was completely empty."

Charlotte knew exactly what he meant.

"Then I went sailing one day and decided I'd much rather deal with wind and waves than the hot air and meltdowns of the blowhards around me."

Again, Charlotte could relate. Not that she knew much about the ocean, but she certainly knew a lot about people behaving badly. She spent most of her time in observation, quite like Jane Goodall and her chimps, witnessing the behavior of the primates who surrounded her.

She picked up her drink and took a slow sip, enjoying the feeling as it went down. Smooth. Calming. She wondered why she'd limited herself to just one drink all these years. Alcohol had the opposite effect of what she'd feared. The more she drank, the clearer things became.

"It's interesting you'd rather deal with the ocean than people. I get it," she said.

"Beyond owning a Main Line McMansion, what else do you want from life?" Jake asked as he rounded the bar and pulled a stool next to hers. "Say you become a partner and buy your house. What will you aim for next?"

Charlotte hadn't thought that far ahead. Suddenly, her dream seemed to be missing something—the next big thing. There wasn't a time in her life when she wasn't striving to achieve a goal. Valedictorian, for acceptance into Penn. High LSAT scores, to get into Harvard Law. Graduating at the top of her class, to land a prestigious job. And now making partner, so she could live in a wealthy suburb. But then...what?

Jake narrowed his eyes. "I'm guessing you're seeking something else. Something you think you'll get from making partner and owning a huge house." He snapped his fingers. "I know. Power. Or respect. Maybe both. You believe it's lacking in your life. People don't respect you now, but if you're a partner, you'll have power, and they'll have to respect you."

He was right. She couldn't wait to be made partner so she could lord it over her asinine co-workers and command their respect.

"Have you ever thought about going out on your own? Being your own partner?" he asked.

"Never." She had zero interest in working anywhere but Jervis Mahoney.

"You should consider it," he said. "There's an attorney here at the shore, a sole practitioner who loves what he does. I can introduce you, if you'd like. You can see what it's like to not have to play the billable hour game."

Charlotte couldn't imagine a life without billable hours. It was all she knew. Accounting for every minute of the day, striving to partake in as many billable activities as possible. It was a matter of survival in a law firm. It was exhausting.

Charlotte's glasses were fogging up from the humidity, so she removed them.

"Do you ever wear contacts?" Jake asked. "Your peepers are too amazing to hide behind glasses."

"Your charm isn't going to work on me, you know."

What had come over her? Was she...*flirting?*

"Sorry. You'd look great either way. As they say, 'Guys make passes at girls with glasses.'"

That was news to Charlotte. No guy had ever made a pass at her. If one tried, she'd likely wallop him with her purse.

"I'll ask you the same question," she said, replacing her glasses. "What do you hope to achieve by sailing around the globe?"

"World domination," he answered.

Hmm. Maybe an Uber ride would be safer than trusting her life with a world-sailing lunatic.

He winked. "JK. I just love sailing. And the opportunity to see the world is priceless."

"Are you running from something?"

"Maybe."

"What?" She placed her hand on his arm. Unusual for her, being someone who wasn't particularly fond of human touch, but probably something a schmoozer would do.

"Life, I guess," he said as he looked at her hand. She yanked it away in case she'd misjudged appropriate social behavior.

He continued. "Nah, I like life. Maybe loneliness. I dunno."

"Won't you be lonelier on a boat?"

Jake hesitated. "I'm pretty lonely here on land, even when surrounded by friends and family."

"I get it," Charlotte said. "I feel lonelier in a crowd than when I'm by myself. Comfortable alone, awkward around people."

"Not you!" Jake said jokingly.

"I hide it well." She punched his arm like someone in a movie would do. Only it was more of a slug. *Hey Tom Jervis— watch me now!*

"I wouldn't think someone who looks like you would ever feel lonely," she said.

"I think many people's first impression is I'm shallow."

"I can't believe people would judge you like that," Charlotte said, despite having just judged him like that. "You certainly can't have problems meeting women."

"The problem isn't meeting them. It's matching interests. I'm thirty-two and single as the day is long. But I have no desire to change that, and people don't get it. Especially my family. They think I'm being picky, but I want to explore the world, experience life outside my immediate surroundings before I settle down. I just haven't met anyone who either wants to join me on that journey or inspires me to stray from it."

"That's not being picky. It's being practical," Charlotte said. "You just haven't met the right person. I want to make partner more than I want someone in my life. When I meet that person who tips those scales, if ever, perhaps I'll feel differently."

"Preach," Jake said, clinking his glass against hers. "My sisters are both married, and my younger brother's getting married next year. They keep trying to set me up with someone for the wedding, hoping it will lead to more, but I'm not going to agree just for the sake of having a date."

"Because that would feel lonelier than going alone."

"You do get it."

Of course, she did. Charlotte never brought a date to the occasional family weddings she attended, mostly because they didn't extend the "plus-one" courtesy. She preferred it that way.

"Maybe I am running away—not so much from loneliness, but expectations," he said. "You sure you're not a shrink?"

"I don't think I'd make a good one. I basically hate people."

"Welcome to the lonely hearts club." Jake clinked his glass with hers. "I guess we're pretty similar that way."

Charlotte almost fell off her chair. Nobody had ever suggested she had commonalities with another humanoid, especially one that looked like, well, *him.*

Jake asked if she wanted another. She shouldn't, but she

rather enjoyed the warm feeling it was giving her, not to mention the ability to talk so freely with someone. Perhaps she didn't need to schmooze more—she just needed to drink more.

The wind-driven rain continued to thrash against the windows, yet she felt safe here on the lower deck with Jake. As he made their drinks, Charlotte wondered what it would be like to run her hands through his wavy hair, guessing it was soft. She couldn't believe this type of specimen would ever feel lonely.

They continued asking each other thought-provoking questions until Jake noted the rain had let up.

"How about one more?" Charlotte suggested.

"Okay, but then I definitely won't be driving you back to Stone Harbor tonight. I'll have to call you an Uber."

Charlotte told him she didn't Uber. He offered to walk her home before she told him her boss's house was thirty blocks away.

"I'll tell you what. I live a couple blocks from here," Jake said. "You can crash in one of my guest rooms. No monkey business."

She considered her options: take a chance on Uber with a driver she knew nothing about, walk to Jervis's house and maybe get there by morning, or take Jake up on his offer. She'd never agree to such a preposterous suggestion when sober, but the drinks lowered her inhibitions and raised her trust. In truth, she felt safer with him than the co-workers she'd known for years or any rideshare driver working this late at night. She just hoped she wouldn't end up as a headline the next morning: "Woman Murdered by Local Sailor; Four Drinks to Blame."

As she walked the darkened street with Jake, Charlotte began second-guessing her decision to go home with a man she'd just met that night, whose last name she didn't even know. What was she thinking? She was about to turn back when they arrived at the driveway of a beachfront home.

"Your parents' house?" she asked, relieved at the prospect others may be there.

"Nope."

"Sure you're not married?"

Jake slapped his forehead. "Oh, God. I forgot—I *am* married! *And* I have four kids."

Charlotte was aghast at the thought she'd been played, until he laughed. Recalling their discussion about their shared singlehood, she reluctantly followed him to the door, expecting the inside of his house to be a pizza-box-infested bachelor pad. Not that she'd ever seen one before, other than in movies. Instead, she was pleasantly surprised to find an open-concept living area awash in neutral hues, looking like it belonged in a design magazine.

Jake grabbed two water bottles and led her to the deck outside. The sky, now clear, was ablaze with stars. One shot across the sky as they watched.

"Shooting star!" Jake exclaimed.

"Actually, it's space debris, heating as it passes through the atmosphere."

"How romantic. Tell me more!" he joked.

"Don't get me started on astronomy."

Later, after Jake got her settled in his guest room, Charlotte worried again that she'd made a colossal mistake agreeing to stay in a stranger's home. But the bed was comfortable, and soon, her trepidation melted away as she was swept peacefully from the scary waking world to safe, sweet slumber.

Marley

MARLEY AND SAM MET KATE AND RYAN AT THE CLINK ON Thursday as planned.

"Let's see this ring!" Marley exclaimed.

Kate held her hand out to display a beautiful emerald-cut diamond.

"Gorgeous." Marley sighed.

"Wow, man, you did great," Sam said.

"I'm here for you for all your future ring-buying needs, dude," Ryan said. "I can even tell you what the four C's are."

"Which are...?" Kate asked, smiling up at her fiancé.

"Carat, clarity, cut...and *crap, there goes my savings.*"

Kate and Ryan laughed.

"The fourth is color, right?" Sam asked.

Kate gave Sam a teasing glance. "How does our boy know so much about rings?"

"It's what I do," he said. "I hang out on Jeweler's Row, and I know things."

After a toast to their engagement, Kate handed Marley and Sam each a shirt box, one wrapped in pink paper, the other navy blue.

"What's this?" Marley asked.

"Open, you'll see."

Inside Marley's box was a framed picture of Kate and Marley on the beach, with the words #bride and #bridesmaid beneath each of them, respectively.

"Are you serious?" she squealed.

"Very," Kate said, nodding.

Marley was pleasantly surprised. Kate had lots of friends,

and she didn't expect to be one of her trusted bridesmaids. "I'm humbled and honored, Kate. Thank you!"

"You've become one of my BFFs. I couldn't imagine doing it without you."

Marley felt the same connection to Kate. She didn't have a lot of female friends after spending the past seven years in the captivating presence of a male BFF. Kate's gesture meant the world to her.

"Yes, Kate, I'll be your bridesmaid, too," Sam joked, holding up his box.

She laughed. "You'll look great in pink."

"No pink for you, my man. Open it." Ryan gave him a playful punch on the arm.

Inside Sam's box was a picture of Ryan and Sam on the beach with their surfboards bearing the words #groom and #groomsman.

Sam gave Ryan a man hug. "Thanks, bruh. Wouldn't miss it for the world."

"So when and where?" Marley asked excitedly.

"June 22 of next year, at Ferry Park."

"What a perfect setting." Marley sighed, recalling the significance of the park. It was where Kate had chased down Ryan as he was heading home on the ferry, after a misunderstanding that almost ended their relationship before it had a chance to begin. "Who else is in the wedding party?"

"Bridesmaids are Delaney, Cleo, and Ryan's sisters, Amy and Lisa. His niece, Bella, is our junior bridesmaid."

"Best man is my brother, Jake, and groomsmen are Kate's brother JJ, my cousin Dalton, and my brothers-in-law, Michael and John," Ryan said.

"Just the important people," Kate said as she squeezed Marley's hand. "We're trying to get the entire wedding party and our families together over New Year's since Delaney and Dalton will be back for the holidays. We're renting out a couple Airbnbs in Cape May and treating you all to tickets for Congress Hall's New Year's Eve gala. Do you think you guys can make it?"

"Wouldn't miss it for the world!" Marley exclaimed.

"Great. We want everyone to get to know one another. Makes the wedding more fun that way."

Back at Marley's condo, she and Kate changed into pajamas and opened a bottle of wine.

"I'm happy you suggested a girls' night," Marley said as they settled on the couch. "We have so much catching up to do, like your trip, the wedding plans, and—"

"Rick being on *The Bachelorette*!" Kate exclaimed. "How are you doing with that?"

Marley had texted Kate when it happened, but they hadn't had a chance to dissect it all.

"I can't believe he's lasted this long. Who would ever have thought he'd continue to get rose after rose each week?" Certainly not Marley.

"I'm sure his days are numbered," Kate said. "Wasn't he shy around his own shadow?"

Marley chuckled. "Yeah, he's not exactly a reality TV heartthrob. I still feel guilty for how it ended between us, and I do want him to find someone, just not on national TV. Hopefully, he won't drag me into it—you know how they love those past-relationship sob stories."

"He wouldn't do that, would he?"

"No," she said with conviction. She never knew Rick to be vengeful, even after their breakup.

"Can we watch the latest episode?" Kate stifled a giggle, hands over her mouth. "Please?"

Marley didn't exactly feel like spending their night together watching TV, but she hadn't seen the latest episode yet. She hoped this would finally be the week he was sent home so he'd no longer harsh their reality TV vibe.

Onscreen, a man entered a room where a group of men were seated on a couch. "Date card!" he announced. "Which lucky guy gets the next one-on-one with Brie? Let's see..." He opened the card. "Rick!"

The men seated on the TV couch appeared confused. The women seated on Marley's couch shared the same puzzled expressions.

"There must be something wrong with her," Kate said. "Look at that couch full of raw male meat, and she chooses Rick?"

"I have no words," Marley muttered.

"Sorry, that was rude. You dated the guy for three years. There must be something special about him."

"He *is* a good guy. But..." She pointed to the other men on the screen. "Seriously?"

Brie and Rick spent the afternoon frolicking with horses at a dude ranch before soaking al fresco in a hot tub. He poured champagne as Brie brought up the topic of past relationships. It was expected of *Bachelorette* participants—the more trauma drama, the better.

"I can't believe you've only had one girlfriend," Brie said.

"I'm brutally shy. It takes a lot for me to talk to a girl."

"What was it about this girl?"

"She was approachable and kind. She lit up every room she walked into."

"Aww," Marley and Kate simultaneously crooned.

"What happened?"

"She broke my heart. I'd been hinting about marriage, but she couldn't commit."

"Why not?"

"She was a law student in Philly, and I lived in Ohio."

"Oh, no—" Marley shot straight up. He'd better not be going there.

"Distance wasn't the only issue. I'd given her a promise ring. Got down on one knee and said, 'Marley, I know you're not ready, but I want to marry you one day.' She thanked me by dreaming about her best friend Sam that night—even calling out his name. Turns out, she'd been in love with him all along."

"You've got to be kidding me!" Marley wailed.

"Oh my god." Kate stared wide-eyed at the screen.

"That asshole just called me out on national TV! He just aired our shit!"

"I'm so sorry—"

Marley spun toward Kate, tears flowing down her face. "He just made me out to be the biggest jerk on the planet!"

Kate pulled her into a hug.

"If the partners find out about this, I'll never get a job offer!"

Pulling back, Kate held her by the arms. "Take a deep breath, girl. I'm guessing the partners at the firm don't watch this crap."

Marley snickered through her tears. "I hope you're right, or I'm royally screwed."

Partners, maybe not. But others—yes. She was accosted in the breakroom the following morning by a group of women.

"Marley! Are you Rick's ex-girlfriend, the one he talked about last night?" one asked.

Oh God.

"You have to be," said another. "How many law students named Marley are there in Philly?"

Her heart pounded, her worst fears realized. Now, everyone knew she was a shitty girlfriend who'd propelled her ex-boyfriend onto a reality TV dating show. It was only a matter of time before the partners found out. Their decision would be made for them even if she scored higher than Sam. Buh-bye, job offer.

"Please..." she begged. "I can't—"

"We need to help Marley out." Sarah came to Marley's rescue. "She's hoping for a job here. Best if we don't spread this around."

"Got it," the admins' supervisor jumped in. "Ladies, you heard her. Mum's the word on this."

"You deserve to work here," her second-in-command said. "In reality, this shouldn't matter, but we know how it works."

"On three," the supervisor said as she thrust out her hand. Others piled theirs on top, counting before exclaiming, "Mum's the word!"

Marley was grateful for female bonding. She felt better for a while. Then Kate called.

"If you haven't been on social media today, I strongly advise you stay off."

"Why?" Marley asked, putting Kate on speaker and going straight to her apps.

Social media trolls had taken to the platforms to air their grievances with Marley. Comment after comment crucified her over her treatment of "poor Rick," challenging her to publicly apologize for breaking his heart.

"Do people not have lives?" Marley asked incredulously, shock turning to anger as she scrolled through the comments, which became increasingly more hostile with each swipe of her finger. "This is ludicrous."

"I'm sorry I said anything, but I didn't want you to be blindsided," Kate said. "You have to ignore it."

"It's bad enough Rick called me out, but now this? I have half a mind to tell 'em all to fuck off."

"Don't," Kate said. "The bigger deal you make of this, the more likely it'll spread. The best you can do is let it roll off your back."

Kate was right. As much as Marley wanted to defend herself, anything she said or did would be held against her in the court of public opinion. All she could do was hope it would die down soon. And that the partners weren't on social media. Or *Bachelorette* fans.

Maxine came into Marley's office at the end of the day, closing the door behind her.

"I'm here to see how you're doing," she said, lowering her thin, angular frame into a chair.

"I'm fine," Marley said, hopeful she wasn't in trouble for something.

Maxine adjusted her glasses. "I know about the social media buzz."

Marley deflated, her heart sinking to her knees. As a senior associate, Maxine had the partners' attention.

"I'm sorry this is happening. I suppose it's not something you wanted," the middle-aged woman continued with a sympathetic smile.

"Please believe me. I had no idea my ex had signed up for a reality show, let alone that he'd drag me into it. I hope it doesn't damage my reputation here..."

"You needn't worry. It's not going beyond me," Maxine said. "I don't think the partners watch the show."

Marley was both grateful and surprised. Maxine wasn't the warm-fuzzy type, yet here she was, presenting as another ally. Girl power, all the way.

"As long as you don't tell anyone I watch the stuff," Maxine said, rising from the chair with a conspiratorial smile on her face.

"Girl Scout's honor. I can't tell you how much this means to me."

"As they say, this too shall pass." She sighed. "It'll only be a matter of time before the trolls shift their focus. Just ride it out."

"Maxine?" Marley called out as the woman reached the door. "If this does get out, do you think it'll affect my chances for employment here?"

"No," she said emphatically.

If only the look in her eyes matched the confidence in her tone.

Charlotte

CHARLOTTE JOLTED AWAKE AS THE MEMORIES FLOODED back. She'd been on a boat. She met a guy. And now, here she was, lying in his spare room like some sort of hussy. She chastised herself for the plethora of poor decisions she'd made the night before. Breaking her one-drink rule. Going to a stranger's home. Agreeing to spend the night. Bad, bad, bad. To top it off, it felt as if someone had sliced her head open with an ax.

At least it wasn't her host.

Charlotte slowly crept through the house, finding Jake at the stove, spatula in hand.

"Good morning," he sang.

He must have seen her reach into her purse. "Whoa, no need for weaponry. I'm unarmed. Except for the delicious breakfast."

"It's only wipes," she said, pulling a pack from her purse and wiping down one of the island stools. He didn't seem to mind or care.

"*Mmm,*" she said, sniffing the air. "Pancakes."

"To match your eyes," he joked.

The delicious aroma calmed her nerves as worry over her bad decisions dissipated. Jake glided around his kitchen with the ease of a practiced chef, sizzling sausage in one pan and scrambling eggs in another. She wondered if this is what it would be like to have a live-in boyfriend—until she remembered she wouldn't want one. Men were messy, but if his clean kitchen was any indication, Jake might be an exception. Maybe she'd just hire him to cook for her once she had her mansion.

Jake slid her two pills and a glass of water. "Advil. I'm guessing you may have a headache."

"Thanks," she said, washing them down. He handed her a copy of the *Wall Street Journal* and launched into a discussion of the Dow's performance as he dished out her breakfast.

Charlotte gobbled the delicious meal, acknowledging it wasn't just whiskey that had compelled her to go home with a stranger. Jake had shown her compassion and interest, one of the few people in her life to do so. He'd shown her friendship.

She could most definitely get used to this—a hired cook capable of engaging in intelligent discourse. Or just a friend. Especially since it appeared he didn't have a propensity toward murder.

Other than his killer pancakes.

Bella

BELLA SAT ON THE FRONT STEPS OF THEIR FAMILY'S VACAtion rental, scrolling through Instagram, pretending to watch Eli while he played. Keeping an eye on the kid was part of her life sentence, and she'd long ago mastered the art of fake-watching him.

"Stop him!" a woman yelled as a dog raced across the yard.

Eli gave chase.

"Get back here, Eli," Bella yelled as she ran after her brother, cursing him under her breath for making her spring to action. He disappeared into someone's fenced-in yard and she followed, finding him talking to a man on the porch.

"Nice looking pooch you got here," the man said. "What's his name?"

"I don't know," Eli said. "It's not my dog. He ran from his owner, and I'm trying to catch him."

The man squatted and rubbed the dog's ears, speaking to him in soft, soothing tones. The dog's tail wagged his approval.

"I think he likes you," Eli said.

"I like him, too." The man cupped the dog's snout with his hand. "Who's a good boy? Wait here. I have something for you."

The old man went inside and returned with treats. "Otis won't mind sharing."

"Is Otis your dog?" Eli asked.

"Was my dog," he said. "He died a month ago."

"Oh, I'm sorry. I'm Eli, by the way."

"Hi, Eli. I'm Hank."

"I'm Bella," she said, waving at the man.

"Nice to meet you, Bella." Hank turned to the dog. "You're always welcome here. I'll leave the gate open in case you want to come back."

They said their goodbyes and returned the dog to its owner, who thanked them and apologized for his behavior.

"He just wanted to go for a walk," Eli said, defending him. "What's his name?"

"Buddy," the woman said. She bent over and wagged a finger at the dog. "Buddy's a bad, bad dog!"

Buddy wagged his tail.

"Thanks for catching him, although if he kept running, I wouldn't care. It's my husband's dog, but he's gone. He left me this mutt."

"I'm sorry your husband died," Eli said.

"He's not dead. He ran away. With another woman."

Awkward!

"I have an idea," Eli said. "I'm down for the summer. Maybe

I could walk Buddy in the mornings?"

The woman regarded him with skepticism. "How much do you charge?"

"I'll do it for free," he said.

She looked surprised but nodded. "That'd be nice."

The woman introduced herself as Mrs. Bigelow and asked if he could come by at ten. Eli agreed.

"You didn't need to offer that," Bella said once they walked away. She would have charged her extra for being so mean to the dog.

"Why not if it helps someone out?" he responded. "Maybe this could be my second good deed."

"If you're doing it for free, I would say it most certainly is a good deed."

"A fun one, too," Eli said as he skipped along. "I love Buddy the dog."

Zachary texted Bella later that afternoon and asked if she wanted to go to the beach movie that night. She had a babysitting gig and, for a split second, considered canceling. She missed hanging out with her friends—particularly Zachary. Thanks to their summer jobs, they rarely saw each other. She missed doing teen things generally, like beach movies, boardwalk crawls, and ice cream meet-ups, but she was making mad bank. If her campaign for an upgrade failed, she'd soon have enough to buy her own damn iPhone. Obvs, getting her parents to buy it vastly benefitted her as she'd have all that money to spend on other things (holla, Hollister!), but she was getting that new iPhone if it was the last thing she did.

She declined his invite just as a text from Sophie came through.

> Callum Tently asked for your number and I gave it to him.

Wait. *What?* Callum Tently was the geekiest kid in their class. Bella had zero interest in him. Sophie had no right to give her number out to him—or anyone.

> Gross! Why would you do that?

> He's not that bad. You'd make a cute couple! This way we can double date since you don't have a boyfriend.

Bella was furious. There was no way she'd consider dating the likes of Callum Tently. She'd rather dive headfirst into a vat of boiling puke. But when Callum texted, she felt bad blowing him off. She engaged in a few friendly text exchanges until he did the unthinkable: he asked her for a date when she returned home after the summer. She sat on it for a couple days, not wanting to be hurtful, but not wanting to accept his offer. On the third day, he texted her again.

> I guess that means no?

Bella considered what to say to let him down easy.

> I'm sorry, Callum. I'm dating someone.

Okay, a lie, but it was better than the truth. Better to nip it in the bud than hurt someone who didn't deserve to be hurt. She texted Sophie next.

> Don't ever do that again. BTW, I DO have a boyfriend.

Another lie, but it made Bella feel better knowing she stood up to Sophie. Hiding behind a text helped—she wouldn't dare stand up to her like that in person.

> Stop being so dramatic. Can't wait to meet this man of yours. :D

Did the smiley face indicate happiness? Or disbelief?

Great. Now she had to find a boyfriend. No biggie—even if winning the Nobel Peace Prize would be slightly more achievable.

July

Marley

S AM'S PARENTS INVITED MARLEY AND SAM TO A GOOD luck picnic a week before the exam.

Best described as a sprawling mansion, their not-so-humble abode was set on nine acres of lush greenery in the Philadelphia suburb of Villanova. Marley, who grew up in a tiny row home in the city, was always a bit intimidated whenever they visited his family. They were warm and welcoming, but she always felt as if she didn't belong.

"Future lawyers are here!" Sam's mother called out as they crossed the manicured lawn to where a large banquet tent stood. His parents greeted them with hugs.

"Ready for the big day?" Mr. Adams asked.

"What big day?" Sam teased.

Marley waved Sam off. "Ignore him."

"I hope you've been studying, son," his dad said, brows furrowed. "No one in this family's ever failed. I hope you're not the first."

Whoa. No pressure.

"Relax, Dad," Sam said.

"Has he been studying, Marley?"

Sam shot her a look.

"Absolutely," she said.

A bald-faced lie. If they'd been tracking their studying hours, Marley would have him beat by a long shot. Sam had an uncanny ability to skate by—not studying much but somehow acing things. It drove Marley crazy, his photographic memory and recall after seeing something once when she had to work her ass off for everything.

Sam's mom ushered everyone under the tent to escape the hot July sun. They gathered around a large table.

"Ready?" one of his cousins asked.

"Oh, God." Sam rolled his eyes.

Under the guise of preparing them for the bar, his older brother and three of his cousins, all lawyers, grilled them on different points of law. Sam's jaw tightened as they fired questions at them. Marley lobbed answers back like a tennis pro, giving justification for her answers as if she were taking the essay portion of the exam. If the bar was anything like this, she'd be fine. Sam, not so much.

Marley hated to admit the feeling of superiority that came over her. Not that she wanted Sam to fail; she just wanted to do better than him. She couldn't help it. They'd always had a bit of a friendly competition going when it came to grades and test scores. Now, jobs.

"I thought we were here to wish them luck, not scare them to death?" Sam's younger brother asked.

"Agreed." Mrs. Adams nodded. "Let's please enjoy our meal together."

"Sooo, Marley," one of Sam's teenage cousins sang out. "Are you the one Rick on *The Bachelorette* was talking about?"

Marley almost spewed her half-chewed coleslaw across the table. She gulped, stunned silent, her brain scrambling for a way to deflect the question. She begged for a tent collapse, a swarm of murder hornets, a flash flood—anything to change the subject. She was horrified to have Sam's family know of her sordid past.

"Yes, it was Marley he was talking about," Sam said. "Rick's her ex-boyfriend."

Marley, meet bus tires. She shot a looks-could-kill glare at Sam, not caring if his family noticed. How dare he out her?

Sam's mother raised her eyebrows and looked down at her lap.

"He's adorbs," the teen continued, smiling as she jabbed her elbow at Sam. "I can't believe you left him for this dork."

"Chicks dig dorks," Sam's eleven-year-old cousin said. "I wanna be one, too. Can you give me pointers, Sammy?"

They laughed and conversation moved on to the boy's upcoming soccer game. Just like that, the topic of Marley's reality TV cameo was old news. To say she was relieved was an understatement of magnanimous proportions. She was shocked they let it go so quickly, half expecting them to banish her ass from their estate.

"Hey, y'all," came a familiar voice from behind Marley. "Here come the Maguires."

She spun in her seat to find her aunt and uncle strolling across the lawn. Her uncle, dressed in a sleeveless white t-shirt and ratty cut-offs, carried a Miller Light thirty-pack on his shoulder. Her aunt looked like an '80s aerobics instructor, sporting a matching bike-shorts-and-workout-bra ensemble, a bottle of Boone's Farm wine in each hand.

Good God. Here come the Maguires, alright.

"Hey," Marley said, nervously chuckling as she rose to greet her tawdry relatives. "What are you guys doing here?"

"I invited your extended family over for dessert so we can get to know each other," Mrs. Adams said. "The more the merrier!"

Oh-ho, lady—you'll soon eat those words.

"Hell, yeah!" her uncle exclaimed, cracking open a beer. Marley was surprised he didn't shotgun it. "Your parents are parking the car."

He looked around as if he were casing the joint. "Nice crib you got here. You rob a bank or something?"

"Don't mind him. Here, I brought the good stuff." Her aunt handed Sam's mom bottles of paint stripper masquerading as wine.

Marley was terror-stricken. Could the extended family invite mean...

No. Sam wouldn't propose here, with her crazy family around. They were good people but rough around the edges (understatement), especially compared to Sam's prim and proper, well-mannered family.

Welp, Adams family, it was nice knowing you. I'll just take my relatives and GTFO.

"Sam!" Marley's six-year-old brother yelled as he barreled across the lawn, leaping into his arms. "I just did the loudest fart on the way over here!"

Sam laughed, always prepared to roll with whatever came out of the mouths of Marley's younger siblings. "My man," he said, giving him a fist bump. "Sorry I missed it."

Her parents and three other brothers sauntered across the lawn, followed by even more extended family. Sam's mom wasn't kidding—she'd invited the entire motley crew. Mrs. Adams loved entertaining, but this was too much.

"God help us," Marley whispered under her breath.

Sam's parents, practiced social hosts they were, welcomed Marley's family like pros, their faces frozen in a mask of feigned acceptance. It was the first time, likely the last, their extended families met. Marley was just relieved she couldn't see the thought bubbles over their heads.

As her family members made themselves at home, she approached Sam, who was smothered in her brothers—one on his shoulder, another wrapped around his leg.

"Think your parents had any idea what they were getting into, inviting everyone here?"

"Well, they do now," he said, laughing. "No worries, Mar. Your family is fun. They're just a little—"

"Mortifying?"

"Different...was what I was gonna say."

The boys ran off. Sam wrapped his arms around her and kissed her forehead.

"I love you, no matter what your family's like. Wait—is he peeing in the bushes?"

Marley whipped her head around to see her youngest brother, pants down to his knees, doing just that.

"Go ahead, break up with me now," she said.

"I'll do no such thing."

One of her uncles brought a transistor radio (yay!) to catch the Phillies game, grabbing the attention of the biggest fans in the group who clustered around him, blending Adamses and Maguires like a gross-looking smoothie.

"Pass me that jawn," Sam called to her ten-year-old brother.

Fluent in Philly-ease, he tossed the football to Sam. A touch football game ensued until her cousin kicked the ball into the potato salad, sending mayo'd shrapnel onto the lap of Sam's grandmother.

After cleaning up the startled matriarch, the Maguire women begged Mrs. Adams for a house tour. Marley was relieved for the break it would give Sam's mom from the circus erupting around them, not to mention her face from its forced smile. Marley joined them to run interference in case intrusive questions or embarrassing comments were forthcoming. As they were—proving you can take the Maguires outta Philly, but you can't take Philly outta the Maguires.

Charlotte

CHARLOTTE HADN'T SEEN THE CREATURE SINCE SHE LEFT for the shore and wondered if it had forgotten about her. Hoped, more like it. But there it was, sitting on her stoop again when she returned home after her weekend.

"You found me," she said.

The cat's big green eyes stared as if demanding to know where she'd been.

"Have you missed me?" she asked.

It looked healthier, and she wasn't as skeeved out as she'd been upon their first meeting. The cat inched closer and rubbed its head against her leg. She smiled, wondering what that meant in cat language.

"Why do you like me?"

It was the same question she'd wanted to ask Jake after he asked for her number so they could keep in touch, fully aware she wasn't the most alluring woman on the planet.

As she sat on the step, the cat settled next to her, and for once she didn't feel as if she were taking her life in her own hands. Even when its paw rested on her leg.

"Aww, you do like me," she whispered. "It doesn't matter why."

The cat purred as it snuggled closer. Charlotte tentatively patted its head.

"How was your weekend?" she asked. "Mine was great. I met a guy."

The cat looked up.

"Okay, not in that way. He's just a—friendly male person. I'll probably never see him again."

Charlotte sat with that thought for a moment, wondering if it bothered her.

The cat's belly rumbled. Animal Control had warned her not to feed it, but there it was, looking up at her like it trusted her. Something tugged at her heart. Retrieving a can of tuna from her kitchen, she peeled back the lid and set it down.

"Sorry about the presentation, but I'm guessing you don't care."

It was something they had in common—outwardly unappealing, yet somehow managing to survive in a world where looks seemed so important. She thought about Jake, whose insides ran deeper than his outward appearance suggested, glad she hadn't written him off as a shallow, pretty boy. Talking with him had been so easy. It was fascinating to discover that someone who looked like him felt just as lost in the world as she did. Too bad they didn't live closer; he'd be a nice friend. For now, she'd have to settle for the furry one next to her.

She patted his head and began talking about her latest case as he listened. Intently, or so it seemed.

Bella

BELLA RAN INTO CUTE DECK GUY AGAIN ONE AFTERNOON, and they flirted a bit deck-to-deck until he asked her to go to the boardwalk with him that night.

"Sure," Bella said, not the least bit "sure" she'd be allowed. Lisa had a way of commandeering her plans. This would likely be one of those times.

"Mama!" she sang as she approached Lisa in the kitchen, giving her mom a rare and suspicious hug.

"What do you want?" Lisa, who suffered no fools, clearly wasn't buying this sudden burst of daughterly affection.

Bella didn't let that derail her. "I made friends with this kid next door, and we're talking about going to the boards tonight."

A slight exaggeration, but better than admitting she'd only really spoken to him for the first time today and didn't know his name.

Lisa assumed warrior stance and narrowed her eyes. "Absolutely not."

"Why?" Bella wailed, all motherlove flying right out the window.

"You don't even know him."

"I'm fifteen! It's time you start trusting me. I'm almost an adult."

"Then start acting like one," Lisa said in her saccharine tone. She patted Bella's head and slid past her like a snake on the hunt for her next prey.

"What does that mean?" Bella demanded, her words echoing off the stainless-steel appliances. Too late. Lisa had disappeared into the next room, undoubtedly bent over a cauldron, conjuring another spell to further destroy her daughter's life.

Today's tally—Lisa: 1, Bella: 0.

This signaled the need for Operation Dad. Or *Daaaa-dee*, as she'd soon call him when she played the cuteness card. John registered slightly higher on the cool scale in Bella's eyes. Not so much to actually make him cool, but definitely more than her Momster. At least he didn't aim a high-powered water hose at every fun idea she had. John was more a disciple of the "Loosen up, Lisa" school of thought when it came to most things Bella.

"*Daaa-dee*," Bella sang out when she found her father sitting on the deck.

"No," he said without hesitation.

That damn Lisa had gotten to him already.

"Just kidding," he said. "I figured you were going to ask me for something."

This was new. Lisa must've forgotten to throw parental armor at John and demand he suit up for battle. Bella decided to leave Cute Deck Guy out of the equation this time.

"I've met friends, and they're going to the boardwalk tonight. I'd love to go. I feel kind of lonely here without anyone my age." Then she sighed for affect as she laid down her ace. "Unless you need me to watch Eli."

That ought to do it.

"Okay," he said, not looking up from his phone. "Be back by ten."

"What?" Lisa shrieked when she heard the news. "John, I said no! I told Eli she'd take him Pokémon hunting tonight."

"Oh, Leese, let Bella be a teenager for one night," John said. "I'll take him."

Bella gratefully accepted his Get Out of Jail Free card, but not before Lisa laid about an hour's worth of rules on her, including staying in touch through texts.

"Oof." Bella gave a dramatic grimace. "I mean, I just hope I have enough bars. My phone doesn't always get the best reception on the boards..."

Another ace. Next stop, new iPhone.

Lisa hooked an eyebrow. "Are you saying you shouldn't go, then?"

Damn. Maybe not the best time for an upgrade pitch. "Nope."

"Good. Don't push me."

She wasn't sure who had it worse—she, having Lisa as a mom, or people on Lisa's caseload, having her as a probation officer.

Definitely Bella. Their probation was temporary.

Bella and Cute Deck Guy, aka Trevor, met up with his friends on the boards for her first official hang-out-with-a-guy attempt since the Robbie Gentry Prom Debacle. It was also the first time a guy held her hand, which quickly progressed to him wrapping his arm around her shoulder, hand dangling dangerously close to her non-boobs. Bella was relieved he didn't try anything—she wasn't quite ready to be felt up on the Ocean City boardwalk by a guy she'd just met.

She was having a great time until the group veered off the boards and trudged through thick sand to sit beyond the glare of lights. Someone lit a joint and passed it around. Bella's heart pounded. She'd never done drugs before and didn't want to start tonight. She considered her options:

A. Go along with it, score a criminal record;
B. Narc on them, end up in a landfill; or...

"Can't," one of the older girls said. "Getting tested for soccer next week."

C. What she said...and pray no one challenged her to a match.

Turns out, no one suspected Bella wasn't a baller—thanks in part to her excellent acting chops. But this little foray into the murky underworld of criminal behavior was no longer fun. If they got caught, she wouldn't be allowed out again until her mid-fifties.

Her phone lit up. It was Eli calling from his baby flip phone. She debated whether she wanted to answer but decided she'd better. Eli never called, only texted.

"What?" she barked.

"Bella?" a deep voice asked.

Not Eli, unless he'd catapulted into puberty in the past hour. Her heart pounded. Who would have his phone?

"Yes?" She scrambled away from the group.

"Bella, it's Jordan—from the Viper? Your brother Eli is here with me."

"Are my parents with him?"

Bella realized how ridiculous that sounded once the words were out of her mouth. Oh, yeah, they're here. I just thought I'd take his phone and call you. *Stupid, Bella. Stupid.*

"He showed up alone to tell me about his good deeds. I was gonna call your parents, but he begged me to call you instead."

"I'll be right there," she said. She ended the call and told the group she had to meet her brother at the Viper.

"Love the Viper!" one of the stoner guys said.

"Let's go!" another called out.

Not that she wanted a posse of potheads following her, but

she was grateful not to walk alone on the darkened beach. If her mother knew she'd strayed from the boardwalk, alone or with this roaming band of delinquents, she'd be hogtied to her bed for decades.

Eli was sitting in the operator's chair when they arrived. "Bella!" he yelled. "I'm running the Viper!"

The group snickered. Bella was disheartened to see Eli wearing his favorite Cowboys t-shirt. Sporting Dallas merch this deep in Eagles territory put a definitive target on his back, as Bella had once warned. It was the kiss of death, an open invitation to have your face pummeled by an unruly, territorial Birds fan. The teams were notorious rivals, and many Eagles fans viewed the Cowboys as evil incarnate. Yet there was Eli, proudly standing by his team.

One of Trevor's friends pointed at Eli's shirt. "Cowboys? Little man, you need to get your priors straight."

"You mean 'priorities,'" soccer girl said, rolling her eyes.

"I like the Cowboys," Eli responded with confidence unbefitting a third grader, much less a Cowboys fan in the middle of bleed-green Ocean City. He seemed unfazed by the snickering Eagles stoners. Bella was impressed.

"I like the Cowboys," one of the guys mimicked.

"I do, too," Jordan said, squaring off with the guy. "Wanna taunt me? Or do you only pick on little kids?"

Trevor gave a maniacal, ugly laugh. "If I knew your brother was a Cowboys fan, I wouldn't have brought you."

"That's not necessary," Jordan said, stepping toward Trevor. His stature and stance caused the others to back up. "Leave the kid alone."

"Yeah, he's *eight*," Bella snapped at them. "Grow the hell up."

Trevor backed away. "Chill, man."

"No, you need to chill," Jordan suggested. "If you're getting on the ride, do it now, or I'll call the police and tell 'em you're trespassing."

"Forget it," one of the kids said.

The group walked away, leaving Bella behind. So much for her "date."

She turned to Eli. "What are you doing out here alone? Where are Mom and Dad?"

"They fell asleep watching a movie. They drank a *whole bottle of wine*, Bella."

Oh, good grief.

"I was bored and wanted to let Jordan know about my good deeds."

Bella turned to Jordan. "Thanks for letting me know about our escapee."

And giving me an excuse to leave the pot party before I was apprehended and sent to juvie.

"No problem."

"I should get him home." Bella took Eli's hand. "Thanks for encouraging him to do good with the promise of a ride. It means the world to him."

"It seems like he's taking it seriously." He gave Eli a high five. "Good job, champ."

She liked the way her brother's face lit up when Jordan spoke. Eli was probably gonna be a lot like this kid when he grew up—a nice guy, an old soul of sorts. With good "priors."

Bella and Eli began making their way back when Jordan called her name.

"They said I could leave. It's slow, and rain's coming. Can I walk you guys home?"

Normally, Bella would've been suspicious of a guy she didn't know offering to walk her home—thanks to Lisa, who had pretty much convinced her she'd be diced into tiny pieces if she so much as looked at a guy she didn't know. Of course, Bella had conveniently forgotten that when it came to Jerk Deck Guy. Jordan didn't seem a threat, especially after he stood up to Trevor and his goon squad.

As they walked, they got to know their new friend. Jordan told them he was working at the shore this summer to save money for a car. When Eli heard that, the boys launched into a discussion of cars like a couple of motorheads. At the house, Bella told Eli to go inside and let their parents know they were home, in case they were having a coronary upon discovering they'd fallen asleep in a drunken stupor and their kids were out roaming the world unsupervised. How funny would it be to call Children and Youth Services on them?

Today's tally—Lisa: 0, Bella: 124 (extra points for adulting).

Bella wasn't anxious to go inside. She still had thirty minutes left of parental furlough, and she intended to use every second of it. A cool ocean breeze swirled around them. It was getting chilly, but she fought through it. She enjoyed talking to Jordan—a welcome break from the immature boys back home.

"I can't believe he snuck out tonight," Bella said. "He's usually a rule-follower."

"I hope you weren't worried."

"I didn't know he'd left the house. I was out with—well. You know."

"Friends of yours?" Jordan asked.

"Some kids I met this week." Bella skipped over the fact it was supposedly a date.

"You gotta watch who you hang out with down here," he said. "You can't trust everyone."

"Yeah, I'm learning that. Anyway, who picks on an eight-year-old?"

As Bella said the words, she realized she'd made a hobby of it herself. The thought made her sad.

"Are you really a Cowboys fan?" she asked.

"Don't tell him, but—" he looked up at the house, dropping his voice to a whisper "—*I can't stand them.* I just didn't want the little guy hanging out there on his own."

If it wasn't evident before, Bella now knew Jordan was a good guy. Being the offspring of die-hard Eagles fans, she knew how hard it must've been to feign Cowboy fandom.

Silence fell between them. Bella shivered.

"I should let you go inside. You look cold."

"I'm fine," Bella said, her teeth chattering.

"Goodnight, Bella. I enjoyed talking with you."

"Me, too." Bella was happy it was dark, so he couldn't see her blushing. She was suddenly very interested in accompanying Eli back to the ride again.

Their eyes met, and Bella did a silent countdown. She once saw an Instagram post stating that if a guy maintained eye contact for more than five seconds, it meant he was interested.

One, two, three...

Bella held her breath.

Four...

Just as she was about to get to *five*, he suddenly glanced skyward and raked a hand through his hair. "I'm looking forward to seeing you guys again. Maybe after his ride, we could get some ice cream. The three of us."

Bella guessed from his expression that his invitation was more about hanging out with her than Eli. Could two guys be asking her out in one day? If so, she should seriously consider moving to New Jersey full-time. Hopefully, the second date would turn out better than the first.

"We'd love to."

Jordan leaned on the railing, and for a split second, she thought he was going to kiss her. She panicked and jogged up a couple steps before turning around.

"See you soon," she said breathlessly.

That was if Lisa didn't turn on her industrial-strength hose and power-wash her plans.

Marley

AR EXAM DAY HAD ARRIVED. MARLEY AWAKENED WITH A potpourri of emotion: excitement, fear, anxiety, and gut-wrenching nausea. She'd asked Sam to sleep at his place the night before, explaining she needed the bed to herself for all her nervous tossing and turning. Truth was, she didn't want Sam's non-studying mojo bringing her down. After sleeping a solid eight hours, she was refreshed and ready to go.

She FaceTimed Sam. "Rise and shine, beautiful!" she sang out.

He was all wild-haired and sleepy-eyed, answering from his bed, and for a split-second Marley regretted not spending the night with him. She wished she could climb into bed with him now instead of doing what they were about to do.

She checked the time. "Sam, you need to get up!"

"I know." He ran his hand through his tousled locks. "Whatcha wanna do today?"

"Let's have our brain matter scooped out and flung onto a standardized test."

"Dude, I was thinking the same thing."

"Great minds…"

"Probably shouldn't have partied with my roommates all night," he said.

"Sam, no! Please tell me you didn't."

"Kidding. I was asleep by ten."

"Good, 'cause it sounds like you'll be disowned if you don't pass."

"You won't disown me, will you?"

"Depends how badly you do."

After they hung up, Marley triple-checked her bag to make sure she had everything she needed for the exam and took a deep breath. It was go time.

As she pushed open the door to her apartment building, she was blinded by flashes from cameras and phones.

"Marley Maguire!" someone called out. "Are you the same Marley Maguire who dated Rick on *The Bachelorette*?"

What?

Marley tried to shield her eyes. The mass of people encroached upon her until she couldn't move.

"Please," she said politely. "I'm about to take the bar exam—"

A reporter shoved a microphone in her face. "Amber Jones, *Daily Celebrity*. I understand you broke Rick's heart when he offered you a promise ring. Can you elaborate?"

Marley looked her square in the face. "No."

She tried to push ahead to a waiting Uber. The more she pushed, the more they crowded.

"Marley, *Gossip Weekly* here. Can you tell us what you did to Rick?"

Did to Rick?

"I didn't murder him, if that's what you mean," she said.

"That's a great headline," one reporter chuckled to another.

She felt defenseless, claustrophobic, afraid she'd pass out—until a strong arm snaked around her shoulders.

"Leave her alone," a man's voice boomed, pushing them away. Felix, her doorman, to the rescue. "Give her space, for fuck's sake."

The sea of reporters parted as Felix led Marley to her Uber.

"Marley, one last question," someone called out as Felix folded her into the back of the car. "Would you marry Rick now?"

She was still trembling when she met Sam outside the Convention Center, where the exam was being administered. She started crying when she saw him and ran into his arms.

"Hey, hey," he whispered. "It's gonna be okay. You're more ready for this than anyone."

"It's. Not. The. Exam." Marley huffed a word with each sob.

"What is it then?" Sam asked, dropping his backpack and cupping her face. "Marley, you're scaring me. What happened?"

She finally caught her breath and told him about the media frenzy.

"That's horrible," he said. Pulling her in, he wrapped his arms tightly around her. "Come on, breathe."

Marley emulated Sam's deep breaths until her heart rate slowed.

"Better?" he whispered in her ear, still holding her tight.

Marley nodded, blotting her tears. "Better."

"I know you're frazzled. Push it out. You only need to think about this exam."

"And the job!" she wailed, a fresh round of tears flowing.

"*Shhh.* It's your job, Marley. No pressure here. Just focus on doing your best."

"Okay," she sniveled, melting further into him. He always knew exactly what to say.

"You got this, Mar." He pulled back, grabbed her shoulders, and stared her down. "So much more than I do. You go in there, and you tell this exam to fuck the fuck off. Because you are the best lawyer I've ever known, and I include all my asshole family members in that assessment. Ain't nothing stopping you now, including this exam. You understand me, counselor?"

Marley was never more grateful to him than she was just then. No matter what happened, she had the love and support of this incredible person. With Sam by her side, there was nothing this exam could do to her.

"I understand."

He kissed her forehead. "Now, let's go do this."

He took her hand, and together, they walked into

Convention Center to tell the Pennsylvania Bar Exam (in the words of Sam Adams) to "fuck the fuck off."

Charlotte

GIVING IN TO AN UNCHARACTERISTIC WHIM, CHARLOTTE asked her co-workers if she could join them for lunch.

"Sure," one of the women said hesitantly. "We're going to the Thai place if that's okay."

It would have to be okay if she wanted to learn how to schmooze over the midday meal.

Once at the restaurant, Charlotte asked her co-workers about their cases. At first, they eyed her with suspicion as if wondering why. She cared not one iota about their cases but could've won an Oscar for her role as "Seemingly Interested Co-worker." After hanging out with Jake on the boat that night, talking with people seemed easier. She even cracked a joke and had them laughing as they left the restaurant.

"Hibachi Grill tomorrow, Charlotte," one said as they returned to the office. "You in?"

Under normal circumstances, she'd rather scale Liberty One skyscraper—naked and in the dead of winter—than hang out with this bunch again. Nonetheless, she agreed.

Returning home that evening, she found a package waiting for her on the porch. On top of the package sat her new friend.

"I guess you know that's for you," she said. She'd broken down and ordered cat food. Feeding him tuna was becoming expensive.

"How was your day?" she asked as she opened the can. She set it down and sat next to him.

Charlotte told him about her lunch experience and how

she had made people laugh—with her, this time. He seemed too hungry to ask for details, so she rambled on about another case of hers, pausing to ask for the feline's advice, which wasn't forthcoming. After consuming the entire can, the cat stretched and kneaded her lap until he curled up and went to sleep.

She chuckled. "Yep, that's the same effect I have on people. But it's okay. You can sleep, friend. You're safe with me."

She continued talking to him until dark, not even pausing to think about the nighttime dangers lurking beyond her porch. Because, for once, she wasn't alone.

August

Marley

BY LABOR DAY WEEKEND, MARLEY FINALLY FELT AS though she could breathe again. The bar exam was a thing of the past. Now, all she had to do was wait. And hope.

It was hard to gauge how she'd done. She'd missed some of the multi-state questions but otherwise felt she'd done okay. Not great, just okay. That was the thing about the bar exam—its results were hard to predict. Marley had been schooled by older classmates to forget about it once the test was over, because two months was a long time to wait for scores. She'd done the best she could, given the media barrage that morning. It was out of her hands.

As the weeks wore on, things began to quiet down on the paparazzi front. Just in case, she donned a disguise whenever she left the building—a head scarf and oversized sunglasses—which seemed to do the trick. Marley had been looking forward to spending Labor Day weekend with Kate in Ocean City to get out of town and away from any lurking media, but Kate had called that morning and canceled—her grandfather had been hospitalized and wasn't expected to make it. Marley consoled her friend, agreeing they'd do it another weekend.

To keep their minds off the exam, Marley and Sam planned a cozy night in. It was the season finale of *The Bachelorette*, and curiosity had gotten the best of her.

More like shock. Rick had made it all the way to the end, one of the last two men standing.

"I'm so here for this," Sam said. "I hope he wins."

"Nah. She's not for him."

"How do you know?"

"I dated the guy for three years. He's too introverted; she's too superficial. She's picking the ex-NFL dude, hands down."

As it turned out, Marley was right. She felt bad watching Rick cry as he walked away from the makeshift proposal venue after Brie shot him down. He'd be fine—according to Kate, he'd gained thousands of followers on Instagram, which cracked Marley up. When they'd dated, he didn't even know what the social media platform was.

The show went to commercial. Sam leaned into her, pushing her into the plush cushions as he brushed his lips against hers.

"Proposals make me horny," he said, breathless, growing hard against her hip.

"Everything makes you horny."

"Only when you're involved," he whispered. "Let's see if we can break the record for the longest kiss."

Kissing Sam sent Marley into another universe, just as it did the first (and every) time. Soft lips, swirling tongues, and occasional moans were all it took. She was ready for more, if only she could stop kissing him.

In the background, the show had come to the final scene, the host's voice breaking through their moans of passion.

"And now we're about to reveal our next bachelor. Are we ready?"

The crowd screamed. A faint chant emerged through their hysteria.

"Your next bachelor is none other than…"

Distracted, they both turned to the TV.

"Richard Alabaster Smith, III. Otherwise known as—"

"Rick?" both Sam and Marley shouted at the same time.

Bella

IT WAS SUNDAY OF LABOR DAY WEEKEND. ELI HAD COM-pleted his final good deed earlier that week when he'd taught a little girl to boogie board. He was flabbergasted when Bella congratulated him.

"You mean that counts?" he asked.

"Of course, it does. Duh!" Bella answered. "You could've been doing your own thing, but you helped someone else learn a skill."

"Wow—if that's the case, doing good is fun! It feels good to help others."

Pretty advanced concept for a kid his age, she had to admit. She was proud of her little brother for embracing the opportunity to help people. She, too, had learned something. Eli was more than an annoying little twerp. He had a good heart, and she was proud to call him brother. At least at this moment (subject to change).

It was finally time for his hard-earned reward. Eli's excitement was infectious as they made their final trip down the boardwalk. Bella understood—she couldn't wait to see Jordan either but for vastly different reasons. She snapped a photo of the ride to add Eli's big adventure to her Insta story. As they approached the queue, Bella was surprised to see another teenager operating the ride. No Jordan in sight.

"Do you see him anywhere?"

Eli craned his neck, searching. "No," he said, seemingly oblivious to the implications of Jordan's absence.

"He said tonight, right?"

"Yep," Eli said, now bouncing in full excitement mode.

Jordan had said he'd be working alone that night, and the height sticklers wouldn't be there. When they got to the front of the line, the ride operator told Eli to stand in front of the height chart. Her brother hesitated.

"Do it," Bella whispered, shoving him forward. Maybe Jordan was somewhere around here, would see Eli, and take over the operation.

Eli stood as tall as he could.

"Nope, too short," the kid said, waving Eli away. "Next!"

"Unacceptable!" Bella barked, both dismayed and elated to be sounding like her own take-no-shit, bellowing Karen of a mother. Okay, maybe not that bad. "Where's Jordan?"

"He called off his shift."

Eli peered at the ride operator, eyes wide with disbelief. Fury ignited in Bella.

"He *what*?" she demanded, continuing to channel her inner-Lisa. She turned to Eli. "Do you have his number? Can you text him?"

"I don't have his number."

Damn. She didn't have it either.

"You guys have to step aside," the operator said.

Bella directed her little brother to a bench so she could figure out her next move. Eli, who'd started the night filled with optimism, sat quietly like a deflated balloon. He leaned his head on her shoulder.

"I'm sad," he said.

"I know, Eli." She wrapped her arm around his little body. "I'm sad, too."

Bella tried to think of something to say to make him feel better, but she, too, felt let down. She was only fifteen, yet in just three months, three guys had treated her poorly. It would be a long time before she trusted another. She felt twice as sorry for Eli, who'd worked hard for this.

"My belly hurts," Eli said.

Bella could tell from his pale complexion he was about to throw up.

"Over here," she directed him to a trash can, where he heaved up his dinner.

Bella, who was normally grossed out by vomit, felt bad for the kid. She knew this was a result of nerves. The kid puked more than any human on the planet, often when he was nervous. She handed him a water bottle so he could rinse his mouth.

"Feel better?" Bella asked as she knelt to his level.

His eyes still looked sad, but he nodded. She wiped a lock of hair from his forehead.

He shrugged. "Well, at least I did some good this summer. I hope I made a difference."

"Of course you did!" Bella assured him. She was forever perplexed how her younger sibling could be so filled with goodness when she wasn't.

"Hey, we still have a couple hours before we have to go home. Let's make the most of this night. What do you want to do?" She had to make it up to the kid so the night wasn't a complete disaster.

"Can we go to the arcade?" Eli asked, eyes lighting up.

If you had asked Bella fifteen minutes earlier to describe the worst place on earth, she would've described a boardwalk arcade. They were loud and discombobulating, filled with thousands of rambunctious Elis.

But all she said was, "I'd love to."

She draped her arm around her little brother's shoulders and went off to spend eternity in the worst place on earth.

Later, on the way home, Bella reached for Eli's hand. "I'm sorry you didn't get to ride the Viper."

"It's probably good Jordan wasn't there tonight," Eli said. "There's still one more good deed I'd like to finish tomorrow."

Bella had to give her brother props for still caring what

Jordan the Jerk thought, even though he'd let Eli down. She wouldn't have given his ridiculous scheme another thought.

When they passed Eli's favorite boardwalk game, he asked if he could play. It involved tossing small plastic rings onto bottlenecks in hopes of ringing a prize winner. Bella despised the game after spending most of her life trying to win the grand prize to no avail—a larger-than-life pink teddy bear.

Eli paid for his bucket of rings and walked the perimeter of the game, developing a strategy. He nailed two bottles, earning him a medium prize, but insisted on going after the major prize. He tossed his last ring. It bounced once, twice, three times before landing on—

"Oh my God! You did it!" Bella screamed.

"I won!" Eli yelled. "I won, I won!"

He bounced up and down while onlookers clapped. The game operator asked Eli which prize he wanted. He pointed to the oversized pink teddy bear.

"That one there," he said. "For my sister. My best friend."

Bella's heart swelled. She hugged her little brother, vowing to be nicer from now on.

The three of them—brother and sister and prized bear—made their way home, stopping for ice cream along the way. It turned out to be an awesome night despite Jordan blowing them off. Ride or no ride, Eli was a winner.

But when he bounded into Bella's room early the next morning, waking her at an ungodly hour, she had a change of heart.

"Why are you here?" she asked, thrusting a pillow over her head.

"I need help with my last good deed."

"I thought we were done with this," she groaned. "I mean, dude blew you off."

In a daring and uncharacteristic move, Eli whipped the covers off Bella.

"Listen to me, Isabella Ann," he growled. "I told you yesterday I had one more good deed to do, and I'm asking you nicely to help. I have tons of intel on you that Mom might be interested in."

Under normal circumstances, this type of behavior on Eli's part would have earned him a pillow to the face. But Bella was too tired for such a showdown. In the end, she knew the penalty for pummeling him was three to five in maximum security lockdown. She also had to admit a bit of fear, wondering what "intel" Eli had on her, whether his threats were credible, and if they'd tank her bid for a new iPhone. Better get up and help the punk.

"Tell me again why we're still doing this?" Bella asked as they walked to Mrs. Bigelow's house.

"I need to leave for the summer knowing I did the best thing for Buddy."

Eli rapped on the door, and Mrs. Bigelow answered, looking surprised to see him.

"I thought yesterday was your last day," she said.

"It was, but I was wondering if you'd like to see the route we take so you can walk him yourself. He really loves it."

Mrs. Bigelow stared him down. "Alright," she finally grumbled. "Let me get my walking shoes."

She emerged with the fugliest pair of shoes on her feet (no wonder she didn't like to walk) and an enthusiastic Buddy on a leash.

"Here's my friend," Eli said, giving the dog a hug. "Let's show your mom where you like to walk."

Bella caught the half-smile spreading across Mrs. Bigelow's face. "No one's ever called me Mom before."

Eli led them to Hank's house, where they found him on the porch. Her little brother introduced the two adults to one another.

"I wanted you two to meet because I have an idea. You miss your dog, Otis," he said to Hank before turning to Mrs. Bigelow. "You can't keep up with Buddy, and you're looking for someone to take him. I was thinking, maybe Buddy can come here to live?"

Hank's eyes were sad as he shook his head. "I'm not ready for a new dog."

"Fair enough," Eli said. "I anticipated that. Here's my Plan B."

Bella caught the smiles they tried to hide.

Eli turned to Mrs. Bigelow. "What if you walk over here with Buddy each day? He can hang out with Hank and play. It'll give you a break and give Buddy someone to play with."

Mrs. Bigelow appeared to consider it. "My doctor says I have to walk more."

"Me, too," Hank said. "How 'bout I meet you halfway, at the park down the street?"

Bella could swear she saw Mrs. Bigelow blush. "That sounds lovely."

She was proud of her little bro for finding a solution for two lonely people using the world's ugliest dog.

"I'm just sad I waited so long to suggest that," Eli said as they walked home. "Maybe that's why Jordan didn't show. He knew I had more to do."

That was it. Bella wasn't about to let some idiot kid ruin her brother's summer. He'd looked so forward to riding the Viper and had worked so hard to make it happen.

"Come on," she said, taking his hand.

"Where are we going?" Eli asked.

"To the Viper."

Jerk or no jerk, Bella was going to get him on that ride if it was the last goddamn thing she did. They stopped at home, where she shoved all her saved babysitting money in her pocket. She'd blow it all on a bribe if she had to. She was prepared to verbally beat the living shit out of anyone who refused; after all, she'd had years of training from the world's biggest Karen.

Screw the iPhone. The kid deserved this.

Minutes later, they stood facing an empty Viper, its only sign of life, a literal sign, flapping in the wind.

CLOSED FOR THE SEASON.

October

Marley

MARLEY WALKED THROUGH THE COBBLESTONED STREETS of Old City as a crisp October sun shined through a canopy of orange and red leaves. It was a beautiful autumn day full of hope and promise. The day she'd hopefully become a lawyer.

As she passed the corner newsstand, she was jolted from her calming walk by Rick's face, peering at her from the cover of *People* magazine. A headline hailed him as "the most genuine" bachelor and promised the "shocking season" would be aired in January. She shook her head in disbelief. Somewhere in the world, Rick was being wooed by beautiful women, making Marley question everything she knew.

She was still pissed at him for sharing their embarrassing breakup with the nation and beyond but was thankful the media outcry had all but disappeared. Thanks, in part, to a famous celebrity who'd left her equally famous husband for a nineteen-year-old Times Square furry, causing social media trolls to lose their fucking minds. Marley wasn't sure she'd want to watch Rick's journey to find love once the show aired, but that was the last thing on her mind right now.

The first: her results.

Returning home, she found her front door unlocked. A wave of panic washed over her. It wasn't Sam—according to his latest text, he'd just left his place and was still on his way. She weighed her options: enter and risk a marauder attack or call the cops and wait longer for bar results.

Screw the marauders, she couldn't wait any longer. Grabbing an umbrella from its holder, she crept along the hallway. She turned the corner and—

"Surprise!"

"Fuck!" she screamed, flinging her umbrella at the unexpected crowd, nearly taking out three souls.

"Marley, language!" Her mom gestured to her younger cousins and brothers, standing in her kitchen instead of at school, where they damn well belonged. "We're here for the big reveal!"

Behind them, her extended family members were squished into the kitchen like the nosy, overbearing lot they were. Sam's parents huddled in the far corner, bewildered, as if they'd been hog-tied and dragged there.

Marley shot a look at Sam, who'd just arrived at her condo, himself. "Were you in on this?"

"No," he responded, looking surprised.

"Here to witness lawyers in the making," an uncle proclaimed.

"The first in our family," said a cousin. "And the last. Y'all can have that school shit!"

Marley's family members burst out laughing. Sam's parents' expressions were equal parts shock and horror, as if wild tigers paced the room. Marly was livid. Her family had no right to do this. They were devoid of boundaries, not to mention common sense.

"Mom, seriously," Marley pleaded. "I don't want an audience. You guys have to go."

"Don't be ridiculous. We pulled the kids out of school for this. Think of all the phone calls you won't have to make now that we're here."

"I'd rather make the calls. What if I don't pass?"

"Oh, silly girl," her mom said, giving her a hug. "Of course, you'll pass."

Marley could tell by the look on Sam's face he was displeased but hid it better than she.

Their phones dinged simultaneously.

"Results are in," Sam said.

Marley's heart raced. They sat at the table, opened their laptops, and signed into their portals while family members huddled around. One of Marley's jokester cousins began a drum roll. Others joined in.

"Could you not?" Marley snapped as they proceeded to ignore her request. Her hands shook as she typed the incorrect password three times.

From across the table, Sam cried out. "I passed!"

Both families erupted in cheers, slapping Sam on the back and giving him hugs. A decade passed, it seemed, before Marley's portal opened. She was so nervous, so focused, she was unable to fully process Sam's announcement.

"Marley?" her mom asked, her voice filled with hope.

The drum roll got louder as the portal popped open.

We regret to inform you...

Marley didn't get beyond the first five words before all oxygen was sucked from the room. Her eyes flooded, and her chest tightened as she felt her heart shatter.

"Marley, you're scaring me!" her mom exclaimed. "Say something!"

"I—" The words choked in her throat. "I didn't pass."

"Oh, Marley..." her mom said, grief-stricken.

Her family members let out a collective, defeated groan. And then...silence.

Sam was the first to reach her. So fast, in fact, Marley wasn't sure if he ran, flew, or slid across the table. He scooped her into his arms, his tears soaking her neck as he mumbled into her shoulder. "I'm sorry, I'm sorry, I'm sorry..."

His sympathetic murmurings reached the pit of her stomach, where they churned and burned and ignited into a furnace of boiling rage.

"Stop saying that!" she screamed, pushing Sam away. He toppled backward, almost taking out one of her cousins.

Overcome by a wave of untamable fury, she swept her arms across the table, sending her laptop crashing to the floor. "You son of a passing bitch!"

Then she turned on her family.

"Are you assholes happy?" she shrieked as if they were the ones responsible for her failure. "Glad you came for this? Did it ever cross any of your pea-sized brains it wasn't a good idea to pull these little fuckers out of school? What, so they could witness failure first-hand?"

Her little cousins were pie-eyed, mouths agape, as her stream of obscenities bounced off her shiny stainless-steel appliances and into their tiny ears. They may not have been in school, but they learned a whole lot that day.

"*She said fuck!*" her five-year-old cousin whispered in apparent awe.

"She says it a lot," her youngest brother replied.

Sam's parents made their way to the door.

"How do you like me now, Adams family?" Marley screamed at their retreating backs. "Still good enough for your precious son?"

One of her idiot cousins guffawed. "Adams Family, that's funny."

"Marley, that's enough." Her father enveloped her in a hug. "We know you're disappointed. We're all feeling your pain right now."

It was all she needed to hear. She broke down crying. Marley could say whatever she wanted about her family, but it didn't stop every pea-brained asshole in the room from surrounding her in a huge Maguire-style hug.

"We love you, Marley," her brother cried out, joined by others.

"We're sorry."

"You're still our favorite lawyer."

Marley felt like the world's biggest jerk for being rude to

her family. She looked up from her dad's tear-stained shirt. "No, I'm sorry. I didn't mean it."

"We know," he said, nodding.

"What happens now?" her mother asked.

"I don't practice law," Marley said.

"Not true," Sam said. "She can take the exam in February." The group was silent.

"We should leave her to process this," Marley's mom said.

Sam slid in and took her dad's place, holding Marley tight as he rubbed her back. He continued holding her long after their families left.

"I can't go through this again," she finally whispered.

"Of course, you can. And you will." Sam was firm in his directive as he held her face. "You just have to get back up and try again, Mar."

"Easy for you to say," she said, trying to keep the vitriol from her voice. "You won. You passed without studying and beat me out of a job."

"This isn't about winning, Marley," Sam said.

"Bullshit. You barely studied. You rich people must be born with built-in legal knowledge, so you can screw off while the rest of us have to work our asses off for everything."

Sam pressed his lips together. He wasn't taking her bait.

"I knew I wasn't worthy of being a lawyer," she said, her lifelong insecurities—borne of a childhood spent feeling like she wasn't smart enough—rearing their ugly head. "This proves it."

"Marley, don't do that," he said quietly. "You're the smartest, most worthy person I know."

Even if that were true, it didn't change the fact that Sam would go on to practice law, and she'd remain in non-lawyer intern purgatory. In perpetuity. Shadowed, as always.

"I need to lie down."

She climbed into her bed and pulled the covers over her

head. Sam followed and held her tight beneath the blankets. She sobbed, succumbing to hopelessness. Devastation. Finally, sleep.

The following morning, Marley put in for a personal day, unable to show her face in the office.

"I won't say anything," Sam promised as he got dressed.

"How will you pull that off?" she snarled. "It's the second question they'll ask."

"You're right," Sam said thoughtfully. "What should I tell them?

"I got hit by a bus."

"Don't even joke about that," Sam said, smiling through sad eyes.

"That's probably next."

Marley pulled the covers over her head again. She was only half-joking. She knew, on some level, her bar failure would someday be a fun party story—how she'd joined the ranks of JFK Jr. and other celebrity lawyers who didn't pass the bar the first time but went on to become successful litigators, nonetheless.

Someday, maybe. Not today.

Marley spent half the day in bed, the other half padding around her apartment in sweats and fuzzy slippers, drowning her sorrows in pretzels and ice cream. She ignored all of Sam's texts inquiring how she was. When Gwen's number flashed across her phone screen, she answered. She'd know exactly what Marley was going through.

"Hey, Mar," Gwen said, her voice dripping with empathy. "I ran into Sam."

"Yeah," Marley sighed. "Hasn't been the best day."

"I know. It totally sucks."

It was comforting to know she was in good company—Gwen had survived this ordeal yet lived to tell about it. "How long did it take you to get over this humiliation?"

"A while." Gwen chuckled. "But then you pull yourself together, move forward, and pass on the second try. As I know you will."

"I'm not taking it again."

Gwen paused. "Tell me again why you want to be a lawyer?"

Marley smiled through her sadness. She knew what her friend was doing.

"To have the title 'Esquire' behind my name," she joked.

"Seriously. I recall you telling me once you wanted to prove something to yourself and others. Think about it. If you and Sam are gonna spend your lives together, how will it feel if he's practicing law and you aren't?"

Gwen was right. It would be brutal to watch Sam practice law if she couldn't.

"You've worked too hard for this. Don't let a stupid test stand in your way. I'd never have found my dream job as an assistant district attorney if I had."

Marley felt a one-eighty coming on. She had no choice—she had to pass the exam if she wanted to be a lawyer. She'd endured three grueling years of law school, but that wasn't enough. Like it or not, she had to take that bitch of a test until she passed. No way was she letting a bunch of little dots on a multiple-choice test stop her from being a lawyer. Fuck the test and all its stupid No. 2 pencils.

Sam came home early with a pizza, but she'd eaten so much junk she wasn't hungry.

"I'm going to bed," Marley announced.

"No, you're not." He grabbed her hand and pulled her back to the kitchen. "We need an M-n-S night."

He put on their soft jazz playlist, dimmed the lights, and climbed on the kitchen island.

Marley relented, joining him. She opened the pizza box to find the words *The law is an ass* written in parm. She couldn't help but smile; they'd often quoted Dickens's famous line in law school.

"I presume everyone knows I'm an utter failure?"

"You're not a failure," Sam said, wincing. "But they know about the results."

She wasn't sure what was worse: learning she'd failed or having others find out. Co-workers. Classmates. Friends. She was embarrassed, humiliated. Eclipsed.

"There's no easy way to say this, so I'm just gonna come out with it," Sam said, his eyes giving away his news.

"They offered you the job."

"Yes. I'm sorry, Marley."

Gut punch.

"I know I said I'd take a job with my dad, but—"

"What's the point? I'm not even in the running," Marley noted, choking back her tears. "You won, fair and square."

Sam flinched. "It wasn't a competition," he said softly.

"Of course it was. The firm saw to that."

Tears welled in his eyes. "Marley, I never wanted this to happen. I saw us both passing and you taking the job. I physically got sick to my stomach after they told me."

"I hope you projectile vomited on them."

"I'll do that tomorrow if it'll make you feel better."

Marley gave him a defeated smile.

"I don't have to take the position if you don't want me to," he said.

"Don't put that on me."

Sam wanted the job as badly as she did. If the tables had been turned—if she'd passed and Sam had failed—she wouldn't be so willing to step aside. But that was the kind of guy Sam was. Better than her. In life and now in law. The fact he was willing to leave a job for her made her realize just how much he loved her. She owed him the same support in return.

"It's okay," Marley whispered, wiping a tear from his cheek. "I know you didn't want this for me, but we'll make it work. Just like we did that night in the B&B from hell."

"You didn't like that place?" Sam teased.

"Loved it, TripAdvisor. Almost as much as I love the fact we'll still be working together, assuming they keep me on as an intern."

"They will." Sam hugged her. "Please don't let this job come between us."

"It won't. I promise."

Charlotte

CHARLOTTE SCURRIED TO GET TO HER OFFICE AS A HUGE gust of wind lifted her hair. She pulled her coat tighter around her neck, relieved it was finally cold enough to wear one. Something about being fully covered in layers of fabric made her feel safe.

Inside the lobby, the elevator door opened as she approached.

"Excuse me," a man mumbled as he emerged, head down.

Something caused her to do a double-take. Just as he did.

"Charlotte?" he asked, his voice incredulous.

It only took a second for Charlotte to place him. It was Jake. Boat Jake. Non-murderous Pancake Jake. She hadn't seen him since that morning at his place three months ago. They'd exchanged numbers and said they'd keep in touch, but she hadn't heard from him. While she was disappointed, she wasn't surprised. Her natural effect on men made her not only invisible, but forgettable. She hadn't reached out to him, either. It wasn't in her DNA to chase a man like some sort of saucy minx.

"This is incredible," he said. "What are the chances?"

"The chances are 0.17199," Charlotte said. She'd done the math one day, contemplating the odds of running into someone she knew in Philadelphia. Namely, Jake. Her research had also revealed the average person will walk past thirty-six murderers in their lifetime. Another reason Charlotte spent most of her time indoors.

"I'm sorry I haven't been in touch," Jake said. "I lost your number."

Sure.

He chuckled, acknowledging her silent disbelief. "I'm serious. I was sailing one day and accidentally dropped my phone in the ocean. I had to get a new one, but for some reason, all the contacts didn't transfer over."

Okay, maybe she could believe that. "What are you doing here?" she asked. "I mean, in this building of all places."

"Meeting with my insurance agent. About my upcoming trip."

"That's right," Charlotte said. "Your plan to sail around the world to achieve world domination."

"You remembered! How's your bid for partner going? Dominating the firm yet?"

"No. They've put off making their decision until the new year."

The partners had announced they needed more time. Charlotte knew, on some level, it had to do with her social ranking. She was the best attorney in the firm—she knew it, they all knew it—but Tom Jervis wanted to see more from her.

"Hey, I'm here until tomorrow. Wanna grab dinner?"

"I have to work late," Charlotte said.

"How late? I'm free all night. You have to eat, right?"

Charlotte considered his offer, recalling how much she'd enjoyed his company. This could be another opportunity to practice being social.

"Okay."

"Great. Before I forget, let's exchange numbers again. I promise I won't drop it in the ocean this time."

She chuckled, agreeing she'd text him when she was ready for a dinner break.

It turned out Charlotte had more work than she'd realized. She tried to cancel dinner, but Jake suggested bringing pizza to the office. She saw no nutritional value in the circular dough product, but schmoozers seemed to like pizza, so she agreed.

She greeted him in the lobby at their agreed upon time. He was wearing a leather jacket, jeans, and a big smile as he stood there holding a large square box. Charlotte's heart almost skipped upon seeing him, until she remembered she preferred men in suits—on the rare occasions she looked up long enough to observe them. A suit meant gainful employment and a healthy 401(k). Not that she was looking to a man for financial support, but a suit was an indication a man took life seriously. Not like the leather jacket-clad boater standing before her who, she had to admit, was nicer than many of the suit-wearing men she knew.

She led him to her office.

"Mmm, love me some pizza," he said, setting the box on her desk and opening it before taking a sniff. "How 'bout you, Char?"

"Oh, yeah," she lied.

Pulling two paper plates from the box, he asked her how many slices she wanted.

"One is fine," she said.

Jake helped himself to two before raising one in the air. "To old friends."

"Yes," Charlotte said, feeling a rush of warmth. "Friends."

She bit into the pizza, expecting to hate it, but the warm, buttery crust delighted her carb-loving senses and the tangy tomato sauce tickled her tastebuds. The gooey, creamy cheese was like nothing she'd tasted before. Her eyes rolled back in her head.

"My God," she moaned instinctively, forgetting her manners.

"Good, huh?"

Charlotte couldn't answer. She was already shoving another bigger bite in her mouth.

Jake watched, an amused expression on his face. She gobbled it up, stopping when she got to the crust.

"Do I eat this too?" she asked.

"It's whatever you want," he said. "Not everyone loves the pizza bones."

"Pizza bones. That's funny," she said through another mouthful.

Jake was about to take another bite but paused. "Charlotte, have you never had pizza before?"

She shook her head. "Once or twice as a kid, but I don't remember it being this good."

Jake laughed out loud. "Your pizza-less days are over."

"I'll say."

Not one, not two, but three slices later, Charlotte sat back, satiated. "That was life-changing. Thank you."

"My pleasure. I've never seen someone enjoy pizza so much. We have to do this again."

"That sounds nice."

"So, these are your digs?" Jake asked, looking around her office.

"Yes." Assuming by "digs" he meant office.

"Very nice. Minimalistic. I like your style."

"I can't stand clutter," Charlotte said. "My work environment must be spotless, or I can't concentrate."

"You'd hate being a sailor, then."

"For more reasons than clutter."

"Such as?"

"Fear of sharks and rogue waves. Motion sickness. The smell of fish makes me gag, and I don't like having more than ten minutes of sunlight on my skin a day."

"How do you feel about garlic?" he teased. "I guess this means you won't be my first mate?"

At first, Charlotte thought he was serious, but then he told her he was kidding.

She breathed a sigh of relief. "Good. I don't mean to be rude, but as they like to say in the movies, 'no fucking way.' Excuse my language."

Jake laughed. "Besides, you have big stuff going on here. How are you feeling now, since our first conversation? Is becoming partner still your main goal in life? Besides your McMansion, of course."

Charlotte wondered if he was making fun of her, but his eyes and smile showed only kindness.

"Yes. I'm trying. They still want me to be more social."

"Would you consider a path where you don't have to try so hard? Maybe a firm that doesn't put so much emphasis on social involvement?"

"I've put in too much time here to quit now."

"Understandable," Jake said, nodding. "If you ever change your mind, don't forget about my lawyer friend. He's talking about retiring but wants to bring someone on who would ultimately take over. Could be a new adventure."

That did sound intriguing until Jake told her his practice was located in Cape May. No thanks. Her whole life was here in Philadelphia. If Charlotte wasn't anything, it was adventurous.

When she arrived home that night, she noticed her furry friend's can of tuna was still full, and he was nowhere in sight. He'd probably already eaten his fair share of mice and was sleeping somewhere, she reasoned, as she tried to dispel the wave of concern washing over her.

Bella

SITTING IN THE HIGH SCHOOL AUDITORIUM, BELLA AND Hanna clasped hands as they waited to learn what show they'd be doing for this year's school production. When the musical director announced they'd be performing *Beauty and the Beast*, the girls squealed with delight.

"We did *Beauty* last summer at camp," Bella exclaimed. "I was only in the chorus, but it's such a great show."

The director announced that auditions would be held in November, rehearsal would begin in January, and the show would be in March. "As you can see, we don't have many upperclassmen participating in theater. Roles are open to all grades."

"You should definitely try out for Belle," Hanna whispered.

"Oh, I don't know..." Bella hedged. She'd been acting since she was a kid but wasn't sure she was ready for a leading role. Still, she couldn't help but hope. Perhaps it was a possibility.

Sophie approached her later that day at her locker. "Hey, Bella. Wanna join us for lunch?"

Bella knew without asking that the "us" Sophie referenced was the band of mean girls she often traveled with. The ones who gathered around Bella now, popping their gum as they gave her the snarled-lip once-over. While Bella wasn't a mainstay of the group, she'd been grandfathered in as Sophie's kindergarten best friend and invited guest whenever it benefitted the leader of the pack in some way.

Sus, perhaps, but Bella overlooked the lurking ulterior motive on Sophie's part. Keeping in the good graces of Belvedere High's popular girls and their queen bee was necessary to the survival of tenth grade. She felt bad blowing off Hanna, with whom she usually lunched, but she'd understand.

"I've decided..." Sophie paused for dramatic effect once seated, her eager followers waiting with bated breath. "I'm auditioning for the role of Belle."

She beamed as the Followers gave tiny claps and squeals of encouragement.

"But you've never been in a play," Bella blurted out before she could stop herself.

There was a definitive pecking order to high school musicals. Lead roles usually went to upperclassmen first, then underclassmen who'd put in their time. Since elementary school, Bella had been cast in small roles in school musicals and had attended theater camp for the past four summers. Conversely, Sophie had never stepped foot on a stage, often mocking Bella for her love of theater, noting it was "cheugy." Not that Bella truly believed she, herself, was worthy of a lead role, but she hoped she'd have a bit of an advantage, knowing how theater worked.

"Where'd you get your shirt, Bella?" Sophie countered, raising an eyebrow at the Hollister shirt she'd given her.

Bella gave her a fake smile. "Goodwill."

"Whatever." Sophie rolled her eyes, the wind from her sails gone. "I've been told my whole life I look just like Belle."

"You *are* Belle," a Follower piped in.

"The OG," another agreed.

Sophie nodded. "I guess that means I should start writing books. Since that's what Belle did."

"Read books," Bella corrected, trying to keep her eye roll in check. "She reads them."

"See, Bella? This is why I need your help," Sophie said, sounding sincere. "You're so smart. I need you to teach me everything there is to know about theater. And run lines with me—maybe Wednesdays after school."

Bella hesitated, not sure she wanted to help, but Sophie's unexpected compliment clouded her judgment. Running lines meant more practice for her, too. Before she knew it, Bella found herself agreeing to help Sophie land the role she wanted for herself.

"Why would you do that?" Hanna hissed when Bella told her later. "She stole Robbie from you, and now she wants you to help her get the role *you* deserve? She's a selfish asshole."

"She's not that bad." Bella recalled her compliment about being the smartest person Sophie knew. They had a history together, and she wasn't about to ditch her for a few infractions.

"She's toxic. You need to cut her off."

"I can't. We've been friends since we were five, and our moms are close. Who knows, maybe if she joins theater, she'll become nicer."

"Yeah, and maybe I'll sprout another head."

Marley

MARLEY WAS MET WITH DOWNCAST EYES AND PITIFUL looks as she entered work the following day.

"Ooh, is this my pity party?" she whispered sarcastically to Sam.

"It's because they care about you," Sam said, squeezing her hand. "Everyone's feeling your pain."

"They don't need to show me. I feel bad enough."

"Stay strong, Mar. You got this." He kissed her and went to his office.

She'd just settled in when someone rapped at her door. It was Sarah, holding a large vase of tulips, surrounded by their female co-workers.

"We figured you could use a little lovin'," Sarah said. "Can we come in?"

Marley teared up when she saw their faces—no longer looked sad, just supportive.

"We love you, Marley," one said. "We're sorry."

"We're here for you, however you need us to be," said another.

"I also didn't pass the first time," an associate added. "I know what you're going through."

"Thank you," Marley said as she hugged them. "This means a lot to me."

"You mean a lot to us. We're not letting you go through this alone."

Marley was blessed to work with such amazing women. It helped to ease the pain, until she and Sam were called into a meeting with Jim Howe, one of the partners.

"Hey, Marley," Jim said, his sympathetic tone like nails on a chalkboard. "I'm sorry about the bar. I'm sure you'll do better next time."

If only she felt as optimistic.

"Obviously, Sam gets the job as a result. We hope you'll stay on as intern—"

Marley perked up, hoping that meant they were reconsidering a second position.

"—until you find something else," he added.

If that wasn't a here's-your-hat-what's-your-hurry invitation, she didn't know what was. She didn't plan to stay forever, but—*sheesh*. At least until she retook the bar exam.

Sam's eyes were downcast. Did he already know about this?

"Should I...be...looking for something right now?" she asked.

"Not immediately, but within the next month or so," Jim said.

A month? That was all she got after two years of service? Fabulous. Now, she'd have to add a job search to her worries.

"In the meantime, you'll be reporting to Sam."

Marley flinched. Sam's eyes shot up to meet Jim's.

"I don't know, Jim—" He clearly didn't seem comfortable with that prospect.

"You two work well together. I have no doubt you'll continue to do so."

"What about Maxine?" Sam asked. "Can't Marley continue reporting to her?"

"Maxine's gone. She received a competitive offer at another firm and gave notice yesterday. With the nature of our business, we needed her to leave immediately."

Go, girl. Run like the wind.

Jim clasped his hand on Sam's shoulder. "You're the boss, now. At least you'll have this fine, intelligent, and accomplished intern under you."

Under you? Jim sounded like he could benefit from a swift kick to the nuts.

After they were excused, Marley stormed to her office, Sam closely in tow. Once the door closed behind them, she spun to face him. "I'm either under you in the bedroom or the boardroom. Not both. Your choice—*boss.*"

"Marley, please," he begged. "I had no idea—"

"Don't. You. Dare." Marley pointed her finger at him. "I don't need you to feign shock over this. You and your good ol' boys network."

"Marley, you and I are a team. You're more of an associate than I'll ever be."

"Tell that to the partners. Oh, right—it doesn't matter because I failed the bar. Oh! And I don't have a swinging dick."

"Marley—"

She held up her hand. "Please, this is humiliating for me, having to 'answer' to you. Are you kidding me?"

"Okay," he said softly. "I'll leave you alone. Let me know when you wanna talk."

He backed out of her office, closing the door behind him.

Marley paced. Tears burned in her eyes, but she was too angry to cry. She'd been expecting to work alongside Sam, not "under" him. Once again, she was haunted by the idea she belonged in someone's shadow, never being worthy of standing on her own.

Her phone dinged with a text from Sam, asking her to come to his office.

Marley rolled her eyes but acquiesced.

"I've just been assigned to the team working the embezzlement case you'd...well. What's it about?"

"Um, embezzlement?" She raised an eyebrow, her voice dripping sarcasm.

"You know what I mean."

Marley wanted to tell him to put in the work as she had, but didn't want to be a jerk to her new "boss." She filled him in on the details.

He furrowed his brow. "Sounds like we'll need to do more research."

We, Sam? Or you?

He jotted down notes and handed them to her. "Would you mind reading up on these items and briefing me?"

Marley wanted to tear the paper in half, but Sam was no more to blame for this weird situation than she was. They'd always worked together as equals, and that wasn't about to change. Her integrity dictated she do the right thing for the case—for them—and stop being a smacked ass about it.

"Sure," she said, then left to do Sam's dirty work.

Soon after, he buzzed her. "Are you finished with that research?"

"Geez, Sam. It's been an hour. If that."

"I'm sitting in on the hearing tomorrow. Just wanna make sure I understand the law."

Marley made haste with the research, not wanting to let Sam down. She created a Word doc with her research results and emailed it to him.

Sam buzzed her again. "I don't understand some of your notes. Can you come here?"

Marley sighed and headed to his office.

"What does this mean?" he asked, pointing to a paragraph where she'd set forth the rule of law on the case.

She gazed at the very elementary, simple-to-understand concept, resisting the urge to explain it to him in the exaggerated tone of an overtly patient kindergarten teacher. It took not one, not two, but three times before he got it, which irked her beyond belief. She knew more about law than Sam apparently did. But here he was, a bona fide attorney, while she was just his knuckle-dragging Igor.

The following day, she asked him if he wanted to do the Reading Terminal Market for lunch.

"Sorry, I'm having lunch with some of the associates," he said.

Marley, who understood the law firm caste system, knew better than to ask to tag along.

Sam left her alone for the rest of the afternoon, which was a relief at first until she started missing him. She was probably making a bigger deal about this than she should. It wasn't Sam's fault she'd failed the bar and was given the position "under" him. She needed to pull her shit together and stop taking it out on him.

At the end of the day, Marley popped into his office.

"Ready to call it a night?" she asked.

"Can't. Too much to do."

"Should I stay and help?"

"Not unless you can upload these files directly into my brain," he joked. He rounded his desk and took her in his arms. "How about I stop by tonight and make it up to you?"

The look in his eyes made her heart melt. She gave him a coquettish gaze. "Isn't it against the rules to sleep with your 'boss'?"

Sam deflated and pulled away. "Marley, don't be like that."

"Like what? I'm just joking."

"You know I feel horrible about this."

"I know," she said, going up on her tiptoes to kiss him. "I'll see you later at my place. Don't work too hard."

Three hours later, when Sam hadn't shown, she texted to see if he was coming.

> Still here. Will have to take a raincheck.

That was new. He'd never made her "take a raincheck" before.

Sam continued growing in his role as supervisor (*read: micro-managing taskmaster*) throughout the week, asking Marley to meet with him at the end of each day to update him on her progress, prepare memos for the cases he'd been assigned to, and do research he should be doing himself.

She'd reached her boiling point one afternoon when he buzzed her. Again.

"Since you're not working on anything important, could you grab me a coffee from Saxby's?"

Which might have been fine had she been planning to go to Saxby's. Which she hadn't been. Nonetheless, she went.

Stepping inside his office with the piping hot coffee, she closed the door behind her.

"You can set it down on my desk," he said, not looking up from his computer.

"And then," she said, setting the cup down, "you can shove it up your ass."

"What was that for?" He swiveled in his chair to face her, eyes wide like he was totally clueless.

"For being an asshole," Marley said.

"How am I an asshole?"

"'Get this, Marley, do that, Marley,'" she said with a snide tone. "'Do my work, bring me coffee, shine my shoes.'"

"I never asked you to shine my shoes."

"I'm sure that's next, Shinola."

"How come when Delaney and Maxine asked us to do the same things, you didn't feel the need to act juvenile?"

"I'm *not* being juvenile," Marley said, picking up the coffee. "Yet."

She crossed the room and poured it into a potted plant.

"Now I am." She tossed the empty cup in the trashcan and wiped her hands together. "Don't bother getting up. I'll see myself out."

Marley was proud of her creative defiance, childish or not. A tiny victory after all she'd been through that week. But as the day wore on and she didn't hear from Sam, triumph melted into a puddle of remorse over her brazen display of rebellion. They'd done plenty of coffee runs for each other in the past. This should've been no different, but for their strange hierarchy.

By five o'clock, Marley had had enough of the guilt-ridden, frankly boring, workday. She texted Sam.

Marley smiled, relieved. He couldn't be that mad if he was joking.

Beware interns bearing hot bevs.

Noted. I'll alert my plants.

Wanna join me for yoga?

Namaste right here.

Yoga proved to be the release she needed to keep her from feeling like a bad downward dog. Back at her condo, Marley had just finished showering when Sam strode through the door with a pizza.

"We need an M-n-S night," he said. "Gotta bring us back to us."

She opened the lid to find his latest parm message: *You owe me a coffee.*

Marley laughed out loud.

The rest of the night was peaceful, with no more talk of work, except when Sam got up to leave. She pouted, disappointed he wasn't staying the night.

"Early morning meeting with the ass—"

Marley knew he was about to say "associates" but stopped himself.

"Okay," she said. "Have a good meeting with the asses."

Pre-lawyer Sam never would have left early to sleep alone. The tentacles of their on-the-job disparity were beginning to wrap a stranglehold on their personal lives, and it was getting harder for Marley to breathe.

The following day, Sam hit her up with five projects, all due at the end of the day, which she delivered.

"Where's the caselaw?" he asked as she handed him the memos she'd created.

"You didn't ask for caselaw," she responded, "you asked for research. These are the results."

"Marley." He sighed as if he were addressing a petulant toddler who'd just thrown her sippy cup across the room. "I need copies of the caselaw. Can you please do that for me?"

Resisting the urge to bark *sir, yessir* before dropping to give him five, she scanned and emailed the caselaw instead of delivering it personally. She couldn't bear to look at him behind his desk, lording his newfound power over her.

By the end of the day, Marley was in dire need of girl time. She met Gwen for drinks after work while Sam stayed back, clamoring to figure out how to practice law on his own.

"It's like he's on some sort of power trip," Marley told Gwen as she sipped a margarita.

"That has to be rough."

"Total insult added to injury. Bad enough I didn't pass the bar, get the job, and have to work 'under' him. He doesn't have to pull rank on me, too."

"Come work for the DA's office. We're hiring interns."

Marley groaned. "I'm tired of interning." Tired of shadowing. Tired of waiting for her life to begin. She was ready to practice law.

"I know, but it would give you a different perspective. Learn some of the tricks of the prosecution trade. Just consider it."

Marley would do no such thing but appreciated the offer.

Charlotte

CHARLOTTE SEARCHED FOR HER LITTLE FRIEND FIRST thing in the morning after noticing his still-untouched food bowl. Concern gave way to low-key panic. Not that she should care about this feral cat, but she'd grown accustomed to him, someone she could practice being "social" with. She was saddened by the possibility something bad might have happened.

She walked up and down her street, looking in patches of grass and behind trash cans. When she entered the small alley next to her row home, she heard a soft meow. She found him hiding behind a discarded bag of trash.

"Oh no!" she exclaimed. A trail of blood ran down the cat's face from its left eye. The lid was drooping, and it appeared to be scratched around the socket as well. The cat's body also had patches of blood where bare skin was exposed.

"What happened to you?" she asked as she kneeled down, tears welling in her eyes.

The cat looked up at her and opened its mouth, but no sound came out.

Charlotte wasn't sure what to do or who to call. Animal Control would probably just euthanize it. She didn't want to touch him for fear it would cause more pain. Then it dawned on her. Jasper had cats—he'd know what to do. She scrolled through her phone contacts to find his number and hit send, pacing as she waited for him to answer.

"Charlotte! How are you?"

The voice, while familiar, wasn't Jasper's. It sounded like—

"Jake?" She must have dialed his number by accident. "I'm sorry. I—"

"Char, are you okay?"

"No," she said, her voice feeble. "But I'm sorry to bother you. I dialed you by mistake."

"It's not a bother," he insisted. "What's going on?"

"My cat—well, it's not my cat, but one I've...befriended," Charlotte began, feeling foolish as she said the words. "He's hurt. Badly. It looks like his eye has been scratched, and he's bleeding. I don't know what to do."

"Is there a veterinarian you could take him to?"

"No. He's feral, so I'm not sure they'd even do anything for him."

Jake chuckled softly. "Let's have a doc make that decision."

"I wouldn't know where to take him. Or how."

"I know a vet. I'll reach out and call you right back."

Charlotte felt badly she'd bothered him with this. "Just give me the number. I can call."

"It's Saturday, and she's not in the office. I'll be in touch." With that, he hung up.

Relieved she was getting help, Charlotte crouched down to her friend, his head resting on his paw as if he was unable to hold it up anymore. The injured eye was now fully closed, and the other was heading that way, too. It looked as if he wasn't going to make it.

Charlotte's heart broke. To ease both their pain, she softly sang "You Are My Sunshine," a song her grandmother used to sing to her when she was sick. The cat's eyes closed fully, but it was still breathing.

"I'm getting you some help, friend. Hang in there with me." The cat shuddered a sigh. "I can't lose you, buddy. I'm sorry for all the mean things I said to you before we became friends."

The ringing vibration of her phone jolted her.

"I'm on my way," Jake said.

"Wait—aren't you in New Jersey?"

"Nope, I was home for my high school reunion. I just ran

into the doc, an old classmate, last night. I'm gonna swing by and pick her up."

"I can't thank you enough, Jake," she said after giving him her address. "I truly appreciate this. I feel bad I'm taking both of you away from your weekend."

"Not a problem, Charlotte," he said. "It's what friends are for."

Friends. The word echoed in her ears long after she hung up. He'd just confirmed what she'd secretly let herself hope: Jake was her friend.

And so was this little guy. Charlotte retrieved an old towel from inside and gingerly laid it on him as she continued singing, relieved he was now sleeping.

Jake arrived not long after with a beautiful brunette dressed in skinny jeans, a tight sweater, and knee-high boots. She was gorgeous, the exact type of woman she assumed Jake dated.

"Charlotte, this is my friend, Dr. Doolittle."

The doctor chuckled at Charlotte's disbelieving glance. "I know, but that's my actual surname. You can call me Diane."

Charlotte wondered how many times a day she had to explain that to people.

The doctor tended to the cat before giving it a shot. She wrapped it in the towel and carefully lifted it up. "Jakey, you good to take us to the animal hospital?"

The cute nickname wasn't lost on Charlotte. She wondered if Dr. Doolittle was more than an old pal from high school.

"Absolutely. Charlotte, wanna come witness the good doc doing what she does best?"

Charlotte agreed, soon discovering why Jake referred to her as a *good doc.* She expertly went to work on the cat, stitching up and dressing its wounds.

"There you go, little fella," Diane said when she was finished. "You should be good now."

Turning to Charlotte, she asked the cat's name.

"Um…" She didn't want to admit the cat was feral, in case there was some sort of kill order in place. The cat looked up at her, one eye patched shut.

"Blinky," she finally said.

Jake and Diane laughed out loud.

"Apropos, if nothing else," she said. "I'm giving you instructions for his care for the next few days."

Shoot. The last thing she had time for was taking care of a pet. But, in the great words of Jake Brady, "That's what friends are for."

Jake dropped Diane off at her house first. Charlotte pulled a crisp twenty from her wallet and handed it to her as she got out of the car.

"For your troubles," she said, feeling like a big spender. Whatever. It was worth it to save a friend.

Diane waved her off. "No worries, it was my pleasure to help the little guy out. You can repay me by taking good care of him."

Charlotte promised she would as she tucked the twenty back in her wallet, impressed by the woman's lack of interest in receiving payment for her services. Obviously, her foremost concern was the cat's well-being. She thanked the good doctor once again.

On their way back to her apartment, Jake asked if she had any plans for Halloween.

"Not giving out candy, that's for sure," she said. One could never be too careful with nighttime marauders posing as children in costume. She told him as much. He just laughed.

"Char, baby, you gotta trust the world a little more. Not everyone is bad."

No thanks. She knew a little bit about the world and its lurking dangers.

"Why don't you come trick-or-treating with me?" he asked.

"Because I'm not a child?" she answered, then immediately regretted her snark.

He laughed. "Well, I am. I take my nieces and nephew and their friends every year. You should join us, get a little fun-spooked and not real-spooked."

"I'll see," she said, uncertain why her heart was racing. Was it over the idea of spending time with Jake...or being slaughtered on the most murderous night of the year? Hard to tell.

Charlotte thanked him when they arrived at her house and asked him to make sure the doc sent her a bill.

"I will, but she won't," Jake said.

"How do you know her?" she asked. "Is she your girlfriend?"

Jake smiled, one hand slung over the steering wheel. "You're pretty perceptive."

Disappointment seeped into her heart. She chastised herself for caring.

"Used to be," he continued. "We're just friends now."

She wasn't sure if she believed it. The good doctor was exactly who she envisioned Jake falling for.

Not that she cared.

Bella

"DID YOU ASK YOUR MOM YET?" HANNA ASKED BELLA AS they picked over the hideous cafeteria food the school had the audacity to call lunch.

"Tonight's the night," she said, swallowing the last of her chicken nuggets, which tasted (and felt) as if they'd been cooked in the 1990s. "It's book club night, which means she'll be good 'n liquored up."

Earlier that week, Sophie had announced a Halloween party was being hosted by a senior lacrosse player on his family's farm, and all were invited. Bella and Hanna were excited at the prospect of hanging out with the host's hot teammates.

Once the last of Lisa's friends left their house that evening, Bella joined her mom in the kitchen.

"Hey, Mom," she sang, lending a hand in cleaning up. "Let me help you with that."

"What do you want, Bella?" Lisa teased, her eyes gleaming with a hint of one too many Chardonnays.

"I just want to help," she said, rolling her eyes. "Why do you always think there's an ulterior motive?"

"Because there always is."

Busted. "So, there's this party Saturday night—"

"Absolutely not."

"You don't even know what I'm gonna say. It's a costume party, and Hanna's parents are letting her go."

Bella knew that was her ace in the hole. Lisa usually trusted Hanna's mom's judgment.

"I really don't care if she's going," Lisa said. "You're not."

"Why?" Bella demanded. "What possible reason could you have?"

Lisa began counting on her fingers. "Alcohol. Drugs. Sexual assault. Shall I go on?"

Ah, the joys of being raised by a probation officer. Good God. You could hand this woman an infant, and she'd see a future serial killer.

Bella stayed the course. "I wish you'd trust me," she said, trying to keep her voice calm and conversational.

"It's not you I don't trust. It's others."

Bella felt the oncoming defeat of a losing battle. "So your plan is to keep me locked away? What are you going to do when I go to college?"

"I'll cross that bridge when we get to it."

"How about crossing it now?" Bella asked, her voice rising against her will to keep calm. "Get used to the fact that I'm growing up. Soon, I'll be out in the world, and I'll have to spot these so-called dangers on my own. How will I learn how to avoid them if I don't start now?"

Bella was impressed by her own argument. Reasonable. Adult-like.

Today's tally—Bella: 1, Lisa: 0.

"No."

"Why do you always do this?" Bella cried, all resolve to be calm gone. She couldn't help it. Her mom brought out the worst in her when she acted like this.

"I'm just trying to protect you while I still can."

"It's not about protection!" she yelled in response to her mom's overbearing grasp on her freedom. "You just want to ruin my life. I hate you for this!"

Not the best way to advance her cause, but whatever. There was no winning this one.

Her dad entered the room. "What's going on?"

"She wants to go to a party, and I said no," Lisa answered.

"Everyone's going," Bella said. "I'm the only one whose mom doesn't trust her."

Tears cascaded down her cheeks but she didn't try to stop them, hoping the waterworks would help soften her dad, who, in turn, would talk sense into her mother. Her parents just didn't understand the pressures on teens these days. Everyone in school would be posting pictures on socials while she rotted away in solitary confinement.

"What kind of party?" her dad asked.

A glimmer of hope.

"An innocent Halloween party," Bella said, catching her breath between sobs. "People will be in costumes, for crying out loud. And the whole school is invited, so it's not like it's me and Hanna and a bunch of drunk guys."

Oops, probably shouldn't have said that.

Her dad looked at her, then at her mom. "I'm sorry, Bella. Gotta back Mom on this one."

Bella growled and stormed away. She felt humiliated, trapped, like she was some sort of juvenile delinquent, her only crime asking to go to a party. She slammed her bedroom door, flung herself on the bed, and sobbed into her pillow.

A few minutes later, someone knocked.

"Go away," she yelled, guessing it was Eli wanting to cheer her up.

"I'm coming in."

Lisa: Prophet of Doom, Slayer of Good Times. Bella wedged her face into her pillow as her mom sat on the edge of her bed.

"Bella, I'd like to talk this out. Can you please look at me?"

"No," she said, her voice muffled.

"I'm sorry you think I'm trying to ruin your life when all I want to do is protect you. I have good reason. Doing what I do for a living, I see how quickly things can go wrong when alcohol's involved."

Bella flopped on her back. "Who said anything about alcohol?"

Lisa cocked her head. "I wasn't born yesterday. My point is, when alcohol gets into the wrong people's hands, especially at your young ages, bad stuff can happen."

"You have to learn to trust me."

"It's not you I don't trust. It's the world and all the jerks in it."

"Thanks to your horror stories and warnings, I'm well aware of what can go wrong."

"I'm sorry, but working in criminal justice, you tend to see the bad before the good."

"Mom, it's different now. I know not to drink because you've terrified me with the ramifications of underage drinking. And the whole spiked drink thing is something they teach us in school, for God's sake. I'm guessing they didn't talk about it back in your day."

"No, they didn't. I'm glad they've opened up the lines of communication. I just—I'm not ready for you to be dealing with this."

Bella placed her hand on Lisa's. "I know, Mom. But you have to. Better I learn now, when I'm here, and we can talk about things, than to keep me locked away until I'm at college, struggling to handle things without your guidance."

Damn, am I good.

Lisa nodded. "That's why I'm here to tell you, you can go to the party. You just have to promise me—no alcohol, no setting your drink down, no going off with some boy. You and Hanna must stick together. Got it?"

Bella smiled and threw herself at her mom, enveloping her with a hug.

"I got it. I promise you can trust me to always use my better judgment. And—thank you. This means a lot to me."

"Are you sure this is appropriate for a high school party?" Lisa asked as Bella climbed into the minivan in a plush Scooby-Doo costume, the humungous dog head taking up most of the front seat. "It seems a little young."

"Well, like you often say, I shouldn't dress provocatively, right?" Bella said, peering at her through the open dog mouth. "I'm guessing no one's coming after me dressed like a cartoon canine."

Little did Lisa know, Scooby was nothing more than a coverup of what lay beneath. Once she was dropped off and her mom was no longer in sight, she planned to shed her outer layer and emerge as a sexy maid. Hella provocative.

Her mom would've never let her out of the house if she knew

of Bella's plan, concocted by Sophie and friends. They'd invited Bella and Hanna to join their posse of sexy vixens: a nurse, a cop, a teacher, and more. The sexier, the better, Sophie had said. Hanna, who wouldn't be caught dead in anything too revealing, opted out. Sophie assigned Bella the maid costume.

Upon arrival, Bella climbed out of the car and waved a giant paw as her mom drove away. As soon as she was out of sight, Bella unzipped Scooby and tossed it into the bushes lining the driveway. Sophie had texted earlier to make sure Bella was wearing her costume and to tell her the party was being moved inside the barn. Bella was forever amazed at how Sophie seemed to have her finger on the pulse of all things Belvedere High despite only being a sophomore herself.

Hanna texted just then to say she was running late and to go in without her.

Bella smoothed her sexy maid skirt, which, now that she looked at it, was more of a tube top than a skirt. Oh well. In the barn, a Drake song was playing at top volume over the excited chatter of classmates. The party was in full swing.

She made her way through the crowd in search of Sophie. People stepped aside, casting double-takes her way. One of the senior boys let out a low whistle.

"Bella baby, I had no idea!" another said.

The crowd parted like she was Moses at the Red Sea. With each step, it became abundantly clear—no one else was in costume. Hiding her growing mortification, Bella kept her head up, looking straight ahead, seeking her sexy-costumed friends.

"Yoohoo, housekeeping!"

She turned to see Sophie and company laughing. In regular clothing.

"Well, bless your little heart. You dressed up, anyway!"

The others, apparently, hadn't.

"Why didn't you tell me you weren't dressing up?" Bella hissed.

"Didn't you get my text?" Sophie's wide eyes feigned innocence. "We decided not to wear ours."

"No, Sophie, your only text reminded me to wear it."

Sophie looked at her phone and chuckled. "LOL, I must've sent the second one to a wrong number. Oops!"

Bullshit. Bella didn't believe it for a second. She knew the truth. Sophie and company had set her up. There was no plan to wear costumes. They just wanted to humiliate her. She blinked back tears as she turned to leave, not wanting them to know they'd gotten the best of her.

"Wait, Bella!" Sophie called out.

She turned back, expecting to hear an apology. An explanation. Something.

"Can we have extra towels?"

Bella pushed through the crowd of bodies. She had to get out of there.

"Sexy maid, come make my bed!" one of the guys called out.

"You can do more than just make it!" another said.

Bella burst through the door into the cool night air and succumbed to tears. She should've known better than to trust Sophie. Lisa had been right—she had no business going to a senior party. Having no other choice, she texted her.

Sobbing as she made her way to the driveway, Bella knew she had a matter of moments to don her Scooby-Doo costume. Lisa would be heading toward her at Mach speed, sensing something was wrong. She couldn't let her mom see what she was really wearing, or she'd never be allowed to leave the house again.

But the costume wasn't in the bushes where she thought she'd thrown it. Pushing the brush aside, she searched for the hideous thing to no avail. Who loses a Scooby-Doo costume with a huge-ass dog head?

Someone who was about to spend her life under house arrest.

Fear mounted as Bella traced her way along the bushes,

becoming increasingly frazzled as she rummaged, no Scooby in sight. Laughter from the barn drew her attention. She turned to find Scooby-Doo entering the party, high-fiving others. Someone had found it first.

Then, a car horn. Her mom was here.

Bella slunk along the bush line before sliding into the back seat, hoping Lisa hadn't seen her barely-there costume. Silence filled the minivan as her mom steered away from the farm, giving Bella hope. If Lisa had seen what she was wearing, she'd be in hysterics by now. But she was silent for too long, which was worse. Bella far preferred a screaming mother to a silent one.

Fan, meet shit.

She dared to look up and caught her mom's eyes in the rearview mirror. Instead of anger, she was met with sadness.

"I had a feeling you weren't really going as Scooby-Doo," Lisa said quietly, her face drenched in disappointment.

Bella's heart lurched as new tears welled in her eyes. "I'm sorry I lied."

"Wanna tell me what happened?"

Bella sighed. "Sophie happened."

Her mom deflated somewhat, and it pushed Bella over the edge.

"They told me they were dressing up in matching outfits," she wept. "But they didn't. I was the only one. They set me up."

"Aww, Bell," her mom said. "What about Hanna? Was she there?"

Shoot, that's right. She'd left before Hanna arrived. She pulled out her phone and texted to let her know about the setup and that she'd left.

Bella waited for the judgment to come, for the *I told you so* lecture to commence, for the mom-regret over letting her go in the first place. For the reprimands that she shouldn't have lied and oh, by the way, don't plan on leaving the house again until you're in menopause.

But her mom said nothing, which made her cry harder. Bella covered her face and let it all out. She knew there'd be some form of punishment coming later (lethal injection, firing squad, stoning), but for now, she was relieved her mom wasn't kicking her when she was down.

The car slowed. Surprised to be home so fast, Bella looked up into the face of a smiling, freckled redhead on a marquee.

"Two Frostys, please," Lisa said into Wendy's drive-up order board.

What was this madness? Bella expected to be punished. Yelled at. Drawn and quartered—maybe even waterboarded. She didn't expect to be rewarded with a delightful treat. Her favorite, no less.

Lisa pulled into a parking spot and climbed into the back seat with Bella, handing her a Frosty. An unexpected giggle bubbled up in Bella. She couldn't remember the last time Perpetually Dieting Lisa ate a carb, much less a cup of fat-laden ice cream. Or sat in the backseat.

Lisa clinked her cup against Bella's. "We're having a mother-daughter bonding moment."

Well, this was new. Unless *bonding* was another word for *big-ass lecture: full speed ahead.*

"I'm sorry that happened," Lisa said as she dipped her spoon into the frozen delicacy and took a lick. "*OhmyGod,*" she purred, her eyes wide. "I haven't had anything this delicious in years. Why have you kept me from this?"

Bella giggled again, tickled to see her mom acting more like a friend than a probation officer/prosecutor/judge/warden/executioner. All of which she expected, none of which would have surprised her.

After a few more bites with corresponding joyful sound effects, Lisa turned to Bella.

"Friends can be real jerks sometimes," she said. "The good news is, the jerks will show you their true colors. And then you can ditch them and go find your people, the ones who have your back and wouldn't dream of purposely hurting you."

"Easier said than done."

"I know," Lisa agreed. "The bad news is, you'll deal with people like this your whole life. Some people never outgrow their own petty childishness. More good news—you'll get better at spotting them earlier on. Same thing with guys."

"I hope so."

"I know so. Did I ever tell you about my so-called 'friend,' Nelly?"

"No," Bella said, eager to hear the story. "Do tell."

Lisa went on to explain how she had a crush on a guy in her junior year, and her friend, whom she trusted, told the guy. A month later, Nelly was dating him.

"That's exactly what Sophie did to me with Robbie," she explained.

Lisa gave her a puzzled look. That's right—she hadn't told her mom about prom. She proceeded to do so now.

Her mom shook her head. "Stay away from her, Bell. Trust me, it won't end well."

"I know, but I don't have many friends. She and I have been together since kindergarten, and she's the most popular girl in school. It's not like I can avoid her."

"Well, it's your choice," Lisa said. "Just watch yourself. I wouldn't trust her as far as I could throw her."

"I thought you were friends with her mom?"

"Only for self-preservation. Her mom's just like Sophie. Better to be friendly than to let them become enemies. But there's a difference between being friendly and being friends. I'm just sorry I've led you to believe they could be trusted."

"The weirdest thing is, she's not always nasty. Sometimes, she's a sweetheart."

Her mom nodded. "The most dangerous kind."

They continued eating their Frostys in silence.

"I could always have her arrested, you know," Lisa finally said. "Jack her up with a felony charge, lock her up in juvie 'til she turns eighteen."

Bella cracked up. Better Sophie than her. "I'll keep that in mind."

When they arrived home, Hanna was standing in their driveway. As soon as Bella emerged from the minivan, her friend ran to hug her.

"I'm so sorry about what happened," she murmured into Bella's hair. "They're all assholes."

Bella hugged her back, reveling in the care of her true friend. The one who had her back. The one who wouldn't purposely hurt her.

"My mom said I can stay over," Hanna said. "I hope you don't mind, Mrs. Baxter."

"Hanna, you're welcome anytime," Lisa said as the three made their way to the house.

"I added that movie you want to see to my watch list. And I brought popcorn. Who wants to spend the night at a stupid party, anyway?"

In the end, it turned out to be a great night, and Bella leaned one more lesson about navigating the dangers (aka mean girls) of the world. And the true meaning of friendship.

Meanwhile, Lisa learned how to let Bella make her own mistakes. And survive.

Marley

MARLEY WAS GROWING MORE AND MORE FRUSTRATED with the dynamics between her and her new "boss.". The final straw came one afternoon when Sam called her on her office phone.

"I could really go for homemade pasta tonight. What do you say?" he asked.

"Mmm, sounds great. Is that what you want for dinner?"

"Yeah, if you're in."

"Of course I'm in," she said. There was more than one way to a woman's heart, but pasta was the fastest. "What are you thinking—Maggiano's or the new Italian place on Walnut?"

"I was thinking home-homemade."

"Oh, *Chef Adams*," she purred. His offer would certainly ease the tension growing between them from their unbalanced job dynamics. Visions of Sam pulling sheets of pasta through a hand-cranked machine were a total turn-on. Better if he wore nothing more than a chef's hat. Her mouth, and other body parts, began to water. "Tell me more."

He chuckled. "I was thinking more Chef Maguire."

"Wait, what?" Record scratch. "You want *me* to make pasta?"

"If you want to..." His voice lingered sexily as if he was trying to entice her.

"Why me?"

"I don't have anything pressing here for you to do. I figured you could leave early and get started."

"Well, one—I've never done it before. Two—we don't have a pasta machine. And three—no! Who do I look like, Mario Batali?"

"Aww, come on, Mar! I'm too busy here."

"So am I."

He paused, his silence pregnant with condescension. She sensed his sneer before it came over the line. "Doing *what*?"

That was it. Ass, meet door.

"Finding a new job."

The following day, Marley arranged to meet with Gwen and the head of the trial division, Assistant District Attorney Wells Abernathy, III, to discuss the open intern position. Donning her navy suit and paparazzi disguise, she made her way to the restaurant where they were meeting. Unfortunately, she didn't see the lone wolf pacing down the street until it was too late.

"Marley, Don Ramsey from *Celebrity Secrets*. How do you feel about Rick being named the next bachelor?"

Marley ignored him. He continued to follow.

"Do you have any regrets breaking up with him?"

She walked faster. He kept pace.

"Marley," he said, his tone defeated. "Please. One quote, and I promise to leave you alone."

She spun on her heels and jabbed a finger into his chest.

"You media motherfuckers are the reason I failed the bar exam! And if you print that, I'll sue every one of your asses!"

Sympathy flooded his brown eyes. "I'm sorry that happened. I didn't know."

His softened tone relaxed her. "What does it matter what I think about Rick? I'm nothing in this story other than a shadow of his past. Can't you keep it that way?"

He nodded and pressed his lips together as he tucked his phone away. "Yes, ma'am. Sorry for the inconvenience. Best of luck to you."

She turned and marched away, fighting to keep the tears from spilling, relieved he'd been one of the decent ones. She was still shaken when she arrived at the restaurant for the meeting but calmed herself before heading inside.

Within a few minutes of meeting with Wells and Gwen, Marley could see herself working on their team. By the time they finished eating, Wells had offered her the position.

"It's an internship at this point, but if we're both a good fit, we'll make it permanent once you pass the bar. We like to get new hires handling their first trial within weeks of starting. Induction by fire. It's the only way."

That pushed Marley over the edge. The idea of handling her own case so soon—a trial, no less—was something she could only dream of if she were working for a private firm. Finally, an opportunity to put everything she'd learned to good use, to step from the shadows and shine in her own light.

After the meeting, Marley headed to the office and typed up her resignation notice. Stepping into Sam's office, she closed the door behind her.

"This isn't working for me," she said. "I'm leaving."

Sam shot up from his chair. "The firm or me?"

"The firm, Sam. Because I don't want to leave you."

Sam raked a hand through his hair. "I'll leave instead. This was your dream firm."

"Not anymore. You heard Jim. They're not holding this position for me."

"This totally sucks. I'm sorry if I've made it worse for you."

"I do think a little power went to your head. We've always been a team, but I felt like I was in your shadow, the exact thing I'm trying not to be. I'm worth more than that. It's time for me to succeed on my own."

"I wish you'd realize—you already do. You're heads and shoulders above me and most people, Marley. You have nothing to prove to anyone. Except yourself, apparently."

Marley shrugged. "I've always been the hardest to impress."

Bella

BELLA WAS EXCITED FOR THEIR ANNUAL TRICK-OR-TREAT outing with Uncle Jake when he'd take her, Eli, and their friends door-to-door in their neighborhood. He would even get into the spirit of the season by dressing in costume himself. This year, her toddler cousins would be joining them, along with Jake's friend Charlotte.

After the sexy maid debacle, Bella wasn't sure she was ready to get back into costume, but she'd better get used to it. Musical auditions were a month away.

She was honored when Jake asked Bella to help find a costume for his friend.

"I have so many options," Bella said as she ushered Charlotte into her bedroom. She sized up the petite woman, noting they were about the same size under the abundant loose-fitting clothing she was draped in.

"I went to theater camp last summer, and we had to make our own costumes. I have Snoopy to Disney princesses and everything in between. Oh, and this." She pulled out her sexy maid costume.

"Oh, my," Charlotte said. "I don't think that's my speed."

"Agreed," Bella said. "Who's your favorite princess?"

"I...don't really have one," Charlotte said.

"Hmm," Bella said, assessing her. "You're giving Cinderella vibes. Your face kinda reminds me of hers, especially your almond-shaped eyes. Then again," she chuckled, "that's every Disney princess."

"I trust your judgment," Charlotte said.

"Cindy it is."

Bella took the gown from her closet, noting the bodice might have to be adjusted to allow for Charlotte's more endowed bust and curvier waistline. She loosened the tacking that the costume designer had added last summer to fit Bella's slimmer mid-section.

"Wow," Bella said when Charlotte emerged after changing. "It fits perfectly. Slay, girl."

Charlotte gave an awkward twirl. "Thanks."

"Now for makeup," Bella said, guiding Charlotte to her vanity. She swept her hair into a Cinderella-esque updo, topped it with a sparkly headband, and applied makeup in the way @MakeupQueenAmelia, her favorite Instagram influencer, tutored.

"How do you know my uncle?" Bella asked as she swirled blush on Charlotte, noting the woman's cheeks instantly became much rosier than warranted by makeup.

"I met him on one of his sunset cruises. My company was on a work retreat, and we ended up chatting."

"You guys dating?" she asked, hopeful. There was something about Charlotte—a genuine, unpretentious nature about her—that Bella instantly liked. It was about time Jake found himself someone real.

Charlotte laughed out loud. "No. We're just...friends."

Bella nodded. "He's a really nice guy. My favorite adult family member next to my Aunt Kate. Did he tell you about his plan to sail around the globe?"

"Yes. It sounds fascinating."

"I wish I could go with him. I can't imagine a better way to learn. I asked my parents if I could take a year off of school, but no, I'll be trapped here for all of eternity, locked away from life."

Charlotte smiled at her. "You'll get your chance to explore the world. Your whole life's ahead of you."

"I can't wait for it to start."

Bella stood back, marveling at her masterpiece. "You're gorgeous," she sighed, handing her a mirror.

Charlotte gasped when she saw her reflection. "Oh, my gosh. I feel like a real princess. You did a great job."

Bella donned her Snow White costume and quickly did her own makeup before grabbing her phone and pulling Charlotte to her side.

"Smile!" she instructed as she snapped the selfie, then dictated a caption aloud as she typed. "'Princesses' Night Out. Hoping our carriage arrives on time.'"

"What are you doing?" Charlotte asked.

"Posting to Instagram. What's your handle? I'll tag you."

"I don't know what that means," Charlotte said.

At first, Bella thought she was joking, but it was obvs the woman had no clue about social media. Bella explained the different platforms and offered to help her create accounts.

"Oh, I don't know," Charlotte said. "I'd probably never use it."

Wow. She clearly wasn't clued into the importance of social media—even Facebook, where the over-thirty dinosaur crowd roamed freely, now that the teens had moved on to much-cooler platforms. She reiterated her offer, but Charlotte didn't seem down with it.

Bella was thrilled to see Jake's reaction when he saw Princess Charlotte in costume. In fact, she'd never seen her uncle look at a woman like that before, which was odd since the man seemed to only date model types. Certainly not someone like Charlotte, despite how pretty she'd become under the spell of Bella's magic wand.

Eli, dressed like Woody from *Toy Story*, joined them.

"Wow, Charlotte," he said, "you look like a real princess!"

"Thank you, Eli," she said. "And you look like a real cowboy."

"Well, I'm not supposed to be real," Eli said. "I'm just a toy."

"Oh. Then you look like a toy cowboy."

Uncle Michael dropped off Bella's two-year-old cousins, Violet and Petunia, both dressed as their namesake flowers. After he left for what he called a "grown-up night out" with Aunt Amy, Jake and company headed out to meet up with Zachary and Hanna.

"You look amazing," Zachary said as he gave Bella a quick hug. "I never knew Snow White was so hot."

Bella flinched at his comment. She'd never heard her friend talk like that.

"Thanks," she said, hesitation edging her voice. "You look...fortified?"

Zachary was dressed as a box of Cheerios.

Swashbuckling pirate Jake led his group from house to house to beg for candy, dressed to the nines. Except for Zachary, who ditched his costume after the third house upon discovering the huge box prohibited him from bending his legs.

"And what are you dressed as?" candy givers would ask as he stood there in street clothes, holding a pillowcase aloft for treats.

"An Epic Costume Fail."

Charlotte

CHARLOTTE COULDN'T BELIEVE HOW...*SLAY*...SHE looked at the hands of a teenage makeup artist. The girl had unbelievable talent, sweeping her mousy hair into a diamond-crowned updo and painting her face to look nothing like herself. She'd have to learn how to do this if she ever decided to care about her outward appearance.

She was slightly embarrassed to admit she had no idea what Bella meant when she asked her what her "handle" was and that she'd "tag" her. It was as if the child were speaking in tongues. Charlotte wasn't sure about joining the social media world. Too peoply with too many opinions. But...if she wanted to be social, perhaps she'd have to take Bella up on her offer and give this thing a try.

Trick-or-treating turned out to be more fun than Jake had promised. Back at the house, the kids plopped themselves down on the living room floor and shook out their bags, making the room look like a candy factory.

"This is totally lit," Bella said, admiring her goody stash.

"Charlotte, what's your favorite?" Eli asked.

"Plain Hershey bars."

"Coming right up."

He ran his hands through his haul, expertly plucking out six miniature bars.

"Here you go," he said as he handed them to her.

"Oh, Eli—that's so sweet, but you don't have to share your candy with me."

"Of course I do," Eli said. "It's not fair you and Uncle Jake took us around the neighborhood and you don't get to reap the rewards. UJ, what's your preference?"

Jake chuckled. "I'm good, E. But thanks for offering."

"Nonsense," the boy said, rummaging through his pile. "If I recall, you're a sucker for suckers."

He gathered a handful of lollipops and crossed the room to Jake, who accepted them graciously. Charlotte couldn't believe how well-mannered and kind the boy was.

Jake held up one of his treats. "Cheers to a successful night," he said.

She clicked her candy against his.

Jake and Charlotte helped the kids check the candy for any suspicious-looking packages and ditched a few that had opened. Michael and Amy arrived to pick up the little girls, and Lisa announced it was bedtime. Eli doled out hugs.

"I really enjoyed hanging out with you, Charlotte," the boy said as he ran a fingertip along the top of her crown. "You make a really pretty princess."

Charlotte's heart warmed. No one had ever given her such a nice compliment. "And you make a great cowboy. Excuse me, toy cowboy."

As Eli clomped from the room on an invisible horse, Bella turned to her uncle. "So, Pirate Jakey, are you taking your princess on a date now?"

Charlotte was sure she turned eight shades of crimson, matching the hue creeping across Jake's cheeks.

"I think you should go out in costume," Bella suggested. "Wawa's giving away free coffee for anyone who dresses up tonight."

Jake laughed. "What do you say, Char? Up for some coffee?"

Charlotte, who never drank caffeinated beverages after six p.m., reluctantly agreed.

After collecting their free Wawa coffee, the pirate and princess sat in the parking lot on the hood of his car and talked for a long time, the conversation flowing as easily as it did the night on the boat.

"Thanks for doing this with me tonight," Jake said. "I had a blast. Love the kids and all, but it was really nice having another adult along."

"The pleasure was all mine." Charlotte meant it. She never knew Halloween was so fun.

"Well, my lady, rumor has it my car will turn into a pumpkin if I don't get you back to your house by midnight. What do you say?"

They returned to Lisa's so Charlotte could change out of her costume. She found her clothing folded neatly on the couch, along with a note.

*Charlotte, I hope you had fun tonight. You make a great
Cindy! Hit me up if you wanna learn more about social
media. XoXo*

Bella had signed off with her number. Charlotte tucked
the note in her purse in case she decided to take her up on
her offer to learn more about Facegram. Instabook. Whatever
they were called.

November

Marley

IN THE MONTH SINCE MARLEY HAD BEGUN INTERNING IN the DA's office, she'd helped prepare a felony drug case, observed an autopsy, and attended law enforcement training on human trafficking. It was fascinating and only made her love criminal law even more. She had no idea working for the prosecution could be so rewarding, especially working with cops. One in particular.

Gabriel Romano, a vice detective, was working the same drug case to which she'd been assigned. He, too, had just graduated from law school and, like Marley, had failed the bar exam—a fact that instantly bonded them. His plan, he explained, was to leave the Philly police department, where he'd served as a detective for the past seven years, and join the rank of prosecutors in the District Attorney's Office.

"I've sat through hundreds of cases, cringing at the prosecutor's inability to follow up with a natural question—one I knew the jury was also asking," he told her. "I believed I could do it better, so I decided to shoot my shot."

He'd attended Temple Law School at night while working for the detective squad during the day.

"That's impressive," Marley exclaimed. "When did you sleep?"

"I found creative ways," he said as he ran his hand through his thick dark hair, mocha eyes twinkling with amusement. "Once in the middle of an exam—needless to say, my score reflected it. Another time during a root canal. And who can forget the time I fell asleep during roll call? The guys can't. They set up a sleeping bag and pillow, complete with teddy bear. All out of love, of course. They were supportive, hoping to see one of their own become an ADA."

Gabriel told her how awful it was the day he got his results. He was in the break room with his supportive brothers, there to cheer him on.

"It was like a bomb went off when my buddy read the results aloud over my shoulder. Everyone scattered like shrapnel. The only one to offer condolences was the guy who'd just announced the results. Within five minutes, he, too, was gone."

"I feel your pain, having an audience at the most embarrassing moment of your life," Marley said. She told him about her experience with her family unceremoniously crashing her bar result reveal.

"Ooh, a family audience sucks even more," Gabriel said. "I'm sure it hurt them more than it hurt you."

"Nah, they don't get it. They never understood why I went to law school in the first place. They're not about higher education."

"Sounds like my fam. They're all 'Why you wanna be a lawyer when you get to be a cop and carry guns and shit?'"

Marley giggled.

"Seriously, an exact quote from my cousin," he clarified. "Who, incidentally, has a rap sheet longer than a CVS receipt."

"When my grandfather found out I was applying to college, he said, 'Women don't need an education. They need to stay home with babies.' Also, an exact quote."

"Ah, so you want to prove him wrong?"

"Him and others in my family like him. Not only that a woman can be more, but *I* can more."

"Don't they believe in you?"

"Not really. I always felt like I dwelled in the shadow of my older cousin, Kelly. One year, we were in a spelling bee—me in sixth grade, she in seventh—and we were the last two standing. When I lost, I overheard my parents saying of course Kelly won. She was the 'smart one.' In so many words, I shouldn't try to compete with her."

Marley recalled the pain she felt that night, believing her parents thought she wasn't smart.

"Did you take that as an invitation to compete?" Gabriel asked.

"Actually, no. I lived with that, thinking she was the star. I dropped out of the spelling bee the following year because I didn't want to go up against her and disappoint my parents. Funny thing is? The word she went out on, I spelled in my head in seconds. When her grades plummeted in high school, I finally saw a chance to be the 'smart one.'"

"Is becoming a lawyer is your way of showing them?"

Marley chuckled. "At first, it was. Now, I think it's more about proving it to myself. A lawyer came to talk to us on high school career day, and I was so impressed. I wanted to *be* her. But that old mantra told me I wasn't smart enough. It took a guidance counselor telling me I could be anything I wanted to be, as long as I worked hard, to change my mindset. So that's what I do—I work my ass off. It's how I've gotten everything good in my life. The bar exam is the first time it didn't pay off."

Marley was contemplative. "Actually, no. I didn't get into my first-choice college or law school despite knocking myself out. Maybe my doubts are warranted."

"Self-fulfilling prophecies are dangerous. You know how you stop them from happening?" He pointed to his head. "Change your thoughts. It changes everything."

"In other words, fake it 'til you make it?"

"You got it, girl. I didn't listen to my own advice last time around. Next time will be different."

Marley nodded. "Wise decision. I'll keep it in mind."

"Some of the best lawyers failed the first time. Conversely, look at all the doofuses we know who passed the first time.

The bar exam isn't a measure of how smart you are."

He was right. She needed to remember that.

"So, whatever became of Kelly?" Gabriel asked. "Is she a Supreme Court Justice or something?"

"No." Marley chuckled. "She dropped out of high school but found her way back. Now, she's a damn fine legal secretary working for one of the biggest firms in Philly. She did well for herself, considering her broken path."

"Which means you're no longer in her shadow," Gabriel noted. "Or anyone's."

"Just the one I cast upon myself," she said. But she was determined to change that.

Marley and Gabriel grew closer through work, discovering they had more in common than a need to prove themselves. They grew up in neighboring parts of the city in large Catholic families—his Italian, hers Irish. Similar upbringings, a shared passion for criminal law, and the humiliation of a failed first bar exam attempt only strengthened their bond.

"Let's study together," Gabriel suggested. "I'll be doing a lot more this time around."

"That'd be nice," Marley said, smiling.

It wouldn't hurt to have a serious prep partner. Maybe this time, her partner would actually show up to their study sessions. And, this time, *both* would pass.

Charlotte

CHARLOTTE GLANCED AT THE TIME ON HER PHONE, ANXious for her call with Jake. Their friendship had continued developing over the past couple months, and they'd fallen into a pattern of calling each other once a week to check in.

They'd also gotten together occasionally whenever he was in the Philadelphia area visiting family.

Her phone rang at five o'clock on the dot.

"How's your week been?" Jake asked. "How's Blinky?"

"Week's been fine, and Blinky's doing well."

Charlotte chuckled that the name she'd given the cat had stuck—especially since his injured eyelid remained droopy. She'd been tending to the little guy, making sure he had fresh food and water each day. She created a cozy bed for him from an old blanket, often finding him there in the morning, awaiting breakfast, or after work, awaiting their daily chat. She'd sit on her porch swing and talk about her day while he listened intently. Occasionally, he'd cuddle next to her.

Jake asked how the firm situation was, and she told him not much had changed. Rhys and Declan were still jerks, and she was still trying to prove herself worthy of partnership. She'd attended a couple more happy hours, often when Tom Jervis was there, to score points. It was getting less brutal as time went on, but she still wasn't loving it.

"How's the trip planning coming along?" she asked, aware she hadn't reciprocated the pleasantry of inquiring how he was.

"Great. I can't believe it's coming together. I've been planning it for years, and now I'm a little more than a year away from leaving.

"You must be so excited," she said, feeling a little deflated herself, uncertain what their communication would be like once he was at sea. She didn't want to lose her friend.

"Don't worry. We'll keep up with our weekly chats," Jake said as if reading her mind. "Maybe not always by phone, but definitely email and social media. Are you on Facebook or Instagram?"

"No," she said. She had yet to take Bella up on her offer. "Are you?"

"I have an account on both, but Instagram is where I'll

document my travels for friends and family. Bella set me up. I bet she'd help you, too."

"She did offer," she admitted. "Maybe I should take her up on it."

Charlotte was relieved to know his departure wouldn't mean the end of their friendship. Giving this social media thing a try might provide one more method of keeping in touch.

"Are you sure you're ready to join the twenty-first century?" Jake asked.

She smiled warmly. No one had ever teased her in a friendly way before. "Listen, funny man. I'm all about the twenty-first century."

"Talk to me when you lose the flip phone," he said, laughing.

She loved joking around with him. Another thing she rarely did pre-Jake.

"Okay, queen of cutting-edge technology. I'll be in town next Saturday. I'll pick you up, and we'll go to my sister's house so you can be introduced to the world of social media by a fifteen-year-old."

"Sounds 'lit.'"

Bella

EACH NOVEMBER, A GET TOGETHER DANCE WAS HELD for high school students from different school districts to meet and make connections outside their normal circles. Bella and Hanna planned to go with Zachary and meet up with friends from his school.

The gym was already crowded by the time the trio arrived. Bella recognized some of the kids from theater camp and other kids she followed on social media. She was excited for the night that lay ahead, full of hope and promise—especially to meet new guys.

When the "Charlie Brown Shuffle" came on, Bella and friends crowded the dance floor, laughing over Zachary's animated dance moves.

"He's cracking me up!" Hanna whispered to Bella. "What's gotten into him?"

"Who knows," Bella said.

After the song, parched from laughter, Bella headed to the refreshment stand to get them drinks. She was standing in line when she heard a voice behind her.

"Bella?"

She turned, expecting to see someone familiar, possibly from theater camp. He was familiar, alright, but not from camp. From the boardwalk.

It was Ride Guy. Jordan. The one who ghosted her months ago.

He laughed. "Wow, I hoped that was you."

No longer sporting a red Viper polo, the guy standing before her was ten out of ten, wearing a slim-fitting black suit, no socks, and loafers. The very look she and her friends swooned over as they swiped through Hot Guys of Instagram.

"Not sure if you remember me. I'm Jordan, from the Viper? On the boardwalk? I met you and your brother Eli this summer."

Eli. Just the mention of her little brother's name brought back the humiliation and anger she felt on the little guy's behalf. He'd spent his summer working toward his coveted prize only to be let down by the one person who could make it happen for him—the boy standing before her. Hot, maybe, but also a basic ass. He had to be for letting that happen.

"Oh, I remember," Bella said, feeling all the feels as she narrowed her eyes at him. "You're the one who promised Eli a ride if he did three nice things, but you weren't there to uphold your end of the bargain. Not sure if you remember that part."

Jordan grimaced. "I do," he said. "I can't tell you how sorry I am. Something came up, and I couldn't work that night."

"Yeah, well, whatever it was, I hope it was super important. Because you broke a little kid's heart."

Little kid's heart, my heart. Who's counting?

Bella wasn't sure how to feel:

A. Hurt and humiliated for trusting another asshole;
B. Protective and angry for dashing Eli's dreams; or
C. Hot and bothered (I mean—look at the guy! Total snack!)

She scolded herself for C. and instead, she chose D. Pretend not to care.

Or notice how his unbroken gaze weakened her knees.

One...Two...

Just then, a girl approached and looped her arm with Jordan's. She was gorgeous, with long blonde hair and big doe eyes. Bella recognized her instantly as @MakeupQueenAmelia—the local Instagram influencer whose makeup tutorials she followed.

"Who's your little friend?" the girl asked.

"This is Bella," Jordan told her. "I met her this summer when I was working."

"Amelia," she said, holding out a limp hand to Bella. "Jordan's girlfriend."

It wasn't as much an introduction as it was a threat. *Don't mess with my man.* She might as well have peed around him to mark her territory. Whatever. The interruption was just what Bella needed to break the spell and dismiss her thirst—for the guy and a beverage.

She found Zachary off to the side of the dance floor, shoving something into his pocket as she approached.

"Hey, where are the drinks?" he asked.

"Eff the drinks. Come with me."

Bella stormed out the side door, looking back to make sure Zachary was following her. He was, but so was Jordan.

"Bella—" Jordan called out.

"Leave me alone!" she snapped. "Go back to your stupid girlfriend."

Zachary laughed, then sobered when he saw the look on Bella's face.

"You heard the girl," he said, turning and puffing his chest at Jordan. If Bella wasn't drowning in her emotions right then, she might have found it amusing—a skinny, five-foot-six-inch sophomore thinking he could take a six-foot senior, especially when Zachary didn't have a threatening bone in his body.

Jordan stopped and held up his hand to ward him off. "No worries, man," he said, then looked at Bella. "I just wish you'd give me a chance to explain."

"Explain this," she said, flipping him the bird before storming out.

Zachary followed her outside. Tripping on a curb, he went down on all fours.

Bella nudged him with her toe. "Get up. I need your help."

Zachary rolled onto his back. Bella sat next to him.

"That was Ride Guy, the one who ghosted me and Eli this summer," Bella said, angrily picking handfuls of grass and tossing them aside.

"That was the guy?" Zachary raised his head toward the door. "I coulda taken him."

"Yeah. No, I'm pretty sure you couldn't."

"I could. In fact, Imma do that right now." Zachary struggled to get up, staggered, and fell again.

"What the hell's wrong with you?" Bella asked. She needed him to pull his shit together and help her out. And not by fighting Jordan, which would be the very definition of a losing battle. What had come over him?

"I'll punch his face for hurting you," Zachary said, his words slurring. "And then I'll kick him in the nuts."

Bella looked at him with alarm. Was he drunk?

"The stars spell out your name," he said, pointing upward.

Bella looked up. There were no stars in the sky. She remembered him shoving something in his pocket earlier. Looking down, she saw a shiny object poking out of his pants. She felt the square of metal.

"Bella! Are you feeling me up?"

"Hell no."

"Why not?" he said, laughing. "You'd be surprised at what I'm packing."

"Shut up. You're being gross."

Seriously. In all their years of friendship, Zachary had never once said or done anything of a sexual nature. They were like brother and sister, with no feelings but pure friendship between them. It made her nauseous to think of him any other way.

"Is that a flask?" she asked.

"It could be. Why don't you reach in and find out?"

"That's it. I'm out." Bella wiped the grass stains from her hands and stood up. She nudged him in the side with her foot again, harder this time. "Have you been drinking?"

"Yes," he said, laughing again. "You should try it. It's fun."

Bella sighed. "Zachary, you could get in huge trouble if they find out you brought alcohol in here."

"They'll never know."

"Except you're acting like a class A drunk. You stay here. I'm gonna get Hanna and some soda so we can sober you up."

"I don't want to sober up," he said.

"Z, you have to. You'll get kicked off the tennis team if they find out."

Zachary had a promising future for a college scholarship, but not if he got busted. He took out the flask, opened it, and turned it over. Nothing came out.

"See?" he said, eyes wide. "No more alcohol."

"Give me that," she said. "Was this full when you left the house?"

"Yeppers!"

She took a sniff and recoiled. "God, that's awful. What was it?"

"I believe it was whiskey."

Bella turned to go get Hanna but remembered hearing you should never let a drunk person lie on their back.

"Sit up," she directed.

He thrust his hands and legs in the air as he waved them around. "I'm a bug. I can't get up. Help me!"

Bella sighed. She took one of his hands to hoist him up. He went dead weight on her. "Come on, Zach, you gotta help me."

"No," he said as he yanked her down.

She fell into his chest, and he wrapped his arms around her.

"Bella," he sighed. "My Bella."

The smell of alcohol wafting from his breath made her want to puke. She struggled to break free from his grasp.

"*Not* my Bella," she said. "Let me go."

He held on and rolled them over until he was on top of her.

"Bella, I love you," he said. "And not just as a friend."

"Stop it," she said.

"I know you like me, too," he said, lowering his lips to hers.

"No, Zachary," Bella begged, tears running down the sides of her face, flooding her ears. "Please."

She pushed at his chest, and he flew off her as if she'd found some adrenaline-fueled strength to defend herself, like a mother whose child was pinned under a car.

Except no. She had help.

"You heard her," a guy said as Zachary landed with a thud feet from her. "Get the fuck off her."

Jordan offered her a hand to help her up. "You okay, Bella?"

"Yes," she breathed, her heart racing.

Physically, maybe, but to have her lifelong buddy turn on her like that was jarring. Thank God Jordan intervened when he did.

"I'm sorry you had to deal with that," he said. "Your boyfriend?"

"Friend. At least, he was," Bella said, looking over at Zachary, who lay there like a slug, a stunned expression on his face. "He drank an entire flask of whiskey tonight."

"Yikes," Jordan said.

Zachary struggled to sit up. "I'm so sorry, Bella," he slurred. "I'm drunk. I know it's not an excuse."

Bella wrapped her arms around her waist and ignored him, too angry to accept his apology.

Moments later, Hanna appeared. "I've been looking for you guys. What's going on?"

She looked from Bella to Jordan to Zachary, who was now puking behind the bushes.

"What's wrong with him?" she asked, a look of alarm on her face.

"He's drunk." Bella, still shaken, whispered, "He tried to kiss me."

Hanna grimaced. "You go. I got this," Hanna said as she went over to him.

Bella was relieved for her friend's presence. Hanna aspired to be an EMT and had volunteered with their local ambulance crew. She'd know exactly what to do.

"Would you like to take a walk? Get some fresh air?" Jordan asked.

Bella nodded. Not that she wanted to spend any more time with the guy who'd blown her off, but she was grateful for his intervention. They walked around the perimeter of the school in comfortable silence until they came upon a playground.

"I have an idea," he said as he headed toward the swings. "There's nothing like a good old-fashioned swing to clear your mind."

They sat and thrust their legs out and back. Out and back, out and back, higher and higher she went, the breeze lifting her hair. She swung until she couldn't see over the top of her feet on the uprise, and nothing but ground on the back swing, Jordan keeping pace. When she'd had enough, she stopped pumping her legs and let gravity bring her down to earth. Jordan let his swing come to a stop and they swayed back and forth for a few moments in silence.

Bella finally felt like she could breathe.

"Thank you," she said, relief coursing through her. "Exactly what I needed."

"We still have a swing set in my backyard from when me and my sisters were kids," Jordan said. "I sometimes still go out there to gather my thoughts."

The vision of six-foot Jordan swinging made Bella giggle, recalling how kind and old-schoolish she'd found him to be last summer.

"I'll have to remember that," she said. "We still have one, although only Eli uses it now."

"You're never too old to play," Jordan said, looking at her intently.

She locked eyes with him, but he quickly looked down. She could tell he wanted to say something.

"You told me you had a good explanation for that night," Bella said, prompting him.

Jordan sighed. "My grandfather passed that day. We were with him all day at his bedside, knowing he was at the end. I was really close to him and too broken up to think straight. I honestly had forgotten all about the ride until later that night. I went through my phone, looking for your number, but realized I'd never asked for it. So, I went to the ride and got there just as it was closing, but obviously, you guys weren't there anymore."

"Oh, Jordan," Bella said, her eyes flooding with tears as his eyes welled too. She was relieved to hear his explanation but felt bad for him. "I'm so sorry to hear about your Grandpa."

"Thanks," he said. "It was rough. It went so fast, and I wasn't ready for it. He's the first person in my life to die, and I was totally shaken."

Still, he went to the ride that night to find them. Bella's heart swooned.

"Of course you were," she said, reaching to take his hand as the anger and humiliation over his disappearing act dissipated.

"I tried to find you online, with no luck. I wanted to apologize to you guys and explain what happened. I couldn't believe it when I saw you standing there tonight."

"I don't think Amelia was too thrilled with me being here," Bella said, then quickly added, "I mean, not that I'm a threat to her."

Jordan gazed at her, his mouth sliding into a half-smile. *Three...Four...*

"I wouldn't exactly say that," he said softly.

Bella's heart pounded with hope—the same feeling she had that summer when he'd asked them out for ice cream. Stop it, heart. Dude has a girlfriend.

"Speaking of which, I'm sorry to have taken you away from her. I'm fine now if you wanna go back."

"I'm in no rush," he said. "Besides, she's fine. Too busy taking selfies with friends to realize I'm not around."

"What school do you go to?" she asked.

"St. John's."

It was the same school Zachary attended.

"How about you?"

"Belvedere."

"It's amazing that we met on the Ocean City boardwalk, but we're from the same area."

Bella agreed. It was amazing.

"Where do you live?" he asked, then shook his head in disbelief when Bella told him. "That's like a mile from me."

They talked about their school activities, sharing their interests and favorite hangouts, wondering if their paths had unknowingly crossed sooner than that night. An hour passed, and they were still deep in conversation when Bella received a text.

"It's Hanna," she said. "She called her mom, and they took Zachary home. He's doing fine, but I'm guessing this isn't going to be an easy few days for him. His parents are pretty strict."

Bella was still upset with Zachary but relieved to hear he was going to be okay.

"I guess I should get back," Jordan said as he checked the time on his phone. "Do you need a ride home?"

"No, I'm fine," she said. "I'll just call my mom."

"We don't mind taking you," he said.

Bella noted his use of the word *we* and definitely didn't want to third wheel her way into their night. She shook her head.

"I hope we run into each other sometime soon," Jordan said.

Bella was tempted to ask for his number and suggest they keep in touch, but she didn't want to throw herself at him, especially when he was dating the beautiful and wildly popular influencer.

"Me, too. Goodnight, Jordan. And—thank you again."

Bella sat on the curb outside the school, waiting for her mom. So much had happened that night, and she needed to unpack it all, starting with Zachary telling her he loved her as more than a friend. It was off-putting because she only ever saw him as a brother. She wasn't sure what his disclosure meant for the future of their friendship.

But the bigger news was Jordan's explanation for the blow-off and his unwavering gaze when they sat on the swings. Not quite five seconds, but close. She decided to obsess over that part of the night above all else. That, and the exhilaration she'd felt swinging up into the stars with him by her side.

Once again, Bella's heart made room for hope. For what, she wasn't sure. It was just there.

Charlotte

JAKE PICKED UP CHARLOTTE THAT SATURDAY, AS PROMised. They arrived at his sister Lisa's house just as her husband, John, pulled in.

"If Charlotte wants pizza, Charlotte's getting pizza," John joked as he emerged from the car with four square boxes.

"Did Charlotte want pizza?" she asked, looking to Jake.

"Don't let her fool you," Jake said.

John shrugged. "He said you wouldn't come unless pizza was involved."

Charlotte laughed and tapped Jake playfully on the arm. She felt embarrassed by this special attention but quickly got over it. Pizza was pizza, and she couldn't wait to sink her teeth into a slice. Or three.

Inside, they collectively dove into the boxes like a bunch of seagulls to a dropped French fry. Eli and Bella each had friends over, and Charlotte enjoyed the happy chatter of children, the laughter of adults, and the feeling of family around her—something she'd never had. If this is what spending a Saturday was like with kids, maybe she'd have to reconsider her plans not to have any. Or, at the very least, find other people's children to entertain her and give them back when she was done. Now, that could work.

"Okay, Char, it's time," Bella said once they were finished eating.

Charlotte felt honored when Bella called her by Jake's nickname for her. The teen patted the chair next to her and pulled out her phone. Charlotte sat obediently, new iPhone in hand. Jake had convinced her it was time for an upgrade.

Within an hour, Bella had shown Charlotte all the features of her new phone, pausing only to *ooh* and *ahh* over it, explaining she was hoping her parents would let her get an upgrade. Bella also set her up on the major social media platforms, showing her how to search for people she knew. Charlotte found two women from college, as well as a few people from work she could actually tolerate. Not that she cared what they did after-hours, but the whole purpose of being on social media was to win work friends and influence partners.

"I'll also ask some of my friends to follow you," Bella offered. "But you have to follow them back. They're all about that."

Bella's thumbs flew across Charlotte's phone screen. "There. That's done."

She slid the phone back to Charlotte and leaned her chin on her cupped hands. "Do you intend to use social media beyond keeping in touch with friends?"

"I'm not sure. Your uncle thought I should get myself out there to—what am I doing this for?"

"To be more social, Charlotte," Jake said. "Stay in touch with people, network. It could even lead to a new job opportunity."

"Oh, then you'll want to check out LinkedIn," Bella said. "That's more for adults, so I don't know much about it—"

"I do," Lisa said, raising her hand. "I'll set you up, Charlotte."

"Look at you, being all tech savvy and stuff," Bella teased her mother. "I had no idea."

"I know a lot more than you realize," Lisa said, ruffling Bella's hair and settling into a chair on Charlotte's other side.

"Doubtful," Bella whispered with a smile.

Lisa schooled her on LinkedIn, and before she knew it, Charlotte Drysdale was an official iPhone-carrying member of the twenty-first century.

Marley

MARLEY AND SAM HADN'T SEEN MUCH OF EACH OTHER lately, thanks to his late work nights. Endeavoring to be one of the first to arrive at work each morning, Marley was often asleep before he even left his office at night. They'd fallen into a pattern where he stayed at his place on weeknights, then made up for lost time on weekends. And then some.

She liked their new arrangement, as it gave her time to be alone with her thoughts. Now both thriving in their respective work environments, their relationship seemed stronger; the tension from working under him was gone. There was something romantic about not seeing each other daily, allowing the passion and longing to build throughout the week. It was new, exciting, especially after spending years in each other's nearly constant presence.

"We should see less of each other more often," Sam joked, breathless, after a particularly erotic session. "I don't really mean that."

One thing they didn't do with their time was discuss work. Marley felt it was important, not to mention ethical, now that they were working on different sides of criminal law. They didn't have any cases together, but both wanted to keep it clean. The less they discussed, the better.

Marley was enjoying her internship. She'd sit in on hearings and trials every chance she got. When not on assignment, she'd stow away in the office law library, poring over briefs and court decisions.

One Friday, Wells called her into his office.

"The drug case you've been working is scheduled for trial in December. I wouldn't typically have a second chair assist for this type of case, but it would be helpful. Most ADAs are busy with their own cases. Would you be interested?"

"Absolutely!" Marley exclaimed. It was like asking a starving person if they wanted a six-course meal.

"Great," he said, sliding a thick file toward her. "Here's a duplicate file. Take it home this weekend, familiarize yourself with the pleadings. The pretrial's in two weeks. Let's meet Monday and discuss."

"Sounds great," she said, picking up the file. "Thanks for trusting me with this. I'm honored."

"You're dedicated, Marley. Exactly what I'm looking for."

She felt a rush of pride. Sam was in Florida for a golf outing, which meant she had the weekend to herself. By Monday morning, she knew everything there was to know about the case, easily discussing details during her meeting with Wells.

"It's more than likely we'll settle before trial," Wells said, explaining he was offering a deal for the defendant to work as a confidential informant in exchange for a reduction of charges.

He glanced at his phone. "Speaking of which, the defense attorney's due any minute to discuss plea offers. Wanna stick around?"

"Sure."

The receptionist knocked and led two men into the room. Not just any two men. Jim Howe, followed by his latest new hire.

Sam Adams.

Marley's mouth dropped; her eyebrows plastered the ceiling. She never expected to see Sam in the District Attorney's

Office. The firm didn't throw new associates into the lion's den until they'd been there for a while. If Atticus Finch himself had strolled into the room, it would've been less shocking.

"Marley Maguire!" Jim exclaimed. "Sorry about the position. Hope there's no hard feelings."

"None at all," she said, smiling to keep Hard Feelings from flooding her face.

Wells and Jim shook hands while Marley and Sam abstained. No one else seemed to notice—except Marley and Sam.

"How do you know my favorite intern here?" Wells asked.

"She was one of our best," Jim said. "Unfortunately, we couldn't offer her a position. You're lucky to have her."

"Your loss, my gain. She's doing a phenomenal job."

Take that, Jim Howe.

Wells waved to the conference table. "Shall we?"

The men took their seats, and by the time Marley snapped out of her stupor, the last seat available was directly across from Sam. Perfect. She kept her eyes focused on Wells as he discussed possible negotiations with the defense team, willing herself not to look at Sam. She didn't want Wells to pick up on the fact they knew each other as personally as they did.

"I'm gonna let Sam take this one," Jim said after Wells presented his offer. "Ultimately, it'll be his case."

Sam cleared his throat. Marley stared at her notes but could sense Sam watching her from across the table.

"Your offer is attractive, but..."

Sam's voice waffled around her at first, but once Marley started listening to what he was saying, she realized he was making good points. Damn good points. Somehow, in her absence, Sam had morphed into an actual lawyer.

Don't look at him. Don't look. Oops! She looked.

Her eyes locked with Sam's. Her heart thudded. He was handsome in his gray Armani suit, leaning back in his chair. Confident and self-assured, it was as if he'd been practicing law for years, telling a top prosecutor all that was wrong with his offer.

Marley fought the urge to crawl across the table and tear off his clothing. That was how turned on she was—hearing him throw around constitutional rights and case holdings as if he were reigning over the Supreme Court itself. Here comes the judge!

Wells countered his offer. Sam responded. Wells added a condition. Marley's head swiveled between their butting heads like a Wimbledon spectator.

Look at you, talking criminal law and shit, was what she'd have said had they been alone. *So freaking hot.*

And he would've grabbed her, kissed her, told her how sexy she looked in her tailored lavender suit as he brushed the files off the table to lay her down, taking all of her. The thought made her smile.

Sam must've seen it because he did a double take, then glanced quickly around the room. Marley did, too, noting everyone's heads were down, taking notes.

Sam's face crinkled with amusement. *What?* he mouthed to Marley through a half-smile.

She gave him a sultry look, hoping to relay her thoughts telepathically. He must've seen her thought bubble. His half-smile turned suggestive as he flashed his eyebrows at her.

"Where were we?" Wells said, putting his pen down and looking up.

Marley and Sam snapped to attention, back to avoiding eye contact. The two sides continued discussing offers until they reached a possible agreement.

"I'll take it back to my client and let you know," Sam said.

As the meeting broke up, Jim and Wells chatted while Sam shook Marley's hand.

"It was a pleasure meeting you," Sam whispered as his middle finger stroked her palm.

"The pleasure was all yours."

He laughed out loud.

"I'm glad we could come to a resolution," Wells said as he turned to shake Sam's hand. "I can tell you're gonna keep me on my toes. Let me walk you guys out."

The men filed from the room, Wells and Jim first.

Sam lingered and whispered in her ear. "Isn't it against the Rules of Professional Conduct to undress opposing counsel with your eyes?"

"Sorry, it was just—*fucking hot* how you handled that."

"You should see what I can do undressed."

"I think I already know."

"If you wanna know more, dial 1-800-HOT-LAWYER."

Marley gazed at him wide-eyed. "Why would I call myself?"

More hearty laughter. Damn, how she missed hanging with him every day.

"Can I take you to dinner tonight?" he asked, voice hushed as they followed the men.

It was tempting, but it was a weeknight, and she wanted to be back in the office early.

"Sure," she found herself saying instead. "I'd like that."

"Great. I'll pick you up at eight. Oh, and Marley?"

She raised her eyebrows in anticipation.

"Try to keep it in your pants this time."

The first thing to greet her when she opened the door was the intoxicating scent of Sam's aftershave. She fought her Pavlovian response to drool and hump his leg. It was, after all, a Monday.

They headed to The Clink and were fortunate to be seated in "their" booth. They finished off a bottle of wine as they discussed Sam's golf weekend and Kate's wedding plans.

Suddenly, Sam bolted upright.

"Hey, man!" he exclaimed as he rose to greet someone who'd approached from behind her. "Good to see you again."

"Sorry to interrupt your date," a familiar voice said. "Just want to thank you for a productive meeting this morning."

Marley turned to find Wells standing there.

"Oh—Marley! I didn't realize that was you," he said, sounding flustered.

Wells looked at Sam, then Marley. "You guys know each other? I mean, other than the case?"

"Yeah, we're—" Marley stopped herself before she blurted out their truth.

Sam's expression mirrored Marley's realization that their truth could spell trouble.

"Friends," Sam said, saving the day. "We used to work together."

Not exactly a lie. They *were* friends beneath everything else.

Wells didn't seem to have a problem with it. There were no rules against opposing lawyers being friends, just not...well. She pushed their reality from her mind.

After Wells left, they headed outside to wait for their Uber. Marley leaned against the brick wall as Sam wrapped his arms around her, warming her from November's chilly air.

"I love you," he whispered as he lowered his lips to hers, crushing her against the wall with the weight of his passion.

It had been a while since they'd kissed like that in public. Doing this outside on a busy street—on a weeknight, no less—made her tingly. For a split second, she worried Wells could still be in the area, witnessing it, but he was probably long gone.

Back in her condo, Marley did to Sam what she'd thought about doing earlier that day. She ravished him. When they finished, he spooned her, the hard muscles of his torso pressed up against her back, their legs entwined, skin on skin. She wondered how she'd made it through these past few weeks without doing this every night.

But then, at four a.m., she jolted awake, heart thudding as scenes from a dream emerged.

She and Sam were kissing outside The Clink when a dark sedan rolled past. A window unrolled to reveal Wells staring them down. The next day, he called a meeting with Marley, the head of HR, and a judge. They fired questions at her about her relationship with Sam, reminding her of potential conflict. She tried to convince them she and Sam would never discuss the case personally. They didn't buy it. The judge declared her in contempt. The HR head told her she had ten minutes to gather her belongings. The last one to speak was Wells, who vowed she'd never get a job in the City of Philadelphia if he had anything to do with it.

Marley lay in bed, panting with anxiety, tears puddling in her eyes. It was just a dream, but one with potential real-life consequences. She knew the rules. As long as she and Sam were working the same case, they couldn't be in an intimate relationship with one another. One of them had to bow out. She'd already bowed out of enough. It was Sam's turn.

She nudged him awake. What she had to say couldn't wait.

"Happy Turkey Day," a sleepy Sam hummed, winding his arms and legs around her as he began singing.

> *A perfect treasure, pure and rare, a Cape May love's beyond compare.*
>
> *A heart this pure, so hard to find; makes me thankful that you're mine.*

Okay, maybe it could wait.

Marley sank into him, the sweet familiarity of his comforting embrace lulling her back to la-la land. Her eyelids became leaden, and she felt herself drifting into unconsciousness, guided by the enveloping warmth of Sam's nakedness. As he snuggled tighter, she felt something warm stirring behind her, hardening, sending shivers of desire throughout her. He snaked his leg around hers and nuzzled her neck with soft, suckling kisses as his lips made their way to her mouth.

"Oh God, Marley," he moaned as he rolled on top of her.

She instinctively wrapped her legs around him as he entered her, his hungry eyes wild with craving. He started moving inside her, dropping his lips to suckle hers as he moaned.

"You feel so good," he whispered as he went deeper, eyes rolling back in his head.

Marley teetered on the edge as Sam's thrusting became more intense. He grunted and took her with him.

"Still better every time," he whispered after he caught his breath.

She got lost in the afterglow as she lay her head on Sam's heaving chest, his hands trailing like feathers along her arm.

"Now, will you marry me?" Sam teased.

She hesitated for just a moment. "Not while we're on the same case."

"I was afraid you'd say that," he said, sighing. "What do we do?"

"For starters, we probably have to stop doing this, at least while the case is going on."

"Hard pass."

"I just had the worst dream. Wells found out and fired me. I can't let that happen."

"Yeah, but...who's gonna know?" he whispered in her ear.

He had a point. Who was gonna know? Besides her conscience, if her dream had anything to say about it.

Shut up, conscience.

Pushing guilt aside, they went for another round.

Bella

BELLA HADN'T SPOKEN TO ZACHARY SINCE THE DANCE. When his text came through on Thanksgiving morning, asking if they could meet up at the park so he could apologize in person, she agreed.

Truth was, she missed his friendship. So many times, over the course of the past few weeks, she'd almost texted him to share a funny meme or an observation. A lifetime of special friendship was too important to lose over one incident. As shocking as it had been, she was ready to receive his apology and move forward.

Zachary was already there when she arrived.

"Hey," he said. His voice matched his expression—sheer embarrassment and remorse. "I'm so sorry, Bella. I never should have said those things or done that to you."

She appreciated him leading off with an apology but wasn't about to tell him it was okay.

"I wasn't lying when I said I had feelings for you beyond friendship, but my execution was reprehensible."

"Yeah, pretty much," Bella agreed.

"I hope, after all these years, you know how much I respect you and cherish your friendship. How much I respect women generally. To try to kiss you against your will was something I'll regret for the rest of my life."

Bella knew he meant it. Zachary was shy, funny, kind—not the type of person who would do that to her or any woman. It had to be the alcohol. That wasn't an excuse, but it may be an explanation for his abhorrent, uncharacteristic behavior.

"I've never seen you drunk before," Bella said.

"I know. I look back on it, and I'm disgusted. I never want to do that again."

Bella paused before asking the question gnawing at her. "Was that the first time?"

"Absolutely."

Bella was relieved. "I'm glad to hear it was a first. Hopefully, a last."

"Facts." He took a deep breath. "I knew deep down you only saw me as a friend, but I'd decided that night I was gonna tell you how I was feeling. I thought it would be a good idea to loosen up with some booze—I just didn't plan on getting so out of hand."

"I'm sorry, Z. You'll be a great boyfriend for someone, just not me. We're too much alike, and while that's great for a friendship, it wouldn't work otherwise."

"Does that mean there's still hope for a friendship?" he asked, looking vulnerable.

"Of course," she said, patting his arm. "Just don't ever do that again, or I'll punch you into next week."

His laughter was a welcome sound.

"And then I'll sic Lisa on you. You won't know what hit you if she gets involved."

"Not Lisa!" he said, fake terror in his voice before his expression softened. "Thanks for meeting me today. I couldn't let Thanksgiving come and go without letting you know just how much you mean to me. I'm thankful for a second chance at friendship."

"I'm thankful for you," Bella said, giving him another hug. She meant it, relieved to have her friend back.

But she wasn't kidding. If he ever tried anything like that again, it would be the end of their friendship. And his kneecaps.

Charlotte

CHARLOTTE WAS FILLED WITH A PROFOUND FEELING OF gratitude that Thanksgiving. Thinking back on the events of the past few months, she felt blessed to have made two new friends—one human, one feline. She was thankful for her job and proud she'd endured brutal social events in her bid for partnership. As a result, she befriended a couple female co-workers and became closer to Jasper.

After enjoying the modest turkey dinner she'd prepared for herself, Charlotte took scraps to the porch for Blinky.

"Happy Thanksgiving, friend," she said as she bent to pet the little guy, whose face was already smushed into the bowl. "Tell me—what are you thankful for?"

She didn't have to ask; his ravenous chomping and bloated belly were enough of a clue. Once skeletal with matted, sparse fur, Blinky had filled out, and his coat appeared healthier.

Charlotte went back inside and returned with a glass of wine and a fuzzy blanket. Cozying up on the porch swing, blanket wrapped around her, she began listing things she was thankful for.

"First off, you, and the fact you're healing quite nicely. Also my friend Jake, who's really nice. You met him once—remember? He and Dr. Doolittle helped you when you were hurt."

The cat stopped eating and looked up at her.

She chuckled. "I know, the name. Ignore it, although she did talk you into getting well after the incident. I bet you're thankful for her—and Jake—as well. Let's see...what else? Oh, I'm thankful for my job, even if I still can't stand my co-workers. Well, some of them. Trust me, you wouldn't like them, either. I'm also thankful for my new iPhone." She held it up. "Pretty cool, right?"

Blinky stepped away from his dish, stretched, and sat next to the pumpkin and mum decorations as if he were posing.

"Photo op!" she exclaimed, snapping a photo of the cat. "My new wallpaper."

Charlotte snuggled back under the blanket and giggled when Blinky jumped up and settled next to her. She raised her phone and snapped a selfie of them. In a burst of euphoria and a corresponding desire to share, she posted the photo to Instagram with the simple caption:

Thankful for small things.

Notifications of "likes" from her modest number of followers began chiming on her phone. With each one, Charlotte's heart grew fuller. Being social, it turned out, was fun.

Her phone rang. It was Jake.

"Look at you being all sosh," he said, sounding impressed. "Go, Char! Tear up that social media!"

She laughed.

"So, tell me, Ms. Charlotte, what has you so thankful this fine Thanksgiving to cause you to go viral on Insta?"

"I'm thankful for my life. It's going well. Getting closer to the partner decision, so that gives me hope. And you?"

"I'm thankful I get to wake up every day on this great planet and spend days doing what I love. I'm thankful for my zany family, even if they can't stop asking me when I'm getting married. And," he took a breath and paused, "our friendship."

She flushed. "Me, too. I've never had a friend like you before."

"It's funny because we're complete opposites in so many ways, yet in others, so similar. In ways that matter."

Charlotte didn't have to ask what he meant because she knew. Two people, alone in the world but not lonely, happy enough with the status quo but wanting something more.

"Speaking of my zany family, I have a question for you," he said.

"I have an answer."

"Kate and Ryan are hosting a New Year's Eve party in Cape May. They asked if I'd be bringing someone. So," he paused, "would I?"

"I don't know," she teased. "Would you?"

A beat. "I think I would. As friends, of course. Unless you already have plans."

Charlotte smiled. She had no holiday plans. In fact, she never had holiday plans.

"Okay," she said, stepping off her comfortable perch of social isolation into a whole new world. One that included a date for New Year's Eve. "Count me in."

First. Time. Ever.

Having a date, and being counted in.

Marley

IT WAS THE MONDAY AFTER THANKSGIVING, AND WELLS had just wrapped up their division meeting when he asked Marley to stick around. After the last of the staff left, Wells closed the door behind them.

"We need to talk," he said, loosening his tie.

Marley's heart leaped into her throat. Was he about to let her go? She sat straight up.

"I saw you and Sam Adams, the defense attorney on the Marcon case, in front of The Clink last week."

Oh shit. Please don't say you saw us kissing. Please don't say—

"Kissing."

Fuuuuuuuck. It was her nightmare come true. Any moment now, a judge and the HR head would be marching in here, telling her to get the hell out. Humiliation coursed through her.

"I don't know what's going on with you guys..."

Marley opened her mouth to explain their relationship, but Wells held up a hand.

"...and I don't want to know. I'm sure you're aware it's a conflict of interest to have anything going on beyond friendship. In public or behind closed doors."

Marley gave him a pleading look, clenching her fists in her lap to keep from passing out. "I know, Wells. I promise it won't happen again."

"I can take you off the case if—"

"No," she interrupted, praying for Sam's future forgiveness. While she loved him, it was important to put her career—herself—first right now. To be respected as an attorney, not a lovestruck woman who couldn't, as Sam would probably say, keep it in her pants. Working this case had given her the confidence she'd been stripped of after The Great Failure. "You needn't worry. I'm fully aware of the rules of ethics."

"Look, we're human. Lots of couples have evolved after being on cases together. But not while the case is going on."

"It won't happen again."

Marley was aware her mouth was writing checks her reality might bounce.

"Good," Wells said, regarding her for a moment before continuing. "I still fully believe Marcon will cooperate. Hopefully, he'll make his decision before the pretrial hearing."

Marley exhaled the breath she'd been holding. Wells continued talking about the case, but his words wafted around her, jumbled and meaningless.

After their meeting, Marley's relief gave way to sadness. She'd betrayed Sam and their relationship by not being honest. But she had to do it or risk losing her assignment. Possibly her job.

Hopefully not Sam.

Marley delivered the news that night by phone, strictly abiding by the *you can't be seeing him* rules laid at her feet.

"Wassup, girl?" Sam asked.

A lump gathered in Marley's throat. "I got bad news."

She proceeded to tell him about Wells's disclosure.

"He reminded me of the ethical rules and warned we can't see each other, 'in public, or behind closed doors,' until the case is over."

"What the fuck," Sam muttered. "You've gotta be kidding me."

Tears welled in her eyes. "It was pretty humiliating. I'm knocking myself out to make a good impression. The last thing I needed was to be reprimanded by my boss about kissing my boyfriend."

"Did you tell him we've been dating since the Ice Age?"

Marley didn't laugh at Sam's attempted joke. "A year isn't exactly an eternity."

"Yeah, but it feels like it. In my heart, I've been dating you since the beginning of time."

Marley's own heart skipped a beat, as it did whenever Sam uttered his dramatic proclamations of love.

"No. I didn't want him to realize it's a bigger problem than it is."

"It *is* a big problem, Marley. I'm dying over here not seeing you much as it is. Why didn't you tell him about us?"

"Because he would've reassigned me, and I don't want to be reassigned."

"So you lied to him."

His verbal slap struck Marley's heart. He was right. She'd lied to her boss by not being honest about their relationship and insulted Sam in the process.

"Maybe if one of us recuses ourselves from the case…"

One of us, meaning you, Sam. Hint, hint.

"Marley, I'm the attorney of record. I can't back out."

"So, I'm supposed to tell my boss I can't be on the case because I'm sleeping with the defense attorney?"

"Is that all this is? Sleeping together?"

"You know what I mean."

"No, actually, I don't. We're in a committed relationship. Can't we just be honest and promise not to talk about the case?"

"It's not that simple."

Why wasn't he getting this? He should be the one most worried. Even without a passing exam, she felt like a better lawyer than Sam.

"Rules of ethics are there for a reason, primarily your client's interests. He deserves zealous representation from you, unencumbered by the fact you're dating someone from the team actively trying to put him behind bars."

She knew she'd made a good point when Sam didn't respond right away.

"Can't you ask to be reassigned?" he asked quietly.

"No. I don't want to jeopardize my job. He specifically chose me for this case, and he tells me every day I'm doing a great job. It's helping restore some of the dignity I've lost. Plus, it's Wells's decision, not mine. Nothing's stopping you from bowing out, though."

"Not gonna happen, Marley. This case is equally important to me. Besides, you're just a member of the team, not attorney of record."

Another blow. What hurt more was, he was right. She was just a lowly intern.

"Sorry," he muttered.

"The pretrial hearing is in five days. We can do this. Hopefully, you'll get him to take the deal before then."

Sam sighed. "I respect your position with regard to the job, but I'll go on record as saying I *absolutely hate* this."

Bella

BELLA STOOD OUTSIDE THE AUDITORIUM WITH A CROWD of other musical hopefuls, waiting for the cast list to be posted.

"I'm so nervous," Sophie whispered.

Bella hadn't exactly taken Lisa's advice and ditched the girl. Sophie had texted the night before auditions to wish Bella luck, apologizing for what she called a "mix-up" with the costumes at the Halloween party, which Bella reluctantly accepted. Belvedere wasn't that big a school that she could easily escape the on-again, off-again friendship of the most popular alpha girl. They'd have to work together if they both made the musical, and Bella wanted to avoid on-stage drama with her most off-stage dramatic classmate.

"I shouldn't be nervous," Sophie continued. "I feel like I totally nailed the role of Belle."

"You were great," Bella agreed. "I'm just hoping I make the chorus."

"Oh, you will. I could definitely see you as one of the spoons."

Gee, thanks, Sophie.

Bella knew Sophie had a good shot. Despite lacking theater experience, Sophie was a natural-born main character while Bella wasn't. She'd also watched her audition. Not only did her friend do well, but she looked like a Disney princess even on a bad day. Bella, meanwhile, had a better shot of being cast as the Beast.

The director emerged from the auditorium and pinned the list to the bulletin board, ducking away before he was crushed to death by the encroaching mob of teenage thespians.

Sophie pushed her way to the front. "You've got to be kidding me!"

Bella made her way through the crowd as Sophie stormed away. Several people turned to look at her, and that was when she saw what had her quasi-friend so torqued up. Sophie hadn't been cast as Belle. In fact, she'd only made the chorus. Instead, across from the role of Belle, was a familiar name.

Her own.

"Oh my God!" Hanna squealed, engulfing Bella in a hug. "You got the lead!"

Bella, shocked, had to blink several times to make sure she was reading it correctly. But Hanna's reaction confirmed her wildest dreams. Bella, a sophomore, had been cast as the lead of the high school musical.

"And I've been cast as a Silly Girl!" Hanna exclaimed, clearly grateful for a minor part.

Bella could barely contain her excitement. She whipped out her phone and took a picture of the cast list so she could send it to her mom.

Hanna gasped, squeezing Bella's arm. "Look who's Beast!"

Robbie Gentry. Oh no...

"That means you have to *kiss him*!"

"Barf, gag. Pass. Total asshole." She still wasn't over what he'd done to her at prom.

"I can't believe we don't start rehearsal until January," Hanna whined as they made their way to Serendipity Café, the popular coffee shop in town. "I don't think I can wait that long!"

Bella could. She planned to use the time to memorize all

her lines and get her Belle on so she could impress the director. She had two more years of musicals after this, and just seeing her name next to the lead character made her want more.

Marley

M ARLEY BARELY MADE IT THROUGH THE WEEK WITHOUT Sam. It felt like an eternity, but pretrial hearing day was here, the day the defendant was expected to accept the prosecution's offer. But a jailhouse lawyer had gotten to him first, convincing him to force a hearing before agreeing to anything. Marley's heart sank. While it was the defendant's right, his insistence on a hearing wasn't a good sign for quick resolution.

She was too nervous to look at Sam as he addressed the court. Nervous for him and for her—that she'd look at him the wrong way and Wells would know there was more to their story than a random kiss outside a restaurant. Nonetheless, she was curious to observe Sam in action.

Lawyer Sam exceeded her expectations. Despite witnessing him in law school moot court competitions, something about the real practice of law brought out the true attorney in him. He was killing it.

At one point, Wells leaned over and whispered to Marley. "This guy's straight-up good."

Not just vertically, either, but Marley kept that thought to herself.

Sam was confident in his address to the court, firm in his legal arguments, and even cracked a joke that made the judge laugh. He was born for the courtroom—a far cry from the aloof, sweatpants-wearing slog he presented as when they first met in college. She was in awe of his talent. He seemed to purposely avoid looking her way throughout the hearing, but as he strode confidently back to counsel table, he gave Marley a quick side glance and a half-smile. Her heart rate shot through the roof.

Sam deserved this. He'd passed the bar had and earned the position. He was a natural. She felt joyful for her friend, the love of her life, despite her own loss. It was what true love was all about—being happy for your partner's success, even at the cost of your own.

"I'll issue my ruling tomorrow," the judge announced when the hearing was over. "Are we still set for trial in December?"

Wells rose to his feet. "As of now, your honor, but if we can't reach a settlement, we'll be asking for a new trial date."

What, now?

"Is defense in agreement with this?" the judge inquired.

Sam shot her a look of pure regret meant for her eyes only. "Yes, your honor," he said, rising from his chair. "We've discussed that possibility."

We have?

Marley deflated as the reality sank in. Anything could happen in law; nothing was a guarantee. Criminal defendants tended to trust their peers above all others, preferring to place their case outcome in the hands of other self-proclaimed legal know-it-alls (aka jailhouse lawyers) than those who'd been formally educated. It was likely Sam's voice in the ear of his client had been drowned out by the jailhouse chatter flooding the other. When that happened, defendants had a propensity to flip the script on their lawyers.

She couldn't wait for this case to be over. She and Sam needed to be together, one way or another.

On the same side of the courtroom—and her Posturepedic.

December

<h1 style="text-align:center">Charlotte</h1>

IT WAS THE DAY OF THE MOST DREADED EVENT OF THE Jervis Mahoney social calendar—the office holiday party. Held each year on the first Friday in December, the party would begin promptly at five o'clock in the lobby of their high-rise office building. The firm's party planning team (which Charlotte was being urged to join by one of her office mates—no thank you) had decided this year's theme was Ugly Holiday Sweaters. Charlotte didn't own any ugly holiday sweaters, just ugly sweaters. But, to show she was a team player, she made her own by tacking green felt Christmas trees to the outside of a red sweater. She was frugal that way; no need to waste money on a ridiculous sweater she'd never wear again. She paired it with a green and red plaid calf-length skirt she'd inherited from her grandmother.

"What's this?" Jasper gasped as she walked in that morning.

"What?" Charlotte asked in defense of her fashion choice. She was proud of her handiwork, looking as festive as she felt.

"Did you get rolled by a bunch of middle-aged elves or something?"

"It's an ugly sweater, made uglier for the holidays," she explained.

Jasper raised his eyebrows. "Emphasis on the ugly."

"I thought that was the point?"

"Ah, hon. By ugly, they mean cute—not 'I've just been run over by a reindeer.'"

Charlotte didn't really care what she looked like. Or what Jasper thought. She just wanted to get through the day and cuddle up at home, après-party, with a good book or old movie.

At five o'clock, she joined her co-workers for the party. Wait staff buzzed around passing hors d'oeuvres as music wafted from speakers in the corner of the room. Tom Jervis worked the room, handing out holiday bonuses.

Declan and Rhys sauntered over to her.

"Where did you get your sweater, Charlotte?" Rhys asked.

She sensed a major insult teeing up. She met it head-on. "Your mom's closet."

Declan laughed and backhanded Rhys on the chest. "Ooh, she gotcha."

"And I got the skirt from your closet, Declan," she said. "I had no idea you were into women's wear."

"Didn't know you were, either," he retorted.

Tom Jervis approached them.

"Let's see, what have we here for these fine folks?"

He pulled three envelopes from the bag. "I hear you've been good boys and girl this year. I'm happy you're getting along so well."

Charlotte forced a smile. "Never better."

"What do you appreciate about each other?" Tom asked, now forcing her hand. "Charlotte, you go first."

"Umm..."

She would've been able to respond quicker if he'd asked her to recite the entire US Constitution by memory. In French.

"I appreciate her style," Declan said, beating her to the punch as he pointed to her sweater, the sarcasm not lost on her.

"I dig his fashionable footwear." Charlotte pointed to Rhys's elf slippers.

"Charlotte has a unique way of seeing the world," Rhys added. When Tom Jervis glanced away, Rhys thrust two middle fingers up before his eyes. He looked so ridiculous, Charlotte laughed out loud.

"You've helped me in that regard," Charlotte responded, returning the favor. Rhys, too, laughed.

Tom, obviously distracted by something going on across the room and therefore oblivious to their childish antics, merely nodded before he redirected his attention to them.

"Among the three of you are the future leaders of the firm. It's important you all get along. Keep up the good work."

Charlotte kept the smile on her face until he was out of earshot.

"Enough bullshit for one night," Declan muttered.

"Yeah, let's go talk to someone more interesting," Rhys added.

As the guys turned away, Charlotte called their names. "What is it you have against me? I've never done anything to warrant you treating me like shit."

Rhys shrugged. "Simple. Competition for partnership. Nothing personal."

"Yeah, but you've made it personal. So how about we just find a way to get along? It'll only benefit the firm in the long run."

Declan was silent for a moment before nodding. "She's right." He turned to Charlotte. "I'm sorry for the crap we've put you through. Like Rhys said, nothing personal. We're just a bit—intimidated by you."

"Yeah," Rhys said, not sounding as convinced. But Charlotte would take it.

"Thanks," she said, trying to sound genuine as she turned to walk away. "You'll be happy you apologized when I become your boss."

Marley

MARLEY WAS DEVASTATED WHEN WELLS TOLD HER A new trial date had been set for January 2nd.

"Isn't Marcon taking the deal?" she asked.

He shrugged. "The ball's in his court. It's up to him to decide whether he's taking the bait or not."

Marley tried to hide her bitter disappointment. If the case wasn't settled prior to the holidays, she and Sam wouldn't be spending them together. She could only hope he'd work his magic and get his client to take the deal before then.

Life without Sam was excruciating. She missed him so much it hurt. So many things had happened in the past few weeks she would've loved to share with him. Mostly the funny things—like the day she was heading to lunch with a co-worker and, not looking where she was going, walked face-first into a lamppost. Sam would've died laughing over that one, whether witnessing it in person or during Marley's animated retelling.

But she loved her job and didn't want to jeopardize her standing with Wells, who would likely be her permanent boss someday. So, instead of sharing stories and hobnobbing with Sam, Marley spent her free time with Gabriel and their books, cramming for the February bar exam.

One Saturday afternoon, Gabriel surprised her with a question. "Would you like to have dinner with me tonight?"

Marley was taken aback. Was he asking her on a date?

"Sounds nice," she hedged, wanting clarification of his intent. "You do know I have a boyfriend, even though we're kind of on a break..."

Gabriel knew Sam from their case but didn't know the dashing attorney was Marley's on-pause boyfriend.

"I know you have a boyfriend," Gabriel said, giving her a conspiratorial smile. "So do I. We're even."

Marley beamed. She'd had no idea her friend was in a relationship. "Great, it's a date."

"Non-date," he laughed. "Circumstances considered."

Back at her place, she decided she should tell Sam in case someone they knew saw her out with another man. He answered on the first ring.

"Hey, girl."

Marley's heart raced hearing his sultry voice.

"Sam..." She cleared her throat. "Just wanted to tell you I'm having dinner with Gabriel tonight. You know, the cop on the case, the one I've been studying with."

"Oh, right. The drop-dead-gorgeous one." His tone was cynical. "Is it a date?"

"No, just friends."

"Got it," he said, sounding as if he didn't.

"What are you up to tonight?" she asked.

"Meeting up with the guys at Murphy's."

"Tell them I said hi."

"Will do." He paused. "Have fun on your *date*."

"Not a date," she reminded him. "Just friends."

"Okay, Mar."

She considered telling him the truth, but Gabriel's personal life wasn't hers to share with others. And anyway, Sam should trust her. She was about to reiterate it was strictly platonic, but Sam had already hung up.

"Ugh," she groaned aloud to her empty apartment.

Was it wrong for her to go out with Gabriel for the simple fact of his maleness? Should she cancel so Sam wouldn't stew in a cauldron of jealousy all night?

No. She'd done the right thing by telling him about the

dinner outing. It was ludicrous to think she couldn't have male friends outside her relationship.

Once at dinner, she was glad she went. The conversation flowed as they got to know each other better and continued after Gabriel suggested an après-dinner drink at The Clink. Marley's stomach flopped at the mere mention of the place, but she went along with it. Sam or no Sam, she wasn't about to stop living her life. After all, the case would soon be re-solved and they'd soon be back to normal.

She and Gabriel found seats at the bar and ordered. When their drinks came, he offered a toast.

"To new friendship, second chances, and stronger self-be-liefs," he said, raising his beer bottle.

"Here, here," Marley said, clinking hers enthusiastically, as if one's toasting abilities might translate to higher bar exam scores.

As she took a sip, a certain someone caught her eye from across the bar.

It was Sam. With a woman.

Marley almost fell off her barstool. He'd told her he was going out with friends, but here he was, laughing with a woman who happened to be the exact type Sam was drawn to back when they were single. It didn't appear he'd noticed Marley gawking from across the bar. All the better to catch him in a lie.

When Gabriel excused himself to use the restroom, she texted Sam.

Having fun?

Sam's eyes drifted from his concubine to his phone. He thumbed a quick response.

Yeppers! You?

Marley decided to mess with him before revealing his secret.

Time of my life. Who you with?

Sam glanced quickly around.

The usual crowd. You still out with that Dick?

He's not a dick.

LOL, I meant Dick as in the old way of saying detective.

Right.

Missing you.

I hope your boys are keeping you company.

Not the same.

True. Especially when they're not with you.

Marley snapped a photo of Sam from across the bar, then attached it to her next message.

Hope that brunette makes up for it!

Sam's head shot up from his phone, eyes darting wildly around the room, finally resting on Marley's glare across the bar. He grabbed his phone, his thumbs flying across the screen.

I can explain.

Don't bother.

It wasn't that she didn't want to hear Sam's explanation, she just didn't want to ruin Gabriel's night by getting in a bar fight with her on-pause boyfriend. Or out their relationship to him.

Sam wasn't giving up. He kept his gaze on Marley, mouthing *call me.*

She shook her head. Gabriel rejoined her as another text came through.

> The boys and I came here after Murphy's. They just left. I was settling our tab when she started talking to me.

> Sure. Have fun on your "date."

Marley glared at Sam and slid her finger across her throat as if to say *enough.*

Her phone rang. She rolled her eyes, knowing he wouldn't stop calling until she answered. Excusing herself from Gabriel, she headed to the back hallway to take his call.

"Did you just threaten me with physical harm?" Sam asked, his tone a combination of humor and feigned fear.

"Yeah. Watch your back. I have a shiv, and I'm not afraid to use it."

"Okay, just wanted to make sure. Just know The Clink has you on security cameras. If I end up beheaded, they'll know it was you."

"Then it's a good thing I disabled the cameras, isn't it?"

"Except I'm one step ahead of you. I re-enabled them."

"That's you, ADT."

"This is seriously not a date," he explained. "I was with the guys, but they left. And I was about to leave, too, when this chick started talking to me."

"I don't believe you. Prove it."

"How?" Sam asked.

"Throw your drink in her face."

"Marley." He sighed, sounding annoyed. "I'd kill for you, but I'm not about to waste a drink on you. It's Jameson's."

"Oh," she relented. "Don't blame you."

"How else can I prove it to you?"

"Hmm, lemme think..."

Marley leaned against the wall, her back to the bar. It was fun flirting with Sam like this. She believed he was telling the truth and decided to give him a pass.

"Have you come up with anything?" he asked.

"Not yet, but I'm thinking. Has to be something good."

"Is this good?" His voice now echoed around her, followed by his fingers snaking around her waist. Spinning her around, he kissed her—lightly at first, then with mounting intensity. Marley's heart pounded, both from desire and fear.

"We can't be doing this," she whispered as he pulled back.

"Fuck ethics." He kissed her again. "I've missed you so much."

It had only been a couple weeks since they were last physically together, but it felt like a lot longer. She couldn't pull away. Being anywhere near this man drew her in like a high-powered magnet.

"I should get back to Gabriel."

"That dick," Sam muttered. "This time, I mean it derogatorily."

Marley cupped Sam's chin. "You have nothing to worry about. He's in a committed relationship, and I love you more than life itself."

She turned to leave. Sam trailed his fingers along her arm, squeezing her hand before he let go.

"Come back to me soon," he said. "I can't stand this."

Charlotte

"I CAN'T BELIEVE YOU DON'T HAVE YOUR TREE UP YET," Jake said one evening as he walked Charlotte home after meeting up for dinner.

"I don't do Christmas trees," she'd said. "Or Christmas."

"Well, that's about to change," he'd said as he steered her off their projected path.

"Where are you taking me?" she asked.

"You'll see."

They came upon a Christmas tree lot a few blocks from Charlotte's house.

"We're getting you a tree."

It wasn't worth arguing with him, especially when he offered to buy it for her.

It felt like they were on the set of a holiday movie. Snow began to fall as they carried the wrapped tree to her house. She made hot chocolate and put one of her grandmother's Christmas albums on the old phonograph record player she'd inherited. After setting up the tree and stringing lights they'd bought at the tree lot, Charlotte asked if he wanted to watch a movie.

"*It's A Wonderful Life* is one of my favorites," she offered.

"Never seen it before."

"Then you must stay and watch it with me. It's amazing."

Charlotte blew the dust off her VHS player, which, miraculously, still worked. She hadn't watched a movie in weeks, now that she was either hanging out with Jake or attending work functions like a social butterfly.

Despite not embracing the holidays themselves, Charlotte loved holiday movies. Especially this one. The ending always made her cry when friends showed up at George Bailey's house in droves, proving he wasn't alone in the world. This time was no different.

"Wow," Jake said, his voice cracking with emotion. "Thanks for sharing this. It makes you think."

"About what it would be like if you were never born?" she asked.

"That, and what we'd do without friends. I hadn't thought about either one before. How about you?"

"I have," Charlotte admitted. "I'm basically alone in the world. If I'd never existed, it would have been easier on my dad. My mom died when I was an infant, so she didn't get to know me. I think the only other person who would have missed me is my Grams. Other than that, I matter to no one. Except maybe him." She pointed to Blinky, curled up on Jake's lap.

"Hello?" Jake teased. "Are you forgetting someone?"

"Right." She nodded. "Rhys and Declan."

Jake laughed. "How 'bout me?"

She shot him a look.

"What?" he asked, meeting her skeptical gaze. "I'm serious. Your friendship means a lot to me. I don't often connect with people as easily as we have."

"Why do you think that is?" She cocked her head to the side. "I mean, we couldn't be any more different."

"We're not that different," he said, shrugging. "We both long for human connection, something we're unable to easily find. For different reasons."

"At least you don't have looks that turn people off. What's your reason?"

"I think my outward appearance tends to attract the wrong people—ones with whom I don't want a connection."

"In other words, we're both judged wrongly for our appearances," she said. "Thanks for not judging me for mine."

Jake shook his head. "I don't know where you get the idea you're unattractive."

"Ask any guy in the tri-state area between the ages of twenty-five to seventy-nine. For some reason, I have no problem attracting the octogenarian crowd. Maybe I should give that a go."

"Are you even looking for a guy?" he asked. "I've sensed you're quite happy with your single life, being on the partner track as you are."

"No, I'm not looking for a guy," Charlotte said hastily. She didn't want him to get the wrong idea. "I'm just saying I don't tend to attract them."

"They say you get back what you put out in the world. If memory serves me correctly, you weren't the most approachable person the night we met. Maybe you're sending the wrong signals."

"What do you mean?" Charlotte exclaimed, half-teasing, half-offended. "I'm approachable!"

Jake raised an eyebrow at her. "You recoiled when I tried to help you up, accused me of stealing your purse, and referred to your co-workers as imbecilic. At one point, I feared you might even Mace me to death."

"You say that like it's a bad thing," she joked.

"I get you don't trust easily, and I don't blame you. But maybe if you were to open up a bit, you'd see more positive responses coming back to you."

Charlotte wasn't sure if she should be offended by his words—or inspired.

"Sorry if that crossed the boundaries," he said. "You have loosened up in the time we've known each other. You're different from when I met you, less guarded."

"Your friendship's certainly helped."

"When it comes to looks, though, you've got nothing to worry about, girl. You have beautiful eyes and a great smile when you allow yourself to do so. And you're genuine. Nothing more attractive than that."

"No, Jake, I won't go out with you if that's what you're asking," Charlotte teased, punching him on the arm. "I do have my standards."

He grinned. "Can't blame a guy for trying."

Was he trying? Charlotte instantly regretted her flirtatiousness, uncertain how to navigate the unfamiliar terrain of male/female friendships. She recalled the assertion of Billy Crystal's character in the movie *When Harry Met Sally*, that men and women couldn't be friends without sex being involved. Hadn't she and Jake been disproving his theory? At least, she hoped so. She didn't want anything to change between them. She enjoyed his friendship and didn't want him to think she was looking for more.

"You're also an attorney, and you're brilliant. If it's true guys overlook you, I'm guessing it's because they're intimidated."

"Intimidated." The same word Declan used. Maybe there was some truth to that.

Jake stood and gave her a hug. "Gotta be on the road early. Thanks for tonight. This was nice."

"Thank *you* for encouraging me to celebrate the holidays. I'm going to enjoy having a tree for the first time since Grams died."

Jake opened the door to let himself out, turning back to look at her.

"Don't forget what Clarence wrote in George's book at the end of the movie," he said.

She smiled. "I forget the exact quote, but something like you can't be a failure if you have friends."

"That's right. See ya, friend."

"Thank you," she whispered as the door closed behind him, "for making me matter."

Bella

BELLA AND HER FRIENDS WERE IN THE MALL FOOD COURT a week before Christmas when Hanna tipped her chin at something going on behind her.

"There's that girl from St. John's who does the makeup tutorials," she said through a mouthful of pizza.

Bella swung around to see Amelia standing in line at Saladworks. She searched the girl's immediate vicinity for Jordan, but he was nowhere in sight. Maybe they'd broken up. Hope flooded her heart.

"And there's her hot boyfriend," Hanna added.

Sure enough, he'd appeared. Hope combusted, leaving her heart deflated.

"Excuse me, ladies," Zachary said as he rose from the table.

"What are you doing?" Bella asked, but it was too late. He was already halfway across the food court.

"Oh, geez," she muttered, turning back around and shielding her eyes. "Please tell me we're not going to have a repeat of the dance."

She peeked through her fingers to see Hanna observing their interaction, an amused expression on her face.

"What's happening over there?" Bella asked.

"Zachary went up to him. Now he's shaking his hand."

"What's Jordan doing?"

"He's—wait, how do you know his name?"

"He's the guy who intervened when Zachary came on to me," Bella whispered as if he could hear her from across the room. "Also known as Ride Guy."

"*That* was Ride Guy?" Hanna asked, nearly choking on her pizza. "Why didn't you tell me he lives around here?"

Bella shrugged. "What's the point? He's dating Amelia."

"That sucks."

"If that's what he's into, I don't stand a chance. What's happening now?"

"They're talking," she said. "Oh, now they're laughing."

Bella was relieved. At least Zachary wasn't squaring off with him as he had that night.

"They're both looking over here," she said, ventriloquizing through her smile. "Turn around and wave."

Bella turned, gave a quick wave, and spun back around. "What could Zachary possibly be saying to him?"

"I dunno, but they're coming over."

Bella's cheeks flushed with embarrassment. Excitement. Something.

"Hey, Bella," Jordan said, smiling as if he was happy to see her.

"Oh, hey!" she said, trying to sound cool like her heart wasn't about to thump out of her chest and onto her 'za.

"It's good to see you again," he said.

"You too. Shopping for Christmas?"

No, Bella, he's here to fix the plumbing. What on earth else would he be doing at the mall the week before Christmas?

"Yeah, last-minute gifts for my fam. And you?"

"Same," she said, praying she didn't have a huge chunk of crust wedged between her teeth.

Amelia arrived just then and re-introduced herself—as if every teen girl in southeast Pennsylvania didn't already know who she was, with her 2.5k Instagram followers.

"Sorry to tear him away, but we still have more shopping to do," she said sweetly.

Bella watched as Jordan walked away, wishing she didn't feel as if he was taking her heart with him. Just as the couple was about to enter a store, he turned, and their eyes met. He gave her a shy smile.

One...Two...Three...Four...

Amelia intercepted the look with a reach for his hand. He quickly glanced away.

"Oh my God, did you see that look?" Hanna squealed.

"What look?" Of course, she saw it. She just wanted to make sure she wasn't dreaming.

"The look of a man who knows what he wants, and it isn't what he has."

Marley

MARLEY HAD ONLY ONE WISH FOR CHRISTMAS THAT year, but it didn't come true.

It was Christmas Eve, Marley and Sam's favorite day of the year. Better than Christmas Day, they'd both agreed, because of the anticipation—a keystone of their relationship. Then... and now.

His client hadn't taken the deal and had insisted on a trial. January 2nd couldn't come fast enough. She hadn't seen Sam since the night at The Clink weeks ago and was elated when he called that night, even if it was against the "rules."

"Merry Christmas, girl," he said softly.

Tears welled in her eyes. She and Sam typically spent Christmas Eve baking cookies and decorating the tree, holiday movies playing in the background, before delivering their treats and joining his family for their annual celebration. Finally returning home to exchange gifts and share intimacy in the soft glow of the lit Christmas tree, jazzy holiday tunes playing in the background.

"I don't care about ethics at this very moment," he said.

"Me either. I miss you so much."

"You belong under my tree, wrapped up in a bow."

"I know, Hallmark Channel. I can't wait for this nightmare to be over."

"What do you think we should do about Kate and Ryan's party?" he asked.

Oh, shit. She'd forgotten about the New Year's Eve shindig in Cape May.

Marley weighed the options. Kate and Ryan had already paid for accommodations and event tickets. It would be rude for either one not to show. Still, she was under Wells's directive. They couldn't be together until the case was over. Then again, attending the same event didn't mean they were "together," especially if they kept their separate thing separate. The trial was scheduled for the day after New Year's, so it wasn't like they couldn't wait a few extra days to be together. In the end, loyalty to her friends won out.

"This party's a big deal for Kate and Ryan," Marley said. "Do you think we can go and still respect boundaries, not cross the line?"

"I guess. What do we tell them about us?"

She thought for a moment. "Nothing. It's between you and me, and I don't want our nonsense raining on their parade. We'll be back to normal before the hangovers wear off. They'll be none the wiser."

"So...we pretend we're together when we're not, but we are? I'm confused."

"We're not gonna lie. We're just gonna withhold some truth. Act normal with others but keep our distance when we're alone."

"Okay." He didn't sound too convinced.

"I'm serious. No crossing the boundaries."

"Got it, Great Wall of China."

"Bruh, it's a couple days. We can do it."

"I can't be responsible for what I'm gonna do to you when

this is all over," Sam said. "Ravish doesn't begin to describe it."

She tingled with anticipation. "Promise?"

Certainly, a weekend getaway would qualify as a violation of the rules. It might have been the eggnog talking, but she didn't care. She'd spent the entire holiday season away from Sam like a goody two shoes. She'd paid her dues, and it was time to loosen her laces.

Bella

ELI BOUNDED INTO BELLA'S ROOM IN THE WEE HOURS OF Christmas morning.

"Get up, get up!" he exclaimed, jumping on her bed. "Let's go see if Santa came!"

Groaning, she rolled over and tipped her phone to check the time. Five-thirty.

"Mom and Dad said not before six," Eli said. "But I can't sleep to save my life."

She chuckled, remembering being eight, when Christmas day was full of hope and promise.

"Okay, buddy. Just give me a minute." She stretched and rubbed her eyes. "One snoopfest, coming up."

It was their tradition, sneaking to the stairway before their parents woke up to peek at the gifts around the tree. Now, as they sat on the steps together, Eli guessed the contents of various boxes, shivering with excitement. "I don't think I can wait any longer."

"We have to, but—wait, what's that?" Bella teased.

She snuck down the steps and turned on the tree lights. Eli followed, and they settled in under the glow of the colorful lights, looking at the gifts. Bella pulled one from the pile.

"This one says 'Eli.'"

"Mom said we can't open anything until they're awake," he whispered, eyes wide with disbelief, as if she was about to commit a major felony.

"Relax, Officer Eli," she said. "This one's from me. I get to say when you open it."

Eli tore at the package. He gasped before lunging at Bella with a hug.

"This is my favorite gift ever!" he exclaimed.

It was a framed photo of Eli's beloved Viper, the one she took the night he was supposed to ride. She'd photoshopped him sitting in a car as it perched at the crest of the steep hill. On the bottom were the words, *Dreams WILL Come True.*

"How did you do this?" he asked, running his hand over the picture. "It's like I was there!"

"It's magic." She waved her fingers in his face. "But that's not all. Whatever happens this year, you're getting on the ride, even if I have to pay someone off. I've earned a lot of money, and I'm not above bribery."

"I'm still sad Jordan didn't show up that night."

Dang, that was right—she'd forgotten to tell him. She explained Jordan lived in their hometown and how she'd run into him.

"That's amazing!" Eli exclaimed. "We should go visit him. Maybe you could date him. You guys would make a cute couple."

She laughed out loud. Eli was so darn adorable at times. Especially now, sitting in his little Grinch jammies, gazing up at her. The hope in his eyes shot straight to her heart, until she remembered Jordan was dating @MakeupQueenAmelia.

"Did he say why he wasn't there that night?"

"His grandfather died that day."

Eli was silent for a moment. "Okay. I forgive him."

Bella suspected on some level her trusting little brother

already had forgiven Jordan, explanation or not.

"You're the best sister a guy could have," Eli said, peering at his gift again.

"And you're the best brother. I love you, baby bro."

Funny thing was, she meant it.

Charlotte

CHARLOTTE WAS FILLED WITH JOY WHEN SHE AWAKENED Christmas morning. Uncharacteristic for the woman who hated the holiday and its forced festivities. Normally, she'd spend the season alone, counting down the days until January when the firm, her co-workers, and the rest of the world finally put down the eggnog and resumed business as usual. This year, however, she wasn't rushing things. Jervis had given the staff time off for the week between Christmas and New Year's, and for the first time ever, Charlotte looked forward to taking vacation. She couldn't wait to curl up on the couch in the soft amber glow of her lit tree and read through the book haul she'd scored from her local indie bookstore. An unusual splurge, her gift to herself.

Getting a tree wasn't the only concession she'd made that year. She'd also had a cat door installed so Blinky could still roam the great outdoors but come in for shelter to escape the bitter cold ushered in by a Polar vortex.

"I got you something," she said to the cat while Perry Como crooned "White Christmas" in the background. Still dressed in her pajamas, she sat on the floor next to where he lay curled up in front of a heating vent. She presented him with a per-sonalized food bowl, the name "Blinky" emblazoned on it, filled with treats and small toys. He reached in with a paw and scooped out a small fabric mouse filled with catnip. It went airborne and he leaped up, swatting at it.

"Wow, they weren't joking," she said. The pet store clerk had told her it would make a great gift. Blinky batted again at the fake mouse, sending it skidding across the floor. Charlotte laughed as her feline friend gave chase, entertaining her with his skillful hunting. When the cat had had its fill, he came to Charlotte and settled onto her lap.

"I'm glad you liked your gift," she said, stroking his head.

He looked up and gave her a slow blink, as if to issue an apology.

"Don't worry if you didn't get me one. You're all the gift I need."

Marley

MARLEY PACED NERVOUSLY AS SHE WAITED FOR SAM TO pick her up for their trip to Cape May. Her Christmas Eve, eggnog–inspired, "screw ethics" resolve had since dissolved into fear she was making a colossal mistake. Would she be able to, as Sam would say, keep it in her pants? She yearned to do the right thing by Wells and the case, but she missed Sam to her core and knew the effect being in such close proximity to him would have on her. It would help if she had her own mode of transportation and didn't have to be trapped with him in an enclosed metal capsule for an hour, but her car was being repaired.

Another thing Marley hadn't considered was that Delaney and Dalton, home for the holidays, would be in Cape May, too. While it seemed a good idea to pretend their ship was status quo, Delaney would recognize the conflict if she found out about their mutual case. Not that she'd take it back to Wells, but Marley didn't want her former boss judging her. She wondered if it was best just to come clean, tell everyone about the conflict, and that she and Sam were on a break. But again, but she didn't want their drama bleeding into what was supposed to be a celebration of Kate and Ryan's upcoming nuptials. In the end, the most logical and least dramatic resolution was just to pretend all was fine and simply mind themselves around each other.

When Sam arrived in faded jeans and a fleece pullover, her heart did a backflip. Not a good start.

"Hey!" he greeted her with his usual enthusiasm, infused with a bit of sarcasm. "Ready for our 'romantic' getaway?"

He ran his hand through his winter hair, now a few sexy shades darker, making his eyes sparkle like Arctic ice. *Breathe, girl.*

"Let me get that," he said, grabbing her overnight bag. Their hands touched, and...*zing!*

He shot her a look as if he'd felt the same thing. This was the last thing she needed. She'd have to keep her distance, or the next couple days would be torture.

"This is going to be one weird weekend," Sam said once they were on the road.

"Yeah."

"What's the face for?"

Marley sighed. "I'm not sure this was a good idea. I'm worried about—you know."

"My untethered sex appeal and your obsession with seducing me?"

"I was thinking more along the lines of Delaney finding out about our case."

"Oh, right. That."

They rode in silence, and soon the rhythmic *ba-dump-ba-dump-ba-dump* of the highway joints lulled her to sleep.

Perhaps her exhaustion was from anxiety, or maybe it was the comfort of Sam's Jeep. Whatever it was, she didn't awaken until they arrived.

"Hey, sleeping beauty. We're here," Sam whispered.

Marley jolted. "Why didn't you wake me?"

"You looked too peaceful."

He grazed his bottom lip with his teeth and gave her That Look—the one that led to more. She looked away, but that didn't stop the *zing!* from racing straight to her nether region. *Stay strong, girl.*

"Just in time for happy hour!" Kate sang as she and Ryan greeted them on the porch. After a round of hugs, Kate announced she had bad news.

"Delaney and Dalton can't make it. Dalton has food poisoning. Bad shrimp, he thinks."

Whew! Sorry, Dalton, but...thanks be to rancid crustaceans. Marley felt her tension dissolving at Kate's announcement.

They dropped their bags in the hall, and Ryan poured a round of drinks. The friends sat around a roaring fire and chatted until Cleo and Nigel arrived.

"Sorry we're late," Cleo said, greeting them with hugs. "We were visiting with Gus."

"How's he doing?" Marley asked. Cleo's friend, Gus, who was like a surrogate grandfather to Cleo, was battling cancer.

"Still full of piss and vinegar. Starting another round of chemo next week. We try to get down to Philly from New York to see the old goat as much as possible."

"Sounds like you could use a drink," Ryan said, mixing another round of gin and tonics.

After toasting the weekend, the couples enjoyed a delicious dinner at the cozy Washington Inn before taking a stroll through the streets of Cape May. They marveled at the Victorian homes ornately adorned with holiday décor, making the town look like a Dickensian Christmas village.

"Cape May's so quaint," Kate cooed, snuggling up to Ryan as they walked.

"Such a cool place, offering a little bit of everything," Sam said. "Something new, something old. Fun and exciting, yet warm and comfortable. Like a good friend."

He slid his fingers between Marley's. *Zing!*

"Wow," he whispered, looking down at her as he squeezed her hand. "You feel that?"

Marley felt it all right but didn't want to encourage him.

"Delaney and Dalton are thinking of buying a house here once they return from the UK," Kate said.

"What do you say, babe?" Nigel asked, nudging Cleo. "Wanna move to Cape May?"

"When I'm old. For now, I'm city girl all the way."

"Maybe we'll end up here, too," Sam whispered to Marley, draping his arm across her shoulders and pulling her close.

Back at the house, the guys picked up the bags and headed toward the stairs when Ryan announced one of the rooms had twin beds. "Whoever takes it can push the beds together."

"Just mind the gap," Sam said under his breath. "Amiright, Mar?"

She laughed out loud, recalling Sam's face lodged between beds that fateful B&B night. The others looked at her strangely.

"No worries," she said. "We'll take the twin room."

Hallelujah. Twin beds would save them from role-playing the "one-bed" trope.

"Nonsense." Cleo waved her off. "We're like an old married couple now. You love birds take the big bed and enjoy your romantic getaway."

"It's fine, Cleo. We see enough of each other at home," Marley said. And to prove her point, she wrapped her arms around Sam's torso.

Zing! It happened again. Sam must've felt it by the look he shot her.

"We insist," Nigel said. "What she's not saying is I've taken up snoring, and she's looking forward to having her own bed."

"Settled," Sam said a little too quickly.

"Why did you give in so fast?" Marley hissed once they were in the room. They should've put up more of a fight.

"You heard the man—Cleo needs a separate bed. Who am I to argue?" Sam gave her a parting smirk as he headed to the bathroom.

Marley laid out a blanket and pillow on the floor for Sam, changed into her pajamas, and crawled into bed. Moments later, she felt the bed move.

"What are you doing?" she asked.

"Getting into bed, what does it look like?"

"Sam, we can't sleep together."

"Why not? You're still my girlfriend, aren't you?"

"Um, the case?"

Sam's stubbled cheek brushed against hers as he whispered in her ear. "Who's gonna know, Mar-mar?"

He traced his fingertips, ever so lightly, down her arm and across her belly, sending shivers through her.

"*I'll* know," she whispered, her breath catching. She removed his hand before it crept lower. "It'll just lead to more, and we can't. Someone has to sleep on the floor."

"I'm guessing that someone is me?" He sulked as he got out of bed and grabbed an Afghan off a rocking chair.

"You got it, Carpet Mart," Marley said. "G'night."

"Mar," he whispered several minutes later. "You awake?"

"I am now."

"Has working for the prosecution made you mean?"

Marley sighed. "What's your point, Sam?"

"You never would've made me sleep on the floor before you worked for them."

She felt bad but didn't want to invite unwelcome advances, as she knew they'd happen.

Still, making him sleep on the floor seemed cruel and unusual.

"Okay," she huffed, tossing the covers aside. "Come back."

Sam slid in next to her, assuming the big spoon. *Zingety-zing-zing.*

"But we're not spooning," she said.

"I'm cold."

Marley was too cold, herself, to argue. It was nice having his arms wrapped around her again, his warm chest pressed up against her back. As she drifted off to sleep, she promised herself she'd disconnect from his smokin' hot body. Just as soon as...

Hours later, she awakened to Sam nuzzling her neck. Too tired to think straight, she went with it as he moved his lips to hers, sighing as he kissed her. Softly at first, then with mounting passion. They were roused by their moans as the kiss became more intense. It wasn't a rarity for them—they'd often wake up in the middle of the night and make love.

"Marley." Sam groaned as he rolled on top of her. She could feel his urgency through the sheet.

"Sam, we can't," she said, even though it was the only thing she wanted to do just then.

"I know," he said, rolling back over. "Actually, I don't. Remind me why?"

"Because your client deserves your zealous and uncompromised representation. Sleeping with the prosecution is not the way."

Sam slapped his forehead. "I wish you'd told me that before I slept with Wells."

Marley smiled before one-upping him. "No worries. I made the same mistake."

The couples met up with Kate and Ryan's other weekend guests for brunch at Mad Batter the next day, followed by a group winery tour. Marley tried to keep her cool with Sam but couldn't help stealing glances. He looked hot in his flannel shirt and faded jeans as he stood laughing with the guys around the fire pit. Every once in a while, he would peer at her over his glass, his gaze intense. Purposeful, as if knowing the effect it would have on her as he licked his lips turned ruby from the reds.

She recalled the sage advice of one Samuel Adams: *Keep it in your pants, girl.*

Back at the house, Marley donned her emerald strapless cocktail dress and glided down the stairs, joining Sam and the others in the living room. His eyes lit as he gave a soft whistle, offering his hand as she stepped from the landing.

"Simply gorgeous."

He'd changed into the tux he'd purchased for a black-tie wedding. He was stunning, looking like he belonged on the red carpet. It took her breath away.

They walked to the party in Congress Hall's ballroom, the same place Delaney and Dalton's reception had been. Marley was hit with all the feels when they entered the room, recalling their first dance as a couple. Her resolve began to melt, but she had to stay strong if she wanted to avoid the magnetic rizz of her handsome boyfriend. If she could do it for six years as friends, she could certainly do it now. She just needed to hang in there for one more night.

Charlotte

CHARLOTTE COULDN'T BELIEVE THE WAY EVERYTHING had worked out to lead her here.

Here in Cape May, for her first New Year's Eve party. With her best bud, Jake.

She marveled at the ballroom adorned in fairy lights and gold and silver balloons. Stations of food and drink were scattered around the room, and a photo booth with props was set off to one side. She'd never been anywhere so festive.

"No way!" Sam exclaimed as he and Marley approached her during cocktail hour. "I had no idea you'd be here, Charlotte!"

Sam hugged her. She stiffened instinctively but didn't back off, having learned during this wretched social experiment that schmoozers loved hugging. She'd better get used to it if she wanted to be one.

"I dunno, Sam," she teased. "I guess I just can't stay away from you."

Sam shot her a look—that was how good her delivery was—before he pointed and laughed. "That's funny, Charlotte!"

Sam and Jake were pulled away by the other groomsmen for a photo booth shoot.

"What's up with you and Jake?" Marley asked. "Are you guys an item?"

"Oh, no," Charlotte said, her cheeks flushing. "We're just friends."

"Sam and I were once 'just friends' too," Marley said, chuckling. "You see how that ended."

Charlotte, blushing, glanced across the room at Jake. He looked handsome in the Irish sweater she'd given him for

Christmas, and for a tiny second, her heart pulsed. He, too, had given her a sweater, along with a friendship bracelet made by Bella. Looking down, she fingered the bracelet and gave a shy smile.

"I guess I could think of worse things," she admitted.

Wait—had she really just made a forward comment about her friend? It had to be the wine talking. She'd better stop, or who knows what else may come out of her mouth?

"I could see it," Marley said with a twinkle in her eye. "You guys would make a cute couple."

Two more firsts. Being referred to as cute and as part of a couple. The thought made her heartbeat quicken once more. Taking a deep breath, she told herself to calm down. She cherished their relationship as it was and didn't want anything to change.

It was definitely the wine.

BELLA AND ELI SETTLED AT A CORNER TABLE, AWAY FROM their drunken relatives. She'd brought some card games to entertain Eli, knowing they'd be the only kids at this jawn. They'd just finished their second game of Uno when Kate approached.

"You guys doing okay? I'm sorry there aren't more kids here to play with."

"It's okay," Eli said. "I have the best date a guy could ask for."

Kate and Bella cracked up.

While not quite as enthusiastic, Bella had to agree it had been a fun night so far. Even if being here meant she was missing out on Sophie's blowout sleepover to which she'd been invited. A blessing in disguise, according to Hanna, who'd texted that the night was a living hell, with Sophie talking nonstop about Robbie.

"It's a shame my brother JJ isn't here, but he had to work tonight," Kate said. "He's about your age, Bella. And he loves Uno. I should fix you guys up."

Hard pass. Any kid her age who *loves Uno* had to be a major loser. Bella didn't dabble in losers. Only hunks. Well, at least that's what she was shooting for, but so far, it hadn't really worked out. Great time for a New Year's resolution.

Marley

A COUPLE HOURS IN, MARLEY BEGAN TO BELIEVE SHE might actually get through the night without being enticed by Sam's uber-hotness. It certainly helped that they'd spent most of the evening surrounded by their friends, never being alone with one another. Until Sam returned from the restroom, and she caught the searing gaze of his *damn, girl!* once-over through the crowd. By the time he got to her, their friends had dispersed, leaving them alone.

"Hello there," he said in a flirtatious tone. "You don't know me. My friends call me Sam. But you can call me...anytime."

"Hi, Anytime," she said, smiling up at him. "I'm Marley. Friends call me Marley McMarley. Sometimes Marley May or even Mar-Mar. But you can call me whatever you want since you will anyway."

"Who you here with, Marley Mar-Mar McMarley?"

She gestured to a big, burly guy in the crowd. "My parole officer."

"Ah, I see. What'd you do time for?"

"Withholding Love and Affection. Felony of the first degree."

"Ooh, that's bad," Sam said. "I know a good defense attorney if you need one."

"Oh, yeah? What makes her so good?"

Sam chuckled, nearly breaking character. "*He*'s good because he knows how to cure someone of their incessant need to break the law in such a heartless manner."

"How?"

He cupped her face, teasing her with his lips. She moaned instinctively at their velvety touch.

"Wow," she breathed. "You do that for all your clients?"

"Only the ones I'm obsessed with," he said, his voice a low growl. He cast her a sultry look as he took a sip of his drink. "So how 'bout we stop breaking the law and get back to this thing of ours?"

"Oooh. I'm flattered, but I have a boyfriend."

"Oh, do you?" he said, a teasing gleam in his eyes. "Lucky guy. I bet he's *hot*."

"Meh, he's alright."

More like *damn fucking hot*, leaning against the bar like a badass, giving serious Bond vibes as he swirled a drink in his upturned palm. His lashes swept down and back up, taking her all in, his teeth grazing his bottom lip as his eyes met hers. It was all she could do to keep herself from pushing him up against the bar and having her way with him right there.

"I bet I can rock your world more than he does," he said.

She returned the once-over. "You think so?"

"I know so. My back aches for you."

Marley laughed, now breaking character herself. "What, from the two seconds you were on the floor?"

"And you hogging the bed all night."

"You had plenty of space," she said, leaning into him and dropping her voice to a whisper. "Plus, you were stuck to me all night, Elmer's Glue."

He set his drink down and clasped his hands around her waist, pulling her close. "I loved every second of it."

Marley got a charge from flirting with him like this. Passion joined the booze coursing through her veins, making her head swimmy with feels. He gave her That Look again just as their favorite song came on. Taking her hand, he pulled her to the dance floor. His arm snaked around her waist and yanked her in tight.

"Enough bullshit. I'm your boyfriend now."

"Oh, okay," she murmured, resting her head on his chest. Where it belonged.

Charlotte

BEFORE CHARLOTTE KNEW IT, THEY WERE COUNTING down the new year. She donned a festive party hat along with other guests.

"I'm having the time of my life," Charlotte said, turning to face Jake just as she was smacked in the nose by his unfurled party blower. She squinted at him. "Just for that..." She blew on hers, hitting him on the cheek.

"Ow, that hurt," he teased. "You better kiss my boo-boo."

Charlotte blushed and looked around. The countdown was at eleven now.

Should she?

Ten, nine, eight...

Kiss his cheek?

Seven, six, five...

But she wasn't a kisser.

Four, three, two...

Then again... *Quand à Rome.* Or Cape May, as the case was. *One!*

Charlotte went up on her tiptoes to kiss his cheek, but at the last moment, he turned his head. Her lips landed awkwardly on his. Her eyes bugged out. So did his.

"Whoa!" He laughed and hugged her.

She didn't pull away. Instead, she stayed there feeling... something. Something that felt like the first cool breeze of autumn. Grilled cheese and tomato soup on a winter's eve. The smell of sunshine on freshly laundered sheets.

The feeling of home.

She would have been mortified had she lunged at a man in such a tawdry way at any other time. But it was midnight on New Year's Eve, when physical connection was not only justified but encouraged. Though she'd never randomly kiss a guy on the lips (preventative hygiene saw to that), she couldn't help the way her lips tingled.

He slid his mouth to her ear and whispered, "Happy New Year, friend."

"You too," she whispered as he pulled back.

"Any resolutions?" he asked. "Besides making partner."

"A million followers on Instagram."

Jake smiled.

"And yours? Other than sailing and world domination, of course."

"Finding a way to stay in touch with you. Wherever life takes us."

Marley

AS THE CLOCK TURNED THE CALENDAR TO A NEW YEAR, Sam wrapped his arm around Marley's waist and dipped her, gazing at her before slowly bringing her back up to a melting embrace.

"I told you the last time we danced together in this room, I was never letting you go," he said, his voice husky. "I mean it. Case or no fucking case."

Confetti and balloons fell from the ceiling as a mass of friends and strangers erupted in celebration around them. Sam cupped her face and kissed her with such intensity she almost fell backward. Marley had few resolutions that year, but the one topping her list just then was to relish this night with Sam.

Back in their room, he swept her into his arms, gliding her around. "I never wanna stop dancing with you, Ginger."

"Then don't, Fred."

Snowflakes fell outside their window. Cast in moonlight's glow, Sam serenaded her.

> *We have a Cape May kind of love, my dear, the kind that lasts beyond our years.*

He laid her gently on the bed, crawling over her, their legs entwining instinctively. She wove her fingers through his hair and pulled him toward her.

"Beyond *all* years," he whispered.

It might have been the drinks, the gaiety of the evening, his sexy with a capital *S* tux. Perhaps it was their flirtatious role play or simply being in the intoxicating presence of this Very Fine Man. Whatever it was, Marley tossed her goody two shoes right out the window. One more day and the conflict would be over.

For now, though...

Her need to be with Sam was raw, animalistic. Greater than anything she'd ever felt—with the exception of their first time. Ethics were the last thing on her mind just then. The first was the smoldering desire in his eyes. She didn't try to stop him when his lips joined hers, and his tongue probed deeper, accompanied by moans of anticipation. Delayed gratification. She proceeded to take, touch, suck, stroke, devour, and savor every last inch of him. And he did the same to her. As to be expected, it was the best it had ever been.

January

Marley

FINALLY. JANUARY 2ND. THE DAY THE CASE WOULD COME to an end. The day Marley and Sam would return to normal. She was about to enter the courtroom when he texted her.

Need to talk.

Before she could respond, she heard a voice behind her.

"I should've figured you'd beat me to court," Wells said. "I just got off the phone with Adams. Plot twist."

He opened the door for Marley. Court was already in session.

"No trial today," he whispered.

Plot twist? More like knife twist. Marley barely registered what he'd said when the judge addressed Wells.

"Counselor, are you ready to proceed?"

Sam was seated at the defense table, a sheepish expression on his face.

"I understand we're here to entertain a motion to continue the case?" the judge asked.

"Correct, Your Honor," Sam said, leaping to his feet. "I was, uh—just informed by my client he wishes to have more time to consider the prosecution's offer. We're requesting the trial be continued to a future date so we can work out a potential plea."

What?

"Does prosecution agree to this?"

"Yes, Judge," Wells said, also rising to his feet. "Can we see you at sidebar?"

The attorneys approached the bench, and that was when Marley knew. Marcon had agreed to work as a confidential informant, a fact which couldn't be disclosed in open court as the streets had ears. She knew the terms of the deal: he had to work for his redemption, wearing a wire, doing deals, helping in the cops' attempt to dragnet bigger fish up the supply chain. If he did everything asked of him by the prosecution, charges would be reduced, and he'd take a plea. If not, they'd proceed to trial.

Either way, Marley and Sam's ethics-driven separation would continue.

The judge consulted her laptop after the attorneys returned to their seats. "My next available date is April fifteenth."

It felt as if the judge had grabbed Marley's heart and flung it across the room. April was three months away. Struggling to breathe, she stared at Sam, who appeared to be doing everything in his power to avoid eye contact. How could he let this happen? If they'd just gone to trial, this would have been over today.

And thus...the crux of a conflict of interest.

Sam had to do what his client wanted, not appease his girlfriend. He'd done the right thing—he had no choice—but that didn't make it any easier. When Sam finally turned to face Marley, his lips were pressed in a straight line, and his sullen eyes begged forgiveness.

Wells handed her a file. "We have a new case starting in five before Judge Dunn. Could end up being your first trial."

Marley, still flabbergasted, followed Wells from the courtroom. They made their way to the elevators, Sam behind them.

"Congrats on getting through to him," Wells said to Sam. "On to the next."

"Yep," Sam said, eyes downcast.

Marley couldn't bear to look at him. Devastation coursed through her. Another three months they'd have to wait to be together. She wasn't sure she could do it again.

Sam stepped into the elevator with them.

"We'll need to go over the details of Marcon's cooperation," Wells suggested.

"Yeah, we'll talk."

"Marley, when are the bar results expected?" Wells asked.

"April twelfth."

Wells laughed. "Perfect timing. If Marcon lets us down and we go to trial, I'll have you do some of the cross-examination."

He turned to Sam. "You'll have to bring your A-game, Adams. Marley promises to be a killer in the courtroom."

Sam gave her a sad smile. "Consider my A-game brought."

Perfect. Going head-to-head with Sam in court was exactly what they needed.

When they arrived at their floor, Sam stepped off the elevator with them.

"What—" Marley caught herself before she could ask why he was following them.

"Any chance we can work out an offer on this next one?" Sam asked.

Marley's worst fears came true as Sam opened the door and followed them to the front of the courtroom. He was on this case, too. A burglary, Wells explained, likely go to trial but not until summer.

"Your bar results will be in by then. I may have you take the lead on this one," Wells said.

She should have been excited, but the thought of another conflict with Sam sucked the living joy from her. All she could think was: *I'm done.*

Somehow, Marley made it through the rest of the court appearance. She couldn't bear to look at Sam. It took every bit of her strength not to break down until she was back in her office. Closing the door behind her, she succumbed to a barrage of tears as she reached her breaking point. She couldn't live without him, but the universe was forcing her to do just that.

The phone rang as she expected it would. She picked up, not caring if he knew she was crying.

"I'm so sorry," he said, his words catching in his throat. "I had no choice in taking on this new case. Jim just assigned me this morning."

"I wasn't expecting this. I—can't do it again."

"Please, Marley," he said, sounding like he was crying.

"What do you expect me to do, Sam? My boss will fire me if you and I are together. I'm not doing this for another three months. Just—not."

"I'll quit the firm," he finally said, his voice wavering.

Marley thought that was what she'd want to hear but knew how much the job meant to him. As much as hers did.

"You can't do that," she whispered, as much as it killed her to say it. "You're too good. I can't ask you to leave and do something you're not passionate about."

"I'm passionate about you. If I stay here, I'll lose you. Not worth it."

"Doesn't matter. The world doesn't want us to be together."

She thought back to their anniversary night at the bed and breakfast and wondered if it was an omen of what was to come; the crevice separating them was no longer just a divide between beds, but between careers. Lives.

"Of course it does. We're meant for each other."

"My heart can't take anymore," she said as she wept. "The bar exam's in six weeks, and I can't deal with this emotional turmoil. I hope you understand. These last few months have been torture for me, between the bar, the job, and this. I've got nothing left to offer."

The sound of his stifled sobs made her cry harder as she cursed their luck. In a city as big as Philly, with as many lawyers as there were, the odds were against them ever being on one case together, let alone two in as many months. Which proved that as long as she worked for the prosecution and he the defense, there'd always be a chance new conflicts would arise. The only way they could guarantee it wouldn't happen again is if one or both left their current jobs.

She wasn't ready for that. Her internship was the only thing keeping her connected to law—especially after Wells suggested she may be assigned to a case heading to trial this summer, finally achieving her ultimate goal.

Leaving her job meant she'd be choosing Sam but losing her dream. Staying meant she'd be choosing herself but losing Sam. A perfect Sophie's Choice.

Marley was left with no other option.

She chose herself.

Charlotte

JAKE CALLED CHARLOTTE TO SAY HE'D BE IN TOWN THE following week and asked if she'd like to have dinner. She suggested he come to her house for a home-cooked meal.

"I'm in!" he said before the words were fully out of her mouth. "What can I bring?"

"How about wine? I don't usually have alcohol here, only on holidays."

"Wine it is. Do you have a preference? Red? White? Blue?"

"Oh, blue!" Then she added, "Wait, do they even make blue wine?"

Jake laughed. "It's a joke, Char."

"Okay, then. Surprise me."

Charlotte was excited to show off her culinary talents to her friend. She made her famous lasagna, garlic bread, and a salad. For dessert, she'd picked up cannoli from the corner Italian bakery. Jake arrived on time, earning more points with Charlotte, who noted he was as punctual as she was.

"Oh my God," he said as they ate. "Unbelievable. This is the best lasagna I've ever had."

Charlotte laughed. "Unbelievable that it's the best, or that I made it?"

"Both," he teased. "No. Seriously delicious."

It was the result she'd hoped for.

"Let me do the dishes," he offered when they finished eating.

"No, I got it. You're my guest. Have more wine."

In truth, Charlotte wouldn't trust anyone but herself to wash the dishes. He joined her at the sink after they cleared the table, helping her dry. That she could handle. They were just finishing up when something outside caught Jake's attention.

"It's snowing!"

Big fluffy flakes twirled outside her window. She turned off the kitchen light so they could see them better.

"That's it," Jake said after a couple minutes. "Suit up, we're going out."

If Charlotte wasn't anything, it was outdoorsy. Certainly not in sub-degree temps. But there was one New Year's resolution she hadn't yet shared with Jake: try new things. Playing in the snow would be one of them.

The friends bundled up and made their way to the small playground across the street. Jake jumped into a snowball fight already in progress between neighborhood kids as Charlotte cheered him on. Soon, the kids were called inside by their parents, leaving Charlotte and Jake alone. She twirled in the falling snow, recalling how much she enjoyed it as a child. A snowflake tumbled onto her outstretched tongue, and she let it melt there, not the least bit concerned it contained acid rain. Jake flopped down on the ground and began sliding his arms back and forth.

Charlotte gasped as a memory came drifting back—that one time in elementary school when her dad took her outside at night to make snow angels. Her heart twanged at the memory. She missed him so much.

"Come on, join me!" Jake called.

Without weighing the risks of contracting a cold, getting frostbite, or freezing to death, Charlotte plopped herself down. There was no way she was allowing risks to outweigh rewards that night. They made their angels, even pausing to take a selfie as they lay there in the snow.

"You gotta send that to Bella," Jake said.

"Already on it," Charlotte assured him, because that was what social media afficionados do.

Jake stood and offered his hand to Charlotte, but his foot slipped on a patch of ice.

"Incoming!" he proclaimed as he went down, landing beside her. They laughed nervously. She expected him to scramble up, but he didn't. Instead, he lay there, staring at her. His hand, which had come to rest on her waist, remained. After a couple slow blinks and what sounded like a sigh, he sat up. "Sorry about that epic fail."

She didn't see it as a fail, more a missed opportunity, as she found herself wondering what his lips would feel like on hers and whether he'd been exposed to any communicable diseases lately.

Had she really just thought that?

If she had, she wasn't about to tell him. Fortunately, his hoisting abilities won out this time, and Charlotte found herself upright, facing him.

Another long stare. He cleared his throat.

"Okay, then. I must be getting on," he said, clearing his throat a second time, alerting Charlotte to the possibility he was, most likely, coming down with something. Thank the good Lord he hadn't tried anything.

"By the way, I'm heading to the Bahamas next week, where I'll be staying for a while, getting a little practice in before the worldwide sail next year."

"Wow," was all she could say.

"It's my annual mini-sailing adventure since there's not much going on in the boating world around here. The Caribbean is wonderful this time of year."

"How long will you be down there?" Charlotte asked, not ready to lose her friend to warmer climes.

"I'll be back in April."

April? Charlotte's heart sank.

He must have seen the look on her face. "Don't worry. I'll keep in touch. I promise."

She deflated once again. She'd be alone for the loneliest months of the winter. Not that she wasn't every year. At least this year, she'd have his long-distance texts to look forward to. And more time to devote to making partner, which was the most important thing in her life.

Wasn't it?

Bella

"STOP RIGHT THERE!" THE DIRECTOR YELLED AS HE marched toward the stage.

Bella pulled back from Robbie after sharing their first awkward stage kiss. She couldn't help the weirdness. Even though Robbie had been kind to her in the past few weeks as they rehearsed together, and had even made her laugh on occasion, the hurt she felt from prom wasn't quick to dissolve.

"I'm not believing Belle and Beast like each other enough to go out for coffee, let alone love each other," the director admonished. "I need to see more passion. More love. Make me feel it, here." He pounded his fist to his chest. "Let's try it again."

Robbie looked down at her as he squeezed her hand, which she now realized he'd been holding since the director stopped the scene. He brushed a lock of hair from her cheek with his other hand, sending unexpected chills down Bella's spine.

"That's more like it," the director said upon witnessing the moment. "Bella, what do you like about this guy?"

"Um..." Bella looked him over. "I like his sneaks."

"Robbie, tell Bella what you like about her."

"I like your strawberry blonde hair."

The director looked back at her. *Think, Bella, think.* "I like your laugh."

"I like the way you make me laugh."

Wow. Robbie took no time in answering.

"I like the fact that you've been typecast," Bella said. "You don't even need a costume to play the Beast."

Robbie and the others laughed, and Bella beamed with pride.

"You, too, have been typecast. As my princess."

"Get it!" yelled one of the guys.

"Except Belle's not really a princess," she pointed out.

"But you are, Beautiful Bella."

That drew an audible swoon from the other cast members. Bella blushed, and Robbie locked eyes with her. She felt all the pre-prom feels flooding back. Thank God Sophie had quit the play and wasn't here to witness this.

"You're kinda hot," Bella said, shocked because where was this confidence coming from? Somehow, being cast as the lead had made her bolder.

"Go on, girl!" yelled one of the female cast members.

"Not only are you hot, but you're funny, smart, and sweet," he said. "And I'm sorry about what happened at prom."

Bella's heart skipped a beat. "Thank you."

He squeezed her hand. "You didn't deserve that."

"Okay, I need more," the director encouraged.

"I had a crush on you back then," Bella admitted. "Not anymore, though."

"That's a shame," he said. "You kinda have me feeling a certain way."

Now her heart was racing. She knew it was all for the sake of the show and that he was still dating Sophie, but it did the trick. Their eyes locked again, this time with more meaning.

"That's more like it!" the director yelled as he clapped his hands together. "Now kiss the girl!"

The cast members began clapping and chanting, "Kiss the girl! Kiss the girl!"

Before Bella could prepare herself, Robbie cupped her face and kissed her, hard, his lips parting as his tongue found hers. She was surprised her heart didn't end up in his mouth. The entire cast was stunned silent.

It might have been a stage kiss, but no one had ever kissed her like that. She felt like she was going to faint if not for the kiss still in progress.

A low "whooo" rose up from the cast members.

"That's it!" the director yelled. "Exactly what I'm looking for!"

"Wow," Robbie whispered after pulling away. "That was amazing."

Ditto.

"Okay, we're gonna wrap up for the day," the director announced, "but I have homework for Belle and Beast. Before our next rehearsal, you're gonna go get coffee or ice cream or whatever it is you kids do. And you're gonna keep talking about what you like about each other so we can get beyond this weirdness I've witnessed between you. Got it?"

"Absolutely," Robbie answered immediately. "Can't wait, actually."

Marley

THE NEXT WEEK WAS NOTHING SHORT OF A NIGHTMARE. Heartbroken, Marley agonized over whether she'd done the right thing, choosing her career over the love of her life. She could barely eat or sleep, to the point she'd begun contemplating a Plan C.

She was nursing her wounds with a bottle of wine one night when he called.

"Sam, I can't do this—"

"I know," he said. "That's not the reason I'm calling. I have something you're not going to believe. Are you sitting down?"

Just the sound of his voice, his whimsical tone, lifted her funk. She missed him terribly.

"I'm assuming you haven't been watching *The Bachelor?*" he asked.

Marley chuckled. "A resounding hell no."

Despite her ex being the newly minted Bachelor, Marley had lost all interest in the show. Not only did it feel creepy watching Rick's new quest for love, but she and Sam had always watched the show together. It reminded her too much of him.

"Take a wild freaking guess who one of the contestants is."

"It's either someone famous or someone we know, I'm guessing," she finally said.

"JENNA!" he yelled, not waiting for her to guess.

"WHAT?"

"I SHIT YOU NOT!" he screamed.

She burst into laughter at the revelation that Sam's ex was a contestant vying for the heart of Marley's former beau. Sam was laughing, too. Pure music.

"No. Freaking. WAY!" she exclaimed, tears of giddiness sliding down her cheeks. It felt good—no, life-affirming—to be laughing with Sam like this.

"Way! In other words, our old flames are on TV searching for love after we cast them aside."

"Hmm," Marley said, sobering. "Somehow, that doesn't seem fair. They'll be getting beaucoup bucks and followers while we—"

She couldn't bring herself to say it.

"Yeah," he said, "which is another reason I called. I'm leaving the firm when these cases are done."

"You better not," she said. "You're too good. And anyway, I beat you to it. I've decided to start looking for another job."

"Marley McMarley. You'd do that for me?"

"Yes, because you're willing to do it for me. For us, actually."

Laughing with Sam like that, sharing a moment of pure joy, was all the confirmation she needed. She had to find a job on the defense side to obliterate the likelihood of future conflicts. First case be damned. There'd be more trials in her future, but there'd never be another Sam.

"I thought you loved the DA's office?"

Marley paused. "Not as much as I love you."

Charlotte

IT HAD BEEN WEEKS SINCE CHARLOTTE HAD HEARD FROM Jake. She knew he was in the Caribbean from the pictures he'd posted on Instagram. In the beginning, she liked and commented on his photos, but when he didn't respond or reach out to her, she stopped reacting. She was confused as to why he'd been incommunicado. Perhaps she'd come on too strong, inviting him for dinner. Or maybe he'd met someone. That had to be it.

Charlotte tried to keep his absence from her mind, but it was hard. She missed him, their weekly calls, and occasional get-togethers. She finally decided to stop being precious about it and sent him a text, asking how he was. Three days later, he still hadn't responded. It was unlike him, as he usually responded right away. Finally, on the fourth day, he wrote.

All's good here. And you?

She stared at the text. If that wasn't a blow-off, she didn't know what was. She decided two could play at this game. She didn't respond. Let him miss her for a change.

"Hey, friend," Charlotte greeted Blinky, heart heavy as she stepped onto her porch after work, where the cat was waiting for her. She poured a couple treats from a container into his empty dish before sinking onto the porch swing, sighing.

Blinky looked up at her, a look of concern on his face (or so she imagined).

"I never thought I'd hear myself say this," she said to her furry friend, "but I think I'm in trouble."

Bella

BELLA AND ROBBIE HEADED TO SERENDIPITY CAFÉ THE following day after school. She wasn't sure what made her more nervous: the fact that she and Robbie were about to go on a forced date, or that Sophie might find out. As mean as she could be, Bella still considered Sophie a friend and didn't want to purposely hurt her. While that might have been

Sophie's nature, it wasn't Bella's.

They found a table in the front window of the café, tucked away from everyone else. Robbie held her chair out for her when she sat.

"I like how you're such a gentleman," she joked.

"I like how you make me want to be one," he said.

"Rehearsal's over," she said. "You can go back to hating me now."

He looked shocked. "I don't hate you."

Bella cocked her head. "But you kinda acted like it at prom last year. Don't you think? Taking me but kissing Sophie?"

Robbie looked down and sighed. "Bella, I'm so sorry about that. I've felt horrible since that night."

"But you went on to date her and still are."

"Kinda," he said, looking up at her. "Not for long. I think I'm gonna break up with her."

If he'd doused her with his cold brew just then, she'd have been less surprised.

"Why?" she asked.

"I dunno. These past few weeks rehearsing with you have been so fun. I meant what I said—you're funny, smart, and sweet, and I like the way you make me laugh. So unlike Sophie. She makes me feel like shit on a daily basis, but you make me feel good."

Bella hoped he couldn't hear her heart thudding away in her chest.

"I'd love to hang out sometime, and not just as a homework assignment," he continued. "What do you think?"

"Break up with Sophie first, and we'll talk. I'm not one to step on another woman's toes."

"See, that's what I mean. You're a decent person. I'm ready to hang with someone like you."

Bella wanted to believe his words but wasn't about to set herself up for disappointment again. She drew a virtual line around herself, labeled it the Friend Zone, and made sure she didn't let her thoughts or feelings leave it. Because if she didn't, she'd die of humiliation. Again.

If Sophie didn't kill her first.

February

$$Marley$$

MARLEY'S SECOND-ATTEMPT BAR EXAM WAS A FEW weeks away. The DA's office had been graciously flexible with her schedule to allow her study time. In what little free time she had, she'd begun a casual search for a new job, to no avail, but would increase her efforts after the exam. As painful as it was without Sam in her life, she had gobs of time to study and was feeling good about the test. She began to see light at the end of the tunnel. It would all be over soon.

One day, Wells summoned her to his office. She was surprised to find the District Attorney herself in his office. More like taken aback. As chief law enforcer of a large metropolitan city, she was more readily seen on the news than in the office.

"Hello, ma'am," Marley said, bowing her head as if she were greeting royalty.

"You can call me Liz," she said warmly.

"This is Marley, the intern I've been telling you about," Wells said.

"I've heard much about you, Marley. Sounds like you're doing a great job."

Her heart soared. Such a compliment coming from Her Royal Prosecutorness.

"I asked you to come in because of the caselaw you found during your search and seizure research," Wells explained. "It's proven to be quite valuable in some tough cases."

Marley smiled. "I'm glad I could be of help."

"It wasn't just helpful, it was impactful," Liz said. "I don't know how you found it, but we've been struggling with that point of law for a while. We knew we were correct in our legal analysis but didn't have the caselaw to back it up. Now, thanks to you, we do."

Marley was elated. She recalled the day a few weeks ago when, during her research, she stumbled upon the rare case from decades ago. It had never been overturned, which meant it was still good law.

"I wanted to thank you personally, Marley," Liz said. "You have a permanent job waiting for you after the bar, as far as I'm concerned. You're quite the shining star."

Marley's glow lasted for hours after the meeting until uncertainty crept in. She'd already made up her mind to leave the DA's office but now wasn't so sure. She needed to talk to someone about it. Gwen was on vacation, so that left Gabriel. She summoned him to The Clink that evening.

"She doesn't dole out compliments to just anyone," he said. "Congrats, girl. You're doing something right."

She hadn't told Gabriel she was planning on leaving. Needing the advice of her good friend, she was about to tell him when Sam walked into the bar. She tried to duck out of his line of vision. Too late. His eyes met hers. Beaming, he approached them.

"Hey, guys," Sam said, his voice like an aphrodisiac. He shook hands with Gabriel and gave her shoulder a friendly squeeze.

"Nice seeing you, Sam," Gabriel said. "Thanks for getting Marcon on board. He's been helpful in our investigations."

"Glad to hear it," Sam said, then turned to Marley. "I haven't seen *you* in a while. Everything good?"

Marley tried to avoid his eye contact as she blushed into her drink. "All good. You?"

"Meh, been better. But them's the breaks, right?"

Marley felt uncomfortable having this discussion in front of Gabriel, who fortunately excused himself to use the restroom. Once out of eyesight, Sam leaned into Marley, his hand on the small of her back, his voice husky in her ear.

"I miss you. Any luck with the job hunt?"

"I miss you too. And no," she said, lifting her eyes to his. Being this close to him after so long made her knees weak. "What brings you here today?"

"Meeting a client."

"Ah, finally, one who's not behind bars?"

Sam laughed. "Yeah, not a criminal case. I'm starting to handle other types because, you know..."

He must still be thinking of leaving the firm.

"Sorry, that's him now. Good seeing you," he said as he squeezed her shoulder again.

Marley watched him walk away, fighting the urge to run after him.

Gabriel returned and picked up his drink. "I have another toast."

"What's this one for?"

"Doing the right thing."

"The right..." Marley followed his gaze. He was looking at Sam.

"This must be hard for you," he said, tipping his chin in Sam's direction.

Her shoulders slunk. Their secret was out. "You knew?"

"Of course. I've been a detective for seven years, trained to read people. I could tell by the look on your face every time he walked into court you had a connection with him. I didn't figure out the boyfriend part until I saw him staring at you when you weren't looking."

"We're that obvious?" She wished she was a better actress.

"Have you been on a break because of the case?"

"You got it, Detective."

"I commend you. Many couples would've stayed together and lied about it. I've even seen it a few times, and in one case, it led to an ineffective assistance of counsel charge."

Marley shivered. That was exactly what she was hoping to avoid.

"I'm thinking of leaving the DA's office," she blurted out as she gazed at Sam across the bar. "He's my person. I can't keep up this charade, pretending not to be in love with him for the purpose of avoiding a conflict."

Gabriel regarded her with sad eyes. "I get it. I couldn't imagine losing someone I love over a case. I'm happy Frank isn't a lawyer."

"Wells doesn't know. I hope you can—"

"Keep a secret?" Gabriel smiled and shrugged. "Kinda my thing. As sad as I'll be if you leave, I think you're doing the right thing."

"Even with the glowing commendation I just received from our boss?" Marley asked. "I feel torn now, like maybe I was meant to be an ADA."

"Marley, you shine wherever you are. You don't need a title or a job description—hell, even a law degree—to make that happen. You're intelligent, kind, funny. If I was your type, you'd precisely be mine."

"That's a huge compliment," she said, leaning over to give her friend a long hug.

From over Gabriel's shoulder, she saw Sam eyeing them up.

"He's looking at us, isn't he?" Gabriel asked.

"Mmm-hmm."

"I'll let him know he has nothing to worry about."

"Thanks, Gabriel. I appreciate that."

"Oh, you think I meant with you?" he said, breaking their embrace, clutching his chest. "I meant with me. Sam's tempting, but Frank's the only man I need."

Marley threw her head back in laughter.

Later that night, Marley recalled the conversation with Liz and how her scrupulous research helped save several cases. She thought about Sam, telling her she was more of a lawyer than he'd ever be and that she didn't need to prove herself to anyone. She thought of her friends' unwavering support, particularly Gabriel's words. It all led to one big revelation.

The only shadow she'd been standing in was the one cast by her own misconceptions about who she was and what she needed. She didn't need to win a spelling bee, pass the bar, or become a lawyer to be someone. Marley was already all she needed to be. She was just the last to know.

Bella

BELLA DIDN'T FEEL LIKE SPENDING A SATURDAY AFTERnoon at a bridal shower. But as junior bridesmaid, she didn't have a choice, according to Lisa.

They arrived early to help the other bridesmaids set up. Marley, whom she'd met at the New Year's Eve party, greeted them with hugs.

"I hear you're playing Belle in your high school musical," Marley said. "So impressive, you must be really good."

Bella blushed. "Thanks."

"I was in musicals in high school, but never as the lead," Marley said. "You'll have to let me know when your show is so I can come see it."

Bella liked Marley, who reminded her of Merida from the Disney movie, *Brave*. She wanted so badly to reach out and wrap one of her curls around her finger but restrained herself.

Despite not wanting to be there, Bella had a good time at the shower. After the luncheon was finished and gifts were unwrapped, Kate gave Bella a hug.

"Thanks so much for coming, Bells. I know you're really busy with the musical. I remember what it was like to be in high school and have so much going on."

Bella appreciated Kate's acknowledgment, wishing her mom could be more empathetic about her schedule. Maybe she'd give her a break from chores.

"Hey, I was serious about introducing you to my brother," Kate said. "Unless you already have a date to the wedding."

Darn. Bella was hoping she'd forgotten. She didn't want to be fixed up with someone. She and Robbie were growing closer every day, and she was planning on inviting him as her plus-one, assuming he was serious about breaking up with Sophie. Not that Bella wanted to jump in on her friend's soon-to-be ex-boyfriend. But Hanna had been encouraging her.

"Sophie knew you liked him and threw herself at him anyway," Hanna said. "In my mind, you were there first. You don't owe her a thing. If he's interested and wants to date you, let him. Screw her."

Hanna was right. Sophie wouldn't show her the same respect, and in fact, purposely disrespected her and their friendship when she decided to stick her tongue down his throat at prom.

"I'm serious. I think you two would make a cute couple," Kate said, jolting her back to the present. At first, Bella thought she was referring to Robbie but realized she was still talking about her dorky, Uno-loving brother.

"That's okay, no need to fix me up for the wedding."

"You sound like someone I know," Kate said, chuckling. "That would be me when my sister tried to fix me up with Ryan for her wedding. And, well, you know how that turned out."

All well and good for Kate and Ryan, but Bella already had her plus-one. She just had to ask him, which she planned to do as soon as he kicked Sophie to the curb.

Marley

I T WAS THE NIGHT BEFORE THE BAR EXAM. SHE HADN'T seen Sam since that night at The Clink but wasn't surprised when the Rocky theme blared from her phone.

"Hey," he said softly.

It was so good to hear his voice. Sadness over their split was being replaced by hope with every step she took. The DA's compliment boosted her self-confidence about the bar exam. She knew, with conviction, she was meant to practice law. As much as she hated the thought of leaving the prosecution and a guaranteed job, she was heading toward something better. Sam.

"How you feelin'?" he asked.

"Good, surprisingly. I thought I was prepared last time, but this time feels different."

"How so?"

"I dunno," she said. "More at peace or something. Calm. Like I survived failure once and know I can do it again. Not that I want to," she quickly added.

Sam chuckled. "I do sense something different. A confidence I didn't see last time."

"Not having the media all over me helps," Marley said. "I shouldn't jinx myself in case they show up tomorrow."

"They'll have to get by me first."

It warmed her to know he still had her back.

"I think I'd made passing the bar this huge, monumental thing in my life. So terrified I'd fail, I didn't give myself a chance."

"What's different this time?"

"Me," Marley said, after a pause. "I've finally realized I don't have to prove myself to anyone. I'm enough."

"You're more than enough. You just keep remembering that as you fill out all those stupid circles tomorrow. To hell with ethics, my spirit will be all the fuck over you."

"Thanks, Sam," she said. "I love you."

He began singing softly.

> *We walk beneath a starry sky, holding hands, just you and I*
> *The lighthouse shines its guiding light, bringing hope to dark of night.*

Well rested. Healthy breakfast. Bag packed. Pencils sharpened.

Media nowhere to be found.

Arrived early. Found seat. Mind sharp, confidence boosted. Gabriel across the room, two thumbs up. Stomach in knots. Puke on cue. Not everything could be perfect.

The timer went off.

She didn't just sit and take the bar for the second time. She bitch-slapped it. Owned it. Kicked it to the curb. Finished early and walked out, head held high. She finally understood what her friends had been trying to tell her. She had nothing to prove to anyone but herself.

And she just did.

March

Charlotte

BEWARE, THE IDES OF MARCH!

The headline screamed from the newspaper perched on the stand, catching Charlotte's eye as she passed by. She took note, hoping her fate wouldn't be as bad as Caesar's.

The month had already not gone well for Charlotte. She still hadn't heard from Jake since the night he'd come to dinner, other than his last dismissive text. While communication was a two-way street, Charlotte wasn't about to reach out again. Especially when he had a shiny new blonde on his arm. Charlotte had seen the photo on his Instagram page the night before.

"Hanging with Tori is the highlight of my week," the caption read.

Tori was a beautiful blonde, exactly the type of woman Charlotte assumed Jake would be interested in. Of course, he'd sail into the Caribbean sunset and find an equally beautiful human. Expected, maybe, but devastating, nonetheless. No wonder he wasn't keeping in touch with her.

Still, as hard as she tried, she couldn't erase from her mind the look on his face when he lay next to her that snowy night.

Tom Jervis greeted her in the hallway as she approached her office.

"Charlotte, can we have a word?"

This was it. The big decision was coming. She could feel it in her bones.

She followed him to his office, where two other partners were waiting. He motioned for her to take a seat and closed the door behind him. He lowered himself into a chair. Charlotte noticed he was no longer making eye contact with her. And that's when she knew.

The Ides of March were upon her.

"I'm sorry..." he began.

Charlotte endeavored to keep her composure. All she heard was, "Not the right choice at this time. Maybe next year."

She simply nodded. After a lifetime of disappointments, she'd honed the skill of pretending she wasn't hurt.

She blinked back the tears threatening to flow as she fled to her office. The only person she wanted to talk to just then was Jake, but she wasn't about to chase someone who was clearly uninterested in keeping in touch with her. Especially after the blow she'd just received.

Dumbfounded, she stood in the middle of her office as the reality set in. She was without a partner offer or a partner. Her best and only friend. The two men in her life she'd trusted the most—her beloved boss and her best friend—had let her down. Served her right. She'd been smart not to trust people all along. Never again. She felt herself crawling back into her chrysalis—alone, naturally.

Now lonely, too.

For the first time in her adult life, Charlotte let herself feel bitter disappointment, no longer able to pretend it didn't matter, that she didn't matter. She sobbed until her tear ducts had nothing left to offer. Exactly what happens when a dream dies.

Bella

BELLA WEPT WITH JOY AS SHE TOOK IN THE OPENING night audience. Everyone was on their feet, cheering for her as she took her curtain call. She'd done it. She'd pulled it off. She never thought she was main character material, but the whoops and cheers from the audience told her otherwise. She grasped Robbie's hand as they took another bow.

The cast members, still in costume, descended upon the lobby to greet audience members. Little girls dressed in Belle costumes lined up for a photo opportunity. Bella stayed in character and interacted with each child until the crowd finally dwindled. After Bella posed with her final fan, she turned to find Sophie standing there, her arms wrapped around Robbie.

"We did it," Robbie said, disengaging from Sophie to give Bella two high fives followed by a hug.

Sophie regarded her with a pained expression as if choking back vomit. "I still think I would have made a better Belle, but good job." She flashed Bella a smile as if to show she was joking, but the smile didn't reach her eyes.

At one time, Sophie's obvious refusal to give Bella props would have been upsetting, but thanks to her conversation with Lisa after the Halloween party, Bella finally saw Sophie for what she wasn't. A true friend. However, she opted to follow her mother's sage advice, deciding it was better to be friendly than create an enemy in someone as socially dangerous as Sophie. "Thank you," was all Bella said.

If Sophie was expecting drama, she wasn't getting it. Not from this main character.

Marley

MARLEY WAS AT HER DESK WHEN HER CELL LIT UP WITH an incoming call. While familiar, she couldn't quite place the number. She answered in case it was a victim on one of their cases.

"Marley," he said after a pause. "It's been too long."

"Rick!" She was genuinely surprised to hear from him. She'd deleted his contact from her phone after they broke up, which was why his name hadn't come up.

"How are you?" he asked.

"Just fine. I guess I don't have to ask how things are going with you," she joked. "Congrats on being the bachelor."

"Thank you. Have you watched the show?"

"I started to watch you on *Bachelorette* until you called me out..."

Rick sighed. "I'm sorry about that."

"Yeah," Marley said. Her tone was casual but serious as she filled him in on the fallout from his shout-out.

"God, Marley, I had no idea," he said.

He probably couldn't have anticipated the media hunting her down, much less on the worst possible day. Still...

"I would've appreciated it if you'd told me prior to the show airing so I was prepared."

"I know. That wasn't fair of me."

At least he was owning up to it.

"The new season finished airing last night," he continued. "I've been sworn to secrecy until the final episode, but I can tell you now. I found my person, at long last."

Marley smiled as the warmth of forgiveness flowed through her. "Congratulations. What's her name?"

He paused and chuckled. "Jenna."

Oh. My. God.

Marley leaped from her seat, and her mouth flew open in a silent scream as she did a jig. It was everything she could do to keep from laughing out loud like she and Sam had when he told her she was a contestant.

Taking a deep breath, she composed herself. "I'm so happy for you," she cooed.

"After we broke up, I didn't think I'd date again. My mom convinced me to audition, and now, I've found love. That wouldn't have happened without you."

"I'm sorry about the way it all went down."

"Things sometimes have a way of working out, even if it doesn't seem so at the time."

Rick's words had a profound effect on her. Perhaps everything she'd been through this year was for a reason. Maybe she was destined for more.

"Are you still with Sam?" he asked.

"We're kind of on a break." She didn't feel like going into details.

Rick paused. "I'm genuinely sorry to hear that."

Marley could only nod, the lump in her throat too big to speak through.

"Funny thing is, Jenna used to date Sam," Rick continued. "How weird is that?"

Marley chuckled. "I know, Rick. Remember? She's the woman Sam ran into last summer, the one I thought he was trying to get back together with."

"That's right. We didn't realize the connection until Jenna and I put two-and-two together."

Marley couldn't resist teasing him. "You do know, we could've just introduced you two. You didn't have to go on national TV to find each other."

Their mutual laughter helped soothe any remaining guilt she'd harbored over breaking Rick's heart. He'd be fine now—better than fine—in the loving arms of Sam's ex. What a strange world it was.

"Thanks for everything, Marley. I wish you only the best. I hope you find your person."

"I already have."

But it wasn't Sam she was talking about. It was Marley.

Charlotte

CHARLOTTE COULD HEAR BLINKY'S YOWLS FROM DOWN the block. A sense of dread came over her as she hurried toward her house and saw a man loading a cage into the back of a utility van. The large white words splayed across the back of his neon vest clued Charlotte into what was going on.

ANIMAL CONTROL.

"Wait!" Charlotte cried out as she ran to the man. "What are you doing?"

"We've had reports of feral cats in the neighborhood, and this one matches the description."

"But he's mine," Charlotte said. There was no mistaking the cat in the cage for Blinky, with his one droopy eye, crying out to her.

"You got proof?" he asked.

Charlotte's brain scrambled for any evidence she might have. She came up with nothing. Except—

"That's my house there," she said, pointing. "His food and water bowl are on my porch if you want to come see. His name is on his bowl. His—name is Blinky."

The man shook his head. "Sorry, lady. That's not good enough."

"Please," Charlotte cried, hoping honesty would sway him. "He was feral, but he's become my pet. My friend. I've been taking care of him, and he's doing so much better as a result. Shouldn't that count for something?"

"I still have to take him in," he said.

"Are you going to kill him?"

The man smiled. "No. We'll scan him for a microchip to see

if he belongs to anyone. If he does, we'll reach out to the owner. If not, we'll neuter and release him. It's a humane way to treat feral cats while also limiting their growing population."

Charlotte was relieved to hear he wasn't going to be euthanized. Still...

"Can't I bring him to a vet myself? He's already been seen by one when he was injured."

"My hands are tied, ma'am. Trust me, though. This is the best thing for him."

Best thing, her ass. Charlotte was the best thing for him, judging by how he'd filled out over the past few months, looking a thousand times healthier now than when she first met him.

"I'll tell you what," the man said after he closed the door to the van. "If we don't find an owner, I'll bring him right back here when it comes time to release him. If what you said is true, I'm sure he'll be looking for a good meal."

Charlotte was relieved the man was being decent about it. Still, it didn't stop her heart from lurching with grief as he drove away with her friend—the last one standing, now that Jake had written her off.

Tears flowed down her face as she climbed the steps to her porch where Blinky's food and water bowls sat, still full from the morning. She couldn't help the feeling creeping through her that she was never going to see Blinky again. In the course of one day, she'd lost her dream and her only friends.

It was official. Charlotte was a failure.

April

Marley

MARLEY PACED AROUND HER APARTMENT ON THE NIGHT before bar exam results were being released, uncertain what to do with herself. Her heart pounded, and her brain scrambled, synapses firing in every direction. Imagining she passed, her body flooded with dopamine, happiness, relief—until her thoughts switched to the other possibility. What if she failed again? How would she ever show her face at work? Or anywhere?

If only she had someone to hang out with, to keep her mind off it, but everyone was busy. She purposefully hadn't told her family when the results were coming out, to avoid what happened last time.

Marley and Gabriel had been keeping a countdown and had sent each other selfies that morning, pointing to their calendars' final crossed-off day. She'd asked him to hang out that night to keep each other's fears from running wild, but he'd just come off a double shift on a murder investigation and was spending a quiet night in with Frank.

Unable to keep her wits about her, Marley decided to eat her feelings. She was rummaging through her fridge in search of a snack when her doorbell rang.

And there he stood.

Bouquet of tulips in one hand. Bag of pretzels in the other. On his head, a gallon of Breyer's Mint Chocolate Chip. Her favorite.

"I wasn't sure if you'd be in a sweet or savory mood, so I brought both," Sam said, grinning from ear to ear. "And your favorite flowers."

He wore his Temple law sweatshirt and jeans, baseball hat on backward, face covered with a light smattering of five o'clock stubble. The sexy weekend look Marley loved.

She laughed out loud, relieved to have someone here to keep her mind off tomorrow—even if it was Sam, and they shouldn't be seeing each other. Yet here he was, looking sexy AF, with a container of her favorite ice cream on his head. Fuck off, ethics.

"Come in, silly man."

She filled a vase with water for the tulips and slid the ice cream into the freezer.

"And this," he said, reaching into his back pocket, pulling out a folded piece of paper.

It looked like an official court document. "Ah, an injunction." She began reading aloud. "'*Marley Maguire v. Her Conscience.* Due to extenuating circumstances in regard to this case, it is hereby ORDERED that Marley Maguire refrain from speculating, insinuating, or otherwise reading into the kind gestures of one Samuel John Adams, on this, the eve of pending Bar Exam Results, as he is only here as a friend, bearing both savory and sweet treats for Ms. Maguire.'"

Marley looked up at Sam, eyes glistening with humor. "That's quite the run-on sentence."

"No shit. The judge struggles with proper grammar and sentence structure."

"I see that." Marley continued reading. "'She is further hereby ORDERED to accept his gracious offerings by not making a Federal Case of the fact that he's here, with no ill-will or ulterior motives, other than to keep her mind off tomorrow. Signed, Judge Olive Branch, this eleventh Day of April.'"

God, how she missed this man. His humor, his joie de vivre, the way he infused light into the most stressful situations.

"This is so sweet, Sam," she said, clutching the injunction

to her chest. "I hereby PROMISE not to do any of the above. Injunction obeyed."

"Good. I didn't want to hold you in contempt of court."

Marley allowed herself the luxury of a quick friend hug. But it wasn't quick, once his aftershave took hold of her olfactory senses. She breathed in clean, fresh Sam, who smelled like a sunny day at the beach despite it being a dark and stormy night—reminding her she couldn't be within five feet of this man without falling under his spell.

The hug lasted longer than she'd intended, especially once he ran his hand up her back to where her curls fell, wrapping a fist around them as he breathed her name into her neck.

She pulled back before they went further. "The flowers are gorgeous," she said, sniffing them—not only because they smelled nice but to keep the scent of Sam from commandeering her senses.

"Turns out, April's the month to find tulips. Who knew?" he asked.

"Uh, everyone?" She chuckled. "That's why I've always wanted to go to Holland in April to see fields of tulips in every color."

"Let's do it. I'll book a flight for the day after tomorrow. We'll celebrate."

"Or jump out of a plane over the Atlantic."

"Nope," Sam said. "You've passed. I feel it in my bones."

If only Marley could feel it, too. It was a done deal. Somewhere in Harrisburg, her results were being uploaded into the computer system for the big reveal tomorrow, which meant others knew her fate before she would. It seemed inherently unfair.

"Got beer?" Sam asked, opening her fridge and retrieving two bottles of Dock Street. He uncapped them and handed her one, clinking his against hers.

"A toast to the news I'm about to deliver."

"Oh boy, what now?"

Sam beamed. "We settled the case."

"Wait, which case?"

"Marcon. The one heading to trial on Monday."

She was flabbergasted. "*What?*"

"Yep. He did what was asked and took a plea to lesser charges. So, whatever this is"—he waved a hand in the space between them—"can finally be the fuck over. If you'll still have me."

"What about the other case?"

Sam gave her a half-smile, relishing the pause. "The defendant fired me. He's gonna represent himself."

"What an idiot!" Marley exclaimed.

"Right? My favorite kind of idiot."

"No, I meant you!" she said, laughing as she slugged his arm. "Why didn't you lead off with all that instead of the injunction?"

"I'd already typed it up before I found out. It was too good to waste, and besides—"

Before he even finished his sentence, reality smacked her in the face. She lunged at him, jumped into his arms, wrapped her legs around his waist. She grabbed his face and kissed him like she'd never kissed him before.

He carried her to the couch.

"Does this mean I can ravish you now?" she asked. "Or do you have other conflicts hidden up your sleeve?"

"Not a one," he said.

He was free. They were free. Free from legal conflict. As they freed themselves of clothing, pure elation combined with nervous energy, combusting into the most powerful passion they'd ever shared.

"And that, ladies and gentlemen, is what months of pent-up sexual frustration will do," Sam said afterward, panting.

Marley's chest was still heaving. "Maybe we should go another three months..."

"Not on your life," Sam said. "Or I'd have to sue you."

"Oh yeah? For what?"

"Withholding Love and Affection. Felony of the first degree."

"Okay, Matlock. I can't spare another strike."

They basked in the afterglow as the feel-good hormones coursed through her, soothing her nerves. She was about to drift off to sleep when Sam kissed her and got up.

"I'm gonna get going," he whispered. "Big day for you tomorrow. Don't wanna keep you up all night."

Marley was disappointed but realized it was best if he wasn't here tomorrow. She didn't want another audience if it was bad news. Even if it was Sam.

He held her for a long time. "I know you probably can't think beyond tomorrow, but I need to get back to M-n-S. I miss you so much it hurts. My life depends upon it."

She knew exactly how he felt.

"Text me immediately when you know," he said as he headed to the door.

"You'll be the first."

As soon as Sam left, anxiety once again kicked into high gear. Unable to sleep, Marley tossed and turned until the sun peeked through the blinds. Before long, her alarm went off.

It was finally time. Months of waiting, now reduced to minutes. She climbed out of bed. Holding her phone with shaky hands, she waited for the text notification that results had been posted. She logged into her portal, which took forever to load. When it finally did, she scrolled down until she saw it...

Her name.

Boldly displayed.

As a passing lawyer.

"I passed!" Marley screamed, leaping up. "I passed, I passed!"

She slunk back down and sobbed—this time, tears of joy— as months of pent-up worry, stress, and anxiety poured out.

She grabbed her phone and texted Sam.

> I PASSED!

No more than twenty seconds later, her door burst wide open, and Sam came tearing in.

"Aaaaahhhhhhhh!" he screamed as if he were Braveheart leading a charge. She didn't even have time to be startled when he grabbed her in a bear hug and lifted her.

"You fucking passed!" he screamed, jumping up and down. "You did it! You passed!"

Marley laughed out loud as Sam lowered her, cupping her face as he smashed his lips into hers. He gave her a long, passionate, no-holds-barred kiss.

"I'm a lawyer, Sam," she whispered, tears streaming down her face as she gazed up at him. "My dreams have come true. I'm a lawyer."

"You're a lawyer," Sam said, his tears matching hers. He threw his head back and yelled, "You're a fucking lawyer!"

"I'm a fucking lawyer!" Marley yelled back at him. "I can sue the shit out of anyone now. Quick—do something I can sue you for!"

"How 'bout this?"

He threw Marley over his shoulder and headed to the bedroom.

"Wait," Marely said, arms dangling as she hung upside down. "How did you get here so fast?"

"I've been waiting outside in my car since five this morning."

He lay her down on the bed, hovering over her. "I wanted to be the first one to hug you, either way."

Marley was blown away, although she shouldn't have been. It was so Sam.

"I've never had sex with a lawyer before," he said in between kisses, his voice husky with desire.

"I guess you'd better change that."

And so, he did. Twice.

Afterward, as they both tried to catch their breath, the endorphins took over.

"I need to text people, but I can't feel my legs."

Sam hopped up and retrieved her phone just as it rang. It was Gabriel. Instead of bursting with her news, she held her breath, hoping his was good, too.

"Sooo?" he asked. The sing-songy tone of his voice hinted it was.

"You go first," she said.

He chuckled, probably sensing from her tone she, too, had passed. "On the count of three, let's say it together."

"One, two, three..."

"I PASSED!" they yelled in unison.

They celebrated their good news, talking a mile a minute and promising to rejoice in person soon. After they hung up, she called home.

"Mama," she whispered into the phone. A sob caught in her throat, remembering her dear, boundary-less mom standing in the kitchen last time, her face filled with hope before it flooded with despair. "*I passed.*"

Her mom let out a blood-curdling scream. "She passed!" she yelled to Marley's dad. "She passed! Our daughter's a lawyer!"

Her dad picked up the other line, his booming laugh filling her ears.

"Way to go, kiddo!" he exclaimed. "You make us both so proud. Whoever would've guessed our daughter would become a lawyer!"

"We've always been so amazed by you," her mom said. "Our shining star."

Marley broke into sobs hearing that from her parents. Perhaps if she'd heard it more, she wouldn't have set the bar so high for her own measurement of success. But none of that mattered now. She'd made them proud, as she had herself.

After she finished texting others, Sam wrapped the down comforter around Marley and snuggled her.

"Don't you have to be in court today?" she asked.

"I took the day off," Sam said. "To be here for you, one way or another."

"That's so sweet."

Relief, joy, and the previous night's sleeplessness got the best of her. Her eyelids drooped. As she drifted off to sleep, she murmured, "I love you, Sam."

"Love you too, sweetheart," he said, kissing her forehead. "Does this mean we're officially back to being a couple?"

"I dunno," Marley teased. "You'll have to win my heart first."

"I've had seven years of practice. I'm just getting started."

Marley giggled and gave him a hug.

"Sleep now, my pretty little lawyer."

And so she did, deeper than she had in months, a huge smile on her face.

Just like a passing lawyer would.

Marley awakened hours later to an empty bed and the distinct scent of pizza wafting in from the kitchen. She checked her phone—it was six in the evening.

She padded to the kitchen, where soft jazz filtered through the room, aglow in candlelight. Sam wrapped his arms around her waist.

"Hey, sleepy little lawyer. It's raining to beat the band, so I thought we'd enjoy our celebratory dinner here."

There was nothing she wanted more than to spend a cozy Friday night with her beautiful boy. They sat on the counter facing each other. Sam poured wine and raised a toast.

"To you, Marley, for achieving your life's goal. And for the criminal justice system, who just gained an excellent lawyer."

Marley opened the pizza box to find the message *Marley Maguire, Esquire* written in parm. She stared in awe. It was the first time seeing the title after her name, a goal she'd had for as long as she could remember. It may have been written in grated cheese, but it was finally real.

Charlotte

CHARLOTTE CALLED FOR BLINKY EACH DAY BEFORE AND after work, hoping he was back. She wasn't sure how long it took Animal Control to do their thing but hoped the man would fulfill his promise to return him to her house. As two weeks turned into three, Charlotte began to lose faith. Until, one day, the same utility van pulled up as she was refilling Blinky's bowl.

"Where's my cat?" she blurted out as the man climbed the steps to her porch, no Blinky in sight.

"With his owner."

"What owner? He's a stray," Charlotte retorted.

"Not according to his microchip. He's registered to a man, a neighbor, not far from here. About two blocks that way," he said, pointing down the street.

Charlotte was flabbergasted to learn her mangy friend had been owned by someone. The person couldn't have cared too much about him, the way the cat once lurked around the neighborhood in search of food, unkempt and unhealthy.

"Anyway, just wanted to let you know he's home. I just dropped him off with the owner. He thought the cat had died."

Shock succumbed to fury. How could the owner have written off his cat so easily?

"I told the owner you took care of him," he said as he turned to leave. "He wanted me to thank you."

She wasn't sure how to feel about Blinky being reunited with his owner. On one hand, it made her happy to know he had a home and an owner, who she hoped would love and care for him now that he'd reincarnated. On the other hand, she was vastly disappointed she wouldn't be caring for him anymore—that he wouldn't be there to talk to. She'd grown accustomed to his captive audience as she broke down the events of her day, unknowingly providing answers to her questions with his various cat looks. Which, if she were honest, were merely varying degrees of disinterest. The same way people regarded her, but somehow much cuter coming from him.

After the man left, Charlotte went to remove The Cat Formerly Known as Blinky's bowls, but something stopped her. She should leave them there in case he returned. She continued to fill his bowls with food and water each day, along with hope.

Bella

BIG NEWS ROCKED THE HALLOWED HALLS OF BELVEDERE High. Robbie and Sophie had officially broken up. Robbie Gentry was a free agent.

Another rumor began to swirl—he'd broken up with Sophie to date Bella. Most likely started by cast members who'd witnessed their onstage kisses leading up to the show, which were *fire* (according to Hanna).

Robbie finally put truth to the week-long rumors as he sat with Bella at Serendipity Cafe, where they'd met under the pretense of celebrating the show's success. He confirmed that he'd officially ended things with Sophie.

"How'd she take it?" Bella asked.

"As you'd expect Sophie to take it. She threw a major hissy fit and the next day slid into one of my friend's DMs. Apparently, they're going out this weekend."

Bella was relieved to hear Sophie was moving on, which would make it easier for her to slide into Robbie's DMs—and his life.

"This has been fun hanging out after rehearsal, but I'd love to make it real," Robbie said as he slid his hand across the table and linked his fingers with hers. "Go out with me Saturday night?"

Bella was thrilled to finally make their secret crush official. She'd never been so confident that a guy liked her—really liked her. Nothing could stop her now from finally snagging her leading man.

Marley

THE DAY AFTER THE BAR EXAM RESULTS, MARLEY SAT ON the beach, hugging her knees as she gazed at the glorious sunset. It had been unseasonably warm for April, until the setting sun ushered in a chilly breeze.

Earlier that day, she'd decided it was time to come clean.

No more hiding, no more lying.

She thought she'd be nervous as she knocked on Wells's door, but experience had taught her honesty was more liberating than controversy avoidance.

"I so appreciate the opportunity you've given me," she'd told Wells after she settled into the chair across from his desk. "But I haven't been honest with you. What you saw outside The Clink that night was me kissing my boyfriend. Sam Adams, the man I'm destined to marry."

Wells gave her a half-smile. "I kinda figured."

"You did?"

"Not at first, but I caught on. I just appreciate you keeping it on the down low."

"We actually cut ties for the sake of the case," she corrected.

He looked surprised. "Wow, that's dedication. And integrity."

She sighed. "But I can't do it anymore. For that reason, I'm resigning."

Wells nodded. "I understand. I hate to see you go, but I get it. A job should never be so important it's worth losing someone you love over. I learned the hard way." His voice trailed off. "Anyway, congrats on the bar. You're already an excellent lawyer."

That meant a lot coming from him. "Thanks for understanding. It's possibly the most embarrassing, unprofessional thing I've ever had to do—quit a job for love."

"It's actually the most well-intentioned resignation I've received," Wells said, shaking her hand. "You got a good guy there, Marley, and he's lucky to have you. Thanks for being honest."

Sam was tied up in court all day, so she couldn't celebrate with him. Instead, she took her newfound freedom to the place that made her heart happiest. Cape May.

Her phone vibrated from inside her hoodie. Sam had texted.

Her phone bleated the Rocky theme.

"Are you serious?" Sam sounded optimistically cautious.

"Yes. It was liberating, finally speaking the truth. I loved working for the prosecution, but there are other things I'd rather do."

"Like what?" Sam asked, his voice hushed.

"Like have you on top of me, gazing at me with those eyes of yours. Kissing me like I'm the most desirable woman on the planet. Making love to you. Waking up tangled in sheets. Sitting on the kitchen island eating parm-messaged pizza. That's how I want to spend my days, not sparring with you from across a courtroom. I never wanna deal with another conflict again. This was the only way."

"Wow." Sam sighed. "I can't believe you did that for us. What will you do now?"

"I dunno. Move to Cape May. Grow tulips. Sit here on Sunset Beach watching sunsets." She chuckled. "No worries. Now that I've passed, I know something will eventually work out."

Charlotte

IT WAS TEN O'CLOCK ON MONDAY MORNING WHEN Charlotte heard the partners coming down the hall for their weekly meeting. They passed her doorway in their fancy suits and polished shoes, laughing about some inside joke only partners share. Among them, Rhys and Declan—the newly minted partners of Jervis Mahoney.

Once again, Charlotte blinked back tears. Once again, she wished she had someone to talk to. From the depths of her soul came a guttural cry.

I can't do this anymore.

For the first time since she'd been with the firm, Charlotte contemplated leaving. Immediately. Walking out on them with no notice, leaving them high and dry on all the cases she'd been juggling.

But Charlotte wasn't impulsive like that. She needed a plan.

Her phone lit up with an incoming call from someone she least expected: Jake. It was as if he could sense her turmoil. Despite her complicated feelings over not hearing from him for so long, she answered.

"Charlotte," he said softly. "It's me, your long-lost buddy. I'm home."

At least he owned up to being long lost. Not so sure about the buddy part, though.

"Hello."

Guard up, she felt shy, vulnerable. Exposed. She hoped her tone wasn't too harsh or, conversely, didn't convey just how much she'd missed him after apparently assigning a greater level of importance to their friendship than he obviously had.

"How's things?" he asked.

"Things have been better, honestly," she said, then added, "I was passed over for partner."

"Oh, Charlotte," Jake exhaled, sounding as sad as she felt. "I know how important that was to you. Did they say why?"

"I'm not sure. I kinda blacked out when I heard the way it was going. I guess I'm still not social enough for their liking."

"But you've come a long way."

"Not far enough, apparently."

Jake's tone turned inquisitive. "How many female partners do they have at the firm?"

"Zero. I would have been the first."

He was quiet for a moment. "You could possibly have a lawsuit on your hands if you believe their refusal to advance you is part of a pattern. Not that I'm telling you anything you don't already know."

Charlotte knew it was a possibility but wouldn't let herself fully believe it. Instead, she'd decided it was her, not them. She just wasn't partner material.

"Maybe making partner at this firm isn't meant to happen because something bigger awaits you."

She hadn't thought about that but would give it consideration.

"So what's your deal?" she blurted out, tired of discussing her misfortune.

"What's my—oh," he said. "Yeah."

He sighed. She waited.

"I met someone."

"Yeah, I saw that on your Instagram. But what does that have to do with me?"

Jake was silent.

"What? You can't maintain a friendship with a woman if you're dating someone?" she demanded. Bold of her, maybe, but she was tired of being the nice guy.

"We're not dating anymore, just friends now. It was a short-lived thing after realizing we weren't right for each other."

Charlotte couldn't help the relief that flooded her, even though she didn't have any right to feel that way.

"This trip allowed me to ponder some things. I think what it all boils down to is that I'm terrified of commitment."

"I wasn't asking you to commit to *me*," Charlotte said.

"I know that, and it was nothing you did. Actually..."

"Actually, what?"

He sighed again. "If I'm completely honest, I was starting to feel conflicted about us. That night you cooked dinner, and we played in the snow... I dunno. It did something to me, made me feel some kinda way. Like I was home or something. Like I could see myself doing that every night. I've never felt like that, and it scared me."

Charlotte didn't know what to say. She knew he'd looked at her differently that night, and if she was honest with *herself*, it scared her as well. She wasn't ready to turn their friendship into something else. She'd never been with a man before, either as a girlfriend or a sexual partner, and the thought terrified her. Not that she didn't want to—there were times Jake's physical attractiveness and kindness allowed her thoughts to venture to intimate areas. She was just brutally inexperienced and painfully shy, not knowing how on earth she'd behave in either role. Above all, she didn't want anything to jeopardize what she and Jake did have.

"I don't want to lose your friendship," he said, mirroring her feelings.

"Then don't." It made perfect sense to Charlotte, but she'd never experienced a friendship like this. All she knew was she loved being Jake's friend, and she'd grown weary of not asking for exactly what she wanted.

He chuckled. "Okay, then. If it's simple to you, it's simple to me."

"Good. Friends again?"

"Always friends. I'm just—sorry I was being weird."

"That's what friends are for," she said. "To be there for each other, through thick and thin. Right?"

"Absolutely. So, now that we got that sorted out, how about dinner next Saturday?"

"Only if it's pizza."

"Nothing else would do," Jake said, laughing. "Friend."

Bella

BELLA WAS EXCITED FOR HER FIRST REAL DATE WITH Robbie. His car was in the shop, so they planned to meet at Serendipity Café since it was within walking distance of both their houses. From there, they'd walk to the movie theater down the street.

From the sidewalk outside, she saw Robbie sitting at their usual table in the front window. But he wasn't alone. He was with Sophie.

Bella's heart sank to her feet. Why was Sophie here? Did she know about their date? Was she here to confront Bella— or beg Robbie to take her back? There was only one way to find out.

Bella pushed her way through the heavy glass door and headed toward the table. Sophie saw her first.

"Bella," she said, a fake smile on her face. "What brings you here?"

Bella shot a glance at Robbie, hoping he'd tell Sophie they were meeting for a date and to get lost. But he just sat there, staring at his lap.

I guess I'm on my own with this.

She took a deep breath and prepared for the battle royale. "I'm here for our date. Robbie asked me out after you guys broke up." She took a deep breath and channeled her inner-Lisa. "May I ask what *you're* doing here?"

Sophie's witch cackle overrode Bella's question. "Broke up?" she screeched, her tinny tone incredulous. "Who said we broke up?"

"Um, everyone?"

"Robbie? Would you say we're broken up?"

He continued to sit there, avoiding her gaze.

"Robbie?" Bella prompted, hoping he'd provide clarification.

There must have been something super interesting going on in that lap of his because he refused to look up.

"If you guys didn't break up, why all the drama these past few weeks?" Bella demanded. "Why does everyone think you're now dating Brandon?"

"Robbie and I had a fight, Isabella. That's all it was. I didn't break up with him, and he didn't break up with me. Right, Robbie?"

Robbie continued looking down. "Right."

His response cut Bella to the core. "You son of a bitch," she hissed.

She wasn't going to stick around to hear the details, find out whether she'd been mistaken about their breakup, or if they'd just gotten back together. Instead, she tore out of the coffee shop and burst into the cool evening air, tears streaming down her face.

"Bella, wait—"

Robbie had followed her outside, but she wasn't going to compromise her dignity by listening to him. She was so over this whole thing. She kept walking.

"Bella, please let me explain," he said, trying to reach for her arm.

"What's there to explain?" Sophie, who'd followed them out, asked. "I'm sorry if you misinterpreted things, but Robbie and I haven't broken up. Right, Robbie?"

Sophie didn't wait for him to answer. "Listen, Bella, I know you've been crushing on him for a long time. But you need to get over it. He's mine, and you just have to deal with it."

Sophie linked her arm with Robbie's and turned him back toward the coffee shop.

"No!" Bella roared, causing the traitors to stop in their tracks. "You listen to *me*, you *fucking bitch*." Her voice sounded gravelly as if she'd been possessed by the devil.

Both Robbie and Sophie spun back around and stared at her in disbelief, bordering on horror. Probably because Bella never spoke back to people, and certainly not in that tone.

Bring it on, Beelzebub.

"You are the worst person I have ever known," Bella growled, pointing her finger at Sophie. "You are a shitty friend and an even shittier person. You are selfish, mean-spirited, narcissistic, and you have no heart. And you, you spineless weasel"—she turned to Robbie—"you're just as disgusting as she is. Worse, if that's even possible. Karma's gonna get you both, and I hope you rot in hell."

And then Bella thrust her two middle fingers—one for Sophie and one for Robbie—into the air. "Fuck off, assholes!"

She turned and banged into the chest of a man.

No, not a man. A younger guy. And not just any guy.

Jordan.

"Whoa," he said, grabbing her elbows and steadying her.

Mortified, she burst into tears. How long had he been there? How much of her tirade had he witnessed?

"Hey, hey," Jordan said, pulling her into a hug. "It's okay. I got you."

Sophie and Robbie had disappeared. Hopefully, the earth had opened up and sucked them into hell.

"Come on, let's get you a drink," Jordan said, guiding her into the coffee shop.

Bella was overtaken by sobs. She was hurt, humiliated. She wished for the comfort of home, where she could hide her face and her imploded self-esteem, but luck was clearly not on her side that day.

Jordan went to order drinks for them as Bella tried to get a hold of herself. By the time he returned to the table, she was wiping the last of her tears away.

"You good?" he asked as he set her drink in front of her and settled into a chair.

Bella nodded, heaving one last shaky sigh. "I'm so sorry about that," she said, finally finding her words.

Jordan raised his eyebrows. "Sorry about what?"

Bella figured he was trying to act like he hadn't witnessed her sidewalk tirade. But she knew he had and didn't want him thinking she flipped off random strangers for fun.

"My public meltdown," she explained, "and letting my freak flag fly. I have good reason."

"I bet you do," he said, giving her a smile. "You don't have to share it with me if you don't feel comfortable, but I'm all ears if you need to vent."

She was relieved for the out he gave her. She didn't feel comfortable telling Jordan about the whole humiliating ordeal, so she remained quiet.

He changed the subject, asking how Eli was doing. Bella told him he was still stretching, hoping to be tall enough for the Viper this year.

"One way or another, we're getting that kid on the ride this summer," Jordan said. Bella's heart filled with joy. Not only for her brother, but for the conspiratorial tone of Jordan's promise—the *we're* part.

Stop it. Dude has a girlfriend. Who, speak of the devil, just walked in. Could this day get any better?

"I'll be on my way," Bella said, raising her drink as she got up to leave. "Thanks for this."

"My pleasure," he said. "Just keep letting that freak flag fly, girl."

Charlotte

A MAN WAS SITTING ON CHARLOTTE'S PORCH STEP AS SHE returned home one evening. Her heart raced as she crept closer, wondering if she should turn and run or call the police. When she was half a block away, he called out to her.

"Charlotte Drysdale?"

He stood. Even from a distance, she could see he was elderly, frail.

"Who wants to know?"

"I'm Gus Rourke," the man said. "Your friendly neighbor. I'm not here to harm you."

Charlotte stared at him with suspicion, wishing she had her Mace.

"I brought your friend," he said, pointing behind him, where a decidedly healthier-looking cat ate from the bowl on her porch.

"Blinky!" Charlotte cried out.

The cat stopped eating and turned to look at Charlotte.

Gus chuckled. "Blinky, is it? Seems appropriate, given the state of his eye. Must have gotten into a fight."

"Yes, he was badly injured. I'd been feeding him for weeks before I found him bleeding and in pain. A friend of a friend, who's a vet, stitched him up good."

"I appreciate all you've done to keep him healthy and safe."

"Someone had to," she said accusatorily. "Why haven't you

been caring for him?"

"He ran away a year ago. Got out when I wasn't looking. I spent weeks searching for him. When I couldn't find him, I figured he'd probably expended all nine of his lives."

Charlotte accepted his explanation but wondered how he could joke about it. She felt bad for the little creature, having to fend for himself. She wondered why the cat chose not to return home but came to her instead.

"I was in the hospital for several weeks after that," Gus explained, as if reading her mind. "I guess he got tired of waiting for me. When the man from Animal Control told me a nice lady had been taking care of him, I let Rex out—that's the name I'd given him—and followed him here."

Rex. She had to admit, he did look like a Rex. Charlotte was happy to see the little guy. She'd been missing him something fierce.

"I don't know how you feel about him now, but I'm wondering whether you'd want to keep him?"

If the man had tackled her and put her in a headlock, she would have been less surprised.

"Why?" was her first response.

The man sighed. "Got cancer. Just a couple months left, that's it. I love this guy, but it's hard enough to care for myself, let alone him. It seems he's done well in your care."

"Are you certain?" she asked, afraid to get her hopes up but not wanting to take away the man's friend.

"Yes. I really did think he was a goner, and I'd gotten used to living by myself again. I'm thrilled to see he survived all those months, thanks to you. I just wanna know that when I'm gone, he has a good home. Seems you'd be the perfect person to care for him."

Charlotte rested her hand on the man's arm. "I don't want to take him from you, but I'd be honored to give him a home."

"Good." Gus nodded. "It's settled then. I just hope you

enjoy his company like I once did. He kept a lonely guy pretty happy."

"He's kept me pretty happy, too," Charlotte said, then had an idea. "I can bring him over to you for visits if you'd like."

Gus smiled. "I'd like that indeed."

After plugging his address into her phone, Charlotte reached out to hug the man before she realized what she was doing. Initiating a hug? What had become of her?

"I can't tell you how happy this makes me, to know you'd trust me with your dear friend," she said. "He's become an important part of my life. I promise to love him like you do."

"That's exactly what I hoped to hear," Gus said, smiling at her. "It means a lot to me that he has someone to love him when I'm gone. You've been a good friend to him. And now, to me as well."

May

Marley

STILL WITHOUT A JOB, MARLEY JUMPED AT HER PARENTS' offer of a celebratory trip to Ireland. She was anxious for the opportunity to travel to their homeland, where they'd stay with family who still lived there. Once word got out, other family members joined them—proving, once again, where one Maguire went, so went them all.

Returning from the Irish countryside ten days later, Marley felt refreshed and ready to renew her job search. The extended family let out a collective swoon as they descended the airport escalator to baggage claim, where a waiting Sam stood, tulips in hand, expectant smile on his face.

Her aunt grabbed her arm. "Oh Lordy, is he here to propose?"

"Airport proposals are so romantic!" her cousin said.

"Sorry to disappoint y'all. He's not here to propose," Marley said. Too minor league for Sam.

She dashed down the remaining steps and leaped into his arms, wrapping her legs around his hips as he spun her around.

"When are you gonna make it official?" an aunt cried out.

"Yeah, Sam—put a ring on it, already!"

"I'm trying," Sam said, grinning. "But first, I have to win her heart."

Marley hugged everyone goodbye and followed Sam to the car. After putting her bag in the back, he leaned her up against the door.

"Welcome home, my love. Happy to have my lucky charm back," he said, kissing her with such yearning she was ready to tear off his clothes right there in the Orange Level of the Terminal A parking garage.

She thought they were heading home until Sam passed the exit.

"Where are we going?" she asked.

"I'm taking you to dinner," he said.

He guided the Jeep into Society Hill, to a block where brick rowhomes were interspersed with boutique-style offices, no restaurant in sight. By the grin on his face, she knew he was up to something.

"What's going on?"

"You'll see." He pulled a scarf from his pocket as he helped her from the car. "But first, I have to blindfold you."

This was it. They were getting engaged.

Marley's heart raced as Sam led her down the sidewalk before removing the blindfold. She blinked and looked straight ahead, seeing nothing but the tree-lined street. A cool breeze gusted, scattering cherry blossoms onto the cobblestoned sidewalk.

He gently lifted her chin. "See it?"

She wasn't sure what he wanted her to see other than a wooden sign swaying above them. Looking closely, she saw it was ornately inscribed with the words *Maguire Adams*.

"That's you and me, baby," Sam whispered. "Our new law firm."

"*What?*" Marley exclaimed, spinning to face him.

"It's been in the works for the past few months," he said. "*Whew*, I can't believe I kept the secret that long."

Marley was flabbergasted. Blown away. She could barely speak.

"What, when, how, who..." Marley's words tumbled out, scrambling to gather facts.

"I can answer that," Sam said, his eyes twinkling. "What? You and me, partners—not only in the bedroom but in the boardroom. Equals, as always. When? I've been working on it since you hinted you may be leaving the DA's office. How? With help from an unlikely source—my dad. He helped me find this building, hired contractors to retrofit it for our needs, and worked out the legalities."

"You've got to be kidding."

Sam laughed. "Who would've seen that coming? He stopped by court one day and saw me do my *thang*. Took me out for drinks afterward and told me I was born to practice criminal law, not corporate. I told him about our ethics quandary. It was actually his idea."

"Why not just bring us into his firm and create a criminal justice division?"

"He thought it'd be best if we learned from the ground up—went through the growing pains of building a client base. Handling cases the way we want to, not how some partner with no experience in criminal law tells us to."

"That makes sense."

Surprise gave way to joy as the reality of Sam's news hit her.

"He also said he can't see me with a better partner—in business or life. He thinks you bring out the best in me."

It made her heart soar to hear that. It was all she wanted, for them to bring out the best in each other.

He handed her a key. "Let's check it out."

Inside, she was greeted by the pleasant smell of new carpeting, furniture, and fresh paint. There were two doors off the foyer, one on either side.

He opened one door and led her into a reception area with a desk and filing cabinets, beyond which a hallway led to four rooms. Sam showed her the conference room first, its walls lined with shelves boasting law books and an oversized oak table in the center surrounded by six overstuffed leather chairs on wheels.

"Here," he said, pulling out a chair.

Marley sat, and he spun her around. "Wee!" she said, giggling.

"Watch this." He plunked himself into another chair and made crab legs as he careened to one side, then the other. "When we're bored, we can have races. Starting...now!"

Sam thrust his chair backward, and Marley followed suit. They raced to the doorway, the wheels of their chairs banging into one another.

"Rubbin's racin'!" Sam exclaimed.

"That's you, *Days of Thunder*."

"Checkered flag. I win!"

"How's that a win?" Marley asked. "I'm an inch closer to the door. Victory is mine!"

"No, victory is mine," Sam said, pulling her up from her chair and onto his lap as he wrapped his arms around her. "I get to work with you every day of my life."

Marley lowered her lips to his, the grin on her face almost making it impossible to kiss him properly.

"I love you so much, Sam Adams."

"I love you too much, Marley Maguire."

She was overcome with emotion. Relief that her job search days were over. Happiness that they'd once again be working together. Awe, that Sam had pulled this off without her knowing.

"What happens to our firm name when we get married?" she asked.

"Who said we're getting married?" he teased, but the look on his face as he gazed up at her—vulnerable, hopeful—answered his own question.

"Up to you," he finally said. "You can keep your maiden name, take mine, or hyphenate them. Your choice."

He tapped her behind and motioned for her to stand up. "Lemme show you the rest."

When he led her into another room, he declared, "This, my lady, is your office."

Marley gasped. It was beautiful. A contemporary glass-top desk and gray leather chair were situated in the center of the room, on the other side of which sat beautifully appointed armchairs in turquoise and gray. Afternoon sunlight poured through a large window, which was flanked by towering palms. A shelf with books and décor lined one of the walls.

"It's gorgeous." Marley sighed.

"You can thank my mom," Sam said. "It was all her doing. Wait 'til you see this."

Sam led her to the hallway and opened a small arched door, revealing a tiny room nestled beneath the staircase. It was brightly decorated with a child-size table and chairs, a shelf filled with colorful books, and a bin of toys.

"Sam, this office is perfect for you!" Marley said.

"Very funny. Another one of Mom's ideas—a playroom for clients who don't have childcare, so they can bring their kids to appointments."

"My God, you guys thought of everything."

Sam wrapped his arms around her. "And it can be where our own kids play while we're working."

The thought made Marley tingle.

Next, he showed her his office, decorated in a similar pattern as hers, only with navy accents instead of turquoise.

"What's this?" Marley crossed the room to a small sign stuck in the pot of a palm—a picture of a coffee cup with a red line through it and the words *Do Not Feed the Palms*.

"That's for you, Folgers," Sam said.

She cracked up, remembering her caffeine-driven act of rebellion back at their old firm.

"Whaddya say?" Sam said as they ended the tour back in the reception area. "Wanna work here with me?"

"Yes."

"Then you'll need to fill out an application." Sam leaned up against the desk.

She stepped in close, kissing him deeply. "How's this for an application?"

"Job's yours," he whispered. "We have dinner reservations at Buddakan at six, but there's one thing I'd like to do first."

Marley could tell by the gleam in his eye what he was thinking. He spun her around and laid her back on the desk, nuzzling her neck. A few fumbles and a groan or two later, their office was officially christened.

On their way out, Marley paused in the foyer. "What's this door for?"

"An upstairs apartment. Owned by us, currently occupied by tenants on a month-to-month basis. We can keep it that way for income. Or, when you're ready, it can be our new home. Easiest commute in the city."

Marley's head was swimming, trying to piece it all together. In one hour, her entire life had changed. She normally wasn't a risk-taker, and worries started to bubble to the surface.

"What about clients?" she asked as they walked to the restaurant, the logistics of owning a law firm dawning on her.

"Dad's already sent us some cases, and he'll help us seek more referrals," Sam said. "Tomorrow, we begin a marketing campaign—ads in local papers, magazines, and a couple billboards."

Oh God. Was she ready for this? Her question must've shown on her face.

"We've been ready since we started our internship, Mar. Remember how we planned it all out during our lunches? Now's the time to take a leap."

Easy for Sam, a compulsive leap-taker, to say. He always jumped first, *then* figured out the landing, while Marley stood on the edge, planning for every possible crash scenario.

Something told her it could work. Her conservative approach to business and law would help balance his eagerness to take risks, while his ability to dive in would pull her worrying, reluctant ass into action. She knew in business, as in love, they'd make great partners.

Charlotte

J AKE ARRIVED AT CHARLOTTE'S PLACE WITH A PIZZA THE following Saturday night. It was her first time seeing him since he'd returned from his sailing trip in the Caribbean. A deep tan made his smile even brighter than usual. He set the pizza down on the small table in her foyer and enveloped her in a warm embrace, which lasted a few beats longer than she suspected was normal between friends.

"Hello, Charlotte," he said softly. "It's so good to see your smile. I've missed it."

"I've missed yours," she said, trying to calm her racing heart.

"I come bearing your favorite meal to make up for all my weirdness."

Her stomach growled at the smell of dough and sauce wafting around them.

After they ate, Jake pointed to a photo album lying on Charlotte's coffee table.

"Mind if I look?" he asked.

Jake perused the photos of her childhood tucked safely behind protective plastic. The album was her most prized possession, the only evidence of the life she'd lived up until then.

"Hey, I know that lighthouse," he said, pointing to a picture. "Cape May, right?"

"My grandmother used to take me every summer. I pretty much grew up there."

He pointed to another picture. "And the sunken ship at

Sunset Beach." He turned to Charlotte. "I can't believe we've never discussed this, but my family spent a lot of time in Cape May once we returned to the States."

Charlotte recalled Jake and his siblings had grown up overseas after the family relocated for their parents' work.

"They rent a house in Cape May for two weeks every summer now," he continued. "They're going next week."

"Why don't they just stay in your Avalon house?"

"Cape May holds a special place in their hearts. It's where my parents met and fell in love. My dad always says he and my mom have a 'Cape May kind of love.'"

"What does that mean?"

"I dunno, to tell you the truth. I think it has something to do with a love based on friendship."

"I like that."

"Random question, but is there anything you've wanted to do in Cape May but haven't?" he asked. "For me, it's climbing the lighthouse."

"You've never done that?" Charlotte asked. Not that she'd ever climbed it, but she had a good excuse. Several actually. Fear of heights. Germy railings. And tiny enclosed spaces.

"Nope. How about you?"

She thought for a moment. "I'd love to see a dolphin or a whale up close."

"Come sailing with me, then," Jake said. "Let me show you my world, where I'll be living for a year or so. I'll get you closer to the water than a cruise, and I guarantee we'll see some sea life out there."

"That's right, you still owe me that 'guaranteed dolphin sighting.'"

"Let's go to the shore next weekend. We'll sail from Avalon to Cape May, then climb the lighthouse."

If the past year had given Charlotte anything, it was a spirit for adventure. She could hardly wait.

Bella

"RISE AND SHINE, SWEET SIXTEEN!"

Bella opened a sleepy eye to find her parents and Eli standing at the foot of her bed, wearing party hats and holding a donut bearing a lit candle. She giggled at the sight of them as they sang to her.

"Thanks, guys," she said, blowing out the candle.

"What did you wish for?" Eli asked, hopping with excitement over his love of birthdays—his and others.

"Another hour of sleep." Bella flopped down on the bed.

"No can do," John said, pulling her arm. "Big plans today. Starting with—"

"IHOP!" Eli exclaimed. Her favorite breakfast joint.

Her dad wasn't kidding when he said they had big plans. After breakfast, they went to the mall, where Bella was allowed to choose any outfit she liked at Hollister.

"But what about your plans to save for my education?" she teased her mom.

"Community college doesn't cost that much since I know you want to keep living with us."

"Am I that obvious?"

"Unfortunately, yes," Lisa said, a gleam in her eye. "I was hoping you'd go far away."

Bella hugged her. "I promise not to go too far. Who else am I gonna fight with?"

The next stop was an unfamiliar strip mall.

"What's here?" Bella asked. She craned her neck to see out the window, her eyes finally resting on the nondescript building with big blue letters.

PennDOT DRIVER'S LICENSE CENTER
Bella squealed. "Are you serious?"

"Who's up for a junior license?" John asked, but she'd already bolted from the car and joined the queue wrapped around the building.

"Darn, I thought if we came later in the day, we'd miss the crowds," Lisa lamented as the fam joined her in line. Bella didn't care. She'd stand there all week if she had to.

"Wait. Don't I need all kinds of forms to do this?" Bella asked, recalling the list they'd learned about in Driver's Ed.

"Got it all right here." Her mom pulled a file from her tote bag. "Including the medical forms, which I had your doc fill out during your last physical."

"You did?" Bella asked. "I had no idea."

"Moms work in mysterious ways." She handed the file to Bella. "Everything you need is in here."

Bella suddenly felt blessed having her as a mother. She gave her a hug. "Thanks, Mom. I love you so much."

An hour later, after having passed the knowledge test with flying colors, Bella posed for a photo holding her prized junior driver's license.

"Here you go," John said, tossing her the keys. "Induction by fire."

"Heaven help us," Eli said softly as he buckled himself into his car seat. "Eight's too young to die."

The family laughed as Bella expertly steered the minivan out of the parking lot, thanks to the hours of practice John had given her over the past few months.

Back at home, Bella gave her parents a hug after they emerged from the car.

"Thank you so much," she said. "This has been one of the best days of my life."

Eli giggled.

"What's so funny?" Bella asked.

Lisa shot Eli a warning glance. Thinking nothing of it, Bella opened the front door and—

"Surprise!"

Before her stood Hanna, Zachary, and a crowd of her closest friends from the musical, theater camp, and other clubs she belonged to. The room was adorned in pink and gold sweet sixteen décor.

"You guys!" she cried out, tears cascading down her face.

Surrounded by her real friends, the party sealed the deal that this was the best day of her life. Hours later, after everyone left, Bella stood at the kitchen island with her parents as they grazed on leftover snacks. Her mom asked if her special day was everything she'd hoped it would be.

"And then some," she said. "I can't tell you guys how much I appreciate everything you did for me today. How much I appreciate *you*. More than you'll ever know."

"Oh, we know," Lisa said.

Behind her, she heard Eli grunting. She turned to see him struggling to get the lid off his Lego box. "A little help?"

"Here, give it," she said, taking the box from him. She popped open the lid, but there were no Legos inside—just a white box adorned with a small silver apple.

"NO. WAY!" Bella screamed, jumping up and down until she burst into tears. Her parents enveloped her in a hug, and Eli joined in.

"Happy birthday, Bells," he said. "Did you like my surprise?"

"I love it!" She wiped the tears away and opened the box to find a brand-new, rose-gold iPhone. The latest model, the one she'd been saving for all year.

"Now you can put your money toward a car," Lisa said.

Bella had never felt as lucky as she did just then to have the family she had. The one she wouldn't trade for all the sweet freedom in the world.

Charlotte

CHARLOTTE GRIPPED THE RAILING FOR DEAR LIFE AS THE sailboat tacked to the left. The whipping wind and sea spray cooled her skin, which had been baking in the late May sun. They shifted direction again, and Charlotte fell to the other side, laughing as she lost her grip.

She was terrified yet euphoric. She'd never experienced something so exhilarating. She was loving Jake's world. It was freeing to be off the coast, away from the soil where all her anxiety was rooted. A pod of dolphins swam so close she could almost touch them.

"This is amazing," she said as they slowed, drifted over rolling waves, relieved to still see land despite enjoying the freedom of not being on it. The best of both worlds.

"Maybe it doesn't seem so crazy now, this goal of mine," he said.

"I never thought it was crazy," Charlotte said, touching his arm. "I think it's really cool."

"You'd be the only one." He smiled and patted her hand. "Are you ready to lose a race to the top of the lighthouse?"

"Are you ready to eat my dust?"

"We'll see about that."

An hour later, Charlotte and Jake began their ascent of the staircase to the top of the lighthouse. With every step, Charlotte picked up her pace.

"Are we racing?"

"Of course!" she said, laughing as she began jogging up the steps. "I'll wait for you at the top!"

Jake grabbed her arm and brushed past her. "I'll be the one waiting!"

They continued jockeying for position as the stairwell narrowed, laughing all the way. They finally made it to the top, declaring a tie just as the sun was about to set. Charlotte, recalling she was terrified of heights, clung to Jake with one hand and the railing with the other as they walked the narrow deck around the perimeter of the lighthouse, stopping to face the bay as the sun slid below the horizon.

"Good night, sun," she said as it took its final dive. "Good night, Cape May."

She looked up to see Jake gazing at her.

"What are you doing on June 22?" he asked abruptly.

The date sounded familiar for some reason. "I don't know. Why? What's June 22?"

"My brother's wedding. I'd be honored if you'd be my plus-one."

A cool breeze gusted and Charlotte shivered with excitement. She'd never been someone's plus-one. But then she remembered why the date was familiar. It was the weekend of the firm's annual retreat, and Tom Jervis had scheduled a dinner party that night. Her attendance was required, even though a large part of her didn't want to go. In fact, she'd been considering whether she even wanted to continue working for the firm. The urge she'd felt to leave that one day hadn't fully left her, yet she vacillated—one day ready to go, the next wanting to stay and make another bid for partner. She wasn't one to give up easily.

Tom Jervis had arranged for his grandson to be her dinner party date but only to ensure an even number of guests—there was no way her boss thought his grandson would be interested in her. Nor did she want to be fixed up with anyone. But she couldn't let Tom Jervis down.

"I'm sorry. I can't," she said and explained about the dinner party.

"Come to the rehearsal dinner with me on Friday night, then."

Charlotte said she didn't think rehearsal dinner dates were a thing. He assured her it was his right, as best man, to determine if it was a thing or not. As far as she knew, Tom Jervis hadn't planned anything for that night.

"Okay, then. I'll be your date for the rehearsal dinner. Just—no monkey business."

"I make no promises."

Hearing that, Charlotte nearly fell off the top of the Cape May Lighthouse.

June

Marley

SIX WEEKS HAD PASSED SINCE MAGUIRE ADAMS OPENED its doors. In that time, they'd built a healthy client list and were swamped with court appearances. After several interviews, they finally settled on a receptionist—Marley's cousin, former seventh-grade spelling bee champ, Kelly. Marley couldn't think of a better person for the job. The person who, unwittingly, inspired her to become a lawyer.

With hard-working Kelly at the administrative helm, Marley and Sam felt confident they could take time off before Kate's wedding for a short romantic getaway. They left on Wednesday morning, giving them two nights alone before wedding duties called.

Marley had hoped this getaway would be when Sam made it official. She'd even gotten her nails done for the standard ring photo, just in case. Whenever Sam suggested a beach walk or a cozy dinner, she was convinced it was happening but had been disappointed each time. She'd been putting him off for so long, but she was finally ready.

One day, out for a beach walk, Sam stopped.

"There's something I have to tell you," he said.

She turned to find him kneeling. Her heartbeat quickened.

"My shoelace is untied."

He gave her a teasing smile as if he knew she was waiting for it.

Sam got her a few more times like that. By the time rehearsal day rolled around, Marley knew it wasn't happening that weekend. He wouldn't dare upstage their friends' wedding.

At the rehearsal, they chatted with Delaney and Dalton and Cleo and Nigel, catching up.

"We've got big news," Delaney announced. "We just purchased a house in Cape May."

"Are you officially moving home?" Marley asked.

"For now, its just a summer home. But maybe next year," Dalton said, putting his arm around Delaney's waist. "To start our family."

"Start talking about it, that is," Delaney joked.

"Congrats on your house, guys," Sam said, raising a toast. "And to us all, being reunited for this special occasion."

Marley felt fortunate to have worked for Delaney's firm, even if she hadn't gotten a job offer in the end. In its place, great friendships had grown.

She recalled Rick's words about things having a way of working out, even if it doesn't seem so at the time. Everything that hadn't worked out in her life led her to exactly where she was. She wouldn't trade it for the world.

Charlotte

CHARLOTTE SAT ON A BENCH AT FERRY PARK, READING her book as the wedding party rehearsed for the ceremony on the grand lawn behind her. She was so engrossed in her story she didn't hear Jake approach.

"Hey, Char, we're done."

Two strong hands squeezed her shoulders. She put her book down and closed her eyes, amazed at how good human touch could feel. Nobody had ever given her a backrub before.

"Please keep doing that."

She leaned her head back as Jake continued to massage her shoulders, easing the tension she was feeling about the night that lay ahead. Even though she and Jake were nothing more than friends and she felt comfortable around his immediate family, she was intimidated to be meeting his extended family that night. There would be lots of them, Jake warned, but assured her they were nice.

"Hey, Charlotte," Kate called out as she and Ryan approached. Charlotte accepted Kate's hug and shook Ryan's hand, having grown accustomed to these social rituals.

"It's good to see you again. We're glad you could join us," Kate said warmly.

As comfortable as the bride and groom made her feel, Charlotte was suddenly self-conscious as they entered the tent where dinner would be served. It seemed everyone was looking at them.

"Welcome to the wide world of my extended family," Jake whispered as they approached their table. "There'll be lots of questions. And opinions. Nobody will accept the explanation we're just friends. Don't let it shake you."

They took their seats. Jake slung his arm across the back of her chair as the questions began. Charlotte thought she'd adequately prepared herself, but now, facing the firing squad, she wasn't quite sure. His family members wanted to know how she and Jake met, if this was their first date, where Charlotte was staying, and other personal questions. They didn't seem to consider any inquiry too bold or probing. Fortunately, she'd had plenty of experience schmoozing. Tom Jervis would be proud.

After the meal, Charlotte excused herself to go to the ladies' room. When she entered, she heard two women talking in the stalls.

"Surprised he would bring her," she heard one say.

"Not his usual type, that's for sure," the other chimed in.

Charlotte knew they were talking about her. She thought

about retreating and using the bathroom later, but she really had to go. She stood her ground and waited for the women to emerge.

She averted her eyes when one of the doors opened, hoping the woman emerging from the stall wouldn't see her. Charlotte was accustomed to people talking about her, even in her presence, as if her plain looks somehow made her invisible. She'd hoped tonight would be different. She didn't want to give people a reason to talk about her, she just wanted to fade comfortably into the background, but that wasn't going to happen. A handsome man bringing a plain Jane as a date was too much to let slide, apparently.

"Oh, hi Charlotte," the woman said loudly upon seeing her, an apparent warning of her presence.

The other woman emerged. Charlotte recalled from introductions they were Jake's cousins.

"Charlotte, I'm not sure what you heard, but I want to clarify."

"Yeah," said the other. "It's just that—well, we were surprised to see Jake with someone. He usually comes solo to these things."

"But when he does bring someone, she's usually—what would you say?" She looked at her cousin for backup.

"Gorgeous," Cousin One said. "No offense."

"Nice." Cousin Two gave an exasperated sigh and rolled her eyes. "What she means is—fake. Good looking, maybe, but plastic as hell."

Charlotte could feel the tears welling in her eyes. She blinked to hold them back. She wanted Jake's family to like her. Not because she wanted to be Jake's girlfriend—she knew that wasn't happening anytime soon. She simply wanted to fit in. For just one night.

They must have seen her tears because Cousin One grabbed her arm. "Oh, honey, don't cry. You may not be his usual type, but we can tell you're real."

Charlotte wiped her tears.

"It's about time that boy finds someone down to earth," a woman emerging from another stall said.

"And smart." Cousin Two added. "She's a lawyer."

"I wanted to go to law school but couldn't get in," a woman behind them claimed.

"Law school?" asked another as she washed her hands. "It's really hard to get in. My brother's girlfriend's cousin was vale-dictorian and even she couldn't get in."

"Jakey said she's the best lawyer in the city," Cousin Two said.

Not entirely accurate, but Charlotte would take it.

"It's about time Jakey found himself a smart girl," another woman piped in.

Charlotte figured she'd better set the record straight. "Jake and I are just friends."

"Sure, you are," Cousin Two said matter-of-factly as she patted Charlotte on the arm and left the bathroom.

After using the restroom, Charlotte made her way back to the tent, where people were milling about. A band had started playing. Jake was talking to a group of men and waved her over, handing her a drink.

"Everything okay?" he asked as he put his arm around her. She leaned her head against his shoulder ever so briefly. It felt nice.

"Everything's fine," she said through a tentative smile.

A slow song came on and Jake offered his hand. "May I?"

He led her to the dance floor and held her the way men do in old movies. Charlotte had danced with precisely two men in her whole life—a cousin and an uncle—both at family weddings. This was the first time she'd danced with a bona fide, unrelated man. Which also meant she didn't know how to dance. She awkwardly tried to move in time to the music.

"Relax," Jake murmured.

She tried, but she was too busy trying not to step on his feet.

"Just follow my lead," he instructed.

Charlotte wasn't sure what that meant. She'd never let someone "lead" her before—on the dance floor or otherwise. Jake must have sensed it.

"Okay, Ms. Lawyer, I know you're used to being in control, but you gotta let me do this. Just relax your muscles and go with the flow."

"I don't want to fall."

"I won't let you."

Charlotte closed her eyes, and Jake swooshed her around the dance floor, expertly missing the other couples swaying around them. Suddenly, they fell into sync.

"That's better," he said. "I'm guessing you don't go dancing too often."

"Obviously, you don't watch *Dancing with the Stars* because I won last season."

"You and Snuffleupagus?"

Charlotte stomped on Jake's foot. "Oops."

They both laughed.

"You have really cute dimples," Jake told her. "You should laugh like that more often."

"Wear contacts, laugh more. Any other suggestions?"

"Yes. Come to the wedding tomorrow."

Charlotte reminded him of her prior commitment. She wished she hadn't agreed to attend the dinner but knew she couldn't get out of it.

When the party ended, Jake and Charlotte took an Uber back to Tom Jervis's house—against her better judgment, of course. To make good on his promise she wouldn't be abducted or murdered, he accompanied her for the ride. It took some convincing and a pretty thorough Wet Ones wipe-down of the back seat, door, and armrests, but Jake was finally able to coax Charlotte into the minivan, where she sat stiffly for the entire ride.

When they arrived at her boss's house, Jake walked Charlotte to the door. She thanked him for a lovely evening.

"I appreciate you coming," Jake said. "I know it was awkward, but I definitely had a much better time with you being there. If you change your mind about tomorrow night, you know where to find me. I'll even pay for your Uber."

"That's nice, but I don't Uber."

"But you"—Jake turned and pointed at the minivan—"just...did?"

"That's because you were with me. And the driver is female, so I felt safer. Women are, statistically speaking, 895% less likely to murder someone."

"Is that a real statistic?"

"It should be," Charlotte joked.

"Okay, hold on."

Jake ran back to the Uber and spoke to the driver.

"She'll be on duty tomorrow night," he said when he returned. "I'm texting you her number. If you change your mind, just give her a ring, and she'll bring you over."

Charlotte laughed. "That's really kind of you, Jake, but I can't get out of dinner. Tom Jervis has set me up to be his grandson's date."

"Ooh, a *date* date?" he teased.

"More like babysitting."

He smiled. "Good."

"It should be a real hoot."

"Well, if it turns out to be anything less than a hoot, come join me."

Jake gave her a peck on the cheek and Charlotte watched her best friend drive away in a (hopefully) non-murderous Uber.

Bella

BELLA WAS NO LONGER THE SLEEPY TEEN WHO'D ARRIVED at the bridal suite that morning in an oversized hoodie and leggings. She'd been transformed into a beautiful princess bridesmaid. Examining herself in the mirror, she appreciated how the strapless pink dress complemented her narrow waist while turning what little boob action she had into—slightly less little boob action. Her makeup was perfectly applied, far better than Amelia's tutorials. She tucked a wayward curl back into her updo as her mom hugged her from behind.

"You look gorgeous, baby girl."

Bella instinctively pulled away but softened when she saw her mom's loving expression.

"Thanks, Mom," she said, patting her hand. "You, too."

She couldn't remember her mother ever looking so pretty— her dress, hair, and makeup were a far cry from the looks she normally sported. When not in her probation-issued uniform, she'd otherwise be found in a harried-mom-baggy-sweats-messy-bun combo that screamed, *I've given up*.

Today's tally—Lisa: 1, Bella: 1.

"You two look like sisters," Kate said as she joined them in a hug.

Bella made a face.

"Gross," Lisa said, beating her to the punch.

A tuxedo-clad Eli bounced into the room and blushed as the women fawned over him. He approached Bella, tie in hand. The fact that Eli sought her help wasn't lost on Bella—he was well-advised not to trust their middle-aged mother with anything having to do with fashion.

Bella cupped his chin in her hand. "You look handsome."

"I know," Eli said matter-of-factly. "Dad said I'd probably pick up some women tonight, but I think they'll be too heavy for me to lift."

Bella tried to stifle a laugh as the door opened, and in came the true stars of the wedding party. Her cousins, Violet and Petunia, tumbled through the room in poufs of white taffeta. They were followed by Uncle Michael, who was in charge of getting them ready so Aunt Amy could enjoy some big girl time with the bridesmaids.

"Okay, Bells, they're all yours!" Uncle Michael said, wiping his hands in jest.

It was Bella's job, as junior bridesmaid, to corral them down the aisle.

The buzz in the bridal suite grew stronger as ceremony time drew near. The adults toasted with champagne while Bella and Eli entertained their toddler cousins. When it was finally go time, the bride and her entourage boarded a trolley to Ferry Park.

Bella felt like a celebrity as the ferry-going public stepped aside to let the wedding party pass, gushing over the bride and bridesmaids. She wished she had her new phone so she could capture this on Snapchat, but Lisa had confiscated it for the ceremony as if it were contraband. For once, though, she understood.

The guests were already seated. Uncle Ryan and his groomsmen lined up beside the wedding arch. Bella struggled to wrangle her toddler cousins as they awaited their turn for the processional. They'd been well-behaved to this point but were starting to get rammy. Eli kept them entertained by making silly faces.

Then it was go-time for Eli. Bella gave him a high five and wished him luck, knowing he wouldn't need it. Eli was the most confident person she knew. After this year, she was more impressed by him than she was jealous. He liked people, and they liked him. He didn't seem to struggle with the social angst Bella often experienced. She wondered if he'd retain his confidence as he entered puberty or whether things would change for him. She hoped his innate belief in himself would remain unshaken during the tumultuous years of middle school that lay ahead, waiting to gobble him up and spit him out. If not? Bully, meet big sister Bella.

Eli made it to the end of the aisle, and then it was Bella's turn. She ushered the girls ahead of her so they could have their moment, hoping they'd make it to the end of the aisle without mishap. The audience chuckled with delight as they toddled along, dropping petals as instructed until Petunia squatted to play in the grass and Violet ran after a seagull.

Too preoccupied with getting herself and the girls down the aisle, Bella couldn't take in the whole wedding scene until she took her place in the line of bridesmaids. It was then Eli caught her eye. Standing at the far end of the groomsmen, he leaned forward and gazed at her, eyes as big as dinner plates, looking as if he'd just seen a ghost. Bella followed his stare to the line of groomsmen and saw what was haunting him.

The ghost of Ride Guy Past. Aka Jordan.

In a tux, standing next to Uncle Jake.

Marley

AS MARLEY WALKED DOWN THE AISLE, BRIDESMAID BOUquet clutched in her hands, she couldn't take her eyes off Sam. He looked beyond handsome in the navy tux Ryan had chosen for the groomsmen. Their eyes met, and Sam's glazed over as everyone else in their surroundings seemed to disappear.

Someday, he mouthed.

Marley giggled with anticipation, hoping someday would be soon. Bar exam passed, career started, law firm thriving—there was nothing stopping them now. She was finally ready, and she could hardly wait to make it official.

Bring it, Sam.

Bella

JORDAN STOOD AMONG HER UNCLE'S GROOMSMEN AS IF he belonged there, looking hotter than the sun in his tux. Bella nearly fainted from the sheer shock of it all. What in the hell was he doing here? Was this some sort of joke? The questions tumbled from her mind, including how a guy could look so fine.

So. Damn. Fine.

But really, how in the—

Hold. Up.

She remembered that Kate had a brother who hadn't attended any of the pre-wedding festivities due to work, including the rehearsal last night. What was his name? Oh, that's right—JJ. Could Jordan be JJ, Kate's Uno-loving brother, the guy Kate was trying to set her up with? He had to be, no other explanation made sense. Jordan, aka JJ, was Kate's brother.

Make that *hot* brother. She might have to let the Uno thing slide.

Jordan stared back at her as if he, too, had seen a ghost.

When the ceremony ended, Kate and Ryan took their celebratory strut up the aisle with the wedding party in tow. Jordan waited for Bella and Eli at the end. Her little brother, who hadn't seen Jordan since before the ride blow-off but couldn't hold a grudge if someone paid him, gave him a hug.

"Are you kidding me?" Jordan cried, arms outstretched in disbelief. "How can this be?"

She wasn't sure what to say or do. Should she:

A. Act enthusiastic to see him;
B. Pretend she didn't care; or
C. Whip out a pack of Uno.

She chose D. Stand there like a tongue-tied doofus.

"This is so weird. I had no idea—who do you know here? Well, duh, obviously Ryan, but—" Jordan tripped over his words, trying to figure out Bella and Eli's relationship to the wedding couple.

"Ryan's our uncle," Bella said, cutting to the chase.

"Kate's my sister," Jordan said. "This is so weird. Unbelievable, really."

Weird didn't begin to describe it.

"Well, as far as I can figure," analyst Eli began with his theory of relativity, "this makes you my uncle-in-law. If there is such a thing. What are the odds? I have to do some calculations." Eli thought for a moment, then snapped his fingers. "Jordan's the guy who wasn't here last night, Bell. Or at the New Year's Eve party. They called him JJ."

"Thanks, Captain Obvious."

Eli turned to Jordan. "I assume your middle name begins with J?"

"That's right, Captain," he said. "Jordan James Ross."

"Well, I'm glad you're here, Jordan James Ross. Bella told me you weren't at the Viper that night because your grandpa died. I'm sorry."

"Appreciate that, little man. And *I'm* sorry. I was looking forward to your ride and having ice cream with you guys. I promise I'll get you on it this summer,"—he paused to look at

Bella, "and whatever else happens."

"I'll definitely take you up on that," Eli said. "I've done more good deeds since then, so maybe I can ride twice."

Jordan laughed as he ruffled Eli's hair. "I think we can make that happen."

"I'm gonna ask Mom and Dad if we can go to the boardwalk tomorrow."

"Maybe Jordan's not available," Bella said.

"Oh, I'm available," Jordan said almost before she'd finished her sentence.

Eli went off in search of their parents. Jordan gazed at her as he ran his hand through his hair. She recognized the look—it was the one he gave her the night he walked them home on the boardwalk. At the dance, as they sat on the swings and talked. At the mall, when he turned back to smile at her. And the night he pretended not to notice her meltdown on the streets of Doylestown.

Three...Four...

"I'm hoping I can have a do-over for ice cream, too," Jordan said.

"I'll get back to you on that," she teased.

But then, reality reared its ugly head, reminding her he had a girlfriend. She just hoped he hadn't brought her as his plus-one.

Bella and Eli were having fun entertaining themselves at their table. She didn't mind hanging out with him during the reception so her parents could drink their faces off and (barf, gag) have some alone time together. Jordan came over just as a slow song came on.

"Hey, pal," he said to Eli, "is it okay if I ask your sister to dance?"

"Only if you promise to treat her right," he said.

Jordan smiled. "I promise. Bella, would you like to dance?"

"Sure." She tried to sound casual like getting asked to dance was No Big Deal. Like dancing with hot guys in tuxes was something she did every day.

"Enjoy yourselves, kids," Eli called out as Jordan led her to the dance floor.

They began swaying awkwardly to the music just as she had a gross thought.

"Wait, this marriage doesn't make us, like, cousins or anything, does it?"

"No." Jordan smiled at her. "I've been thinking about it. No relation. Which makes me happy."

Don't get too comfy. Dude has a girlfriend.

"How's Amelia?" she asked, to keep herself from melting into him. Not that she really cared to know, but it was a good reminder not to enjoy this dance too much. Even if his arms tightening around her waist could have been taken as a sign he, too, was enjoying it.

"I wouldn't know," he said, giving her a shy half-smile. "We broke up."

Bella felt the heavens open up, and the angels began singing. The excitement coursing through her veins nearly caused her to burst like a firework.

"It happened right after I saw you at the coffee shop. That time you ripped those kids a new one."

So he *had* witnessed it.

"I heard everything you said, and it was all I could do to keep from cheering you on. Right down to the two-gun salute. I'm guessing whatever they did, they deserved it."

"Pretty much."

"Amelia and I broke up a couple days later," he said. "She just wasn't for me, especially when someone else had been capturing my full attention every time I ran into her."

"Wow..." Bella didn't know what else to say. Thank God he was holding on so tight or she would have puddled at his feet.

"While I enjoyed your epic meltdown, I was devastated to see you cry like that. I wanted to do whatever I could to put that beautiful smile back on your face. I never felt like that with Amelia, probably because she had so much other stuff on her face."

Bella giggled, guessing he was referencing her hours-long makeup routine.

"So..." he began, his tone shy. "Please tell me you don't have a boyfriend."

"I don't." For the first time in forever, Bella wasn't ashamed to admit it. "That night was supposed to be a first date, but destiny had different plans."

"I'm glad," he said, not shifting his gaze. He pulled her in closer and whispered in her ear. "Eli's a great kid and all, but I was really looking forward to hanging out with you."

This time, she allowed herself to melt into him, and he did the same with her. She hoped the song would never end. When it did, they parted wistfully, but he held her hand as they returned to the table where they were greeted by Kate and Ryan.

"I'm happy to see you guys hitting it off. I had a feeling you would," Kate said, beaming.

Jordan smiled at his sister and held up Bella's hand. "Kate, this is the girl I was telling you about."

Bella shot him a look. He'd told his sister about her?

"Wait," Kate said, holding up her hand. "Bella's the girl?" To say she seemed shocked was an understatement of epic proportions. "The reason you didn't want me fixing you up for the wedding?"

"She's the one."

Kate's mouth gaped as she clasped a hand to her forehead. "I can't believe this. It's happening again."

"What's...going on?" Bella asked, blue eyes wide as her gaze shifted between the two.

"Kate's been trying to fix me up with 'Ryan's niece' for the wedding," he said, giving air quotes for emphasis. "She wanted me to have a date for the wedding. Someone who wasn't Amelia."

"Never liked her," Kate said, shaking her head.

"She told me I'd really like 'Ryan's niece,' but I told her I'd already met someone I was interested in. Someone I kept running into and hoped I'd run into again so I could ask her to the wedding."

Kate gazed at Jordan. "Neither one of us ever mentioned her name, I guess, or maybe we would have realized..." Kate closed her eyes and shivered. "My God, I have chills."

"It was you, Bella," Jordan said. "You're the girl I've been looking for. I just didn't know you were the one my sister wanted me to meet."

Bella was speechless. For the first time ever, her crush liked her back—without her having to be someone she wasn't or accept less than she deserved. She just had to be herself. She might have only been sixteen, but it didn't take her long to realize he was more than a plus-one. He was *the* one.

"And so, destiny strikes again," Kate sighed, "Pure serendipity."

Charlotte

CHARLOTTE DRYSDALE WAS NOT HAVING A HOOT. She'd spent most of her boss's dinner party sitting by herself while her blind date, a drunken Cal Jervis, flirted with their waitress. Cal was crass and full of himself, nothing like his grandfather, and she was immediately turned off upon meeting him. He looked right through her when they were introduced, and while Charlotte was accustomed to that response from males, she didn't feel it was warranted that night. Because she knew she looked good.

Earlier that day, Tom's wife, Tiffany, had asked Charlotte what she was planning on wearing. When Charlotte showed her the skirt and cardigan she'd selected, Tiffany suggested it wasn't appropriate for meeting one of Philly's most eligible bachelors. Charlotte wondered why, if he was so "eligible," he was free on a Saturday night. Not that she knew much about the social calendars of bachelors. Nonetheless, she agreed to a trip to Stone Harbor's 96th Street shopping district to select a more "appropriate" dinner party outfit.

Tiffany had a much different definition of appropriate, it turned out, selecting a sleek black cocktail dress for Charlotte to try, which she immediately refused. With off-shoulder sleeves, a plunging neckline, and a hem that fell at mid-thigh, it looked more like a slutty Halloween costume than a cocktail dress. It took some convincing, but Charlotte finally gave in and tried it on.

She was shocked at what she saw. She looked—pretty. The dress fit her perfectly and was far less revealing on her body than it appeared on the hanger.

"Oh my God, doll," Tiffany exhaled when she emerged from the dressing room. "You have the cutest figure. Who knew, under all that fabric? Those legs should be seen and not hidden by long-ass skirts."

The dress was nothing she'd ever pick out for herself, considering the high price tag and, conversely, the diminutive amount of fabric that went along with it. Tiffany found a pair of black strappy sandals to go with the dress, as well as a small clutch purse. Charlotte, who only ever wore flats, had to walk around the shop a few times to see if she was able to navigate on stilts without breaking a limb. Which was proving more challenging without glasses after Tiffany convinced her that she "had" to wear her contacts or, in Tiffany's words, she may as well "just wear a trash bag."

Charlotte had no choice but to go along with Tiffany's advice, an obvious expert in this area. She didn't want Tom's wife reporting back to him that she was being difficult.

"I have to make sure this purse holds all the items I need," Charlotte said.

She carefully placed her phone, tissues, hand sanitizer, and travel Wet Ones in the clutch. Including her glasses, which she'd insist on taking with her in case something flew into her eye during dinner. She was relieved it all fit.

Back in the dressing room, Charlotte couldn't take her eyes off the mirror.

"I look like an actual woman," she commented to herself.

"I know, right?" Tiff must have heard her as she cracked her gum from outside the dressing room curtain. "You're stunning, girl. You should definitely go shopping with me more often."

Charlotte would have to give that serious consideration.

After shopping, Tiffany took her to a salon—yes, despite swearing she'd never patronize another one. This time, the stylist swept Charlotte's mousy brown hair into a French twist. She swiveled the chair so Charlotte could observe the finished product. She almost didn't recognize the sophisticated woman looking back at her in the mirror.

But now, sitting at the table while her co-workers mingled with one another, Charlotte wondered why she had wasted all that time and Tiffany's money trying to look so nice. She was more appropriately dressed for a wedding than a—

Hmm. What an unfortunate time for an intestinal flare-up!

That was exactly what she told the Jervises as she apologized for leaving the party early. Slipping outside, Charlotte dialed the number Jake had gotten from their Uber last night. Within minutes, the familiar female driver pulled up, waiting patiently as Charlotte wiped down the back seat.

Her heart pounded as she stepped from the minivan and walked toward the big tent on the lawn of Ferry Park. She'd never done anything so bold as to show up at a place—a wedding, much less—unannounced. She hesitated for a moment, not sure if she should go in.

No, she shouldn't. She turned to let the driver know she'd changed her mind, but the minivan was gone. She'd have to call the driver back.

Or—she could take a chance. Follow her New Year's resolution to try new things.

Charlotte took a deep breath, trusting that Jake wanted her here or he wouldn't have asked. As she approached, a group of guys passed her. One whistled, and another turned.

"Hey, cutie!" he called to her.

Charlotte was certain the guy must have been talking to someone else, but no one else was around. The catcall was for her. Another first.

"Thanks," Charlotte replied, surprised at the confidence in her own voice. "Have a great night!"

"You too, sweetheart!" The guy blew her a kiss and turned to join his friends.

That gave Charlotte a much-needed boost of confidence. She was ready to experience a social outing as the New and Improved Charlotte before the Cinderella effect turned her back into a dowdy lawyer at midnight.

"Hello, beautiful," a man said as she made her way along the walkway. "Here for the Ross/Brady wedding?"

He gestured to the tent where the reception was in full swing. She looked around for Jake, but finding the bar first, she ordered a drink. As she drained the glass, someone bumped into her from behind.

"Oh, I'm sorry," a familiar voice said as he grabbed her waist to steady her.

"It will cost you," she joked, turning to find Jake.

"Wait, *Charlotte?*" He sounded as shocked as she'd felt when she saw herself in the mirror earlier. "What the *what?*"

Charlotte enjoyed seeing the look of surprise flash across Jake's face. The last time he saw her, she was draped in yards of fabric, but tonight's outfit hugged her slim waist and accentuated body parts even Charlotte was surprised to discover.

"Good God, you're *stunning!*"

It was the same word Tiffany had used in the shop. Charlotte had no idea dressing up could make you feel so good.

"Not that you weren't already," Jake quickly backtracked. "I mean, I always thought you were pretty, under all that clothing and those glasses and all, but—" He bit his lip and took a step back. "*Wow.*"

Charlotte smiled. Coming here had definitely been the right choice.

"Hey, remember the attorney I was telling you about? He's here, and I'd love to introduce you."

Jake began to lead her to a table when they were stopped by Jake's nephew.

"Uncle Jakey!" the boy cried out. "Wait 'til you hear this!"

Eli told them how he was going to ride his favorite roller coaster for the first time tomorrow. Charlotte asked how he knew it was his favorite if he'd never been on it before.

"You make a good point, ma'am," he said as if he were an eighty-year-old man trapped in an eight-year-old's body. "I believe it's the things we can't have that we want the most."

Charlotte was taken aback by his insightful answer. She knew exactly what he meant.

"I've dreamed of going on this ride for *years,*" he said, thrusting out his hands, emphasizing the word as if it were decades. "I was never tall enough. I had high hopes for last summer but was still a smidge too short."

Charlotte tried to hide a smile. This kid was definitely an old soul, something she knew a lot about. She'd often been told she, too, was an old soul—not belonging to her generation while oddly possessing wisdom beyond her years. Only not as cute.

"Have you grown this year?" she inquired.

"I think so."

"What if you're still a smidge too short?"

"That kid over there? The one dancing with my sister? He works for the ride, and he promised if I did three good deeds last summer, I could go on it. So I did three good deeds, and I was supposed to go on Labor Day, but his grandpa died that day and he didn't show up. But now he's friends with my sister, and well, they promised I could do it tomorrow."

"Whoa, kiddo," Jake laughed as he rubbed Eli's shoulder, "take a breath!"

Charlotte was sincerely impressed with Eli's work ethic. "That's great. It's so important to work hard for your dreams and make them come true."

Even as she said it, Charlotte began doubting her own dreams. Was making partner really what she wanted? Jake's questions from so long ago reverberated in her mind. *You make partner, buy your mansion, and...then what?*

A roller coaster goal was different. You do it, and you've achieved your dream, the end result. Was being partner in a firm she hated really the end result she sought?

She couldn't think on it too long because Eli held up his hand, and Charlotte found herself reciprocating her first high five ever, despite that she viewed the gesture as garish and germ-ridden. Especially from someone who, at his age, already qualified as a walking petri dish. But she was armed and ready with hand sanitizer, vowing to use it as soon as she walked away.

"I like you, Eli," she told him.

"I like you too, Miss Charlotte," the boy said as he skipped off.

Jake led her to a table and introduced her to Bob Stevens, a thin man with gray hair, wire-rimmed glasses, and a firm handshake. Laugh lines surrounded kind brown eyes, and there was an ease about him, a confidence that was neither boastful nor rude. Charlotte liked him instantly, finding him easy to talk to, especially when they discussed their areas of practice. She told him about her work and asked questions about his. Jake wandered off at one point, but Charlotte's attention was fully focused on Bob and his business. She was fascinated to learn he handled a wide variety of legal matters for his local clients. Everything from adoptions to estates, bankruptcy to business start-ups. Nothing was off limits. It sounded interesting, fun—a new challenge every day.

Try something new.

What impressed Charlotte the most about Bob Stevens were testimonials from others at the table—neighbors and friends who, at one point or another, were also clients. They spoke of Bob's personalized service and treatment of his clients as if they were family. They told stories of him going the extra mile, making house calls for legal matters, and kayaking through coastal flood waters to rescue clients' pets after storms. They clearly loved their country lawyer for his treatment of their legal and personal matters and his ability to obtain successful results in their cases.

Charlotte couldn't tear herself away from the conversation. Bob seemed to possess a love for his work she lacked for her own. She was envious of the joy he displayed as his clients regaled him with praise.

Jake returned with a drink for Charlotte. Realizing she was monopolizing the attorney's time, she thanked him for the conversation.

"It's been my pleasure. Jake, thanks for letting me chew your friend's ear off."

"I loved it!" Charlotte said. "Besides, I've got another to spare."

Everyone laughed, taking her by surprise. She felt a camaraderie she'd never felt before, with a group of random people she'd just met. She wished her clients were more like this. More like family.

"I'm glad you two met," Jake told Bob. "She's gunning for partnership at a big Philly firm, but I thought she'd enjoy hearing about your practice, see how the other legal half lives."

Bob's eyes lit up. "I'm retiring soon, Charlotte. I'm looking for someone to come on board and eventually take over. We should talk. Maybe you'd be interested in learning more about my practice. I have a feeling you and I would work well together."

Charlotte didn't know it at the time, but it would become the comment that changed the entire trajectory of her career.

And her life.

Bella

JORDAN AND BELLA DUCKED AWAY FROM THE RECEPTION for a beach walk. They were deep in conversation when she realized they'd been gone for over an hour, which meant Lisa had likely issued an APB. Any minute now, the Coast Guard would arrive.

To keep her mom's search and rescue mission at bay, Bella shot her a text to let her know where she was. Lisa texted right back and told her to enjoy the walk. She was likely into a few glasses of wine by now, which meant Bella could probably demand the car keys and a wad of cash to gamble away in Atlantic City, and her mom would go along with it. But she'd rather be right where she was, sitting in a lifeguard stand with Jordan.

She sent her mom another text, complete with heart-eye emojis, and told her she loved her.

Neither she nor Jordan were in any rush to return to the reception. It was a perfect night, and the sky was ablaze with stars.

"There's one!" Bella exclaimed as she pointed to a flash of light shooting across the night sky. Her first shooting star.

She turned to see if Jordan saw it too, but he was looking at her instead.

Five.

And there, in that lifeguard stand, Jordan James Ross gave Isabella Ann Baxter her first kiss. This one, real.

Charlotte

AFTER THE WEDDING RECEPTION, JAKE ASKED CHARLOTTE if she wanted to Uber back to Tom Jervis's house or whether she wanted to "crash," as he put it, in his room. Charlotte was concerned about being on the road after bars closed when "the drunks," as she put it, were out. Therefore, the idea of Uber-ing was stricken for cause—especially since her earlier driver was most likely off her shift by then.

She wasn't willing to "crash" in other ways, either. She was enjoying their friendship and wasn't interested in crossing lines tonight—if that's what Jake had in mind. As luck would have it, there was a last-minute cancellation, and Charlotte was able to get her own room.

The following morning, they met up in the hotel lobby to join Jake's family for brunch at the Blue Pig. As they headed toward the restaurant, Charlotte stopped in her tracks.

"I don't know if I should go in," she said, chewing her lip. "They're going to think we...you know."

"They won't think anything," Jake said, taking her hand. "I'll set the record straight. But you are joining me for brunch, I insist. It's the best, with farm-to-table ingredients grown here on the Cape."

Of course, this meant she had to do the walk of shame into the hotel restaurant, still wearing clothing from the night before.

As soon as they entered, Jake grabbed a spoon and tapped it on a glass. The room suddenly became quiet, and everyone turned toward them.

"I'd like to make an announcement. Charlotte and I are just friends, for any of those who notice she's still wearing her dress from last night. She stayed in her own room but didn't bring a change of clothing. She doesn't want you to think we slept together in the same room. Although I must admit to trying—"

Charlotte felt her cheeks burst into flames. That wasn't the case at all. Jake had been a perfect gentleman, walking her to her room and giving her only a hug and a kiss on the cheek. Good thing, too, since she didn't have her Mace.

She gave him a playful slap on the arm now. Slug, more like it.

"I have my standards, after all," she said.

His family members erupted in laughter. Charlotte was proud of herself for not wallowing in mortification, using humor to deflect her embarrassment. She'd have to remember that life hack going forward.

Lisa waved Jake and Charlotte to the empty seats at their table.

"Is today still the big day?" Jake asked as he squeezed Eli's shoulders.

"Yeah, we're going to the boardwalk right after brunch. You have to come with us, Uncle Jake. You too, Aunt Charlotte!"

Jake gave her a smile. Charlotte melted at her new title.

"What do you say, Aunt Char?" Jake asked. "Feel like going on a roller coaster today?"

She waved dismissively. "I don't do roller coasters."

"I didn't either until today," Eli said. "But I promise—if I can do it, you can do it too. If you're scared, you can ride with me!"

Like the Grinch on Christmas Day, Charlotte's heart grew two sizes bigger. She decided right then and there that if an eight-year-old was willing to try something new, she could too.

After brunch, she made her way to the lobby to check out, where she ran into Bob Stevens.

"Hey, Charlotte," he said, seeming delighted to see her. "I got to thinking after our talk last night. If you're in town tomorrow, we could meet up at my office, and I can show you around—give you a taste of what I do."

Charlotte considered his offer. It wouldn't hurt to check out her options.

Try something new.

"I'm serious about retiring soon," he continued. "I don't know how you feel about being a small-town lawyer or if your heart is set on the big-city firm, but the invitation's open. No pressure. If you're not interested in a future partnership, at least let me treat you to lunch."

Charlotte smiled. "You know, Bob, I think I may just take you up on that."

She shook his hand, and they made plans to meet up the next day.

For once, she didn't even think to reach for sanitizer.

One look at the tarnished handlebar of the old wooden roller coaster, and Charlotte instinctively backed up, right into Jake. She regretted agreeing to this ride.

She was relieved when Eli decided to ride with his sister, happy not to sit next to a little germ factory. But the handlebar was another story. Without having to ask, Jake held out his hand. Charlotte retrieved Wet Ones from her purse and handed one over.

"I may agree with you on the germ thing when it comes to ride handles," he said, valiantly scrubbing.

It dawned on her then that she hadn't worried about handle germs on Jake's sailboat. Or at the top of the lighthouse. But a roller coaster...much different story.

"And..." Charlotte pointed to the seat.

Without a word, Jake wiped the seat down, too. She waited for Jake to make fun of her, to say something derogatory about her obsession with germs. But he didn't.

"That better?" he asked, without a hint of annoyance in his voice. Charlotte nodded. In all her life, she couldn't recall anyone so accommodating when she displayed her foibles.

The longer they sat there waiting for the ride to start, the more Charlotte rued her decision.

"I'm going to vomit," she announced.

"You're gonna be fine," he assured her as he put his arm around her.

"How do you know?"

"Because I'm here, and you wouldn't dare throw up on a friend."

She smiled, wondering if she'd ever get used to hearing that word.

"Tell you what," he said. "If you puke, you buy me lunch on the boards before you head home. If you don't, it's my treat."

"Deal." A good incentive not to vomit, considering how expensive boardwalk food was.

"What time are you heading home today?" he asked.

She'd forgotten to tell Jake her big news. "I'm not, actually. I have a hot lunch date with Bob Stevens tomorrow."

"Char, that's great!"

"But wait—the plot thickens."

"There's a plot?"

"Of course. It's impetuous, I know, but I called Tom Jervis and told him I'm taking a personal day tomorrow. I'm staying at Congress Hall tonight so I can see Bob's firm in action."

"How will you get home?"

"My Uber driver, Ellen."

Charlotte had contacted the driver to make sure she was available for a Philly run when she was done with Bob, agreeing to pay a handsome tip. Maybe five dollars this time.

"So, we went from not taking Uber to having a personal driver in less than seventy-two hours? Impressive."

"I know, right?" Charlotte giggled, sounding more like a teenager than a respectable attorney. "I don't know what happened, but since knowing you, I'm seeing things in a new light. Different opportunities, things I hadn't considered before."

But inside, Charlotte knew exactly what had happened. She'd made a friend, something that hadn't happened since she was a child. A friend who helped her look beyond her blinders to see the world around her. A world rich with opportunity.

"Me, too." Jake looked at her for a moment before his face broke into a smile. "I'm happy for you, Char."

"Do high-five with me, friend," Charlotte said, suddenly losing all self-control. She held up her palm, and Jake tapped it lightly.

"Now a low five," he said.

"Don't press your luck."

Charlotte turned to face forward, hands wrapped around the handlebar. As the roller coaster jolted to a start and the car slowly ascended the hill, Charlotte's feelings of dread dissipated into a feeling of excitement. Possibility.

On this side of the hill (which, by the way, went on forever) was all she knew. A job with people she couldn't stand. Living to work, not working to live. Dwelling in a gritty city. Alone.

On the other side lay the great unknown. A possible new career path and geographical relocation. Although she couldn't see what lay ahead, she knew with a friend by her side, she could handle anything life had to offer.

They reached the pinnacle, and the car slowed before it began its descent.

Charlotte said a silent goodbye to the old, threw her hands in the air, and welcomed the new. Squealing for the first time in her life.

Charlotte Drysdale was finally happy to be right where she was.

Eli and his best friend Bella

ON SUNDAY, JUNE 23, AT PRECISELY 1:07 PM EASTERN Standard Time, Elijah "Eli" Baxter, age eight years, nine months, three weeks and six days, climbed into the front row seat of the Viper with his big sister and best friend, Bella, by his side.

One day shy of his ninth birthday, he conquered the Almighty Viper, soaring to the highest heights of his young life.

And he didn't even throw up.

<h1 style="text-align:center">Epilogue</h1>

THE LATE SEPTEMBER BREEZE HINTED OF APPLES AND pumpkin spice as Marley, Delaney, Kate, and Cleo made their way to the beach. Summer was on pause before fall ushered in the cooler weather, giving the couples one last glorious weekend together at Delaney and Dalton's new shore house in Cape May. The women would be spending that Friday on the beach while the guys golfed. Sam was tied up with a court appearance in Philly, but he'd be down later that night.

Once they were settled into their beach chairs, Delaney passed around White Claws and offered a toast. "I'm thankful for your friendship and a shore house for us to gather as our families grow. What are y'all thankful for?"

"That you were all a part of our big day," Kate jumped in.

"No more studying!" Marley exclaimed.

Cleo nodded, pensive for a moment. "For Gus, my friend. Somehow still hanging on, but I know he won't be with me much longer. I've loved every second of our friendship. He's been a guardian angel to me, the one who convinced me to give some guy a chance. That guy being Nigel."

They made another toast. "To Gus."

Plentiful sunshine and a cool sea breeze had lured fellow beachgoers to enjoy the waning summer. The women spent the day catching up. Before long, Sam texted Marley to say he was on his way and would be there in an hour.

"Perfect timing," Kate said. "Ryan just texted to say they finished golfing."

"We should order pizza and hang out here until dark," Marley suggested. It was one of their favorite things to do for happy hour—cocktails and pizza on the beach as the sun set.

"Count me in," Cleo said.

"It's a plan," Delaney agreed.

Marley closed her eyes, soaking up summer's last rays. She took a deep breath of salt air, relishing the warm sun and cool sea breezes swirling around her.

"Excuse me."

Marley opened her eyes to find a man standing before them, holding his phone.

"Would you ladies mind taking a video for me? I'm about to propose to my girlfriend, but our videographer couldn't make it."

"Oh my God, yes!" Delaney exclaimed as she sat straight up and took the man's phone.

Kate clapped. "Wee! I love proposals!"

"Where is she now?" Marley asked.

He pointed to a woman standing at the water's edge. "I'm gonna talk to her first, so turn on the video at any point. Just make sure you capture it."

"We're on it!" Delaney giggled.

They followed him, keeping enough distance until he dropped to his knee.

Marley exhaled. "So romantic!"

As they made their way closer, the man began singing.

I wished upon a star above and found a Cape May kind of love.

His voice was perfect, like a professional singer. It wasn't until the third line that Marley realized it was the song Sam had been singing on and off for the past year.

"Sam loves this song," she said to Kate. "I wish he was here to witness this!"

Suddenly, the prospective bride began singing, too. A man

with a metal detector joined in, followed by a woman walking a dog. Others popped up from beach chairs, all singing.

And now, all walking toward them.

Soft summer breezes, sky so blue; something old and something new.

Delaney turned the phone on Marley.

"What's happening?" she whispered to Kate, whose eyes welled with tears.

"Turn around."

Marley turned to see a path outlined in tulip petals and flickering candles leading to her. Sauntering toward her in the middle of it all was Sam. She gasped as the singing crowd around her grew, closing in on them.

"Surprise," he said, grinning.

"What—"

"Shh," he said, placing his finger on her lips. "I have something to say."

Marley giggled, looking down at his shoelaces, remembering his earlier jokes.

"This one's for real," he said, sounding more nervous than ever.

Marley's heart pounded with anticipation. Passion. Pizzazz.

"I've been waiting a long time for this, Marley." He took a breath and blinked back tears. "Since the moment I met you, I knew you were it. You make me whole. You bring out the best in me, even at my worst. You're everything to me. Like the song says, you're a summer breeze, a salty kiss, a boardwalk stroll, a heart of bliss. It's time we took this loyal friendship, joyful humor, and burning passion of ours to the next level."

Tears streamed down Marley's face as she followed Sam's gaze. A banner plane flew over the waves with the words *Marry Me Marley* flapping in the wind.

Sam went down on one knee and held open a ring box. Inside, a sparkling diamond.

"Marley May Maguire, will you make me the happiest man on this planet and finally, *finally,* let me marry the hell out of you?"

"Yes!" Marley whispered through her tears. "A thousand times, yes!"

The crowd erupted in cheers. Marley sank to her knees and hugged Sam as they broke into sobs—hugging, kissing, and hugging some more. Their friends gathered around them. Someone popped a bottle of champagne and passed out glasses.

"Were you guys all in on this?" Marley asked, simultaneously laughing and crying.

"Of course," Kate said, then gestured behind her. "So were they."

Sam and Marley's co-mingled family members emerged from the beach path, cheering and high-fiving one another. Like one big happily blended family. Marley laughed through her tears as their families enveloped them with hugs.

"These guys were in on it too." Delaney pointed to the fake proposal couple and the rest of the singing crowd. "Actors from Cape May Stage."

"The whole purpose for this weekend getaway was to witness true love at its finest," Cleo said, hugging her. "I'm such a believer now."

"We weren't golfing today," Ryan admitted. "We were helping our man here capture the heart of the woman he loves. About damn time."

"Consider me captured," Marley said, still in awe over the magnificent, Sam-style production.

After more revelry, Sam took Marley's hand and addressed the group. "Thanks for all your help, folks, but I'd love some time alone with my bride now."

Bride. Over the course of seven years, they'd gone from classmates, to friends, to secret admirers. From partners in love, to partners in law. And now, bride and groom.

The crowd dispersed as he led her back up the tulip-lined path to a blanket adorned with flickering candles. On it, a box of pizza. Marley opened the lid to find the words *At Last* drawn with parmesan cheese.

"You're the love of my life," Marley said, pulling him in for a kiss.

They sat on the blanket, sipping champagne as the sun set behind them. Before them, a glimpse into their future played out as families posed for beach portraits, little kids scrambled into lifeguard stands to see how far they could jump, and couples young and old held hands as they strolled along the shore.

Another banner plane approached. The sounds of cheers came from down the beach.

"Aww, another proposal!"

Sam gave her a half-smile as the plane flew closer with a banner that read, *She said YES!!*

Marley laughed out loud. "Pretty presumptuous, wouldn't you say?"

"Hopeful," he said, leaning his forehead on hers as he serenaded her.

> *We strolled along the sand, and she...said yes when I dropped on one knee;*
>
> *My quest for love is finally done. It's in Cape May we'll become one.*

"That song is beautiful. It fits us perfectly. Who wrote it?"

Sam gave her a shy smile. "I did."

Marley laughed, thinking he was joking, but he looked serious.

"I loved that Delaney and Dalton had a special song," he

explained. "I figured we needed one of our own. I wrote the lyrics and hired a musician to record it."

"You wrote that?" Marley shook her head in disbelief. "My God, Sam. You blow my mind."

"But have I won your heart?"

"Yes," she breathed. "Hate to tell you, though. You've had it all along."

"I know. But I'll still try to win it every day of our lives."

Fireworks exploded above them. Marley laughed and kissed her fiancé as bursts of pure energy and light matched the joy in her heart. Two fireworks erupted in the shape of hearts, linking as the breeze pushed them together.

The breeze, a friendship. Attraction, longing. Hearty laughter and sizzling passion. Criminal justice, pizza parm messages, reality TV dating shows. Destiny.

A Cape May kind of love.

Just like Marley and Sam.

WHEN THE CLOCK STRUCK TWELVE ON NEW YEAR'S DAY 2023, I wished it would be the year I'd finally become a published author. I never imagined that in a little over a year later, I'd have not one, but two book babies out in the world, and working on the third. I've truly found my passion.

I'd like to thank my beloved editor, Emily Ohanjanians, for her continued belief in me, my stories and characters. Your sage advice, based upon your years of professional experience and stellar writing talent, have helped give my characters believable lives, my books interesting plots, and my dreams a chance to be realized. You've given me the best advice an author could ask for, encouragement to keep going, and most of all hope for continued success. It has been my greatest joy throughout this publishing journey to have found you. Ready for the next?

Many thanks to Jessica Kleinman, my amazing cover art and book designer, who has guided me on matters well beyond just the aesthetics of my books. It has truly been a blessing working with you and I hope we continue to do so. Also, a big shout-out to Jen Boles, fellow attorney and proofreader extraordinaire, for helping to fine tune this book.

From the moment I envisioned this series, I saw my books sitting on shelves in seaside bookshops. I'd shopped these stores for years searching for a local beach read, to no avail, when I finally decided to write one myself. Between Philly and the Jersey shore, there were ten indie bookstores who decided to take a chance on this first-time author with my debut novel, *The Way to Cape May*, and for that I owe you much gratitude. To my Pennsylvania shops—Reads and Company in Phoenixville, Firefly Bookstore in Kutztown, and Narberth Bookshop in Narberth—thank you for helping to support this local author. To my Jersey indies, many thanks for not only carrying my books, but for promoting them and giving me feedback when your readers responded positively. If you're a vacationer, local or day tripper to the Jersey Cape, please help support independent bookstores by purchasing your summer reads from the following: Sun Rose Words and Music in Ocean City, Dalrymple's and Book Nook in Sea Isle City, Barrier Island Books and Art in Stone Harbor and West Cape May, Hooked on Books in Wildwood, Beachlove Cape May, and Congress Hall's Tommy's Folly Café in Cape May. You were instrumental in putting my first book in the hands of beach readers along the southern Jersey shore and getting me closer to my ultimate goal, which is to see someone reading one of my books on the beach. Thanks to you, I just may get there this summer.

To my dear Mom and Dad, I cannot thank you enough for supporting me, encouraging me, and giving me wings to fly in my writing career and beyond. You have been there for me throughout all these years, and I feel so blessed to have you both in my life. Dad, thank you for taking "Sam's" song and putting it to music. I cannot wait to share it with the world and make it Jersey-famous like the original song that served as inspiration for *The Way to Cape May*. You amaze me with your talent and the joy you find in music. And, Mom, the joy you find in all of us.

Thank you also to my two partners in crime—my daughter Julia and husband Dan—for all your love and support as I chase my wildest dreams from our dining room table. I promise to soon clear up my many drafts so we can eat here again (or not!)

Last, but certainly not least, I want to thank the readers and book club members who have become fans of my work. I hope to keep connecting with you as I continue my writing journey. Please stay in touch with me through my website, KimberlyBrighton.com, and share your stories as inspiration for future novels. Who knows—your love story could be my next book.

Go forth with love in your hearts and be kind to one another!

Reader's Guide

ABOUT THIS BOOK

BOOK CLUB QUESTIONS

About this Book

WHEN I ORIGINALLY ENVISIONED THE FIRST BOOK IN THIS series, *The Way to Cape May*, it featured six main characters trying to find (and keep) love as they traveled to a Cape May wedding. The vibe I was going for was the movie, *Love Actually*, meets the popular TV series, *This is Us*. I loved the idea of an ensemble cast with interwoven plots, providing readers with the opportunity to peel back layers of each character's past to understand their present. After consulting with beta readers, editors, and other book professionals, it was determined six point-of-view characters were too many for a novel. That meant I had to banish two of the characters, Charlotte and Bella, who resurfaced here in the second book of this series.

As I drafted plots and character arcs, I kept asking myself, "what if...?" I used a combination of real-life stories and my own wild imagination to weave a tapestry of interesting developments that would cause my characters to challenge their self-beliefs, purge themselves of destructive thought patterns, and achieve their goals through the joy of fresh perspective. Before long I saw the need to turn this one book into a series of three so I could fully explore the lives of these six characters and how they all find their happy endings at the tip of the Jersey Cape—Exit 0 of the Garden State Parkway—in quaint Cape May.

Which begs the question: is Exit 0 the end of the road...or the beginning?

This being the second book in the series, that can only mean one thing. With any luck and many steaming mugs of coffee, a third book will be coming soon to a bookstore near you.

Book Club Questions

THIS BOOK TELLS THE STORY OF THREE MAIN CHARACTERS and their journey to find what truly matters to them, as each harbors self-beliefs that hold them back from achieving their goals. Through their journeys, each character has to learn a lesson about themselves, first, before they find their place in the world, the place they long to be.

This reader's guide is meant to promote discussion and self-reflection. I hope some of these questions will inspire robust conversation among your book club members or other fellow readers, as well as helpful discovery about yourself and your relationships. There are no right or wrong answers here, just yours, and all thoughts are welcome and appreciated.

1. Each of our characters began their story with a self-belief thwarting their ability to reach their full potential. What would you say is each characters' unproductive belief, and how does it limit their chances to achieve their individual dreams and goals?

2. How do each of our characters' beliefs about themselves and/or relationships in general impact their ability to find and keep love?

3. What happens between Marley's first ill-fated attempt to pass the bar, and her second one, to give her the confidence she needs to succeed? Did any of the other characters help her, and if so, how?

4. What do you think Sam means when he refers to their relationship as "a Cape May kind of love?" What does that mean to you?

5. Why is becoming a partner in her firm so important to Charlotte? What do you think she really seeks?

6. Do you think Charlotte and Jake are better off as friends, or should they become more?

7. Why do you think Bella accepts hurtful treatment from Sophie and Robbie? What happens to cause her to ultimately reject these two bad actors in her life?

8. What caused Bella's feelings toward Eli to change throughout the book?

9. Did any of the characters' stories cause you to make discoveries about your own life?

10. What would you like to see happen for each of our characters in a sequel? (This is where I'd love to hear your feedback—please head on over to KimberlyBrighton. com to share!)

READ ON FOR
AN EXCERPT FROM

Cape May Ever After

BOOK THREE IN THE
CAPE MAY SERIES

MARLEY TRIED TO SHIELD HER EYES FROM THE BLINDING spotlights as she stepped onto the stage of the Channel Six news studio, wishing she could be anywhere but here.

"You good?" Sam asked as he squeezed her elbow.

"I'm gonna pass out," she announced, trying to steady her wobbling knees as she struggled to breathe. While she was accustomed to being center stage in a courtroom—thrived on it, actually—any other type of public appearance was terrifying. Especially knowing she was about to have millions of eyes upon her, given the expansive girth of the station's viewing area and the wild popularity of its upcoming segment, *PheelGoodPhilly*.

"Do we really have to do this?" she pleaded with Sam.

"Come on, Mar. It'll be fun. Where's your sense of adventure?"

"At home. Under the covers, where I should be."

"Good thing I got enough for both of us, then," Sam said, grinning, as he clasped a strong hand around hers.

The assistant producer directed them to join five other couples already lined up onstage. All of them here for the same reason: to compete in the first annual "Battle of the Betrothed."

It wasn't in Marley's plan to wage war against other wedding-bound couples. Nope, this was all Sam's brilliant idea. He'd entered a poetry contest without her knowledge, beating out thousands of other engaged couples after submitting the lyrics to his song, "A Cape May Kind of Love." He'd written the award-winning (in his words) song and had a local artist put it to music so he could serenade Marley in the months leading up to their engagement.

Marley had to agree with Sam—the song was, without a doubt, worthy of award. It was sweet and romantic, sweeping Marley off her feet whenever Sam sang it to her. But it belonged between the two of them, not sweeping throughout southeast Pennsylvania. While she loved the song, she didn't love the fact it had catapulted them to the semi-finals as one of six contestant couples who would be competing for the grand prize: a free wedding and a bunch of cash.

"Cold, *hard* cash," Sam emphasized when he broke the news to her earlier that morning—that he'd not only entered the contest, but they'd been selected as finalists. And she'd better hurry and dress nicely as they were about to go on live TV.

She barely had time to register what was happening when she found herself in a City Line Avenue newsroom, getting mic'd up beneath the sweltering glare of studio lights, at o'dark-thirty on a Monday.

"You got this," Sam whispered as he guided her to the end of the line.

"Okay, guys—listen up," the producer addressed the couples. "First off, I want to congratulate you on getting to this point. As a result of your winning poems, you six couples will go on to the final round of the competition. The purpose of today's broadcast is to introduce you to our viewers who, ultimately, will decide your fate. With that—"

She swept her arm in the direction of a woman perched on a director's chair. "I'm sure you're all familiar with the host of *PheelGoodPhilly*, Amanda Bacharach."

Marley wasn't. But whatever.

A chorus of greetings arose from the couples. Amanda, who was inspecting her fingernails as if she might find the body of Jimmy Hoffa under one of them, cast them a look of undeniable disinterest. Apathetic AF, as if she'd rather be swimming in shark-infested waters than there on the set with a bunch of pie-eyed contest hopefuls.

I hear ya, girl.

"We're going live in three minutes, so I want to give you a rundown of what to expect today," the producer continued. "Amanda will kick off the segment by introducing Battle of the Betrothed to our audience and explain what the contest involves. Then, we'll go down the line so you can introduce yourselves. You'll give your first names, the town you live in, and why you think you should win. After that, we'll invite our audience to tune in every week to vote for their favorite couple. Finally, we'll wrap up the segment with your first challenge. Questions? Comments?"

From her periphery, Marley saw Sam raise his hand. "Who in each couple gets to do the introductions?" he asked, wagging a finger between the two of them.

The producer shot Sam a puzzled glance. Marley followed with one of her own. Really? That was the burning question in his mind? How about: why on God's green earth are we doing this?

Besides the cash, of course.

"I guess it's between the two of you to decide," the producer said hesitatingly, then chuckled as she looked from one to the other. "Hopefully that's something you can agree upon."

She sounded polite enough, but Marley could see the veritable thought bubble over her head, questioning how good a team could they be if they were about to spar over something as trivial as introductions. And whether they should even be in this contest, let alone get married.

The producer moved down the line to adjust another contestant's mic. Marley noticed Sam's fist pumping up and down between them, signaling the onslaught of a rock-paper-scissors battle.

"What are you doing?" she whispered.

"Seeing which one of us gets to speak. On three."

On two, he thrust out a flattened palm. Without thinking, she instinctively followed with rock.

"You lose," he proclaimed smugly as he smothered her fist with his hand.

"Oh my God, Sam," she muttered. They always had a bit of a competitive thing going between them, but this was ridiculous. "Have at it. It's all yours."

"You sure?"

"If I have to open my mouth on live TV, I'm gonna puke. So, yah."

"I won't let us down, Mar," then added, "but do me a fave. If they do make you speak, please turn the other way. I gotta be in court in an hour, and all my other suits are at the drycleaners."

The producer began counting down from five, getting ready to signal to Amanda. Who, up until now, couldn't have appeared any more bored, but who sprang to life with the point of a finger.

"Hey, everyone, Amanda here with *PheelGoodPhilly*, the hap-hap-*happy* show brought to you by Channel Six news." She sang out with such enthusiasm, it was as if someone had shot Red Bull directly into her veins. "Now, if you've ever planned a wedding or are currently doing so, you know what a drain on your budget that can be." Then, under her breath, she added, "Not that I would know, having never been engaged, before. Thank you, Jason."

Uncomfortable! The couples glanced around the room, looking from one to another in an attempt to figure out who Jason was and why he was responsible for someone—most likely, himself—not putting a ring on it.

"But I *am* told by my friends who've snagged a man that between the venue, the professionals, and *all* the things, costs can really add up to rob you of the hap-hap-*happi*ness you deserve. That's why Channel Six has partnered with local wedding vendors to make you feel good, Philly, with its latest contest, 'Battle of the Betrothed.' Over the course of the next six months, these six...*lucky* couples will compete in various wedding prep challenges to win an all-expenses-paid wedding and $10,000 cash."

"Oh, yeah! Bring it," a man called out.

How crass. Marley frowned down the line to see which uncouth lowbrow was responsible for the outburst, until she realized it had come from the mouth of the man she was standing aside. Her very own groom.

Amanda took a deep breath, eyelids fluttering in an apparent attempt to keep them from rolling back into her head. Through a forced smile, she explained the rules. Each month, the contestants would compete in a wedding prep challenge, and the audience would vote for their favorite couple. Whoever received the lowest number of votes each month would be eliminated until there was only one standing.

The couples' challenge: woo the audience and get the most votes.

Marley's challenge: get eliminated in the first round.

She didn't have time for such folly. She had real work to do—not only running a law firm but planning their wedding. They'd agreed upon a two-year engagement because they'd recently opened their law firm and wanted to make sure it was well established before they shifted their focus to wedding planning. Their date was a year away, but most everything still had to be done, with the exception of two biggies: the venue and the memory makers.

Their intended venue, Congress Hall, often booked up years in advance. Upon learning it was available for their chosen date, they nabbed it right away. Same with the memory makers, who were none other than South Jersey's premiere photographer/videographer husband-and-wife team, Elle+Ross.

Also highly sought after. Marley and Sam hastily hired the couple through their online portal without meeting them in person. They didn't have to, based upon what they'd done for the wedding of their good friends, Kate and Ryan. Their work spoke for itself. To Marley, hiring the best photographer and videographer was of paramount importance, even if their cost was equivalent to the sticker price of a brand-new sportscar. Photos and videos would be the only physical manifestations of the memories they'd share with their kids and grandkids of their special day. Based upon that alone, Elle+Ross were well worth it.

That left everything else. Shopping for her dress. Compiling the guest list. Creating table décor and favors. As Amanda had said, *all* the things. It made Marley's head swim just thinking about it. But now, instead of serious wedding planning, they'd be engaging in mind-numbing nuptial nonsense for a rare chance at winning.

Then again, (light bulb!) maybe a free wedding and wads of cash weren't such bad things to shoot for. Especially given the high price tag attached to Elle+Ross's memory-making services. In fact, Marley had learned upon entering the studio that they were one of the vendors who'd be providing services to the winning couple. Free of charge.

Hmm. She'd have to give this some thought. For the first time since Sam had sprung it on her that morning, Marley felt herself entertaining his zany plan.

Amanda turned the mic on the couples. Each one introduced themselves and gave a cutesy pitch as to why they should win. One couple recited lines from their poem. Another announced they were expecting a child. A third promised to donate the cash to charity. All tough to top, but Marley had unshakeable faith in Sam, knowing he'd pull something equally spectacular out of his ass. An eloquent trial attorney who thought fast on his feet, not to mention a hopeless romantic himself, Sam would surely come up with something that would drop the mic on the others.

It was finally Sam's turn. He raked a hand through his sunkissed surfer hair, aqua eyes twinkling at Marley before he cast a sultry stare at the camera. Marley grinned expectantly, preparing to "*in yo' face*" the other contestants.

"Hi, I'm Sam," he said, his tone as smooth as melted butter. "And this is my gorgeous bride-to-be, Marley. We live in Society Hill and we're here to win this challenge because..."

Uh oh.

Sam's eyes locked with the camera lens. His mouth dropped open and he made a gurgling sound as if he'd just been stabbed in the neck. Marley had never seen this look before. Sam was a natural-born ham under normal circumstances, but this would be his first time on TV before an audience of millions. And it must've just hit him.

"Because why, Sam?" the host tittered nervously.

"Uhhh..." His unwavering, non-blinking gaze was accompanied by a swallow so hard, his Adam's apple nearly popped onto the stage. "That's why," he croaked.

The others laughed. Amanda looked amused for the first time since the airing began, while Sam looked like someone had just thrown a pie in his face.

"Well, members of the viewing audience, you heard it," she said, recovering like a pro as she turned to the camera. "Marley and Sam should win because...that's why."

She smiled, then added, "sounds like a meme waiting to happen."

"That was *so hot*, Sam," Marley teased under her breath. "*Damn*, you have a way with words."

"I froze, Mar," he whispered.

"No shit, Elsa."

"I'm sorry, I fucked up."

"Let it go," she joked.

Amanda spun to them and spoke from the side of her mouth. "You guys do know you're mic'd, right?"

"Oh, shit," Sam blurted out, then clamped his hand over his mouth. "Sorry."

The other contestants laughed again. Amanda gave a terse smile, her thought bubble reading like the drink order she'd no doubt be making when this was all over.

"So those are your six couples, ladies and gentlemen, yet I'm the one standing here without a ring. Thanks again, Jason."

Awkward! Every eye in the studio was drawn to the man behind Camera One, who'd just gone into an epic coughing fit. Presumably, Jason-the-Non-Engager himself.

"Switch to Camera Two," the producer hissed.

Amanda gave Camera Two a big, fake smile. "To give you a little preview of what to expect with this competition, we're going to head right into our first challenge. Everyone ready?"

"Yes!" the couples answered enthusiastically.

"No!" Marley screamed. To herself...or so she thought. Apparently not, as all heads in the studio swiveled toward her.

"*Heh heh*, just kidding," she muttered, making a street gesture with her hands, as if she were signaling fellow gang members. "Keepin' it real, Philly."

Dear God, strike me down now.

Amanda crossed the stage to a table where six small gift bags were neatly lined up, casting a look of appreciation at Marley—as if they were partners in crime, sisters from another mister, kindred spirits who also saw the contest for the silliness it was. Or, perhaps, merely hoping to enlist Marley's apparent gang connections to off Jason.

"Since our audience didn't get to witness your proposals, we're going to have you reenact them right here. But there's a twist. In each of these bags are three items that you're going to use during your proposal. Men, I'd like you to each come pick out a gift bag."

The men shuffled to the table, all looking nervous, with the exception of Sam. He didn't shuffle, he sauntered. With all that natural swag, boy couldn't help it. Marley caught the side eye he shot the camera, the one he considered his "sexy look"—head down, brows slightly raised, suggestive half-smile. Seemingly over his crippling stage fright, Sam was already working the audience, trying to win votes. Marley wasn't sure if she should be embarrassed by his showmanship, or proud of it.

"He's dreamy," the woman next to her whispered to Marley as she squeezed her hand.

"Please. Don't encourage him."

Nonetheless, the woman's comment pushed her over the edge with pride. Marley's own competitive tendencies clicked into place so strongly it almost made a sound.

Work it, Sam! Let's win this thing!

The men claimed their bags as Amanda continued. "Your challenge is to give a three-sentence proposal using the items in your bag. I'll give you a moment to compose your thoughts."

Sam rejoined her and opened the bag, a mixed look of concern and humor on his face.

"We're screwed," he said. "Literally." He held up a six-inch screw.

"Sam. No." She shook her head as if she were admonishing a toddler.

He gave her a lascivious grin. "Dare me?"

Oh boy. She saw the bold gleam in his eye.

He wouldn't dare. As an attorney and otherwise respectful member of modern society, Sam would know better than to break FCC rules by being brazenly suggestive on live daytime TV. Or so she hoped.

The other men worked their random objects into clunky proposal lines, but none appeared to have the same gift of gab as Sam. Filled with adrenaline over the thrill of competition and excited by the prospect of winning (with a dash of cautious trepidation thrown in for good measure), Marley said a silent prayer Sam would kill it.

He gave a mischievous grin as he went down on one knee before her.

"It would be *knife* if you would be my wife," he said as he held up the knife, smiling at her. Marley laughed out loud at the adorable look on his face, the teasing gleam in his eye.

He pulled out the spoon. "And I'm over the moon whenever we *spoon*."

OMG. Could he be any cuter?

He reached in the bag for the screw. "But most of all, what I love to do...."

Don't do it. Don't do it, Sam. Think of the children. Think of the money! Marley prepared to apologize to the FCC and bid the Battle bye-bye.

Sam cast a naughty glance at the camera and held up his last object, to the collective gasp of contestants and studio personnel alike, and opened his mouth to speak.

About the Author

KIMBERLY BRIGHTON IS A FORMER CRIMINAL LAWYER, INCI-dental humorist, and asparagus enthusiast from the Philadelphia area. She studied satirical writing and screenwriting at The Second City and is the author of *The Shore Blog,* a travel website, and *BlaBlaBlog,* a humor website. *A Cape May Kind of Love* is the second of three books in her Cape May Series, following *The Way to Cape May.* When not dreaming up swoony romance plots, she spends her time searching for food expiration labels and sitting at red lights. Married for 25 laugh-filled years, she's discovered the key to a lasting marriage: takeout.

To stay in touch and learn about upcoming book releases, sign up for her newsletter at KimberlyBrighton.com.